NIGHTSIDE THE LONG SUN

The first volume of a new masterpiece of science fiction

The Book of the Long Sun

NIGHTSIDE THE LONG SUN

GENE WOLFE

A TOM DOHERTY ASSOCIATES BOOK
NEW YORK

NIGHTSIDE THE LONG SUN

Copyright © 1993 by Gene Wolfe

Cover art by Richard Bober

A Tor Book
Published by Tom Doherty Associates, Inc.
175 Fifth Avenue
New York, N.Y. 10010

Tor® is a registered trademark of Tom Doherty Associates, Inc.

ISBN: 0-812-51625-7
Library of Congress Catalog Card Number: 92-21568

First edition: April 1993
First mass market edition: December 1993

Printed in the United States of America

0 9 8 7 6 5 4 3 2

This book is dedicated to Joe Mayhew
for at least a dozen reasons.

NIGHTSIDE THE LONG SUN

Chapter 1

THE MANTEION
ON SUN STREET

Enlightenment came to Patera Silk on the ball court; nothing could ever be the same after that. When he talked about it afterward, whispering to himself in the silent hours of the night as was his custom—and once when he told Maytera Marble, who was also Maytera Rose—he said that it was as though someone who had always been behind him and standing (as it were) at both his shoulders had, after so many years of pregnant silence, begun to whisper into both his ears. The bigger boys had scored again, Patera Silk recalled, and Horn was reaching for an easy catch when those voices began and all that had been hidden was displayed.

Few of these hidden things made sense, nor did they wait upon one another. He, young Patera Silk (that absurd clockwork figure), watched outside a clockwork show whose works had stopped—tall Horn reaching for the ball, his flashing grin frozen in forever.

—dead Patera Pike mumbling prayers as he slit the throat of a speckled rabbit he himself had bought.

—a dead woman in an alley off Silver Street, and the people of the quarter.

—lights beneath everyone's feet, like cities low in the

night sky. (And, oh, the rabbit's warm blood drenching Patera Pike's cold hands.)

—proud houses on the Palatine.

—Maytera Marble playing with the girls, and Maytera Mint wishing she dared. (Old Maytera Rose praying alone, praying to Scalding Scylla in her palace under Lake Limna.)

—Feather falling, not so lightly as his name implied, shoved aside by Horn, not yet quite prone on the crumbling shiprock blocks, though shiprock was supposed to last until the end of the whorl.

—Viron and the lake, crops withering in the fields, the dying fig and the open, empty sky. All this and much else besides, lovely and appalling, blood red and living green, yellow, blue, white, and velvet black, with minglings of other colors and of colors he had never known.

Yet all these were as nothing. It was the voices that mattered, only the paired voices (though there were more, he felt sure, if only he had ears for them) and all the rest an empty show, shown to him so that he might know it for what it was, spread for him so that he might know how precious it was, though its shining clockwork had gone some trifle awry and must be set right by him; for this he had been born.

He forgot the rest at times, though at others all these things would reoccur to him, rough truths cloaked in a new certainty; but he never forgot the voices that were in fact but one voice, and what they (who were one) had said; never forgot the bitter lesson, though once or twice he tried to push it away, those fell words heard as Feather fell, poor little Feather, as the rabbit's hot blood spilled from the altar, as the First Settlers took up the homes prepared for them in this familiar Viron, as the dead woman seemed to stir, rags fluttering in the hot wind born halfway 'round the whorl, a wind that blew ever stronger and wilder as clock-work that had never really stopped began to turn again.

"I will not fail," he told the voices, and felt he lied, yet felt the approbation, too.

And then.

And then . . .

His left hand moved, snatching the ball from Horn's very fingers.

Patera Silk spun about. The black ball flew like a black bird, straight through the ring at the opposite end of the ball court. It struck the hellstone with a satisfying thump and an irruption of blue sparks, and threaded the ring a second time as it bounced back.

Horn tried to stop him, but Patera Silk knocked him sprawling, caught the ball again, and smoked it in for a second double. The monitor's chimes sang their three-note paean, and its raddled gray face appeared to announce the final score: thirteen to twelve.

Thirteen to twelve was not a bad score, Patera Silk reflected as he took the ball from Feather and stuffed it into a trousers pocket. The bigger boys would not be too downcast, while the smaller boys would be ecstatic.

This last, at least, was already quite apparent. He repressed the impulse to hush them and lifted two of the most diminutive onto his shoulders. "Back to class," he announced. "Class for all of you. A little arithmetic will do you good. Feather, throw Villus my towel, please."

Feather, one of the larger small boys, obliged; Villus, the boy perched upon Silk's right shoulder, managed to catch it, though not deftly.

"Patera," Feather ventured, "you always say there's a lesson in everything."

Silk nodded, mopping his face and rubbing his already disheveled yellow hair. He had been touched by a god! By the Outsider; and although the Outsider was not one of the

Nine, he was an undoubted god nevertheless. This, *this* was enlightenment!

"Patera?"

"I'm listening, Feather. What is it you want to ask?" But enlightenment was for theodidacts, and he was no holy theodidact—no gaudily painted gold-crowned figure in the Writings. How could he tell these children that in the middle of their game—

"Then what's the lesson in our winning, Patera?"

"That you must endure to the end," Silk replied, his mind still upon the Outsider's teaching. One of the hinges of the ball-court gate was broken; two boys had to lift the gate to swing it, creaking, backward. The remaining hinge would surely break too, and soon, unless he did something. Many theodidacts never told, or so he had been taught in the schola. Others told only on their deathbeds; for the first time he felt he understood that.

"*We* endured to the end," Horn reminded him, "but we lost just the same. You're bigger than I am. Bigger than any of us."

Silk nodded and smiled. "I did not say that the only object was to win."

Horn opened his mouth to speak, then shut it again, his eyes thoughtful. Silk took Goldcrest and Villus from his shoulders at the gate and dried his torso, then reclaimed his black tunic from the nail on which he had hung it. Sun Street ran parallel to the sun, as its name indicated, and as usual at this hour it was blazing hot. Regretfully, he pulled his tunic over his head, smelling his own sweat.

"You lost," he remarked to Villus once the stifling tunic was in place, "when Horn got the ball away from you. But you won when everyone on our team did. What have you learned from that?"

When little Villus said nothing, Feather answered, "That winning and losing aren't everything."

The loose black robe followed the tunic, seeming to close about him. "Good enough," he told Feather.

As five boys shut the court gate behind them, the faint and much-diffused shadow of a Flier raced down Sun Street. The boys glared up at him, and a few of the smallest reached for stones, though the Flier was three or four times higher than the loftiest tower in Viron.

Silk halted, raising his head to stare upward with a long-felt envy he struggled to suppress. Had he been shown the Fliers, among his myriad, leaping visions? He felt he had—but he had been shown so much!

The disproportionate, gauzy wings were nearly invisible in the glare of the unshaded sun, so that it seemed that the Flier flew without them, arms outstretched, feet together, an uncanny figure black against the burning gold.

"If the Fliers are human," Silk admonished his charges, "it would surely be evil to stone them. If they are not, you must consider that they may be higher than we are in the spiritual whorl, just as they are in the temporal." As an afterthought he added, "Even if they *are* spying on us, which I doubt."

Had they, too, achieved enlightenment, and was that why they flew? Did some god or goddess—it would be Hierax, perhaps, or his father, sky-ruling Pas—teach those he favored the art of flight?

The palaestra's warped and weathered door would not open until Horn had wrestled manfully with its latch. As always, Silk delivered the smaller boys to Maytera Marble first. "We won a glorious victory," he told her.

She shook her head in mock dismay, her smooth oval face, polished bright by countless dustings, catching the sunlight from the window. "My poor girls were beaten, alas, Patera. It seems to me that Maytera Mint's big girls grow quicker and stronger with each week that passes. Wouldn't you think our Merciful Molpe would make my smaller ones quicker, too? Yet it doesn't seem she does it."

"By the time they're quicker, they'll be the big girls, perhaps."

"That must be it, Patera. While I'm only a small girl myself, snatching at every chance to put off the minuends and subtrahends for as long as possible, always willing to talk, never willing to work." Maytera Marble paused, her work-worn steel fingers flexing the cubit stick while she studied Silk. "You be careful this afternoon, Patera. You must be tired already, after scrambling around up there all morning and playing with the boys. Don't fall off that roof."

He grinned. "I'm finished with my repairs for today, Maytera. I'm going to sacrifice after manteion—a private sacrifice."

The old sib tilted her gleaming head to one side, thus lifting an eyebrow. "Then I regret that my class will not participate. Will your lamb be more pleasing to the Nine, do you think, without us?"

For an instant Silk was tempted to tell her everything there and then. He drew a deep breath instead, smiled, and closed the door.

Most of the larger boys had already gone into Maytera Rose's room. Silk dismissed the rest with a glance, but Horn lingered. "May I speak with you, Patera? It'll just take a minute."

"If it *is* only a minute." When the boy said nothing, Silk added, "Go ahead, Horn. Did I foul you? If I did, I apologize—it certainly wasn't intentional."

"Is it . . ." Horn let the question trail away, staring at the splintering floorboards.

"Speak up, please. Or ask your question when I come back. That would be better."

The tall boy's gaze moved to the whitewashed mud-brick walls. "Patera, is it true that they're going to tear down our palaestra and your manteion? That you're going to have to go someplace else, or noplace? My father heard that yesterday. Is it true?"

"No."

Horn looked up with new hope, though the flat negative had left him speechless.

"Our palaestra and our manteion will be here next year, and the year after that, and the year after *that* as well." Suddenly conscious of his posture, Silk stood straighter, squaring his shoulders. "Does that put your mind at rest? They may become larger and better known, and I hope that they will. Perhaps some god or goddess may speak to us through our Sacred Window again, as Pas once did when Patera Pike was young—I don't know, though I pray for it every day. But when I'm as old as Patera Pike, the people of this quarter will still have a manteion and a palaestra. Never doubt it."

"I was going to say . . ."

Silk nodded. "Your eyes have said it for you already. Thank you, Horn. Thank you. I know that whenever I'm in need I can call on you, and that you'll do all that you can without counting the cost. But, Horn—"

"Yes, Patera?"

"I knew all that before."

The tall boy's head bobbed. "And all the other sprats, too, Patera. There are a couple of dozen that I know we can trust. Maybe more."

Horn was standing as straight as a Guardsman on parade now. With a slight shock of insight, Silk realized that this unaccustomed perpendicularity was in imitation of his own, and that Horn's clear, dark eyes were very nearly level with his.

"And after that," Horn continued, "there will be others, new boys. And men."

Silk nodded again, gravely reflecting that Horn was already a grown man in every way that mattered, and a man far better educated than most.

"And I don't want you to think I'm mad about it— knocking me over like that, Patera. You hit me hard, but that's the fun of the game."

Silk shook his head. "That's merely how the game is played. The fun comes when someone small knocks down someone larger."

"You were their best player, Patera. It wouldn't have been fair to them if you hadn't played as well as you can." Horn glanced over his shoulder at Maytera Rose's open door. "I have to go now. Thanks, Patera."

There was a line in the Writings that applied to the game and its lessons—lessons more important, Silk felt, than any Maytera Rose might teach; but Horn was already almost to the doorway. To his back, Silk murmured, " 'Men build scales, but the gods blow upon the lighter pan.' "

He sighed at the final word, knowing that the quotation had come a second too late, and that Horn, too, had been too late; that Horn would tell Maytera Rose that he, Patera Silk, had detained him, and that Maytera Rose would punish him nevertheless without bothering to find out whether it was true.

Silk turned away. There was no point in remaining to listen, and Horn would fare that much worse if he tried to intervene. How could the Outsider have chosen such a bungler? Was it possible that the very gods were ignorant of his weakness and stupidity?

Some of them?

The manteion's rusty cash box was bare, he knew; yet he must have a victim, and a fine one. The parents of one of the students might lend him five or even ten bits, and the humiliation of having to beg such poor people for a loan would certainly be beneficial. For as long as it took him to close the unwilling door of the palaestra and start for the market, his resolution held; then the only-too-well-imagined tears of small children deprived of their accustomed supper of milk and stale bread washed it away. No. The sellers would have to extend him credit.

The sellers must. When had he ever offered a single sacrifice, however small, to the Outsider? Never! Not one in his entire life. Yet the Outsider had extended infinite credit to him, for Patera Pike's sake. That was one way of looking at it, at least. And perhaps that was the best way. Certainly he would never be able to repay the Outsider for the knowledge and the honor, no matter how hard or how long he tried. Small wonder, then . . .

As Silk's thoughts raced, his long legs flashed faster and faster.

The sellers never extended a single bit's credit, true. They gave credit to no augur; and certainly they would not extend it to an augur whose manteion stood in the poorest quarter of the city. Yet the Outsider could not be denied, so they would have to. He would have to be firm with them, extremely firm. Remind them that the Outsider was known to esteem them last among men already—that according to the Writings he had once (having possessed and enlightened a fortunate man) beaten them severely in person. And though the Nine could rightly boast . . .

A black civilian floater was roaring down Sun Street, scattering men and women on foot and dodging ramshackle carts and patient gray donkeys, its blowers raising a choking cloud of hot yellow dust. Like everyone else, Silk turned his face away, covering his nose and mouth with the edge of his robe.

"You there! Augur!"

The floater had stopped, its roar fading to a plaintive whine as it settled onto the rutted street. A big, beefy, prosperous-looking man standing in its passenger compartment flourished a walking stick.

Silk called, "I take it you are addressing me, sir. Is that correct?"

The prosperous-looking man gestured impatiently. "Come over here."

"I intend to," Silk told him. A dead dog rotting in the gutter required a long stride that roused a cloud of fat blue-backed flies. "*Patera* would be better mannered, sir; but I'll overlook it. You may call me 'augur' if you like. I have need of you, you see. Great need. A god has sent you to me."

The prosperous-looking man looked at least as surprised as Horn had when Silk had knocked him down.

"I require two—no, three cards," Silk continued. "Three cards or more. I require them at once, for a sacred purpose. You can provide them easily, and the gods will smile on you. Please do so."

The prosperous-looking man mopped his streaming brow with a large peach-colored handkerchief that sent a cloying fragrance to war with the stenches of the street. "I didn't think that the Chapter let you augurs do this sort of thing, Patera."

"Beg? Why, no. You're perfectly correct, sir. It's absolutely forbidden. But there's a beggar on every corner— you must know the kinds of things they say, and that's not what I'm telling you at all. I'm not hungry, and I have no starving children. I don't want your money for myself, but for a god, for the Outsider. It's a major error to restrict one's worship to the Nine, as I— Never mind. The Outsider must have a suitable offering from me before shadedown. It's absolutely imperative. You'll be certain to gain his favor by supplying it."

"I wanted—" the prosperous-looking man began.

Silk raised his hand. "No! The money—three cards at

least, at once. I've offered you a splendid opportunity to gain his favor. You've lost that now, but you may still escape his displeasure, if only you'll act without further delay. For your own sake, give me three cards immediately!" Silk stepped closer, scrutinizing the prosperous-looking man's ruddy, perspiring face. "Terrible things may befall you. Horrible things!"

Reaching for the card case at his waist, the prosperous-looking man said, "A respectable citizen shouldn't even stop his floater in this quarter. I simply——"

"If you own this floater, you can afford three cards easily. And I'll offer a prayer for you—many prayers that you may eventually attain to . . ." Silk shivered.

The driver rasped, "Shut your shaggy mouth and let Blood talk, you butcher." Then to Blood, "You want me to bring him along, Jefe?"

Blood shook his head. He had counted out three cards, and now held them in a fan; half a dozen ragged men stopped to gawk at the gleaming gold. "Three cards you say you want, Patera. Here they are. Enlightenment? Was that what you were going to ask the gods to give me? You augurs are always squeaking about it. Well, I don't care about that. I want a little information instead. Tell me everything I want to know, and I'll hand over all three. See 'em? Then you can offer this wonderful sacrifice for yourself if you want to, or do whatever you want with the money. How about it?"

"You don't know what you're risking. If you did——"

Blood snorted. "I know that no god's come to any Window in this city since I was a young man, Patera, no matter how you butchers howl. And that's all I need to know. There's a manteion on this street, isn't there? Where Silver Street meets it at an angle? I've never been in that part of this quarter, but I asked, and that's what I was told."

Silk nodded. "I'm augur there."

"The old cull's dead, then?"

"Patera Pike?" Silk traced the sign of addition in the air. "Yes. Patera Pike has been with the gods for almost a year. Did you know him?"

Ignoring the question, Blood nodded to himself. "Gone to Mainframe, eh? All right, Patera. I'm not a religious man, and I don't pretend to be. But I promised my—well, I promised a certain person—that I'd go to this manteion of yours and say a few prayers for her. I'm going to make an offering, too, understand? Because I know she'll ask if I did. That's besides these cards here. So is there somebody there who'll let me in?"

Silk nodded again. "Maytera Marble or Maytera Mint would be delighted to, I'm sure. You'll find them both in the palaestra, on the other side of our ball court." Silk paused, thinking. "Maytera Mint's rather shy, though she's wonderful with the children. Perhaps you'd better ask for Maytera Marble, in the first room to your right. She could leave one of the older girls in charge of her class for an hour or so, I would think."

Blood closed his fan of cards as if about to hand them over to Silk. "I'm not too crazy about chemical people, Patera. Somebody told me you've got a Maytera Rose. Maybe I could get her, or isn't she there any more?"

"Oh, yes." Silk hoped his voice did not reflect the dismay he felt whenever he thought of Maytera Rose. "But she's quite elderly, sir, and we try to spare her poor legs whenever we can. I feel sure that Maytera Marble would prove completely satisfactory."

"No doubt she will." Blood counted his cards again, his lips moving, his fat, beringed fingers reluctant to part from each wafer-thin, shining rectangle. "You were going to tell me about enlightenment a minute ago, Patera. You said you'd pray for me."

"Yes," Silk confirmed eagerly, "and I meant it. I will."

Blood laughed. "Don't bother. But I'm curious, and I've never had such a good chance to ask one of you about it before. Isn't enlightenment really pretty much the same as possession?"

"Not exactly, sir." Silk gnawed his lower lip. "You know, sir, at the schola they taught us simple, satisfying answers to all of these questions. We had to recite them to pass the examination, and I'm tempted to recite them again for you now. But the actualities—enlightenment, I mean, and possession—aren't really simple things at all. Or at least enlightenment isn't. I don't know a great deal about possession, and some of the most respected hierologists are of the opinion that it exists potentially but not actually."

"A god's supposed to pull on a man just like a tunic—that's what they say. Well, some people can, so why not a god?" Watching Silk's expression, Blood laughed again. "You don't believe me, do you, Patera?"

Silk said, "I've never heard of such people, sir. I won't say they don't exist, since you assert that they do, although it seems impossible."

"You're young yet, Patera. If you want to dodge a lot of mistakes, don't you forget that." Blood glanced sidelong at his driver. "Get on these putts, Grison. Make them keep their paws off my floater."

"Enlightenment . . ." Silk stroked his cheek, remembering.

"That ought to be easy, it seems to me. Don't you just know a lot of things you didn't know before?" Blood paused, his eyes upon Silk's face. "Things that you can't explain, or aren't allowed to?"

A patrol of Guardsmen passed, their slug guns slung and their left hands resting on the hilts of their swords. One touched the bill of his jaunty green cap to Blood.

"It's difficult to explain," Silk said. "In possession there's always some teaching, for good or ill. Or at any rate that's what we're taught, though I don't believe— In enlightenment, there's much more. As much as the theodidact can bear, I would say."

"It happened to you," Blood said softly. "Lots of you say it did, but from you it's lily. You were enlightened, or you think you were. You think it's real."

Silk took a step backward, bumping against one of the onlookers. "I didn't call myself enlightened, sir."

"You didn't have to. I've been listening to you. Now you listen to me. I'm not giving you these cards, not for your holy sacrifice or for anything else. I'm paying you to answer my questions, and this is the last one. I want you to tell me—right now—what enlightenment is, when you got it, and why you got it. Here they are." He held them up again. "Tell me, Patera, and they're yours."

Silk considered, then plucked them from Blood's hand. "As you say. Enlightenment means understanding everything as the god who gives it understands it. Who you are and who everyone else is, really. Everything you used to think you understood, you see with complete clarity in that instant, and know that you didn't really understand it at all."

The onlookers murmured, each to his neighbor. Several pointed toward Silk. One waved over the drawer of a passing handcart.

"Only for an instant," Blood said.

"Yes, only for an instant. But the memory remains, so that you know that you knew." The three cards were still in Silk's hand; suddenly afraid that they would be snatched away by one of the ragged throng around him, he slipped them into his pocket.

"And when did this happen to you? Last week? Last year?"

Silk shook his head, glancing up at the sun. The thin black line of the shade touched it as he watched. "Today.

Not an hour ago. A ball—I was playing a game with the boys . . .

Blood waved the game away.

"And it happened. Everything seemed to stand still. I really can't say whether it was for an instant, or a day, or a year, or any other period of time—and I seriously doubt that any such period could be correct. Perhaps that's why we call him the Outsider: because he stands outside of time, all the time."

"Uh-huh." Blood favored Silk with a grudging smile. "I'm sure it's all smoke. Just some sort of daydream. But I've got to admit it's interesting smoke, the way you tell it. I've never heard of anything like this before."

"It's not exactly what they teach you in the schola," Silk conceded, "but I feel in my heart that it's the truth." He hesitated. "By which I mean that it's what I was shown by him—or rather, that it's one of an endless panorama of things. Somehow he's outside our whorl in every way, and inside it with us at the same time. The other gods are only inside, I think, however great they may appear inside."

Blood shrugged, his eyes wandering toward the ragged listeners. "Well, they believe you, anyhow. But as long as we're in here too, it doesn't make a bad bit's difference to us, does it, Patera?"

"Perhaps it does, or may in the future. I don't know, really. I haven't even begun to think about that yet." Silk glanced up again; the sun's golden road across the sky was markedly narrower already. "Perhaps it will make all the difference in the whorl," he said. "I think it will."

"I don't see how."

"You'll have to wait and see, my son—and so shall I." Silk shivered, as he had before. "You wanted to know why I received this blessing, didn't you? That was your last question: why something as tremendous as this should happen to someone as insignificant as I am. Wasn't that it?"

"Yes, if this god of yours will let you tell anybody."

Blood grinned, showing crooked, discolored teeth; and Silk, suddenly and without in the least willing it, saw more vividly than he had ever seen the man before him the hungry, frightened, scheming youth who had been Blood a generation before.

"And if you don't gibbe yourself, Patera."

"Gibbe?"

"If you've got no objections. Don't feel like you're stepping over his line."

"I see." Silk cleared his throat. "I've no objection, but no very satisfactory answer for you, either. That's why I snatched my three cards from your hand, and it's why I need them, too—or a part of it. It may be only that he has a task for me. He does, I know, and I hope that that's all it is. Or, as I've thought since, perhaps it's because he means to destroy me, and felt he owed this to me before he struck. I don't know."

Blood dropped to his seat in the passenger compartment, mopping his face and neck with his scented handkerchief, as he had before. "Thanks, Patera. We're quits. You're going to the market?"

"Yes, to buy him a fine victim with these cards you've given me."

"Paid you. I'll have left your manteion before you get back, Patera. Or anyhow I hope I will." Blood dropped into the floater's velvet seat. "Get the canopy up, Grison."

Silk called, "Wait!"

Blood stood again, surprised. "What is it, Patera? No hard feelings, I hope."

"I lied to you, my son—misled you at least, although I didn't intend to. He—the Outsider—told me why, and I remembered it a few minutes ago when I was talking with a boy named Horn, a student at our palaestra." Silk stepped closer, until he was peering at Blood over the edge of the half-raised canopy. "It was because of the augur who had our manteion when I came, Patera Pike. A very good and very holy man."

"He's dead, you said."

"Yes. Yes, he is. But before he died, he prayed—prayed to the Outsider, for some reason. And he was heard. His prayer was granted. All this was explained to me, and now I owe it to you, because it was part of our bargain."

"Then I may as well have it explained to me, too. But make it as quick as you can."

"He prayed for help." Silk ran his fingers through his careless thatch of straw-colored hair. "When we—when you pray for his help, to the Outsider, he sends it."

"Nice of him."

"But not always—no, not often—of the sort we want or expect. Patera Pike, that good old man, prayed devoutly. And I'm the help—"

"Let's go, Grison."

The blowers roared back to life. Blood's black floater heaved uneasily, rising stern first and rocking alarmingly.

"—the Outsider sent to him, to save the manteion and its palaestra," Silk concluded. He stepped back, coughing in the billowing dust. Half to himself and half to the shabby crowd kneeling around him, he added. "I am to expect no help from him. I *am* help."

If any of them understood, it was not apparent. Still coughing, he traced the sign of addition and muttered a brief formula of blessing, begun with the Most Sacred Name of Pas, Father of the Gods, and concluded with that of his eldest child, Scylla, Patroness of this, Our Holy City of Viron.

As he neared the market, Silk reflected on his chance encounter with the prosperous-looking man in the floater. Blood, his driver had called him. Three cards was far, far too much to pay for answers to a few simple questions, and in any case one did not pay augurs for their answers; one made a donation, perhaps, if one was particularly grateful. Three full cards, but were they still there?

He thrust a hand into his pocket; the smooth, elastic surface of the ball met his fingers. He pulled it out, and one of the cards came with it, flashing in the sunlight as it fell at his feet.

As swiftly as he had snatched the ball from Horn, he scooped it up. This was a bad quarter, he reminded himself, though there were so many good people in it. Without law, even good people stole: their own property vanished, and their only recourse was to steal in turn from someone else. What would his mother have thought, if she had lived to learn where the Chapter had assigned him? She had died during his final year at the schola, still believing that he would be sent to one of the rich manteions on the Palatine and someday become Prolocutor.

"You're so good-looking," she had said, raising herself upon her toes to smooth his rebellious hair. "So tall! Oh, Silk, my son! My dear, dear son!"

(And he had stooped to let her kiss him.)

My son was what he had been taught to call laymen, even those three times his own age, unless they were very highly placed indeed; then there was generally some title that could be gracefully employed instead, Colonel or Commissioner, or even Councillor, although he had never met any of the three and in this quarter never would—though here was a poster with the handsome features of Councillor Loris, the secretary of the Ayuntamiento: features somewhat scarred now by the knife of some vandal, who had slashed his poster once and stabbed it several times. Silk felt suddenly glad that he was in the Chapter and not in politics, though politics had been his mother's first choice for him. No one would slash or stab the pictured face of His Cognizance the Prolocutor, surely.

He tossed the ball into his right hand and thrust his left into his pocket. The cards were still there: one, two, three. Many men in this quarter who worked from shadeup to dark—carrying bricks or stacking boxes, slaughtering, hauling like oxen or trotting beneath the weighty litters of the rich, sweeping and mopping—would be fortunate to make three cards a year. His mother had received six, enough for a woman and a child to live decently, from some fund at the fisc that she had never explained, a fund that had vanished with her life. She would be unhappy now to see him in this quarter, walking its streets as poor as many of its people. She had never been a happy woman in any case, her large dark eyes so often bright with tears from sources more mysterious than the fisc, her tiny body shaken with sobs that he could do nothing to alleviate.

("Oh, Silk! My poor boy! My son!")

He had at first called Blood *sir,* and afterward, *my son,* himself scarcely conscious of the change. But why? *Sir* because Blood had been riding in a floater, of course; only the richest of men could afford to own floaters. *My son* afterward. "The old cull's dead, then? . . . It doesn't make a bad bit's difference to us, does it, Patera? . . . Nice of him." Blood's choice of word and phrase, and his almost open contempt for the gods, had not accorded with the floater; he had spoken better—far better—than most people in this quarter; but not at all like the privileged, well-bred man whom Silk would have expected to find riding in a private floater.

He shrugged, and extracted the three cards from his pocket.

There was always a good chance that a card (still more, a cardbit) would be false. There was even a chance, as Silk admitted to himself, that the prosperous-looking man in the floater—that this odd man Blood—kept false cards in a special location in his card case. Nevertheless all three of these appeared completely genuine, sharp-edged rectangles two thumbs by three, their complex labyrinths of gold encysted in some remarkable substance that was almost indestructible, yet nearly invisible. It was said that when two of the intricate golden patterns were exactly alike, one at least was false. Silk paused to compare them, then shook his head and hurried off again in the direction of the market. If these cards were good enough to fool the sellers of animals, that was all that mattered, though he would be a thief. A prayer, in that case, to Tenebrous Tartaros, Pas's elder son, the terrifying god of night and thieves.

Maytera Marble sat watching, at the back of her class. There had been a time, long ago, when she would have stood, just as there had been a time when her students had labored over keyboards instead of slates. Today, now—in whatever year this might be . . . Might be . . .

Her chronological function could not be called; she tried to remember when it had happened before.

Maytera Marble could call a list of her nonfunctioning or defective components whenever she chose, though it had been five years or fifty since she had so chosen. What was the use? Why should she—why ever should anyone—make herself more miserable than the gods had chosen to make her? Weren't the gods cruel enough, deaf to her prayers through so many years, so many decades and days and languid, half-stopped hours? Pas, Great Pas, was god of mechanisms, as of so much else. Perhaps he was too busy to notice.

She pictured him as he stood in the manteion, as tall as a talus, his smooth limbs carved of some white stone finer grained than shiprock—his grave, unseeing eyes, his noble brows. Have pity on me, Pas, she prayed. Have pity on me, a mortal maid who calls upon you now, but will soon stop forever.

Her right leg had been getting stiffer and stiffer for years, and at times it seemed that even when she sat so still—

A boy to a girl: *"She's asleep!"*

—that when she sat as still as she was sitting here, watching the children take nineteen from twenty-nine and get nine, add seven and seventeen and arrive at twenty-three—that when she sat so still as this, her vision no longer as acute as it once had been, although she could still see the straying, chalky numerals on their slates when the children wrote large, and all children their age wrote large, though their eyes were better than her own.

It seemed to her that she was always on the point of overheating any more, in hot weather anyway. Pas, Great Pas, God of Sky and Sun and Storm, bring the snow! Bring the cold wind!

This endless summer, without snow, with no autumn rains and the season for them practically past now, the season for snow nearly upon us, and no snow. Heat and dust and clouds that were all empty, yellow haze. What could Pas, Lord Pas, Husband of Grain-bearing Echidna and Father of the Seven, be thinking of?

A girl: *"Look—she's asleep!"*

Another: *"I didn't think they slept."*

A knock at the Sun Street door of the palaestra.

"I'll get it!" That was Asphodella's voice.

This was Ratel's. *"No, I will!"*

Fragrant white blossoms and sharp white teeth. Maytera Marble meditated upon names. Flowers—or plants of some kind, at least—for bio girls; animals or animal products for bio boys. Metals or stones for us.

Both together: *"Let me!"*

Her old name had been—

Her old name had been . . .

A crash, as a chair fell. Maytera Marble rose stiffly, one hand gripping the windowsill. "Stop that this instant!"

She could bring up a list of her nonfunctioning and defective parts whenever she chose. She had not chosen to do so for close to a century; but from time to time, most often when the cenoby lay on the night side of the long sun, that list came up of itself.

"Aquifolia! Separate those two before I lose my temper."

Maytera Marble could remember the short sun, a disk of orange fire; and it seemed to her that the chief virtue of that old sun had been that no list, no menu, ever appeared unbidden beneath its rays.

Both together: *"Sib, I wanted—"*

"Well, neither of you are going to," Maytera Marble told them.

Another knock, too loud for knuckles of bone and skin. She must hurry or Maytera Rose might go, might answer that knock herself, an occasion for complaint that would outlast the snow. If the snow ever arrived.

"I am going to go myself. Teasel, you're in charge of the class until I return. Keep them at their work, every one of them." To give her final words more weight, Maytera Marble paused as long as she dared. "I shall expect you to name those who misbehaved."

A good step toward the door. There was an actuator in her right leg that occasionally jammed when it had been idle for an hour or so, but it appeared to be functioning almost acceptably. Another step, and another. Good, good! Praise to you, Great Pas.

She stopped just beyond the doorway, to listen for an immediate disturbance, then limped down the corridor to the door.

A beefy, prosperous-looking man nearly as tall as Patera

Silk had been pounding the panels with the carved handle of his walking stick.

"May every god favor you this morning," Maytera Marble said. "How may I serve you?"

"My name's Blood," he announced. "I'm looking at the property. I've already seen the garden and so on, but the other buildings are locked. I'd like you to take me through them, and show me this one."

"I couldn't possibly admit you to our cenoby," Maytera Marble said firmly. "Nor could I permit you to enter the manse alone. I'll be happy to show you through our manteion and this palaestra—provided that you have a valid reason for wishing to see them."

Blood's red face became redder still. "I'm checking the condition of the buildings. All of them need a lot of work, from what I've seen outside."

Maytera Marble nodded. "That's quite true, I'm afraid, although we do everything that we can. Patera Silk's been repairing the roof of the manteion. That was most urgent. Is it true—"

Blood interrupted her. "The cenoby—is that the little house on Silver Street?"

She nodded.

"The manse is the one where Silver Street and Sun come together? The little three-cornered house at the west end of the garden?"

"That's correct. Is it true, then, that this entire property is to be sold? That's what some of the children have been saying."

Blood eyed her quizzically. "Has Maytera Rose heard about it?"

"I suppose she's heard the rumor, if that's what you mean. I haven't discussed it with her."

Blood nodded, a minute inclination of his head that probably escaped his own notice. "I didn't tell that towheaded butcher of yours. He looked like the sort to make trouble. But you tell Maytera Rose that the rumor's true, you hear me? Tell her it's been sold already, sib. Sold to me."

We'll be gone before the snow flies, Maytera Marble thought, hearing her future and all their futures in Blood's tone. Gone before winter and living somewhere else, where Sun Street will be just a memory.

Blessed snow to cool her thighs; she pictured herself sitting at peace, with her lap full of new-fallen snow.

Blood added, "Tell her my name."

Chapter 2

THE SACRIFICE

As it was every day except Scylsday, "from noon until the sun can be no thinner," the market was thronged. Here all the produce of Viron's fields and gardens was displayed for sale or barter: yams, arrowroot, and hill-country potatoes; onions, scallions, and leeks; squashes yellow, orange, red, and white; sun-starved asparagus; beans black as night or spotted like hounds; dripping watercresses from the shrinking rivulets that fed Lake Limna; lettuces and succulent greens of a hundred sorts; and fiery peppers; wheat, millet, rice, and barley; maize yellower than its name, and white, blue, and red as well, spilling, leaking, and overflowing from baskets, bags, and earthenware pots—this though Patera Silk noted with dismay that prices were higher than he had ever seen them, and many of the stunted ears were missing grains.

Here still despite the drought were dates and grapes, oranges and citrons, pears, papayas, pomegranates and little red bananas; angelica, hyssop, licorice, cicely, cardamom, anise, basil, mandrake, borage, marjoram, mullein, parsley, saxifrage, and scores of other herbs.

Here perfumers waved lofty plumes of dyed pampas grass to strew the overheated air with fragrances matched to every conceivable feminine name; and here those fragrances warred against the savory aromas of roasting meats and bubbling stews, the stinks of beast and men and of the excrements of both. Sides of beef and whole carcasses of pork hung here from cruel-looking hooks of hammered iron; and here (as Silk turned left in search of those who dealt in live beasts and birds) was the rich harvest of the lake: gap-mouthed fish with silver sides and starting eyes, mussels, writhing eels, fretful black crawfish with claws like pliers, eyes like rubies, and fat tails longer than a man's hand; sober gray geese, and ducks richly dressed in brown, green, black, and that odd blue so seldom seen elsewhere that it is called teal. Folding tables and thick polychrome blankets spread on the trampled, uneven soil held bracelets and ornamental pins, flashing rings and cascading necklaces, graceful swords and straight-bladed, double-edged knives with grips of rare hardwoods or colored leathers, and hammers, axes, froes, and scutches.

Swiftly though he shouldered his way through the crowd, greatly aided by his height, his considerable strength, and his sacred office, Silk lingered to watch as a nervous green monkey picked fortunes for a cardbit, and to see a weaver of eight or nine tie the ten thousandth knot in a carpet, her hands working, as it seemed, without reference to her idle, empty little face.

And at all times, whether he stood watching or pushed through the crowd, Silk looked deep into the eyes of those who had come to buy or sell, and tried to look into their hearts, too, reminding himself (whenever such prompts were needed) that each was treasured by Pas. Great Pas, with an understanding far beyond that of mere men, accounted this faded housewife with her basket on her arm more precious than any figurine carved from ivory; this sullen, pockmarked boy (so Silk thought of him, though the youth was only a year or two the younger), standing ready to snatch a brass earring or an egg, worth more than all the goods that all such boys might ever hope to steal. Pas had built the whorl for Men, and not made men, or women, or children, for the whorl.

"Caught today!" shouted half a dozen voices, by the goodwill of Melodious Molpe or the accident of innumerable repetitions for once practically synchronized. Following the sound, Silk found himself among the sellers he sought. Hobbled deer reared and plunged, their soft brown eyes wild with fright; a huge snake lifted its flat, malevolent head, hissing like a kettle on the stove; live salmon gasped and splashed in murky, glass-fronted tanks; pigs grunted, lambs baaed, chickens squawked, and milling goats eyed passersby with curiosity and sharp suspicion. Which of these, if any, would make a suitable gift of thanks to the Outsider? To that lone nebulous god, mysterious, beneficent, and severe, whose companion he had been for a time that had seemed less than an instant and longer than centuries? Motionless at the edge of the seething crowd, one leg pressed against the unpeeled poles that confined the goats, Silk ransacked the whole store of dusty knowledge he had acquired with so much labor during eight years at the schola; and found nothing.

On the other side of the goat pen, a well-marked young donkey trotted in a circle, reversing direction each time its owner clapped, bowing (a foreleg stretched forward, its wide forehead in the dust) when he whistled. Such a trained animal, Silk reflected, would make a superb sacrifice to any god; but the donkey's price would be nearer thirty cards than three.

A fatted ox recalled the prosperous-looking man called Blood, and Blood's three cards might well obtain it after a session of hard bargaining. Many augurs chose such victims whenever they could, and what remained after the sacrifice would supply the palaestra's kitchen for at least a week, and feed Maytera Rose, Maytera Mint, and himself like so many commissioners as well; but Silk could not believe that a mutilated and stall-fed beast, however sumptuous, would be relished by a god, nor did he himself often indulge in meats of any kind.

Lambs, unrelieved black for Stygian Tartaros, Deathly Hierax, and Grim Phaea, purest white for the remainder of the Nine, were the sacrifices most frequently mentioned in the Chrasmologic Writings; but he had offered several such lambs already without attracting a divine presence to the Sacred Window. What sort of thanks would such a lamb— or even an entire flock of such lambs, for Blood's cards put a sizable flock within his reach—be now to the veiled god who had, unbribed, so greatly favored him today?

This dog-headed ape, trained to light its master's way with cresset or lantern, and (according to a badly lettered placard) to defend him from footpads and assassins, would cost at least as much as the donkey. Shaking his head, Silk walked on.

A Flier—perhaps the same Flier—sailed serenely overhead, his widespread, gauzy wings visible now, his body a dark cross against the darkening streak of the sun. The burly, bearded man beside Silk shook his fist, and several persons muttered maledictions.

"Don't nobody ever want it to rain," the nearest of the sellers of beasts remarked philosophically, "but everybody wants to go on eatin'."

Silk nodded his agreement. "The gods smile on us, my son, or so it is written. It's a wonder they don't laugh aloud."

"Do you think they're really spyin' on us, Patera, the way the Ayuntamiento keeps tellin' us? Or do they bring on rain? Rain and storms, that's what my old father used to say, and his before him. I've noticed myself that it's true pretty often. Lord Pas must know that we could use some these days."

"I really don't know," Silk confessed. "I saw one around noon today, and it hasn't rained yet. As for spying upon Viron, what could a Flier see here that any foreign traveler couldn't?"

"Nothin' I know about." The seller spat. "That's supposed to bring on rain, too, Patera. Let's hope it works this time. Lookin' for a good sacrifice, are you?"

Silk's face must have betrayed his surprise, because the seller grinned, revealing a broken front tooth. "I know you, Patera—that old manteion on Sun Street. Only you went right on past the sheepfold today. Guess they haven't been workin' out for you."

Silk endeavored to appear indifferent. "I'll recognize the beast I want when I see it."

" 'Course you will—so let me show you mine." The seller raised a soiled finger. "No, wait a bit. Let me ask you one question first. I'm just an ignorant man, Patera, but isn't a child the best sacrifice of all? The very best gift that a man or even a whole city can make to the gods? The greatest and the highest?"

Silk shrugged. "So it's written, though no such victim has been offered here within living memory. I don't believe that I could do it myself, and it's against the law in any case."

"Exactly what I'm gettin' at!" Like a conspirator, the seller glanced warily from side to side. "So what's nearest to a child, eh? Only on the right side of the law? What is it, I ask you, Patera—you and me bein' flash grown men and not no sprats—that half those high-bred females up on the Palatine is givin' suck to on the side? A catachrest, isn't that it?"

With a showman's flourish, the seller reached beneath the stained red cloth that draped his table and produced a small wire cage containing an orange-and-white catachrest. Silk was no judge of these animals, but to him it appeared hardly more than a kitten.

The seller leaned forward, and his voice dropped to a hoarse whisper. "Stolen, Patera. Stolen, or I couldn't possibly sell it, even to you, for—." He licked his lips, his restless gaze taking in Silk's faded black robe and lingering on his face. "For just six little cards. It talks. It walks on its hind legs sometimes, too, and it picks up things to eat with its little paws. It's exactly like a real child. You'll see."

Looking into the animal's melting blue eyes (the long, nycterent pupils were rapidly narrowing in the sunlight) Silk could almost believe him.

The seller tested the point of a long-bladed knife with his finger. "You recollect this, don't you, Tick? Then you better talk when I tell you to, and not try to get away, neither, when I let you out."

Silk shook his head.

If he had seen the motion, the seller ignored it. "Say *shop*. Talk for the rev'rend augur, Tick. Say *shop!*" He prodded the unhappy little catachrest with the point of his knife. "*Shop!* Say it!"

"Never mind," Silk told the seller wearily. "I'm not going to buy him."

"It'd make you a fine sacrifice, Patera—the finest you could have, inside of the law. What was it I told you? Seven cards, was that it? Tell you what. I'll make it six, but only for today. Just six cards, because I've heard good things about you and hope to do more business with you in the future."

Silk shook his head again.

"Told you Tick was boilin', didn't I? I knew it, and believe me I put crimp on the lad that did it, or I wouldn't have got Tick here half so cheap. Talked about rollin' him over to Hoppy and all that."

"It doesn't matter," Silk said.

"So now I'm goin' to let you steal him off me. Five cards,

Patera. You can—talk, you little faker, say somethin'—you can go through the whole market, if you like, and if you can find a nice catachrest like this any cheaper, bring me there and I'll match the price. Five cards, we'll say. You won't be able to touch one half this good for five cards. I promise you that, and I'm a man of my word. Ask anybody."

"No, my son."

"I need the money bad, Patera. I guess I shouldn't say that, but I do. A man has to have some money to buy animals so he's got somethin' to sell, see?" His voice fell again, so low this time that it was scarcely audible. "I put mine into a few cold 'uns. You take my meanin', Patera? Only they warmed up an' went bad on me 'fore I could move 'em. So here's what I say—five cards, with one of 'em chalked. How's that? Four down, see, right now. And a card next time I see you, which I will on Molpsday after this comin' Scylsday, Patera, I hope."

"No," Silk repeated.

"Word," the little catachrest said distinctly. "Shoe word, who add pan."

"Don't you call me a bad man." Sliding the slender blade between the wires, the seller prodded the catachrest's minute pink nose with the point of his knife. "The rev'rend augur's not interested in seein' any cully bird, you flea-bit little pap-sucker." He glanced up hopefully at Silk. "Are you, Patera? It *is* a talkin' bird at that. Naturally it doesn't look exactly like a child. It's a good talker, though—a valuable animal."

Silk hesitated.

"Berry add word," the catachrest told him spitefully, gripping the wire mesh of his cage. "Pack!" He shook it, minute black claws sharper than pins visible at the tips of his fuzzy white toes. "Add word!" he repeated. "Add speak!"

No god had spoken through the Sacred Window of the

old manteion on Sun Street since long before Silk had been born, and this was an omen beyond question: one of those oracular phrases that the gods, by means no mere human being could ever hope to understand, insert at times into the most banal speech. As calmly as he could manage, Silk said, "Go ahead and show me your talking bird. I'm here, so I might just as well have a look at it." He glanced up at the narrowing sun as if on the point of leaving. "But I've got to get back soon."

"It's a night chough, Patera," the seller told him. "Only night chough I've had this year."

This cage as well appeared from under the table. The bird crowded into it was large and glossy black, with bright red legs and a tuft of scarlet feathers at its throat; the "add speak" of the catachrest's omen was a sullen crimson, long and sharp.

"It talks?" Silk asked, though he was determined to buy it whether it could or not.

"They all do, Patera," the seller assured him, "all of these here night choughs. They learn from each other, don't you see, down there in the swamps around Palustria. I've had a few before, and this 'un's a better talker than most, from what I've heard it say."

Silk studied the bird with some care. It had seemed quite plausible that the little orange-and-white catachrest should speak: it was in fact very like a child, despite its fur. There was nothing about this downhearted fowl to suggest anything of the kind. It might almost have been a large crow.

"Somebody learned the first 'un back in the short sun time, Patera," the seller explained. "That's the story they tell about 'em, anyhow. I s'pose he got sick of hearin' it jabber an' let it go—or maybe it give him the air, 'cause they're dimber hands for that—then that 'un went home an' learned all the rest. I bought this 'un off of a limer that come up from down south. Last Phaesday, just a week ago it was. I give him a card for it."

Silk grinned. "You've a fine manner for lying, my son, but your matter gives you away. You paid ten bits or less. Isn't that what you mean?"

Sensing a sale, the seller's eyes brightened. "Why, I couldn't let it go for anything under a full card, don't you see, Patera? I'd be losing on it, an' just when I need gelt so bad. You look at this bird, now. Young an' fit as you could ask for, an' wild bred. An' then brought here clean from Palustria. A bird that'd cost you a card—every bit of one an' maybe some over—in the big market there. Why this cage here, by itself, would cost you twenty or thirty bits."

"Ah!" Silk exclaimed, rubbing his hands. "Then the cage is included in the price?"

The clack of the night chough's bill was louder than its muttered, "No, no."

"There, Patera!" The seller seemed ready to jump for joy. "Hear it? Knows everythin' we're sayin'! Knows why you want him! A card, Patera. A full card, and I won't come down by one single bit, I can't afford to. But you give me back what I paid the limer and this bird's yours, as fine a sacrifice as the Prolocutor himself might make, and for one little card."

Silk feigned to consider, glancing up at the sun once more, then around him at the dusty, teeming market. Green-shirted Guardsmen were plying the butts of their slug guns as they threaded the crowd, no doubt in pursuit of the lounging youth he had noticed earlier.

"This bird's stolen property, too, isn't he?" Silk said. "Otherwise you wouldn't have been keeping him under your table with the catachrest. You talked of threatening the poor wretch who sold you that. Roll him over to Hoppy, isn't that what you said, my son?"

The seller would not meet Silk's eyes.

"I'm no flash cull, but I've learned a little cant since I've been at my manteion. It means you threatened to inform on him to the Guard, doesn't it? Suppose that I were to threaten you in the same way now. That would be no more than just, surely."

The seller leaned closer to Silk, as he had before, his head turned to one side as if he himself were a bird, though possibly he was merely conscious of the garlic that freighted his breath. "It's just to make 'em think they're gettin' a bargain, Patera, I swear. Which you are."

The hour for the palaestra's assembly was striking when Silk returned with the night chough. A hurried sacrifice, he decided, might be worse than none, and the live bird would be a ruinous distraction. The manse had doors on Sun and Silver Streets, but he kept them bolted, as Patera Pike had. He let himself in by the garden gate, and trotted down the graveled path between the west wall of the manteion and the sickly fig tree, swung left between the grape arbor and Maytera Marble's herb garden, and took the manse's disintegrating steps two at a time. Opening the kitchen door, he set the birdcage on the shaky wooden table, pumped vigorously until the water gushed forth clear and cold, and left a full cup within easy reach of the big bird's crimson beak. By then he could hear the students trooping into the manteion. Smoothing his hair with a damp hand, he darted off to address them at the conclusion of their day.

The low door at the rear of the manteion stood open for ventilation. Silk strode through it, up a short stair whose treads had been sloped and hollowed by the hastening feet of generations of augurs, and into the dim sanctum behind the Sacred Window. Still thinking of the market and the morose black bird he had left in the kitchen of the manse, fumbling mentally for something of real significance that he might say to seventy-three students whose ages ranged

from eight to almost sixteen, he verified power and
scanned the Sacred Window's registers. All were empty.
Had Great Pas actually come to this very Window? Had any
god, ever? Had Great Pas, as Patera Pike had averred so
often, once congratulated and encouraged him, urging
him to prepare, to stand ready for the hour (soon to come,
or so Pas had appeared to intimate) when this present
whorl would vanish, would be left behind?

Such things seemed impossible. Testing connections
with an angled arm of the voided cross he wore, Silk prayed
for faith; and then—stepping carefully across a meander-
ing primary cable whose insulation was no longer to be
relied upon—drew a deep breath, stepped from behind the
Window, and took his place at the chipped ambion that
through so many such assemblies had been Patera Pike's.

Where slept Pike now, that good old man, that faithful
old servant who had slept so badly, who had nodded off for
a moment or two—only a moment or two—at each meal
they had shared? Who had both resented and loved the tall
young acolyte who had been thrust upon him after so many
years, so many slow decades of waiting alone, who had
loved him as no one had except his mother?

Where was he now, old Patera Pike? Where did he sleep,
and did he sleep well there at last? Or did he wake as he
always had, stirring in the long bedroom next to Silk's own,
his old bed creaking, creaking? Praying at midnight or past
midnight, at shadeup with the skylands fading, praying as
Viron extinguished its bonfires and its lanterns, its many-
branched candelabras, praying as they were forfeited to the
revealed sun. Praying as day's uncertain shadows reappeared and resumed their accustomed places, as the morning glories flared and the long, white trumpets of the night
silently folded themselves upon themselves.

Sleeping beside the gods, did old Patera Pike waken no
longer to recall the gods to their duties?

Erect at Patera Pike's ambion, beside the luminous gray vacuity of the Sacred Window, Silk took a moment to observe the students before he began. All were poor, he knew; and for more than a few the noon meal that half a dozen mothers had prepared in the palaestra's kitchen had been the first of the day. Yet most were almost clean; and all—under the sharp gaze of Maytera Rose, Maytera Marble, and Maytera Mint—were well behaved.

When the new year had begun, he had taken the older boys from Maytera Mint and given them to Maytera Rose: the reverse of the arrangement Patera Pike had instituted. As he ran his eyes over them now, Silk decided it had been unwise. The older boys had, for the most part, obeyed timid Maytera Mint out of an odd, half-formed chivalry, enforced when necessary by leaders like Horn; they had no such regard for Maytera Rose, and she herself imposed an inflexible and merciless order that might very well be the worst possible example to give the older boys, young men who would so soon (so very, very quickly) be maintaining order in families of their own.

Silk turned from the students to contemplate the images of Pas and his consort, Echidna: Twice-Headed Pas with his lightnings, Echidna with her serpents. It was effective; the murmur of young voices faded, dying away to an expectant hush. At the back of the manteion, Maytera Marble's eyes gleamed like violet sparks beneath her coif, and Silk knew that those eyes were on him; however much she might approve of him, Maytera Marble did not yet trust him to speak from the ambion without making a fool of himself.

"There will be no sacrifice today, at this assembly," he began, "though all of us know that there should be." He smiled, seeing that he had their interest. "This month began the first year for eleven of you. Even so, you probably know by now that we rarely have a victim for our assembly.

"Perhaps some of you are wondering why I've mentioned

it today. It's because the situation on this particular day is somewhat different—there will be a sacrifice, here in this manteion, after you have gone home. All of you, I feel quite certain, recall the lambs."

About half nodded.

"I bought those, as I think you know, using money I had saved while I was at the schola—money that my mother had sent to me—and with money I had saved here from the salary I receive from the Chapter. Do all of you realize that our manteion operates at a loss?"

The older ones did, as was plain from their expressions.

"It does," Silk continued. "The gifts we receive on Scylsday, and at other times, aren't enough to offset the very small salaries paid to our sibyls and me. Our taxes are in arrears—that means we owe money to the Juzgado, and we have various other debts. Occasionally animals are presented by benefactors, people who hope for the favor of the merciful gods. Perhaps your own parents are among them, and if they are we are very grateful to them. When no such victims are presented, our sibyls and I pool our salaries to buy a victim for Scylsday, generally a pigeon.

"But the lambs, as I said, I bought myself. Why do you think I did that, Addax?"

Addax, as old as Horn and with coloring nearly as light as Silk's own, stood. "To foretell the future, Patera."

Silk nodded as Addax resumed his seat. "Yes, to know the future of our manteion. The entrails of those lambs told me that it is bright, as you know. But mostly because I sought the favor of various gods and hoped to win it by gifts." Silk glanced at the Sacred Window behind him. "I offered the first lamb to Pas and the second to Scylla, the patroness of our city. Those, so I thought, were all that I had funds for—a single white lamb for All-powerful Pas, and another for Scylla. And I asked, as I should tell you, for a particular favor —I asked that they appear to us again, as they did of old. I longed for assurances of their love, not thinking how needless they would be when ample assurances are found throughout the Chrasmologic Writings." He tapped the worn book before him on the ambion.

"Late one evening, as I read the Writings, I came to understand that. I'd read them from boyhood—and never learned in all that time how much the gods love us, though they had told me over and over. Of what use was it, in that case, for me to have a copy of my own? I sold it, but the twenty bits it brought would not have bought another white lamb, or even a black lamb for Phaea, whose day this is. I bought a gray lamb instead, and offered it to all the gods, and the entrails of the gray lamb held the same messages of hope that I had read in the white lambs. Then I should have known, though I did not, that it was not one of the Nine who was speaking to us through the lambs. Today I learned the identity of that god, but I won't tell you that today; there is still too much I have not understood." Silk picked up the Writings and stared at the binding for a moment before he spoke again.

"This is the manteion's copy. It's the one that I read now, and it's a better one—a better printed copy, with more extensive notes—than my old one, the one I sold so that I might make a gift to all the gods. There are lessons there, and I hope that every one of you will master them. Wrestle with them a while, if they seem too difficult for you at first, and never forget that it was to teach you these wrestlings that our palaestra was founded long ago.

"Yes, Kit? What is it?"

"Patera, is a god really going to come."

Some of the older students laughed. Silk waited until they were quiet again before he replied. "Yes, Kit. A god will come to our Sacred Window, though we may have to wait a very long time. But we need not wait—we have their love and their wisdom here. Open these Writings at any point, Kit, and you'll find a passage applicable to your present condition—to the problems you have today, or to the ones you'll have to deal with tomorrow. How is this possible? Who will tell me?" Silk studied the blank faces before him before calling on one of the girls who had laughed loudest. "Answer, Ginger."

She rose reluctantly, smoothing her skirt. "Because everything's connected to everything else, Patera?" It was one of his own favorite sayings.

"Don't you know, Ginger?"

"Because everything's connected."

Silk shook his head. "That everything in the whorl is dependent on every other thing is unquestionably true. But if that were the answer to my question, we ought to find any passage from any book as appropriate to our condition as one from the Chrasmologic Writings. You need only look into any other book at random to prove that it isn't so. But," he tapped the shabby cover again, "when I open *this* book, what will we find?"

He did so, dramatically, and read the line at the top of the page aloud: " 'Are ten birds to be had for a song?' "

The clarity of this reference to his recent transaction in the market stunned him, afrighting his thoughts like so many birds. He swallowed and continued. " 'You have daubed Oreb the raven, but can you make him sing?'

"I'll interpret that for you in a moment," he promised. "First I wish to explain to you that the authors of these Writings knew not only the state of the whorl in their time—and what it had been—but what was yet to come. I'm referring," he paused, his eyes lingering on every face, "to the Plan of Pas. Everyone who understands the Plan of Pas understands the future. Am I making myself plain? The plan of Pas *is* the future, and to understand it and follow it is the principal duty of every man, and of every woman and each child.

"Knowing the Plan of Pas, as I said, the Chrasmatists knew what would best serve us each time this book would be opened—what would most firmly set your feet and mine upon the Aureate Path."

Silk paused again to study the youthful faces before him; there was a flicker of interest here and there, but no more than a flicker. He sighed.

"Now we return to the lines themselves. The first, 'Are ten birds to be had for a song?' bears three meanings at least. As you grow older and learn to think more deeply, you'll learn that every line of the Writings bears two meanings or more. One of the meanings here applies to me personally. I'll explain that meaning in a moment. The other two have application to all of us, and I'm going to deal with them first.

"To begin, we must assume that the birds referred to are of the singing kind. Notice that in the next line, when the singing kind isn't intended, that is made plain. What then, is signified by these ten singing birds? Children in class— that is to say yourselves—provide an obvious interpretation, surely. You're called upon to recite for the good sibyls who are your teachers, and your voices are high, like the twitterings of songbirds. To buy something for a song is to buy it cheaply. The meaning, as we see, is: *is this multitude of young scholars to be sold cheaply*? And the answer is clearly, no. Remember, children, how much Great Pas values, and tells us over and over again that he values, every living creature in the whorl, every color and kind of berry and butterfly—and human beings above all. No, birds are not to be sold for a song; birds are precious to Pas. We don't sacrifice birds and other animals to the immortal gods because they are of no value, do we? That would be insulting to the very gods.

" 'Are ten birds to be had for a song?' No. No, you children are not to be sold cheaply."

He had their interest now. Everyone was awake, and many were leaning forward in their seats. "For the second, we must consider the second line as well. Notice that ten singing birds might easily produce, not ten, but tens of thousands of songs." For a moment the picture filled his mind as it had once, perhaps, filled that of the long-dead Chrasmologic author: a patio garden with a fountain and many flowers, its top covered with netting—bulbuls, thrushes, larks, and goldfinches, their voices weaving a rich fabric of melody that would stretch unbroken through decades and perhaps through a century, until the netting rotted and the birds flew free at last.

And even then, might they not return at times? Would they not surely return, darting through rents in the ruined netting to drink at that tinkling fountain and nest in the safety of the patio garden, their long concerto ended yet continued beyond its end, as the orchestra plays when the audience is leaving a theater? Playing on and on for the joy of the music, when the last theater-goer has gone home, when the yawning ushers are snuffing the candles and the guttering footlights, when the actors and actresses have washed away their makeup and changed back into the clothing they ordinarily wear, the plain brown skirts and trousers, drab blouses and tunics and coats worn to the theater, worn to work as so many other drab brown garments, as plain as the bulbuls' brown feathers, were worn to work?

"But if the birds are sold," Silk continued (actors and actresses, theater and audience, garden, fountain, net, and songbirds all banished from his consciousness), "how are songs to be had? We, who were so rich in songs, are now left poor. It will not help us, as the foreknowing authors point out in the next line, to daub a raven, smearing a black bird with the delicate beauties of the lark or the decent brown of the bulbul. Not enough, even, to gild it like a goldfinch. It is still a raven."

He drew a deep breath. "Any ignorant man, you see, my children, may find himself in a position of veneration and authority. Suppose, for example, that some uneducated man—let us say an upright and an honorable man, one of you boys in Maytera Marble's class taken from her class and brought up with no further education—were by some chance to be thrust into the office of His Cognizance the Prolocutor. You would eat and sleep in His Cognizance's big palace on the Palatine. You would hold the baculus and wear the jeweled robes, and all the rest of us would kneel for your blessing. But you could not provide us with the wisdom that it would be your duty to supply. You would be a croaking raven daubed with paint, with gaudy colors."

While he counted silently to three, Silk stared up at the manteion's dusty rafters, giving the image time to sink into the minds of his audience. "I hope that you understand, from what I've said, why your education must continue. And I hope, too, that you also understand that though I took my example from the Chapter, I might just as easily have taken it from common life, speaking of a trader or a merchant, of a chief clerk or a commissioner. You have need of learning, children, in order that the whorl will someday have need of you."

Silk paused once more, both hands braced upon the old, cracked stone ambion. The tarnished sunlight that streamed through the lofty window above the wide Sun Street door was perceptibly less brilliant now. "Thus the Writings have made it abundantly clear that your palaestra *will not* be sold—not for taxes, or any other reason. I've heard that there is a rumor that it will be, and that many of you believe it. I repeat, that is not the case."

For a moment he basked in their smiles.

"Now I'll tell you about the meaning that this passage

holds for me. It was I who opened the Writings, you see, and so there was a message for me as well as for all of us here. Today, while you were studying, I went to market. There I purchased a fine speaking bird, a night chough, for a private sacrifice—one that I shall make when you have gone home.

"I've already told you how, when I bought the lambs you enjoyed so much, I hoped that a god, pleased with us, would come to this Window, as gods appeared here in the past. And I tried to show you how foolish that was. Another gift, a far greater gift, was given me instead—a gift that all the lambs in the market could not buy. I've said that I'm not going to tell you about it today, but I will tell you that it wasn't because of my prayers, or the sacrifices, or any other good work of mine that I received it. But receive it I did."

Old Maytera Rose coughed, a dry, sceptical sound from the mechanism that had replaced her larynx before Silk had spoken his first word.

"I knew that I, and I alone, must offer a sacrifice of thanks for that, though I had already spent all of the money that I had on the lambs. I would like very much to explain to you now that I had some wise plan for dealing with my dilemma—with my problem—but I didn't. Knowing only that a victim was necessary, I dashed off to the market, trusting in the merciful gods. Nor did they fail me. On the way I met a stranger who provided me with the price of an excellent victim, the speaking night chough I told you about earlier, a bird very like a raven.

"I found out, you see, that birds are not sold for a song. And I was given a sign—such is the generosity of the gracious gods to those who petition them—that a god will indeed come to this Sacred Window when I have made my sacrifice. It may be a long time, as I told Kit, so we must not be impatient. We must have faith, and remember always that the gods have other ways of speaking to us, and that if our Windows have fallen silent, these others have not. In omens and dreams and visions, the gods speak to us as they did when our parents and grandparents were young. Whenever we are willing to provide a victim, they speak to us plainly through augury, and the Writings are always here for us, to be consulted in a moment whenever we have need of them. We should be ashamed to say, as some people sometimes do, that in this age we are like boats without rudders."

Thunder rumbled through the windows, louder even than the bawlings of the beggars and vendors on Sun Street; the children stirred uneasily at the sound. After leading them in a brief prayer, Silk dismissed them.

Already the first hot, heavy drops of the storm were turning the yellow dust to mud beyond the manteion's doors. Children scurried off up or down Sun Street, none lingering this afternoon, as they sometimes did, to gossip or play.

The three sibyls had remained inside to assist at his sacrifice. Silk jogged from the manteion back to the manse, pulled on leather sacrificial gauntlets, and took the night chough from its cage. It struck at his eyes like an adder, its long, crimson beak missing by a finger's width.

He caught its head in one gauntleted hand, reminding himself grimly that many an augur had been killed by the victim he had intended to sacrifice, that scarcely a year passed without some unlucky augur, somewhere in the city, being gored by a bull or a stag.

"Don't try that again, you bad bird." He spoke half to himself. "Don't you know you'll be accursed forever if you harm me? You'll be stoned to death, and your spirit handed over to devils."

The night chough's bill clacked; its wings beat vainly until he trapped its struggling body beneath his left arm.

* * *

Back in the dim and airless heat of the manteion, the sibyls had kindled the sacrificial fire on the altar. When Silk entered, a solemn procession of one down the central aisle, they began their slow dance, their wide black skirts flapping, their tuneless voices lifted in an eerie, ritual wail that was as old as the whorl itself.

The fire was a small one, and its fragrant split cedar was already burning fast; Silk told himself that he would have to act quickly if his sacrifice were not to take place when the flames were dying, always a bad omen.

Passing the bird quickly over the fire, he pronounced the shortest invocation and gave his instructions in a rush of uncadenced words: "Bird, you must speak to every god and goddess you encounter, telling them of our faith and of our great love and loyalty. Say too how grateful I am for the immense and undeserved condescension accorded me, and tell them how earnestly we desire their divine presence at this, our Sacred Window.

"Bird, you must speak thus to Great Pas, the Father of the Gods.

"Bird, you must speak thus also to Sinuous Echidna, Great Pas's consort. You must speak so to Scalding Scylla, to Marvelous Molpe, to Black Tartaros, to Mute Hierax, to Enchanting Thelxiepeia, to Ever-feasting Phaea, to Desert Sphigx, and to any other god that you may encounter in Mainframe—but particularly to the Outsider, who has greatly favored me, saying that for the remainder of my days I will do his will. That I abase myself before him."

"No, no," the night chough muttered, as it had in the market. And then, "Please, no."

Silk pronounced the final words: "Have no speech with devils, bird. Neither are you to linger in any place where devils are."

Grasping the frantic night chough firmly by the neck, he

extended his gauntleted right hand to Maytera Rose, the senior among the sibyls. Into it she laid the bone-hilted knife of sacrifice that Patera Pike had inherited from his own predecessor. Its long, oddly crooked blade was dull with years and the ineradicable stains of blood, but both edges were bright and keen.

The night chough's beak gaped. It struggled furiously. A last strangled half-human cry echoed from the distempered walls of the manteion, and the wretched night chough went limp in Silk's grasp. Interrupting the ritual, he held the flaccid body to his ear, then brushed open one blood-red eye with his thumb.

"It's dead," he told the wailing women. For a moment he was at a loss for words. Helplessly he muttered, "I've never had this happen before. Dead already, before I could sacrifice it."

They halted their shuffling dance. Maytera Marble said diplomatically, "No doubt it has already carried your thanks to the gods, Patera."

Maytera Rose sniffed loudly and reclaimed the sacrificial knife.

Little Maytera Mint inquired timidly, "Aren't you going to burn it, Patera?"

Silk shook his head. "Mishaps of this kind are covered in the rubrics, Maytera, although I admit I never thought I'd have to apply those particular strictures. They state unequivocally that unless another victim can be produced without delay, the sacrifice must not proceed. In other words, we can't just throw this dead bird into the sacred fire. This could just as well be something that one of the children picked up in the street."

He wanted to rid himself of it as he spoke—to fling it among the benches or drop it down the chute into which Maytera Marble and Maytera Mint would eventually shovel the still-sacred ashes of the altar fire. Controlling himself with an effort, he added, "All of you have seen more of life than I. Haven't you ever assisted at a profaned sacrifice before?"

Maytera Rose sniffed again. Like her earlier sniff, it reeked of condemnation; what had happened was unquestionably Patera Silk's fault, and his alone. It had been he and none other (as the sniff made exquisitely plain), who had chosen this contemptible bird. If only he had been a little more careful, a little more knowledgeable, and above all a great deal more pious—in short, much, much more like poor dear Patera Pike—nothing of this shameful kind could possibly have occurred.

Maytera Marble said, "No, Patera, never. May I speak with you when we're through here, on another topic? In my room in the palaestra, perhaps?"

Silk nodded. "I'll meet you there as soon as I've disposed of this, Maytera." The temptation to berate himself proved too strong. "I ought to have known better. The Writings warned me; but they left me foolish enough to suppose that my sacrifice might yet be acceptable, even if our Sacred Window remained empty. This will be a salutary lesson for me, Maytera. At least I certainly hope it will be, and it had better be. Thank Phaea that the children weren't here to see it."

By this time Maytera Mint had nerved herself to speak. "No one can ever know the mind of the Outsider, Patera. He isn't like the other gods, who take counsel with one another in Mainframe."

"But when the gods have spoken so clearly—" Realizing that what he was saying was not to the point, Silk left the thought incomplete. "You're right, of course, Maytera. His desires have been made plain to me, and this sacrifice was not included among them. In the future I'll try to confine myself to doing what he's told me to do. I know I can rely upon all of you to assist me in that, as in everything."

Maytera Rose did not sniff a third time, mercifully contenting herself with scratching her nose instead. Her nose, her mouth, and her right eye were the most presentable parts of her face; and though they had been molded of some tough polymer, they appeared almost normal. Her left eye, with which she had been born, seemed at once mad and blind, bleared and festering.

While trying to avoid that eye, and wishing (as he so often had since coming to the manteion) that replacements were still available, Silk shifted the night chough from his left hand to his right. "Thank you, Maytera Rose, Maytera Marble, Maytera Mint. Thank you. We'll do much better next time, I feel certain." He had slipped off his sacrificial gauntlets; the hated bird felt warm and somehow dusty in his perspiring hands. "In the palaestra, in five minutes or so, Maytera Marble."

Chapter 3

TWILIGHT

"In here, Patera!"

Silk halted abruptly, nearly slipping as the wet gravel rolled beneath his shoes.

"In the arbor," Maytera Marble added. She waved, her black-clad arm and gleaming hand just visible through the screening grape leaves.

The first fury of the storm had passed off quickly, but it was still raining, a gentle pattering that settled like a benediction upon her struggling beds of kitchen herbs.

We meet like lovers, Silk thought as he regained his balance and pushed aside the dripping foliage, and wondered for an instant whether she did not think the same.

No. As lovers, he admitted to himself. For he loved her as he had loved his mother, as he might have loved the older sister he had never had, striving to draw forth the shy smile she achieved by an inclination of her head—to win her approval, the approbation of an old sibyl, of a worn-out chem at whom nobody, when he had been small and there had been a lot more chems around, would ever have troubled to glance twice, whom no one but the youngest children ever thought interesting. How lonely he would have been in the midst of the brawling congestion of this quarter, if it had not been for her!

She rose as he entered the arbor and sat again as he sat. He said, "You really don't have to do that when we're alone, sib. I've told you."

Maytera Marble tilted her head in such a way that her rigid, metal face appeared contrite. "Sometimes I forget. I apologize, Patera."

"And I forget that I should never correct you, because I always find out, as soon as it's too late, that you were right after all. What is it you want to talk to me about, Maytera?"

"You don't mind the rain?" Maytera Marble looked up at the overarching thatch of vines.

"Of course not. But you must. If you don't feel like walking all the way to the palaestra, we could go into the manteion. I want to see if the roof still leaks, anyway."

She shook her head. "Maytera Rose would be upset. She knows that it's perfectly innocent, but she doesn't want us meeting in the palaestra, with no one else present. People might talk, you know—the kind of people who never attend sacrifices anyway, and are looking for an excuse. And she didn't want to come herself, and Maytera Mint's watching the fire. So I thought out here. It's not quite so private— Maytera can see us through the windows of the cenoby— and we still have a bit of shelter from the rain."

Silk nodded. "I understand."

"You said the rain must make me uncomfortable. That was very kind of you, but I don't feel it and my clothes will dry. I've had no trouble drying the wash lately, but it takes a great deal of pumping to get enough water to do it in. Is the manse's well still good?"

"Yes, of course." Seeing her expression, Silk shook his head. "No, not of course. It's comforting to believe as children do that Pas won't resist his daughter's pleas in our behalf much longer, and that he'll always provide for us. But one never knows, really; we can only hope. If we must have new wells dug, the Church will have to lend us the money, that's all. If we can't keep this manteion going without new wells, it will have to."

Maytera Marble said nothing, but sat with head bowed as though unable to meet his eyes.

"Does it worry you so much, Maytera? Listen, and I'll tell you a secret. The Outsider has enlightened me."

Motionless, she might have been a time-smoothed statue, decked for some eccentric commemorative purpose in a sibyl's black robe.

"It's true, Maytera! Don't you believe me?"

Looking up she said, "I believe that you believe you've been enlightened, Patera. I know you well, or at least I think I do, and you wouldn't lie about a thing like that."

"And he told me why—to save our manteion. That's my task." Silk stumbled after words. "You can't imagine how good it feels to be given a task by a god, Maytera. It's wonderful! You know it's what you were made for, and your whole heart points toward that one thing."

He rose, unable to sit still any longer. "If I'm to save our manteion, doesn't that tell us something? I ask you."

"I don't know, Patera. Does it?"

"Yes! Yes, it does. We can apply logic even to the instructions of the gods, can't we? To their acts and to their words, and we can certainly apply logic to this. It tells us two things, both of major importance. First, that the manteion's in danger. He wouldn't have ordered me to save it if it weren't, would he? So there's a threat of some sort, and that's vital for us to know." Silk strode out into the warm rain to stare east toward Mainframe, the home of the gods.

"The second is even more important, Maytera. It's that our manteion can be saved. It's endangered, not doomed, in other words. He wouldn't have ordered me to save it if that couldn't be done, would he?"

"Please come in and sit down, Patera," Maytera Marble pleaded. "I don't want you to catch cold."

Silk re-entered the arbor, and she stood.

"You don't have—" he began, then grinned sheepishly. "Forgive me, Maytera. Forgive me, please. I grow older, learning nothing at all."

She swung her head from side to side, her silent laugh. "You're not old, Patera. I watched you play a while today, and none of the boys are as quick as you are."

"That's only because I've been playing longer," he said, and they sat down together.

Smiling she clasped his hand in hers, surprising him. The soft skin had worn from the tips of her fingers long ago, leaving bare steel darkened like her thoughts by time, and polished by unending toil. "You and the children are the only things at this manteion that aren't old. You don't belong here, neither of you."

"Maytera Mint's not old. Not really, Maytera, though I know she's a good deal older than I am."

Maytera Marble sighed, a soft *hish* like the weary sweep of a mop across a terrazzo floor. "Poor Maytera Mint was born old, I fear. Or taught to be old before she could talk, perhaps. However that may be, she has always belonged here. As you never have, Patera."

"You believe it's going to be torn down, too, don't you? No matter what the Outsider may have told me."

Reluctantly, Maytera Marble nodded. "Yes, I do. Or as I ought to say, the buildings themselves may remain, although even that appears to be in doubt. But your manteion will no longer bring the gods to the people of this quarter, and our palaestra will no longer teach their children."

Silk snapped, "What chance would these sprats have—without your palaestra?"

"What chance do children of their class have now?"

He shook his head angrily, and would have liked to paw the ground.

"Such things have happened before, Patera. The Chapter will find new manteions for us. Better manteions, I think, because it would be difficult to find worse ones. I'll go on teaching and assisting, and you'll go on sacrificing and shriving. It will be all right."

"I received enlightenment today," Silk said. "I've told no one except a man I met in the street on my way to the market and you, and neither of you have believed me."

"Patera—"

"So it's clear that I'm not telling it very well, isn't it? Let me see if I can't do better." He was silent for a moment, rubbing his cheek.

"I'd been praying and praying for help. Praying mostly to the Nine, of course, but praying to every god and goddess in the Writings at one time or another; and about noon today my prayers were answered by the Outsider, as I've told you. Maytera, do you . . ." His voice quavered, and he found that he could not control it. "Do you know what he said to me, Maytera? What he told me?"

Her hands closed upon his until their grip was actually painful. "Only that he has instructed you to preserve our manteion. Please tell me the rest, if you can."

"You're right, Maytera. It isn't easy. I had always thought enlightenment would be a voice out of the sun, or in my own head, a voice that spoke in words. But it's not like that at all. He whispers to you in so many voices, and the words are living things that show you. Not just seeing, the way you might see another person in a glass, but hearing and smelling—and touch and pain, too, but all of them wrapped together so they become the same, parts of that one thing.

"And you understand. When I say he showed me, or that he told me something, that's what I mean."

Maytera Marble nodded encouragingly.

"He showed me all the prayers that have ever been said to any god for this manteion. I saw all the children at prayer from the time it was first built, their mothers and fathers too, and people who just came in to pray, or came to one of our sacrifices because they hoped to get a piece of meat, and prayed while they were here.

"And I saw the prayers of all you sibyls, from the very beginning. I don't ask you to believe this, Maytera, but I've seen every prayer you've ever said for our manteion, or for Maytera Rose and Maytera Mint, or for Patera Pike and me, and—well, for everyone in this whole quarter, thousands and thousands of prayers. Prayers on your knees and prayers standing up, and prayers you said while you were cooking and scrubbing floors. There used to be a Maytera Milkwort here, and I saw her praying, and a Maytera Betel, a big dark woman with sleepy eyes." Silk paused for breath. "Most of all, I saw Patera Pike."

"This is wonderful!" Maytera Marble exclaimed. "It must have been marvelous, Patera." Silk knew it was impossible, that it was only their crystalline lenses catching the light, but it seemed to him that her eyes shone.

"And the Outsider decided to grant all those prayers. He told Patera Pike, and Patera Pike was so happy! Do you remember the day I came here from the schola, Maytera?"

Maytera Marble nodded again.

"That was the day. The Outsider granted Patera Pike enlightenment that day, and he said—he said, here's the help that I'm—that I'm . . ."

Silk had begun to weep, and was suddenly ashamed. It was raining harder now, as if encouraged by the tears that streaked his cheeks and chin. Maytera Marble pulled a big, clean, white handkerchief out of her sleeve and gave it to him.

She's always so practical, he thought, wiping his eyes and nose. A handkerchief for the little ones; she must have a child sobbing in her class every day. The record of her days is written in tears, and today I'm that sobbing child. He managed to say, "Your children can't often be as old as I am, Maytera."

"In class, you mean, Patera? They're never as old. Oh, you must mean the grown men and women who were mine when they were boys and girls. Many of them are older than you are. The oldest must be sixty, or about that. I was—didn't teach until then." She called her memorandum file, chiding herself as she always did for not calling it more often. "Which reminds me. Do you know Auk, Patera?"

Silk shook his head. "Does he live in this quarter?"

"Yes, and comes on Scylsday, sometimes. You must have seen him. The large, rough-looking man who sits in back?"

"With the big jaw? His clothes are clean, but he looks as if he hasn't shaved. He wears a hanger—or perhaps it's a hunting sword—and he's always alone. Was he one of your boys?"

Maytera Marble nodded sadly. "He's a criminal now, Patera. He breaks into houses."

"I'm sorry to hear that," Silk said. For an instant he had a mental picture of the hulking man from the back of the manteion surprised by a householder and whirling clumsily but very quickly to confront him, like a baited bear.

"I'm sorry, too, Patera, and I've been wanting to talk to you about him. Patera Pike shrove him last year. You were here, but I don't think you knew about it."

"If I did, I've forgotten." To quiet the hiss of the wide blade as it cleared the scabbard, Silk shook his head. "But you're right, Maytera. I doubt that I knew."

"I didn't learn about it from Patera myself. Maytera Mint told me. Auk still likes her, and they have a little talk now and then."

Blowing his nose in his own handkerchief, Silk relaxed a trifle. This, he felt certain, was what she had wanted to speak to him about.

"Patera was able to get Auk to promise not to rob poor

people any more. He'd done that, he said. He'd done it quite often, but he wouldn't any more. He promised Patera, Maytera says, and he promised her, too. You're going to lecture me now, Patera, because the promise of a man like that—a criminal's promise—can't be trusted."

"No man's promise can be trusted absolutely," Silk said slowly, "since no man is, or can ever be, entirely free from evil. I include myself in that, certainly."

Maytera Marble pushed her handkerchief back into her sleeve. "I think Auk's promise, freely given, can be relied on as much as anybody's, Patera. As much as yours, and I don't intend to be insulting. That was the way he was as a boy, and it's the way he is as a man, too, as well as I can judge. He never had a mother or a father, not really. He— but I'd better not go on, or I'll let slip things that Maytera's made me promise not to repeat, and then I'll feel terrible, and I'll have to tell both of them that I broke my word."

"Do you really believe that I may be able to help this man, Maytera? I'm surely no older than he is, and probably younger. He's not going to respect me the way he respected Patera Pike, remember."

Rain dripping from the sparkling leaves dotted Maytera Marble's skirt; she brushed at the spots absently. "That may be true, Patera, but you'll understand him better than Patera Pike could, I think. You're young, and as strong as he is, or almost. And he'll respect you as an augur. You needn't be afraid of him. Have I ever asked a favor of you, Patera? A real favor?"

"You asked me to intercede with Maytera Rose once, and I tried. I think I probably did more harm than good, so we won't count that. But you could ask a hundred favors if you wanted to, Maytera. You've earned that many and more."

"Then talk with Auk, Patera, some Scylsday. Shrive him if he asks you to."

"That isn't a favor," Silk said. "I'd do that much for

anyone; but of course you want me to make a special effort for this Auk, to speak to him and take him aside, and so on; and I will."

"Thank you, Patera. Patera, you've known me for over a year now. Am I lacking in faith?"

The question caught Silk by surprise. "You, Maytera? Why—why I've never thought so. You've always seemed, I mean to me at least—"

"Yet I haven't had the faith in you, and the god who enlightened you, that I should've had. I just realized it. I've been trusting in merely human words and appearances, like any petty trader. You were saying that the god had promised Patera Pike help, I think. Could you tell me more about that? I was only listening with care before. This time I'll listen with faith, or try to."

"There's more than I could ever tell." Silk stroked his cheek. He had himself in check now. "Patera Pike was enlightened, as I said; and I was shown his enlightenment. He was told that all those prayers he had said over so many years were to be granted that day—that the help he had asked for, for himself and for this manteion and the whole quarter, would be sent to him at once."

Silk discovered that his fists were clenched. He made himself relax. "I was shown all that; then I saw that help arrive, alight as if with Pas's fire from the sun. And it was me. That was all it was, just me."

"Then you cannot fail," Maytera Marble told him softly.

Silk shook his head. "I wish it were that easy. I can fail, Maytera. I dare not."

She looked grave, as she often did. "But you didn't know this until today? At noon, in the ball court? That's what you said."

"No, I didn't. He told me something else, you see—that the time has come to act."

Maytera Marble sighed again. "I have some information

for you, Patera. Discouraging information, I'm afraid. But first I want very much to ask you just one thing more, and tell you something, perhaps. It was the Outsider who spoke to you, you say?"

"Yes. I don't know a great deal about him, however, even now. He's one of the sixty-three gods mentioned in the Writings, but I haven't had a chance to look him up since it happened, and as I remember there isn't a great deal about him anyway. He told me about himself, things that aren't in the Writings unless I've forgotten them; but I haven't really had much time to think about them."

"When we were outside like him, living in the Short Sun Whorl before this one was finished and peopled, we worshipped him. No doubt you knew that already, Patera."

"I'd forgotten it," Silk admitted, "but you're right. It's in the tenth book, or the twelfth."

"We chems didn't share in sacrifices in the Short Sun Whorl." Maytera Marble fell silent for a moment, scanning old files. "It wasn't called manteion, either. Something else. If only I could find that, I could remember more, I think."

Without understanding what she meant, Silk nodded.

"There have been many changes since then, but it used to be taught that he was infinite. Not merely great, but truly without limit. There are expressions like that—I mean in arithmetic. Although we never get to them in my class."

"He showed me."

"They say that even the whorl ends someplace," Maytera Marble continued, "immense though it is. He doesn't. If you were to divide him among all the things in it, each part of him would still be limitless. Didn't you feel awfully small, Patera, when he was showing you all these things?"

Silk considered his answer. "No, I don't think I did. No, I didn't. I felt—well, great. I felt that way even though he was immeasurably greater, as you say. Imagine, Maytera, that His Cognizance the Prolocutor were to speak to me in person, assigning me some special duty. I'd feel, of course, that he was a far greater man than I, and a far, far greater man than I could ever be; but I'd feel that I too had become a person of significance." Silk paused, ruminating. "Now suppose a Prolocutor incalculably great."

"I understand. That answers several questions that I've had for a long while. Thank you, Patera. My news—I want to tell you why I asked you to meet me."

"It's bad news, I assume." Silk drew a deep breath. "Knowing that the manteion's at risk, I've been expecting some."

"It would appear to indicate—mistakenly, I feel sure, Patera—that you've failed already. You see, a big, red-faced man came to the palaestra while you were away. He said that he'd just bought it, bought the entire property from the city." Maytera Marble's voice fell. "From the Ayuntamiento, Patera. That's what he told me. He was here to look at our buildings. I showed him the palaestra and the manteion. I'm quite sure he didn't get into the cenoby or the manse, but he looked at everything from the outside."

"He said the sale was complete?"

She nodded.

"You're right, Maytera. This sounds very bad."

"He'd come in a floater, with a man to operate it for him. I saw it when we were going from the palaestra to the manteion. We went out the front, and along Sun Street past the ball court. He said he'd talked to you before he came here, but he hadn't told you he'd bought it. He said he'd thought you'd make trouble."

Silk nodded slowly. "I'd have hauled him out of his floater and broken his neck, I think, Maytera. Or at least I would have tried to."

She touched his knee. "That would have been wrong, Patera. You'd go to the Alambrera, and into the pits."

"Which wouldn't matter," Silk said. "His name's Blood, perhaps he told you."

"Possibly he did." Maytera Marble's rapid scan seldom functioned now; she fell silent as she searched past files, then said, "It's not a common name at all, you know. People think it's unlucky. I don't believe I've ever had a single boy called Blood."

Silk stroked his cheek, his eyes thoughtful. "Have you heard of him, Maytera? I haven't, but he must be a wealthy man to have a private floater."

"I don't think so. If the sale is complete, Patera, what can you do?"

"I don't know." Silk rose as he had before. A step carried him out of the arbor. A few drops of rain still fell through sunshine that seemed bright, though the shade had more than half covered the sun. "The market will be closing soon," he said.

"Yes." Maytera Marble joined him.

The skylands, which had been nearly invisible earlier, could be seen distinctly as dawn spread across them: distant forests, said to be enchanted, and distant cities, said to be haunted—subtle influences for good or ill, governing the lives of those below. "He's not a foreigner," Silk said, "or at least he doesn't talk like any foreigner I've ever met. He sounded as though he might have come from this quarter, actually."

Maytera Marble nodded. "I noticed that myself."

"There aren't many ways for our people here to become rich, are there, Maytera? I wouldn't think so, at least."

"I'm not sure I follow you."

"It doesn't matter. You wanted me to speak with this man Auk. On a Scylsday, you said; but there are always a dozen people waiting to talk to me then. Where do you think I might find Auk today?"

"Why, I have no idea. Could you go and see him this

evening, Patera? That would be wonderful! Maytera Mint~
might know."

Silk nodded. "You said that she was in the manteion,
waiting for the fire to die. Go in and ask her, please, while
you're helping her purify the altar. I'll speak with you again
in a few minutes."

Watching them from a window of the cenoby, Maytera
Rose grunted with satisfaction when they separated. There
was danger there, no matter how Maytera and Patera might
deceive themselves—filthy things she could do for him, and
worse that he might do to her. Undefiled Echidna hated
everything of that kind, blinding those who fell as she had
blinded her. At times Maytera Rose, kneeling before her
daughter's image, felt that she herself was Echidna, Mother
of Gods and Empress of the Whorl.

Strike, Echidna. Oh, strike!

It was dark enough already for the bang of the door to
kindle the bleared light in one corner of Silk's bedroom,
the room over the kitchen, the old storeroom that old
Patera Pike had helped clean out when he arrived. (For Silk
had never been able to make himself move his possessions
into Pike's larger room, to throw out or burn the faded
portraits of the old man's parents or his threadbare, too-
small clothing.) By that uncertain glow, Silk changed into
his second-best robe. Collar and cuffs were detachable in
order that they might be more easily, and thus more frequently, laundered. He removed them and laid them in the
drawer beside his only spare set.

What else? He glanced in the mirror; some covering for
his untidy yellow hair, certainly. There was the wide straw
hat he had worn that morning while laying new shingles on
the roof, and the blue-trimmed black calotte that Patera
Pike had worn on the coldest days. Silk decided upon both;
the wide straw would cast a strong shadow on his face, but

might blow off. The calotte fit nicely beneath it, and would supply a certain concealment still. Was this how men like this man Auk felt? Was it how they planned?

As reported by Maytera Marble, Maytera Mint had named half a dozen places in which he might come across Auk; all were in the Orilla, the worst section of the quarter. He might be robbed, might be murdered even though he offered no resistance. If Blood would not see him . . .

Silk shrugged. Blood's house would be somewhere on the Palatine; Silk could scarcely conceive of anyone who rode in a privately owned floater living anywhere else. There would be Civil Guardsmen everywhere on the Palatine after dark, Guardsmen on foot, on horseback, and in armed floaters. One could not just kick down a door, as scores of housebreakers did in this quarter every night. The thing was impossible.

Yet something must be done, and done tonight; and he could not think of anything else to do.

He fingered his beads, then dropped them back into his pocket, removed the silver chain and voided cross of Pas and laid them reverently before the triptych, folded two fresh sheets of paper, put them into the battered little pen case he had used at the schola, and slipped it into the big inner pocket of his robe. He might need a weapon; he would almost certainly need some sort of tool.

He went downstairs to the kitchen. There was a faint stirring from the smelly waste bin in the corner: a rat, no doubt. As he had often before, Silk reminded himself to have Horn catch him a snake that might be tamed.

Through the creaking kitchen door, he stepped out into the garden again. It was almost dark, and would be fully dark by the time he reached the Orilla, eight streets away. The afternoon's rain had laid the dust, and the air, cooler than it had been in months, was fresh and clean; perhaps autumn was on the way at last. He should be tired, Silk told himself, yet he did not feel tired as he unlocked the side door of the manteion. Was this, in sober fact, what the Outsider wanted? This rush to battle? If so, his service was a joy indeed!

The altar fire was out, the interior of the manteion lit only by the silver sheen of the Sacred Window and the hidden flame of the fat, blue-glass lamp between Echidna's feet—Maytera Rose's lamp, burning some costly scented oil whose fragrance stirred his memory.

He clapped his hands to kindle the few lights still in working order, then fumbled among the shadows for the long-hafted, narrow-bladed hatchet with which he split shingles and drove roofing nails. Finding it, he tested its edge (so painstakingly sharpened that very morning) before slipping its handle into his waistband.

That, he decided after walking up and down and twice pretending to sit, would not do. There was a rusty saw in the palaestra's supply closet; it would be simple to shorten the handle, but the hatchet would be a less useful tool, and a much less serviceable weapon, afterward.

Stooping again, he found the rope that had prevented his bundle of shingles from sliding off the roof, a thin braided cord of black horsehair, old and pliant but still strong. Laying aside robe and tunic, he wound it about his waist, tied the ends, and slid the handle of the hatchet through several of the coils.

Dressed again, he emerged once more into the garden, where a vagrant breeze sported with the delectable odor of cooking from the cenoby, reminding him that he ought to be preparing his own supper at this very moment. He shrugged, promising himself a celebratory one when he returned. The tomatoes that had dropped green from his vines were still not ripe, but he would slice them and fry them in a little oil. There was bread, too, he reminded himself, and the hot oil might be poured over it afterward to flavor and soften it. His mouth watered. He would scrape out the grounds he had reused so long, scrub the pot, and brew fresh coffee. Finish with an apple and the last of the cheese. A feast! He wiped his lips on his sleeve, ashamed of his greed.

After closing and carefully locking the side door of the manteion, he made a wary study of the cenoby windows. It would probably not matter if Maytera Marble or Maytera Mint saw him leave, but Maytera Rose would not hesitate to subject him to a searching cross-examination.

The rain had ended, there could be no doubt of that; there had been an hour of rain at most, when the farmers needed whole days of it. As he hurried along Sun Street once more, east this time and thus away from the market, Silk studied the sky.

The thinnest possible threads of gold still shone here and there among scudding clouds, threads snapped already by the rising margin of the ink-black shade. While he watched, the threads winked out; and the skylands, which had hovered behind the long sun like so many ghosts, shone forth in all their beauty and wonder: flashing pools and rolling forests, checkered fields and gleaming cities.

Lamp Street brought him to the Orilla, where the lake waters had begun when Viron was young. This crumbling wall half buried in hovels had been a busy quay, these dark and hulking old buildings, warehouses. No doubt there had been salting sheds, too, and rope walks, and many other things; but all such lightly built structures had disappeared before the last caldé, rotted, tumbled, and at last cannibalized for firewood. The very weeds that had sprouted from their sites had withered, and the cellar of every shiprock ruin left standing was occupied by a tavern.

Listening to the angry voices that issued from the one he approached, Silk wondered why anyone went there. What sorts of lives could they be to which fifty or a hundred men and women preferred this? It was a terrifying thought.

He paused at the head of the stair to puzzle out the drawing chalked on the grimy wall beside it, a fierce bird with outstretched wings. An eagle? Not with those spurs. A gamecock, surely; and the Cock had been one of the places suggested by Maytera Mint, a tavern (so Maytera Marble had said) she recalled Auk's mentioning.

The steep and broken stairs stank of urine; Silk held his breath as he groped down them, not much helped by the faint yellow radiance from the open door. Stepping to one side just beyond the doorway, he stood with his back to the wall and surveyed the low room. No one appeared to pay the least attention to him.

It was larger than he had expected, and less furnished. Mismatched deal tables stood here and there, isolated, but surrounded by chairs, stools, and benches equally hetero-dox on which a few silent figures lounged. Odious candles fumed and dribbled a sooty wax upon some (though by no means all) of these tables, and a green and orange lampion with a torn shade swung in the center of the room, seeming to tremble at the high-pitched anger of the voices below it. The backs of jostling onlookers obscured what was taking place there.

"Hornbus, you whore!" a woman shrieked.

A man's voice, slurred by beer yet hissing swift with the ocher powder called rust, suggested, "Stick it out your skirt, sweetheart, an' maybe she will." There was a roar of laugh-ter. Someone kicked over a table, its thud accompanied by the crash of breaking glass.

"Here! Here now!" Quickly but without the appearance of haste, a big man with a hideously scarred face pushed through the crowd, an old skittlepin in one hand. "OUT-side now! OUTside with this!" The onlookers parted to let two women with dirty gowns and disheveled hair through.

"Outside with *her!*" One woman pointed.

"OUTside with both." The big man caught the speaker expertly by the collar, tapped her head almost gently with the skittlepin, and shoved her toward the door.

One of the watching men stepped forward, held up his hand, and gestured in the direction of the other woman, who seemed to Silk almost too drunk to stand.

"Her, too," the big man with the skittlepin told her advocate firmly.

He shook his head.

"Her too! And you!" The big man loomed above him, a head the taller. "OUTside!"

Steel gleamed and the skittlepin flashed down. For the first time in his life, Silk heard the sickening crepitation of breaking bone; it was followed at once by the high, sharp report of a needler, a sound like the crack of a child's toy whip. A needler (momentarily, Silk thought it the needler that had fired) flew into the air, and one of the onlookers pitched forward.

Silk was on his knees beside him before he himself knew what he had done, his beads swinging half their length in sign after sign of addition. "I convey to you, my son, the forgiveness of all the gods. Recall now the words of Pas—"

"He's not dead, cully. You an augur?" It was the big man with the scarred face. His right arm was bleeding, dark blood oozing through a soiled rag he pressed tightly against the cut.

"In the name of all the gods you are forgiven forever, my son. I speak here for Great Pas, for Divine Echidna, for Scalding Scylla, for—"

"Get him out of here," someone snapped; Silk could not tell whether he meant the dead man or himself. The dead man was bleeding less than the big man, a steady, unspectacular welling from his right temple. Yet he was surely dead; as Silk chanted the Final Formula and swung his beads, his left hand sought a pulse, finding none.

"His friends'll take care of him, Patera. He'll be all right."

Two of the dead man's friends had already picked up his feet.

". . . and for Strong Sphigx. Also for all lesser gods." Silk hesitated; it had no place in the Formula, but would these people know? Or care? Before rising, he finished in a whisper: "The Outsider likewise forgives you, my son, no matter what evil you did in life."

The tavern was nearly empty. The man who had been hit with the skittlepin groaned and stirred. The drunken woman was kneeling beside him just as Silk had knelt beside the dead man, swaying even on her knees, one hand braced on the filthy floor. There was no sign of the needler that had flown into the air, nor of the knife that the injured man had drawn.

"You want a red ribbon, Patera?"

Silk shook his head.

"Sure you do. On me, for what you done." The big man wound the rag about his arm, knotted it dexterously with his left hand, and pulled the knot tight with his left hand and his teeth.

"I need to know something," Silk said, returning his beads to his pocket, "and I'd much rather learn it than get a free drink. I'm looking for a man called Auk. Was he in here? Can you tell me where I might find him?"

The big man grinned, the gap left by two missing teeth a little cavern in his mirth. "Auk, you say, Patera? Auk? There's quite a few with that name. Owe him money? How'd you know I'm not Auk myself?"

"Because I know him, my son. Know him by sight, I should have said. He's nearly as tall as you are, with small eyes, a heavy jaw, and large ears. I would guess he's five or six years younger than you are. He attends our Scylsday sacrifices regularly."

"Does he now." The big man appeared to be staring off into the dimness of the darkest corner of the room; abruptly he said, "Why, Auk's still here, Patera. Didn't you tell me you'd seen him go?"

"No," Silk began. "I—"

"Over there." The big man pointed toward the corner, where a solitary figure sat at a table not much larger than his chair.

"Thank you, my son," Silk called. He crossed the room, detouring around a long and dirty table. "Auk? I'm Patera Silk, from the manteion on Sun Street."

"Thanks for what?" the man called Auk inquired.

"For agreeing to talk with me. You signaled to him somehow—waved or something, I suppose. I didn't see it, but it's obvious you must have."

"Sit down, Patera."

There was no other chair. Silk brought a stool from the long table and sat.

"Somebody send you?"

Silk nodded. "Maytera Mint, my son. But I don't wish to give you the wrong impression. I haven't come as a favor to her, or as a favor to you, either. Maytera was doing me a favor by telling me where to find you, and I've come to ask you for another one, shriving."

"Figure I need it, Patera?" There was no trace of humor in Auk's voice.

"I have no way of knowing, my son. Do you?"

Auk appeared to consider. "Maybe so. Maybe not."

Silk nodded—understandingly, he hoped. He found it unnerving to talk with this burly ruffian in the gloom, unable to see his expression.

The big man with the wounded arm set an astonishingly

delicate glass before Silk. "The best we got, Patera." He backed away.

"Thank you, my son." Turning on his stool, Silk looked behind him; the injured man and the drunken woman were no longer beneath the lampion, though he had not heard them go.

"Maytera Mint likes you, Patera," Auk remarked. "She tells me things about you sometimes. Like the time you got the cats' meat woman mad at you."

"You mean Scleroderma?" Silk felt himself flush, and was suddenly glad that Auk could not see him better. "She's a fine woman—a kind and quite genuinely religious woman. I was hasty and tactless, I'm afraid."

"She really empty her bucket over you?"

Silk nodded ruefully. "The odd thing was that I found a scrap of—of cats' meat, I suppose you'd call it, down my neck afterward. It stank."

Auk laughed softly, a deep, pleasant laugh that made Silk like him.

"I thought it an awful humiliation at the time," Silk continued. "It happened on a Thelxday, and I thanked her on my knees that my poor mother wasn't alive to hear about it. I thought, you know, that she would have been terribly hurt, just as I was myself at the time. Now I realize that she would only have teased me about it." He sipped from the graceful little glass before him; it was probably brandy, he decided, and good brandy, too. "I'd let Scleroderma paint me blue and drag me the whole length of the Alameda, if it would bring my mother back."

"Maytera Mint was the nearest to a real mother I ever had," Auk said. "I used to call her that—she let me—when we were alone. For a couple of years I pretended like that. She tell you?"

Silk shook his head, then added, "Maytera Marble said

something of the sort. I'm afraid I didn't pay a great deal of attention to it."

"The Old One brought up us boys, and he raised us hard. It's the best way. I've seen a lot that didn't get it, and I know."

"I'm sure you do."

"Every so often I tell myself I ought to stick my knife in her, just to get her and her talk out of my head. Know what I mean?"

Silk nodded, although he could not be certain that the burly man across the table could see it. "Better than you do yourself, I think. I also know that you'll never actually harm her. Or if you do, it won't be for that reason. I'm not half as old as Patera Pike was, and not a tenth as wise; but I do know that."

"I wouldn't take the long end of that bet."

Silk said nothing, his eyes upon the pale blur that was Auk's face, where for a moment it seemed to him that he had glimpsed the shadow of a muzzle, as though the unseen face were that of a wolf or bear.

Surely, he thought, this man can't have been called Auk from birth. Surely "Auk" is a name he's assumed.

He pictured Maytera Mint leading the boy Auk into class on a chain, then Maytera Mint warned by Maytera Rose that Auk would turn on her when he was grown. He sipped again to rid himself of the fancy. Auk's mother had presumably named him; the small auks of Lake Limna were flightless, thus it was a name given by mothers who hoped their sons would never leave them. But Auk's mother must have died while he was still very young.

"But not here." Auk's fist struck the table, nearly upsetting it. "I'll come Scylsday, day after tomorrow, and you can shrive me then. All right?"

"No, my son," Silk said. "It must be tonight."

"Don't you trust—"

"I'm afraid I haven't made myself entirely clear," Silk interposed. "I haven't come here to shrive you, though I'd be delighted to do it if you wish, and I'm certain it would make Maytera Mint very happy when I told her I had. But you must shrive me, Auk, and you must do it tonight. That is what I've come for. Not here, however, as you say. In some more private place."

"I can't do that!"

"You can, my son," Silk insisted softly. "And I hope you will. Maytera Mint taught you, and she must have taught you that anyone who is himself free of deep stain can bring the pardon of the gods to one who is in immediate danger of death."

"If you think I'm going to kill you, Patera, or Gib over there—"

Silk shook his head. "I'll explain everything to you in that more private place."

"Patera Pike shrove me one time. Maytera got after me about it, so I finally said all right. I told him a lot of things I shouldn't have."

"And now you're wondering whether he told me something of what you told him," Silk said, "and you think that I'm afraid you'll kill me when I tell you that I told someone else. No, Auk. Patera told me nothing about it, not even that it took place. I learned that from Maytera Marble, who learned it from Maytera Mint, who learned of it from you."

Silk tasted his brandy again, finding it difficult to continue. "Tonight I intend to commit a major crime, or try to. I may be killed, in fact I rather expect it. Maytera Marble or Maytera Mint could have shriven me, of course; but I didn't want either of them to know. Then Maytera Marble mentioned you, and I realized you'd be perfect. Will you shrive me, Auk? I beg it."

Slowly, Auk relaxed; after a moment he laid his right

hand on the table again. "You don't go the nose, Patera, do you?"

Silk shook his head.

"If this's a shave, it's a close one."

"It's not a shave. I mean exactly what I say."

Auk nodded and stood. "Then we'd better go somewhere else, like you want. Too bad, I was hoping to do a little business tonight."

He led Silk to the back of the dim cellar room, and up a ladder into a cavernous night varied here and there by pyramids of barrels and bales; and at last, when they had followed an alley paved with refuse for several streets, into the back of what appeared to be an empty shop. The sound of their feet summoned a weak green glow from one corner of the overlong room. Silk saw a cot with rumpled, soiled sheets; a chamber pot; a table that might have come from the tavern they had left; two plain wooden chairs; and, on the opposite wall, what appeared to be a still-summonable glass. Planks had been nailed across the windows on either side of the street door; a cheap colored picture of Scylla, eight-armed and smiling, was tacked to the planks. "Is this where you live?" he asked.

"I don't exactly live anywhere, Patera. I've got a lot of places, and this is the closest. Have a seat. You still want me to shrive you?"

Silk nodded.

"Then you're going to have to shrive me first so I can do it right. I guess you knew that. I'll try to think of everything."

Silk nodded again. "Do, please."

With speed and economy of motion surprising in so large a man, Auk knelt beside him. "Cleanse me, Patera, for I have given offense to Pas and to other gods."

His gaze upon the smiling picture of Scylla—and so well away from Auk's heavy, brutal face—Silk murmured, as the ritual required, "Tell me, my son, and I will bring you his forgiveness from the well of his boundless mercy."

"I killed a man tonight, Patera. You saw it. Kalan's his name. Gurnard was set to stick Gib, but he got him . . ."

"With his skittlepin," Silk prompted softly.

"That's lily, Patera. That's when Kalan come out with his needler, only I had mine out."

"He intended to shoot Gib, didn't he?"

"I think so, Patera. He works with Gurnard off and on. Or anyway he used to."

"Then there was no guilt in what you did, Auk."

"Thanks, Patera."

After that, Auk remained silent for a long time. Silk prayed silently while he waited, listening with half an ear to angry voices in the street and the thunderous wheels of a passing cart, his thoughts flitting from and returning to the calm, amused and somehow melancholy voices he had heard in the ball court as he had reached for the ball he carried in a pocket still, and to the innumerable things the owner of those voices had sought to teach him.

"I robbed a few houses up on the Palatine. I was trying to remember how many. Twenty I can think of for sure. Maybe more. And I beat a woman, a girl called—"

"You needn't tell me her name, Auk."

"Pretty bad, too. She was trying to get more out of me after I'd already given her a real nice brooch. I'd had too much, and I hit her. Cut her mouth. She yelled, and I hit her again and floored her. She couldn't work for a week, she says. I shouldn't have done that, Patera."

"No," Silk agreed.

"She's better than most, and high, wide and handsome, too. Know what I mean, Patera? That's why I gave her the brooch. When she wanted more . . ."

"I understand."

"I was going to kick her. I didn't, but if I had I'd probably have killed her. I kicked a man to death, once. That was part of what I told Patera Pike."

Silk nodded, forcing his eyes away from Auk's boots. "If Patera brought you pardon, you need not repeat that to me; and if you refrained from kicking the unfortunate woman, you have earned the favor of the gods—of Scylla and her sisters particularly—by your self-restraint."

Auk sighed. "Then that's all I've done, Patera, since last time. Solved those houses and beat on Chenille. And I wouldn't have, Patera, if I hadn't of seen she wanted it for rust. Or anyhow I don't think I would have."

"You understand that it's wrong to break into houses, Auk. You must, or you wouldn't have told me about it. It is wrong, and when you enter a house to rob it, you might easily be killed, in which case you would die with the guilt upon you. That would be very bad. I want you to promise me that you will look for some better way to live. Will you do that, Auk? Will you give me your word?"

"Yes, Patera, I swear I will. I've already been doing it. You know, buying things and selling them. Like that."

Silk decided it would be wiser not to ask what sorts of things these were, or how the sellers had gotten them. "The woman you beat, Auk. You said she used rust. Am I to take it that she was an immoral woman?"

"She's not any worse than a lot of others, Patera. She's at Orchid's place."

Silk nodded to himself. "Is that the sort of place I imagine?"

"No, Patera, it's about the best. They don't allow any fighting or anything like that, and everything's real clean. Some of Orchid's girls have even gone uphill."

"Nevertheless, Auk, you shouldn't go to places of that kind. You're not bad looking, you're strong, and you have some education. You'd have no difficulty finding a decent girl, and a decent girl might do you a great deal of good."

Auk stirred, and Silk sensed that the kneeling man was looking at him, although he did not permit his own eyes to leave the picture of Scylla. "You mean the kind that has you shrive her, Patera? You wouldn't want one of them to take up with somebody like me. You'd tell her she deserved somebody better. Shag yes, you would!"

For a moment it seemed to Silk that the weight of the whole whorl's folly and witless wrong had descended on his shoulders. "Believe me, Auk, many of those girls will marry men far, far worse than you." He drew a deep breath. "As penance for the evil you have done, Auk, you are to perform three meritorious acts before this time tomorrow. Shall I explain to you the nature of meritorious acts?"

"No, Patera. I remember, and I'll do them."

"That's well. Then I bring to you, Auk, the pardon of all the gods. In the name of Great Pas, you are forgiven. In the name of Echidna, you are forgiven. In the name of Scylla, you are forgiven . . ." Soon the moment would come. "And in the name of the Outsider and all lesser gods, you are forgiven, by the power entrusted to me."

There was no objection from Auk. Silk traced the sign of addition in the air above his head.

"Now it's my turn, Auk. Will you shrive me, as I shrove you?"

The two men changed places.

Silk said, "Cleanse me, friend, for I am in sore danger of death, and I may give offense to Pas and to other gods."

Auk's hand touched his shoulder. "I've never did this before, Patera. I hope I get it right."

"Tell me . . ." Silk prompted.

"Yeah. Tell me, Patera, so that I can bring you the forgiveness of Pas from the well of bottomless mercy."

"I may have to break into a house tonight, Auk. I hope that I won't have to; but if the owner won't see me, or won't do what a certain god—the Outsider, Auk, you may know of him—wishes him to do, then I'll try to compel him."

"Whose—"

"If he sees me alone, I intend to threaten his life unless he does as the god requires. But to be honest, I doubt that he'll see me at all."

"Who is this, Patera? Who're you going to threaten?"

"Are you looking at me, Auk? You're not supposed to."

"All right, now I'm looking away. Who is this, Patera? Whose house is it?"

"There's no need for me to tell you that, Auk. Forgive me my intent, please."

"I'm afraid I can't, my son," Auk said, getting into the spirit of his role. "I got to know who this is, and why you're going to do it. Maybe you won't be running as big of a risk as you think you are, see? I'm the one that has to judge that, ain't I?"

"Yes," Silk admitted.

"And I see why you looked for me, 'cause I can do it better than anybody. Only I got to know, 'cause if this's just some candy, I got to tell you to go to a real augur after you scrape out, and forget about me. There's houses and then there's Houses. So who is it and where is it, Patera?"

"His name is Blood," Silk said, and felt Auk's hand tighten on his shoulder. "I assume that he lives somewhere on the Palatine. He has a private floater, at any rate, and employs a driver for it."

Auk grunted.

"I think that he must be dangerous," Silk continued. "I sense it."

"You win, Patera. I got to shrive you. Only you got to tell me all about it, too. I need to know what's going on here."

"The Ayuntamiento has sold this man our manteion."

Silk heard Auk's exhalation.

"It was bringing in practically nothing, you realize. The

income from the manteion is supposed to balance the loss from the palaestra; tutorage doesn't cover our costs, and most of the parents are behind anyway. Ideally there should be enough left over for Juzgado's taxes, but our Window's been empty now for a very long while."

"Must be others doing better," Auk suggested.

"Yes. Considerably better in some cases, though it's been many years since a god has visited any Window in the city."

"Then they—the augurs there—could give you a little something, Patera."

Silk nodded, remembering his mendicant expeditions to those solvent manteions. "They have indeed helped at times, Auk. I'm afraid that the Chapter has decided to put an end to that. It's turned our manteion over to the Juzgado in lieu of our unpaid taxes, and the Ayuntamiento has sold the property to this man Blood. That's how things appear, at least."

"We all got to pay the counterman come shadeup," Auk muttered diplomatically.

"The people need us, Auk. The whole quarter does. I was hoping that if you—never mind. I intend to steal our manteion back tonight, if I can, and you must shrive me for that."

The seated man was silent for a moment. At length he said, "The city keeps records on houses and so on, Patera. You go to the Juzgado and slip one of those clerks a little something, and they call up the lot number on their glass. I've done it. The monitor gives you the name of the buyer, or anyhow whoever's fronting for him."

"So that I could verify the sale, you mean."

"That's it, Patera. Make sure you're right about all this before you get yourself killed."

Silk felt an uncontrollable flood of relief. "I'll do as you suggest, provided that the Juzgado's still open."

"They wouldn't be, Patera. They close there about the same time as the market."

It was hard for him to force himself to speak. "Then I must proceed. I must act tonight." He hesitated while some frightened portion of his mind battered the ivory walls that confined it. "Of course this may not be the Blood you know, Auk. There must be a great many people of that name. Could Blood—the Blood you know—buy our manteion? It must be worth twenty thousand cards or more."

"Ten," Auk muttered. "Twelve, maybe, only he probably got it for the taxes. What's he look like, Patera?"

"A tall, heavy man. Angry looking, I'd say, although it may only have been that his face was flushed. There are wide bones under his plump cheeks, or so I'd guess."

"Lots of rings?"

Silk struggled to recall the prosperous-looking man's fat, smooth hands. "Yes," he said. "Several, at least."

"Could you smell him?"

"Are you asking whether he smelled bad? No, certainly not. In fact—"

Auk grunted. "What was it?"

"I have no idea, but it reminded me of the scented oil—no doubt you've noticed it—in the lamp before Scylla, in our manteion. A sweet, heavy odor, not quite so pungent as incense."

"He calls it musk rose," Auk said dryly. "Musk's a buck that works for him."

"It is the Blood you know, then."

"Yeah, it is. Now be quiet a minute, Patera. I got to remember the words." Auk rocked back and forth. There was a faint noise like the grating of sand on a shiprock floor as he rubbed his massive jaw. "As a penance for the evil that you're getting ready to do, Patera, you got to perform two or three meritorious acts I'll tell you about tonight."

"That is too light a penance," Silk protested.

"Don't weigh feathers with me, Patera, 'cause you don't know what they are yet. You're going to do 'em, ain't you?"

"Yes, Auk," Silk said humbly.

"That's good. Don't forget. All right, then I bring to you, Patera, the pardons of all the gods. In the name of Great Pas, you're forgiven. In the name of Echidna, you're forgiven. In the name of Scylla, of Molpe, of Tartaros, of Hierax, of Thelxiepeia, of Phaea, of Sphigx, and of all the lesser gods, you're forgiven, Patera, by the powers trusted to me."

Silk traced the sign of addition, hoping that the big man was doing the same over his head.

The big man cleared his throat. "Was that all right?"

"Yes," Silk said, rising. "It was very good indeed, for a layman."

"Thanks. Now about Blood. You say you're going to solve his place, but you don't even know where it is."

"I can ask directions when I reach the Palatine." Silk was dusting his knees. "Blood isn't a particular friend of yours, I hope."

Auk shook his head. "It ain't there. I been there a time or two, and that gets us to one of those meritorious acts that you just now promised me about. You got to let me take you there."

"If it isn't inconvenient—"

"It's shaggy—excuse me, Patera. Yeah, it's going to put me out by a dog's right, only you got to let me do it anyhow, if you really go to Blood's. If you don't, you'll get lost sure trying to find it. Or somebody'll know you, and that'll be worse. But first you're going to give Blood a whistle on my glass over there, see? Maybe he'll talk to you, or if he wants to see you he might even send somebody."

Auk strode across the room and clapped his hands; the monitor's colorless face rose from the depths of the glass.

"I want Blood," Auk told it. "That's the buck that's got the big place off the old Palustria Road." He turned to Silk. "Come over here, Patera. You stand in front of it. I don't want 'em to see me."

Silk did as he was told. He had talked through glasses before (there had been one in the Prelate's chambers at the schola), though not often. Now he discovered that his mouth was dry. He licked his lips.

"Blood is not available, sir," the monitor told him imperturbably. "Would someone else do?"

"Musk, perhaps," Silk said, recalling the name Auk had mentioned.

"It will be a few minutes, I fear, sir."

"I'll wait for him," Silk said. The glass faded to an opalescent gray.

"You want to sit, Patera?" Auk was pushing a chair against the backs of his calves.

Silk sat down, murmuring his thanks.

"I don't think that was too smart, asking for Musk. Maybe you know what you're doing."

Still watching the glass, Silk shook his head. "You had said he worked for Blood, that's all."

"Don't tell him you're with me. All right?"

"I won't."

Auk did not speak again, and the silence wrapped itself about them. Like the silence of the Windows, Silk thought, the silence of the gods: pendant, waiting. This glass of Auk's was rather like a Window; all glasses were, although they were so much smaller. Like the Windows, glasses were miraculous creations of the Short-Sun days, after all. What was it Maytera Marble had said about them?

Maytera herself, the countless quiescent soldiers that the Outsider had revealed, and in fact all similar persons—all chems of whatever kind—were directly or otherwise marvels of the inconceivably inspired Short-Sun Whorl, and in time (soon, perhaps) would be gone. Their women rarely conceived children, and in Maytera's case it was quite . . .

Silk shook his shoulders, reminding himself severely that in all likelihood Maytera Marble would long outlive him— that he might be dead before shadeup, unless he chose to ignore the Outsider's instructions.

The monitor reappeared. "Would you like me to provide a few suggestions while you're waiting, sir?"

"No, thank you."

"I might straighten your nose just a trifle, sir, and do something regarding a coiffeur. You would find that of interest, I believe."

"No," Silk said again; and added, as much to himself as to the monitor, "I must think."

Swiftly the monitor's gray face darkened. The entire glass seemed to fall away. Black, oily-looking hair curled above flashing eyes from which Silk tore his own in horror.

As a swimmer bursts from a wave and discovers himself staring at an object he has not chosen—at the summer sun, perhaps, or a cloud or the top of a tree—Silk found that he was looking at Musk's mouth, lips as feverishly red and fully as delicate as any girl's.

To damp his fear, he told himself that he was waiting for Musk to speak; and when Musk did not, he forced himself to speak instead. "My name is Patera Silk, my son." His chin was trembling; before he spoke again, he clenched his teeth. "Mine is the Sun Street manteion. Or I should say it isn't, which is what I must see Blood about."

The handsome boy in the glass said nothing and gave no sign of having heard. In order that he might not be snared by that bright and savage stare again, Silk inventoried the room in which Musk stood. He could glimpse a tapestry and a painting, a table covered with bottles, and two elaborately inlaid chairs with padded crimson backs and contorted legs.

"Blood has purchased our manteion," he found himself explaining to one of the chairs. "By that I mean he's paid the taxes, I suppose, and they have turned the deed over to him. It will be very hard on the children. On all of us, to be sure, but particularly on the children, unless some other arrangement can be made. I have several suggestions to offer, and I'd like—"

A trooper in silvered conflict armor had appeared at the edge of the glass. As he spoke to Musk, Silk realized with a slight shock that Musk hardly reached the trooper's shoulder. "A new bunch at the gate," the trooper said.

Hurriedly, Silk began, "I'm certain for your sake—or for Blood's, I mean—that an accommodation of some sort is still possible. A god, you see—"

The handsome boy in the glass laughed and snapped his fingers, and the glass went dark.

Chapter 4

NIGHTSIDE

It had been late already when they had left the city. Beyond the black streak of the shade, the skylands had been as clear and as bright as Silk (who normally retired early and rose at shadeup) had ever seen them; he stared at them as he rode, his thoughts drowned in wonder. Here were nameless mountains filling inviolate valleys to the rim with their vast, black shadows. Here were savannah and steppe, and a coastal plain ringing a lake that he judged must certainly be larger than Lake Limna—all these doming the gloomy sky of night while they themselves were bathed in sunlight.

As they had walked the dirty and dangerous streets of the Orilla, Auk had remarked, "There's strange things happen nightside, Patera. I don't suppose you know it, but that's the lily word anyhow."

"I do know," Silk had assured him. "I shrive, don't forget, so I hear about them. Or at least I've heard a few very strange stories that I can't relate. You must have seen the things as they occurred, and that must be stranger still."

"What I was going to say," Auk had continued, "was that I never heard about any that was any stranger than this, what you're going to do, or try to do. Or seen anything stranger, either."

Silk had sighed. "May I speak as an augur, Auk? I realize

that a great many people are offended by that, and Our Gracious Phaea knows I don't want to offend you. But this once may I speak?"

"If you're going to say something you wouldn't want anybody to hear, why, I wouldn't."

"Quite the contrary," Silk had declared, perhaps a bit too fervently. "It's something that I wish I could tell the whole city."

"Keep your voice down, Patera, or you will."

"I told you a god had spoken to me. Do you remember that?"

Auk had nodded.

"I've been thinking about it as we walked along. To tell the truth, it's not easy to think about anything else. Before I spoke to—to that unfortunate Musk. Well, before I spoke to him, for example, I ought to have been thinking over everything that I wanted to say to him. But I wasn't, or not very much. Mostly I was thinking about the Outsider; not so much what he had said to me as what it had been like to have him speaking to me at all, and how it had felt."

"You did fine, Patera." Auk had, to Silk's surprise, laid a hand on his shoulder. "You did all right."

"I don't agree, though I won't argue with you now. What I wanted to say was that there is really nothing strange at all about what I'm doing, or about your helping me to do it. Does the sun ever go out, Auk? Does it ever wink out as you or I might snuff out a lamp?"

"I don't know, Patera. I never thought about it. Does it?"

Silk had not replied, continuing in silence down the muddy street, matching Auk stride for stride.

"I guess it don't. You couldn't see them skylands up there nightside, if it did."

"So it is with the gods, Auk. They speak to us all the time, exactly as the sun shines all the time. When the dark cloud that we call the shade gets between us and the sun, we say it's night, or nightside, a term I never heard until I came to Sun Street."

"It don't really mean night, Patera. Not exactly. It means... All right, look at it like this. There's a day way of doing, see? That's the regular way. And then there's the other way, and nightside's when you do this other way—when everything's on the night side of the shade."

"We're on the night side of the shade for only half the day," Silk had told him. "But we are on the night side of whatever it is that bars us from the gods almost constantly, throughout our whole lives. And we really shouldn't be. We weren't meant to be. I got that one small ray of sunshine, you see, and it shouldn't be strange at all. It should be the most ordinary thing in the whorl."

He had expected Auk to laugh, and was surprised and pleased when he did not.

They had rented donkeys from a man Auk knew, a big gray for Auk and a smaller black for Silk. "Because I'll have to lead him back," Auk had said. "We got to get that straight right now. He don't stay with you."

Silk had nodded.

"You're going to get caught, like I told you, Patera. You'll talk to Blood, maybe, like you want. But it'll be after they get you. I don't like it, but there it is. So you're not going to need him to ride back on, and I'm not going to lose what I'm giving this donkey man to hold, which is double what he'd cost in the market."

"I understand," Silk had assured him.

Now, as they trotted along a narrow track that to him at least was largely invisible, with the toes of his only decent shoes intermittently intimidated by the stony soil, Auk's words returned to trouble him. Tearing his eyes from the skylands, he called, "You warned me that Blood was going to catch me, back there in the city while you were renting these donkeys for us. What do you think he'll do to me if he does?"

Auk twisted about to look at him, his face a pale blur in the shadow of the crowding trees. "I don't know, Patera. But you're not going to like it."

"You may not know," Silk said, "but you can guess much better than I can. You know Blood better than I do. You've been in his house, and I'm sure you must know several people who know him well. You've done business with him."

"Tried to, Patera."

"All right, tried to. Still you know what kind of man he is. Would he kill me, for breaking into his house? Or for threatening him? I fully intend to threaten his life if he won't return our manteion to the Chapter, assuming that I get that far."

"I hope not, Patera."

Unbidden and unwanted, Musk's features rose from Silk's memory, perfect—yet corrupt, like the face of a devil. So softly that he was surprised that Auk heard it, Silk said, "I have been wondering whether I shouldn't take my own life if I am caught. If I am, I say, although I hope not to be, and am determined not to be. It's seriously wrong to take one's own life, and yet—"

A chain or more ahead, Auk chuckled. "Kill yourself, Patera? Yeah, it could be a good idea. Keep it in mind, depending. You won't tell Blood about me?"

"I've sworn," Silk reminded him. "I would never break that oath."

"Good." Auk turned away again, his posture intent as his eyes sought to penetrate the shadows.

Clearly Auk had been less than impressed by his mention of suicide, and for a moment Silk resented it. But Auk was right. How could he serve any god if he set out determined to resign his task if it became too difficult? Auk had been correct to laugh; he was no better than a child, sallying forth with a wooden sword to conquor the whorl—something that he had in fact done not too many years ago.

Yet it was easy for Auk to remain calm, easy for Auk to mock his fears. Auk, who had no doubt broken into scores of these country villas, was not going to break into this one, or even to assist him in doing it. And yet, Silk reminded himself, Auk's own position was by no means impregnable.

"I would never violate my solemn oath, sworn to all the gods," Silk said aloud. "And besides, if Blood were to find out about you and have you killed—he didn't strike me as the type who kill men themselves—there would be no one to help me escape him."

Auk cleared his throat and spat, the sound unnaturally loud in the airless stillness of the forest. "I'm not going to do a shaggy thing for you, Patera. You can forget about that. You're working for the gods, right? Let them get you out."

Almost whispering, because he was saddened by the knowledge, Silk said, "Yes, you will, Auk."

"Sneeze it!"

"Because you couldn't ever be certain that I wouldn't tell, eventually. I won't, but you don't trust me. Or at least not that much."

Auk snorted.

"And since you're a better man than you pretend to be, the knowlege that I—not I particularly perhaps, but an augur who had been a companion of sorts, if only for this one night—required your help would devour you, even if you denied it a hundred times or more, as you very probably would. Thus you'll help me if you can, Auk, eventually and possibly quite quickly. I know you will. And because you will, it will go much better for me if Blood doesn't know about you."

"I'd crawl a long way in for a while, maybe, but that's all.

Maybe go see Palustria for a year or three till Blood was gone or he'd forgotten about me. People ain't like you think, Patera. Maybe you studied a long time, but there's a lot that you don't know."

Which was true enough, Silk admitted to himself. For whatever inscrutable reasons, the gods thrust bios into the whorl knowing nothing of it; and if they waited until they were so wise as to make no mistakes before they acted, they waited forever. With sudden poignancy Silk wished that he might indeed wait forever, as some men did.

And yet he felt certain that he was right about Auk, and Auk wrong about himself. Auk still returned at times to talk with little Maytera Mint; and Auk had killed a man that evening—a serious matter even to a criminal, since the dead man had friends—because that man had been about to kill the big man called Gib. Auk might be a thief and even a murderer; but he had no real talent for murder, no innate bent toward evil. Not even Blood had such a bent, perhaps. He, Silk, had seen someone who did in Blood's glass, and he promised himself now that he would never again mistake mere dishonesty or desperation for it again.

"But I know you, Auk," he said softly. He shifted his weight in the vain hope of finding a more comfortable spot on the crude saddle. "I may be too trusting of people in general, as you say; but I'm right about you. You'll help me when you think that I require it."

Auk made a quick, impatient gesture, barely visible in the gloom. "Be quiet there, Patera. We're getting pretty close."

If there had ever been a real path, they were leaving it. With seeing feet, the donkeys picked their way up a rock-strewn hillside, often unavoidably bathed in the eerie sky-light. At the top, Auk reined up and dismounted; Silk followed his example. Here the faintest of night breezes stirred, as stealthy as a thief itself, making away with the mingled scents of post oak and mulberry, of grass and fern withered almost to powder, of a passing fox, and the very essence of the night. The donkeys raised their long muzzles to catch it, and Silk fanned himself with his wide straw hat.

"See them lights, Patera?" Auk pointed toward a faint golden glimmer beyond the treetops. "That's Blood's place. What we did was circle around behind it, see? That's what we been doing ever since we got off the main road. On the other side, there's a big gate of steel bars, and a grass-way for floaters that goes up to the front. Can you see that black line, kind of wavy, between us and the house?"

Silk squinted and stared, but could not.

"That's a stone wall about as high as that little tree down there. It's got big spikes on top, which I'd say is mostly for show. Could be if you threw your rope up there and caught one, you could climb up the wall—I don't know that anybody's ever tried it. Only Blood's got protection, understand? Guards, and a big talus that I know about for sure. I don't know what else. You ever done anything like this before, Patera?"

Silk shook his head.

"I didn't think so. All right, here's all that's going to happen, probably. You're going to try to get over that wall, with your rope or whatever, only you're not going to make it. Along about shadeup, you're going to start hiking back to the city, feeling worse than shit in the street and thinking that I'm going to laugh myself sick at you. Only I'm not. I'm going to sacrifice 'cause you came back alive, understand? A black ram to Tartaros, see? A good big one, at your manteion the day after tomorrow, you got my word on that."

Auk paused for breath.

"And after my sacrifice is over, I'm going to make you swear you'll never try anything this stupid ever again. You think you can make Blood swear to give back your manteion, which you can't. And you think he'll stick with whatever he swore to afterward, which he wouldn't, not for every god in Mainframe. But I can make you swear, Patera, and I'm going to—see if I don't. And I know you'll stick. You're the kind that does."

Silk said gratefully, "This is really very good of you, Auk. I don't deserve it."

"If I was really good I wouldn't have hired us these donkeys, Patera. I'd have hiked out here with you and let you tire yourself—that way you'd come back that much quicker."

Troubled, Auk paused, running his fingers through his hair. "Only if you do get inside, it'd be all queer if you was tired. You don't work when you're fagged out, not in my trade, only when you're cold up and full of jump. Only I've done a hundred or more, and I wouldn't try to solve this one for a thousand goldboys. Good-bye, Patera. Phaea smile on you."

"Wait a moment." Silk took him by the sleeve. "Haven't you been inside that house? You said you had."

"A couple of times on business, Patera. I don't know anything much about it."

"You said that I was certain to be caught, and I'll concede that you may very well be correct. Nevertheless, I don't intend to be caught; and if I am, I will have failed the Outsider, the god who has sent me, just as I will have failed him if I don't make the attempt tonight. Can't you see that? Haven't you ever been caught yourself, Auk? You must have been."

Auk nodded reluctantly. "Once, Patera, when I was just a sprat. He winnowed me out. By Phaea's sow, I thought he was going to kill me. And when he was through, he kicked me out into the street. That was right in our quarter. I'll show you the house sometime."

He tried to pull free, but Silk retained his grip on his

sleeve. "How were you caught, Auk? What was it that you did wrong? Tell me, please, so I won't make the same mistake."

"You done it already, Patera." Auk sounded apologetic. "Look here. I'd solved a few places, and I got pretty hot on myself and thought I couldn't get caught. I had some picks, know what I mean? And I showed 'em off and called myself a master of the art, thinking Tartaros himself would pull his hat off to me. Got to where I never troubled to look things over the way a flash buck ought to."

Auk fell silent, and Silk asked, "What was the detail you overlooked?"

"Debt, Patera." Auk chuckled. "That don't go with Blood, 'cause it's not him you got to worry about."

"Tell me anyway," Silk insisted.

"Well, Patera, this bucko that had the house had a good lay, see? Taking care of all the shoes and such like up at Ermine's. You know about Ermine's? A goldboy or maybe two for supper. Gilt places like that deal on Scylsday, 'cause Sphigxday's their plum night, see? So I gleaned once he'd got off he'd put down a few and snoodge like a soldier. If I was to flush his fussock—rouse up his wife, Patera—she'd stave her broom getting him off straw, and I'd beat the hoof to my own tune. Only he owed 'em, you see? Up to Ermine's. They're holding his lowre back on him, so he was straight up, or nearly. So he napped me and I owed it."

Silk nodded.

"Now you tonight, Patera, you're doing the same thing. You're not flash. You don't know who's there or who ain't, or how big the rooms might be, or what kind of windows. Not a pip of the scavy you got to have right in your hand."

"You must be able to tell me something," Silk said.

Auk adjusted the heavy hanger he wore. "The house's a tidy stone place with a wing to each side. Three floors in 'em, and the middle's two. When you come in the front like

I did, there's a big front room, and that's the farthest I got. Him that told me about floors says there's a capital cellar and another underneath. There's guards. You saw one of that quality in my glass. And there's a tall ass, begging your pardon, Patera. Like what I told you already."

"Have you any idea where Blood sleeps?"

Auk shook his head, the motion scarcely visible. "But he don't sleep a hour, nightside. The flash never do, see? His business'll keep him out of bed till shadeup." Sensing Silk's incomprehension, Auk elaborated. "People coming to talk to him like I did, or the ones that work for him with their hats off so he can tell where they come from and where they're going, Patera."

"I see."

Auk took the reins of the smaller donkey and mounted his own. "You got four, maybe five hours to shadeup. Then you got to get back. I wouldn't be too close to that wall then if I was you, Patera. There might come a guard walking the top. I've known 'em to do that."

"All right." Silk nodded, reflecting that he had some ground to cover before he was near the wall at all. "Thank you again. I won't betray you, whatever you may think; and I won't get caught if I can help it."

As he watched Auk ride away, Silk wondered what he had really been like as a schoolboy, and what Maytera Mint had found to say to that much younger Auk that had left so deep an impression. For Auk believed, despite his hard looks and thieves' cant; and unlike many superficially better men, his faith was more than superstition. Scylla's smiling picture on the wall of that dismal, barren room had not come to its place by accident. Its presence there had revealed more to Silk than Auk's glass: deep within his being, Auk's spirit knelt in adoration.

Inspired by the thought, Silk knelt himself, though the sharp flints of the hilltop gouged his knees. The Outsider had warned him that he would receive no aid—still, it was licit, surely, to ask help of other gods; and dark Tartaros was the patron of all who acted outside the law.

"A black lamb to you alone, kindly Tartaros, as quickly as I can afford another. Be mindful of me, who come in the service of a minor god."

But Blood, too, acted outside the law, dealing in rust and women and even smuggled goods, or so Auk had indicated; it was more than possible that Tartaros would favor Blood.

Sighing, Silk stood, dusted off the legs of his oldest trousers, and began to pick his way down the rocky hillside. Things would be as they would be, and he had no choice but to proceed, whether with the aid of the dark god or without it. Pas the Twice-Seeing might side with him, or Scalding Scylla, who wielded more influence here than her brother. Surely Scylla would not wish the city that most honored her to lose a manteion! Encouraged, Silk scrambled along.

The faint golden lights of Blood's house soon vanished behind the treetops, and the breeze with them. Below the hill, the air lay hot and close again, stale, and overripe with a summer protracted beyond reason.

Or perhaps not. As Silk groped among close-set trunks, with leaves crackling and twigs popping beneath his feet, he reflected that if the year had been a more normal one, this forest might now lie deep in snow, and what he was doing would be next to impossible. Could it be that this parched, overheated, and seemingly immutable season had in actuality been prolonged for his benefit?

For a few seconds the thought halted him between step and step. All this heat and sweat, for him? Poor Maytera Marble's daily sufferings, the children's angry rashes, the withered crops and shrinking streams?

No sooner had he had the thought than he came close to falling into the gully of one, catching hold by purest luck to a branch he could not see. Cautiously he clambered down the uneven bank, then knelt on the water-smoothed stones of the streambed to seek water with his fingers, finding none. There might be pools higher or lower, but here at least what had been a stream could be no drier.

With head cocked, he listened for the familiar music of fast-flowing water over stones. Far away a nightjar called; the harsh sound died away, and the stillness of the forest closed in once more, the hushed expectancy of the thirsting trees.

This forest had been planted in the days of the caldé (or so one of his teachers at the schola had informed him) in order that its watershed might fill the city's wells; and though the Ayuntamiento now permitted men of wealth to build within its borders, it remained vast, stretching more than fifty leagues toward Palustria. If its streams were this dry now, how long could Viron live? Would it be necessary to build a new city, if only a temporary one, on the lakeshore?

Wishing for light as well as water, Silk climbed the opposite bank, and after a hundred strides saw through the bare, close-ranked trees the welcome gleam of skylight on dressed and polished stone.

The wall surrounding Blood's villa loomed higher and higher as he drew nearer. Auk had indicated a height of ten cubits or so; to Silk, standing before its massive base and peering up at the fugitive glints of skylight on the points of its ominous spikes, that estimate appeared unnecessarily conservative. Somewhat discouraged already, he uncoiled the thin horsehair rope he had worn about his waist, thrust the hatchet into his waistband, tied a running noose in one end of the rope as Auk had suggested, and hurled it up at those towering points.

For a moment that seemed at least a minute, the rope hung over him like a miracle, jet black against the shining skylands, lost in blind dark where it crossed the boundless, sooty smear of the shade. A moment more, and it lay limp at his feet.

Biting his lips, he gathered it, reopened the noose, and hurled it again. Unlooked-for, the last words of the dying stableman to whom he had carried the forgiveness of the gods a week earlier returned, the summation of fifty years of toil: "I tried, Patera. I tried." With them, the broiling heat of the four-flight bedroom, the torn and faded horsecloths on the bed, the earthenware jug of water, and the hard end of bread (bread that some man of substance had no doubt intended for his mount) that the stableman could no longer chew.

Another throw. The ragged, amateurish sketch of the wife who had left when the stableman could no longer feed her and her children . . .

One last throw, and then he would return to the old manse on Sun Street—where he belonged—and go to bed, forgetting this absurd scheme of rescue with the brown lice that had crept across the faded blue horsecloths.

A final throw. "I tried, Patera. I tried."

Descriptions of three children that their father had not seen since before he, Silk, had been born. All right, he thought, just one more attempt.

With this, his sixth cast, he snared a spike, and by this time he could only wonder whether someone in the house had not already seen his noose rising above the wall and falling back. He heaved hard on the rope and felt the noose tighten, wiped his sweating hands on his robe, planted his feet against the dressed stone of the wall, and started up. He had reached twice his own considerable height when the noose parted and he fell.

"Pas!" He spoke more loudly than he had intended. For three minutes or more after that exclamation he cowered in silence beside the base of the wall, rubbing his bruises and listening. At length he muttered, "Scylla, Tartaros, Great Pas, remember your servant. Don't treat him so." And stood to gather and examine his rope.

The noose had been sliced through, almost cleanly, at the place where it must have held the spike. Those spikes were sharp-edged, clearly, like the blades of swords, as he ought to have guessed.

Retreating into the forest, he groped among branches he could scarcely see for a forked one of the right size. The first half-blind blow from his hatchet sounded louder than the boom of a slug gun. He waited, listening again, certain that he would soon hear cries of alarm and hurrying feet.

Even the crickets were silent.

His fingertips explored the inconsiderable notch in the branch that his hatchet had made. He shifted his free hand to a safe position and struck hard at the branch again, then stood motionless to listen, as before.

Briefly and distantly (as he had long ago, a child and feverish, heard through a tightly closed window with drawn curtains, from three streets away, the faint yet melodious tinklings of the barrel organ that announces the gray beggar monkey) he caught a few bars of music, buoyant and inviting. Quickly it vanished, leaving behind only the monotonous song of the nightjar.

When he felt certain it would not return, he swung his hatchet again and again at the unseen wood, until the branch was free and he could brace it against its parent trunk for trimming. That done, he carried the rough fork out of the darkness of the trees and into the skylit clearing next to the wall, and knotted his rope securely at the point where the splayed arms met. A single hard throw sent the forked limb arching above the spikes; it held solidly against them when he drew it back.

He was breathless, his tunic and trousers soaked with sweat, by the time he pulled himself up onto the slanting capstone, where for several minutes he stretched panting between the spikes and the sheer drop.

He had been seen, beyond doubt—or if he had not, he would inevitably be seen as soon as he stood up. It would be utter folly to stand. As he sought to catch his breath, he assured himself that only such a fool as he would so much as consider it.

When he did stand up at last, fully expecting a shouted challenge or the report of a slug gun, he had to call upon every scrap of self-discipline to keep from looking down.

The top of the wall was a full cubit wider than he had expected, however—as wide as the garden walk. Stepping across the spikes (which his fingers had told him boasted serrated edges), he crouched to study the distant villa and its grounds, straightening his low-crowned hat and drawing his black robe across the lower half of his face.

The nearer wing was a good hundred cubits, he estimated, from his vantage point. The grassway Auk had mentioned was largely out of sight at the front of the villa, but a white roadway of what appeared to be crushed ship-rock ran from the back of the nearer wing to the wall, striking it a hundred strides to his left. Half a dozen sheds, large and small, stood along this roadway, the biggest of them apparently a shelter for vehicles, another (noticeably high and narrow, with what seemed to be narrow wire-covered vents high in an otherwise blank wall) some sort of provision for fowls.

What concerned Silk more was the second in size of the sheds, whose back opened onto an extensive yard surrounded by a palisade and covered with netting. The poles of the palisade were sharpened at the top, perhaps partly to hold the netting in place; and though it was difficult to judge by the glimmering skylight, it seemed that the area enclosed was of bare soil dotted with an occasional weed. That was a pen for dangerous animals, surely.

He scanned the rest of the grounds. There appeared to be a courtyard or terrace behind the original villa; though it was largely hidden by the wing, he glimpsed flagstones, and a flowering tree in a ceramic tub.

Other trees were scattered over the rolling lawns with studied carelessness, and there were hedges as well. Blood had built this wall and hired guards, but he did not really fear intrusion. There was too much foliage for that.

Although if his watchdogs liked to lie in the shadows, an intruder who sought to use Blood's plantings to mask his approach could be in for an ugly surprise; in which case an uncomplicated dash for the villa might be best. What would an experienced and resolute housebreaker like Auk have done in his place?

Silk quickly regretted the thought; Auk would have gone home or found an easier house to rob. He had said as much. This Blood was no common magnate, no rich trader or graft-swollen commissioner. He was a clever criminal himself, and one who (why?) appeared more anxious than might be expected about his own security. A criminal with secrets, then, or with enemies who were themselves outside the law—so it appeared. Certainly Auk had not been his friend.

At the age of twelve, Silk had once, with several other boys, broken into an empty house. He remembered that now, the fear and the shame of it, the echoing, uninhabited rooms with their furniture swathed in dirty white dustcovers. How hurt and dismayed his mother had been when she had found out what they had done! She had refused to punish him, saying that the nature of his punishment would be left to the owner of the house he had violated.

That punishment (the mere thought of it made him stir uneasily on top of the wall) had never arrived, although he had spent weeks and months in dread of it.

Or possibly had arrived only now. That deserted house,

after all, had loomed large in the back of his mind when he had gathered up his horsehair rope and his hatchet and gone out looking for Auk, then only a vague figure recalled from Scylsdays past. And if it had not been for Auk and Maytera Mint, if it had not been for the repairs he had been making on the roof of the manteion, but most of all if it had not been for that well-remembered house whose rear window he had helped to force—if it had not been for all those things together, he would never have undertaken to break into this villa of Blood's. Or rather, into an imagined house on the Palatine belonging to Blood. On the Palatine where, as he realized now, the respectable rich would never have allowed such a man as Blood to live. Instead of this preposterous, utterly juvenile escapade, he would have . . .

Would have what? Have penned another appeal to Patera Remora, the coadjutor of the Chapter, perhaps, although the Chapter had, as seemed clear, already made its decision. Or have sought an interview with His Cognizance the Prolocutor—the interview that he had tried and failed to get weeks before, when it had at last become apparent to him (or so he had thought at the time) exactly how serious the manteion's financial situation was. His hands clenched as he recalled the expression of His Cognizance's sly little prothonotary, his long wait, ended only when he had been informed that His Cognizance had retired for the night. His Cognizance was quite elderly, the prothonotary had explained (as though he, Patera Silk, had been a foreigner). His Cognizance tired very easily these days.

And with that, the prothonotary had grinned his oh-so-knowing, vile grin; and Silk had wanted to strike him.

All right then, those possibilities had been explored already, both of them. Yet surely there was something else he might have done, something sensible, effectual, and most significantly, legal.

He was still considering the matter when the talus Auk had mentioned glided ponderously around a corner of the more remote wing, appearing briefly only to vanish and reappear as its motion carried it from skylight into shadow and from shadow into bright skylight again.

Silk's first thought was that it had heard him, but it was moving too slowly for that. No, this was no more than a routine patrol, one more among the thousands of circuits of Blood's high, crenelated villa it must have made since Blood engaged its services. Nervously, Silk wondered how good the big machine's vision was, and whether it routinely scanned the top of the wall. Maytera Marble had told him once that hers was less acute than his own, though he had worn glasses for reading since turning twelve. Yet that might be no more than the effect of her great age; the talus would be younger, although cruder as well. Certainly movement was more apt to betray him than immobility.

And yet he found immobility more and more difficult to maintain as the talus drew nearer. It appeared to wear a helmet, a polished brazen dome more capacious than many a respectable tomb. From beneath that helmet glared the face of an ogre worked in black metal: a wide and flattened nose, bulging red eyes, great flat cheeks like slabs of slate, and a gaping mouth drawn back in a savage grin. The sharp white tusks that thrust beyond its crimson lips were presumably mere bluster, but the slender barrel of a buzz gun flanked each tusk.

Far below that threatening head, the talus's armored, wagon-like body rolled upon dark belts that carried it in perfect silence over the close-sheared grass. No needler, no sword, and certainly no hatchet like the one he grasped could do more than scratch the talus's finish. Met upon its own terms, it would be more than a match for a whole platoon of armored Guardsmen. He resolved—fervently—

never to meet it on its own terms, and never to meet it at all if he could manage it.

As it neared the pale swath that was the white stone roadway, it halted. Slowly and silently, its huge, frowning head revolved, examining the back of the villa, then each of the outbuildings in turn, then staring down the roadway, and at last looking at the wall itself, tracing its whole visible length (as it appeared) twice. Silk felt certain that his heart had stopped, frozen with fear. A moment more and he would lose consciousness and fall forward. The talus would roll toward him, no doubt, would dismember him with brutal steel hands bigger than the largest shovels; but that would not matter, because he would already be dead.

At length it seemed to see him. For a long moment its head ceased to move, its fierce eyes staring straight at him. As smoothly as a cloud, as inexorably as an avalanche, it glided toward him. Slowly, so slowly that he would not at first permit himself to believe it, its path inclined to the left, its staring eyes left him, and he was able to make out against its rounded sides the ladders of bent rod that would permit troopers to ride into battle on board its flattened back.

He did not move until it had vanished around the corner of the nearer wing; then he stepped across the spikes again, pulled his rope and the forked limb free, and jumped after them. Although he struck the drought-hardened ground with bent knees and rolled forward, putting back into practice the lessons of boyhood, the drop stung the soles of his feet and left him sprawled breathless.

The rear gate, to which the white roadway ran, was a grill of bars, narrow and recessed. A bellpull beside it might (or might not, Silk reflected) summon a human servant from within the house. Suddenly reckless, he tugged it, watching through the four-finger interstices to see who might appear, while the bell clanged balefully over his head. No dog barked at the sound. For a moment only, it seemed to him that he caught the flash of eyes in the shadow of a big willow halfway between the wall and the house; but the image had been too brief to be trusted, and the eyes (if eyes they had been) at a height of seven cubits or more.

The talus itself threw open the gate, roaring, *"Who are you!"* It seemed to lean forward as it trained its buzz guns at him.

Silk tugged his wide-brimmed straw hat lower. "Someone with a message for Blood, your master," he announced. "Get out of my way." Quickly, he stepped under the gate, so that it could not be dropped again without crushing him. He had never been so close to a talus before, and there seemed no harm in satisfying his curiosity now; he reached out and touched the angled plate that was the huge machine's chest. To his surprise he found it faintly warm.

"Who are you!" the talus roared again.

"Do you wish my name or the tessera I was given?" Silk replied. "I have both."

Though it had not appeared to move at all, the talus was nearer now, so near that its chest plate actually nudged his robe. *"Stand back!"*

Without warning, Silk found himself a child once more, a child confronting an adult, an uncaring, shouting giant. In a story his mother had read to him, some bold boy had darted between a giant's legs. It would be perfectly possible now; the seamless black strips on which the talus stood lifted its steel body three cubits at least above the grass.

Could he outrun a talus? He licked his lips. Not if they were as fast as floaters. But were they? If this one chose to shoot, it would not matter.

Its chest plate shoved him backward, so that he reeled and nearly fell. *"Get out!"*

"Tell Blood I was here." He would surely be reported; it

might be best if he appeared to wish it. "Tell him that I have information."

"*Who are you?*"

"Rust," Silk whispered. "Now let me in."

Suddenly the talus was rolling smoothly back. The gate crashed down, a hand's breadth in front of his face. Quite possibly there was a tessera—a word or a sign that would command instant admittance. But *rust* certainly was not it.

He left the gate, discovering with some surprise that his legs were trembling. Would the talus answer the front gate also? Very probably; but there was no harm in finding out, and the back of the villa seemed unpromising indeed.

As he set off upon the lengthy walk along the wall that would take him to the front gate, he reflected that Auk (and so by implication others of his trade) would have attempted the rear; a foresighted planner might well have anticipated that and taken extra precautions there.

A moment later he rebuked himself for the thought. Auk would not have dared the front gate, true; but neither would Auk have been terrified of the talus, as he had been. He pictured Auk's coarse and frowning face, its narrowed eyes, jutting ears, and massive, badly shaved jaw. Auk would be careful, certainly. But never fearful. What was still more important, Auk believed in the goodness of the gods, in their benign personal care—something that he, whose own trade it was to profess it, could only struggle to believe.

Shaking his head, he pulled his beads from his trousers pocket, his fingers reassured by their glassy polish and the swinging mass of the voided cross. Nine decades, one with which to praise and petition each major divinity, with an additional, unspecified decade from which the voided cross was suspended. For the first time it occurred to him that there were ten beads in each decade as well. Had the Nine been the Ten, once? He pushed the heretical thought aside.

First the cross. "To you, Great Pas . . ."

There was a secret in the empty, X-shaped space, or so one of his teachers had confided, a mystery far beyond that of the detachable arms he showed the smallest boys and girls at the palaestra and used (as every other augur did) to test and tighten sacred connections. Unfortunately, his teacher had not seen fit to confide the secret as well, and probably had not known it himself—if any such secret actually existed. Silk shrugged aside the memory, ceased fingering the enigmatic emptiness of the voided cross, and clasped it to his chest.

"To you, Great Pas, I present my poor heart and my whole spirit, my mind and all my belief . . ."

The grass thinned and vanished, replaced by odd little plants like multilayered, greenish umbrellas that appeared healthy and flourishing, yet crumbled to mere puffs of dust when Silk stepped on them.

Blood's front gate was less promising than the other, if anything, for an eye in a black metal box gleamed above the top of its arch. Should he ring here, Musk or someone like him inside would not only see him, but interrogate him, no doubt, speaking through a mouth in the same box.

For five minutes or more, sitting on a convenient stone while he rubbed his feet, Silk considered the advisability of submitting himself to the scrutiny of that eye, and thus of the unknown inquisitor who would examine him through it. He knew himself to be a less than competent liar; and when he tried to concoct a tale that might get him into Blood's presence, he was dismayed at how feeble and un-convincing even the best of his fabrications sounded. Even-tually he was driven to conclude, with a distinct sense of relief, that the prospect was hopeless; he would have to get into the villa by stealth, if he got into it at all.

Retying his shoes, he rose, advanced another hundred

paces along the wall, and once more heaved the forked limb over its spikes.

As Auk had indicated, there was a central building of two stories, with wings whose rows of windows showed them to be three, although the original structure was nearly as tall as they. Both the original structure and its wings appeared to be of the same smooth, grayish stone as the wall, and all three were so high that throwing the limb onto the roof of any appeared quite impossible. To enter them directly, he would have to discover an unbolted door or force one of the ground-floor casements, exactly as he and the other boys had broken into the deserted house a few years before he left home to attend the schola. He winced at the thought.

On the farther end of the wing on the right, however (the structure most remote from his old vantage point), was a more modest addition whose decorative merlons appeared to stand no more than a scant ten cubits above the lawn; the size and close spacing of its numerous windows suggested that it might be a conservatory. Silk noted it for future use and turned his attention to the grounds.

The broad grassway that curved so gracefully up to the pillared portico of Blood's villa was bordered with bright flower beds. Some distance in front of that entrance, a fine porcelain Scylla writhed palely among the sprays of an ostentatious fountain, spewing water alike from her woman's mouth and her upraised tentacles.

Scented water, in fact; sniffing the almost motionless air like a hound, Silk caught the fragrance of tea roses. Postponing judgement on Blood's taste, he nodded approvingly at this tangible evidence of pious civic feeling. Perhaps Blood was not really such a bad man after all, no matter what Auk thought. Blood had provided three cards for a sacrifice; it might well be that if Blood were approached in the right way he would be amenable to reason.

Possibly the Outsider's errand would come to no more than that, in the end. Giving rein to this pleasing line of thought for a second or two, Silk imagined himself comfortably seated in some luxurious chamber of the villa before him, laughing heartily over his own adventures with the prosperous-looking man with whom he had spoken in Sun Street. Why, even a contribution toward necessary repairs might not be entirely out of the question.

On the farther side of the grassway . . .

The distant roar of an approaching floater made him look around. With running lights blazing through its own dust, it was hurtling along the public road in the direction of the main gate. Quickly he stretched himself flat behind the row of spikes.

As the floater braked, two figures in silvered conflict armor shot away from the portico on highriders. At the same moment, the talus rounded the conservatory (if that was what it was) at full tilt, dodging trees and shrubs as it rolled across the lawn nearly as fast as the highriders; after it bounded half a dozen sinuous, seemingly tailless beasts with bearded faces and horned heads.

While Silk watched fascinated, the thick metal arms of the talus stretched like telescopes, twenty cubits or more to catch hold of a ring high in the wall near the gate. For a second they paused. An unseen chain rattled and creaked. They shrank, drawing the ring and its chain with them, and the gate rose.

The shadow of a drifting cloud from the east veiled the pillars of the portico, then the steps at their bases; Silk murmured a frantic appeal to Tartaros and tried to judge its speed.

There was a faint and strangely lonely whine from the blowers as the floater glided under the gate's rounded arch. One of the horned beasts sprang onto its transparent canopy, appearing to crouch upon empty air until it was driven off snarling by the armored men, who cursed and brandished their short-tubed slug guns as if to strike it. The drifting shadow had reached Scylla's fountain by the time the horned beast sprang away.

The talus let the heavy gate fall again as the floater swept proudly up the darkening grassway, escorted by the high-riders and accompanied by all six horned beasts, which rose upon their hind legs again and again to peer inside. It halted and settled onto the grass before the wide stone steps of the villa, and the talus called the horned beasts from it with a shrill shuddering wail that could have issued from no human throat.

As the brilliantly dressed passengers disembarked, Silk leaped from the wall and dashed across the lawn toward the conservatory, with a desperate effort flung the forked limb over its ornamental battlement, and swarmed up the horsehair rope, over the battlement, and onto the roof.

Chapter 5

THE WHITE-HEADED ONE

For what seemed to him the greater part of an hour, Silk lay behind the battlement trying to catch his breath. Had he been seen? If the talus or one of the armored men had seen him, they would have come at once, he felt certain; but if one of Blood's guests had, it might easily be ten minutes or even longer before he decided that he should report what he had seen, and reached the appropriate person; it might be that he would not so much as try until prompted by another guest to whom he mentioned the incident.

Overhead the skylands sailed serenely among broad bars of sterile cloud, displaying countless now-sunlit cities in which nobody at all knew or cared that one Patera Silk, an augur of faraway Viron, was frightened almost to death and might soon die.

The limb, too, might have given him away. He was sure that he, on the ground, had heard it thump down on the warm, tarred surface of the roof; and anyone in the conservatory below must have heard it very distinctly. As he sought to slow the pounding of his heart by an effort of will, and to force himself to breathe through his nose, it seemed to him that anyone who had heard that thump would realize at once that it had been made by an intruder who had climbed onto the roof. As the thunder of his own pulse faded away, he listened intently.

The music he had heard so faintly from the wall was louder now. Through it, over it, and below it, he heard the murmur of voices—the voices of men, mostly, he decided, with a few women among them. That piercing laugh had been a woman's, unless he was greatly mistaken. Glass shattered, not loudly, followed by a moment of silence, then a shout of laughter.

His black rope was still hanging over the battlement. He felt that it was almost miraculous that it had not been seen. Without rising from his back, he hauled it in hand over hand. It would be necessary, in another minute or two, to throw the limb again, this time onto the roof of the wing proper. He was not at all sure he could do it.

An owl floated silently overhead, then veered away to settle on a convenient branch at the edge of the forest. Watching it, Silk (who had never considered the lives of Echidna's pets before) suddenly realized that the building of Blood's wall, with the cleared strip on its forest side and the closely trimmed lawn on the other, had irrevocably altered the lives of innumerable birds and small animals, changing the way in which woodmice foraged for food and hawks and owls hunted them. To such creatures, Blood and his hired workmen must have seemed the very forces of nature, pitiless and implacable. Silk pitied those animals now, all the while wondering whether they did not have as much right, and more reason, to pity him.

The Outsider, he reflected, had swooped upon him much as the owl would stoop for a mouse; the Outsider had assured him that his regard for him was eternal and perfect, never to be changed by any act of his, no matter how iniquitous or how meritorious. The Outsider had then told him to act, and had withdrawn while in some fashion remaining. The memory, and the wonder of the Outsider's love and of his own new, clean pride in the Outsider's regard, would make the rest of his life both more meaningful and more painful. Yet what could he do, beyond what he was doing?

"Thank you," he whispered. "Thank you anyway, even if you never speak to me again. You have given me the courage to die."

The owl hooted from its high branch above the wall, and the orchestra in Blood's ballroom struck up a new tune, one Silk recognized as "Know I'll Never Leave You." Could that be an omen? The Outsider had indeed warned him to expect no help, but had never (as well as Silk could remember, at any rate) actually told him that he would never be vouchsafed omens.

Shaking himself, his self-possession recovered and his sweat dried, he lifted his knees and rolled into a crouch behind one of the merlons, peering through the crenel on its left. There was no one on that part of the grounds visible to him. He readjusted the long handle of the hatchet while changing position slightly in order to look out through the crenel on the right. Half the grassway was visible from that angle, and with it the gate; but there was no floater on that section of the grassway, and the talus and the horned beasts that had come at its call had gone elsewhere. The skylands were brightening as the trailing edge of the cloud that had favored him left Viron for the west; he could make out the iron ring the talus had pulled to raise the gate, to the left of the arch.

He stood then and looked about him. There was nothing threatening or even extraordinary about the roof of Blood's conservatory. It was level or nearly so, a featureless dark surface surrounding an abatjour for the illumination of the conservatory, itself enclosed on three sides by chest-high battlements. The fourth was defined by the south wall of the wing from which the conservatory extended; the sills of its second-story windows were three cubits or a trifle less above the conservatory roof.

Silk felt a thrill of triumph as he studied the windows. Their casements were shut, and the rooms that they lighted, dark; yet he felt an undeniable pride in them that was not unrelated to that of ownership. Auk had predicted that he would get roughly this far before being captured by Blood's guards—and now he had gotten this far, doing nothing more than Auk, who clearly knew a great deal about such things, had expected. The manteion had not been saved, or even made appreciably safer. And yet . . .

Boldly, he leaned over the nearest battlement, his head and shoulders thrust beyond the merlons. One of the horned beasts was standing at the base of the conservatory wall, directly below him. For an instant he was acutely conscious of its amber stare; it snarled, and cat-like padded away.

Could those fantastic animals climb onto the roof? He decided that though possible it was unlikely—the walls of the villa were of dressed stone, after all. He leaned out farther still, his hands braced on the bottom of the crenel, to reassure himself about the construction of the wall.

As he did, the talus rolled into view. He froze until it had passed. There was a chance, of course, that it had concealed, upward- or rearward-directed eyes; Maytera Marble had once mentioned such features in connection with Maytera Rose. But that, too, seemed less than probable.

Leaving his limb and horsehair rope where they lay, he walked gingerly across the roof to the abatjour and crouched to peer through one of its scores of clear panes.

The conservatory below apparently housed large bushes of some sort, or possibly dwarfed trees. Silk found that he had unconsciously assumed that it had supplied the low-growing flowers that bordered the grassway. That had been an error, now revealed; while examining the plants below, he cautioned himself against making any further unconsidered assumptions about this villa of Blood's.

The panes themselves were set in lead. Silk scraped the lead with the edge of his hatchet, finding it as soft as he could wish. With half an hour's skillful work, it should be possible, he decided, to remove two panes without breaking them, after which he could let himself down among the lush, shining leaves and intertwined trunks below—perhaps with an undesirable amount of noise, but perhaps also, unheard.

Nodding thoughtfully to himself, he rose and walked quietly across the conservatory roof to examine the dark windows of the wing overlooking it.

The first two he tested were locked in some fashion. As he tugged at each, he was tempted to wedge the blade of his hatchet between the stile and casing to pry them open. The latch or bolt would certainly break with a snap, however, if it gave at all; and it seemed only too likely that the glass would break instead. He decided that he would try to throw the limb onto the roof two stories above him (diminished by a third, that throw no longer appeared nearly as difficult as it had when he had reconnoitered the villa from the top of its surrounding wall) and explore that roof as well before attempting anything quite so audacious. Circuitous though it seemed, removing panes from the abat-jour might actually be a more prudent approach.

The third casement he tried gave slightly in response to his tentative pull. He pushed it back, wiped his perspiring palms on his robe and tugged harder. This time the casing moved a trifle farther; it was only jammed, apparently, not locked. A quick wrench of the hatchet forced it open enough for him to swing it back with only the slightest of protests from the neglected hinges. Vaulting with one hand upon the sill, he slid headfirst into the lightless room beyond.

The gritty wooden floor was innocent of carpet. Silk explored it with his fingertips, in ever-wider arcs, while he knelt, motionless, alert for any sound from within the room. His fingers touched something the size of a pigeon's egg, something spherical, hard, and dry. He picked it up— it yielded slightly when squeezed. Suspicious, he lifted it to his nostrils and sniffed.

Excrement.

He dropped it and wiped his fingers on the floor. Some animal was penned in this room and might be present now, as frightened of him as he was of it—if it was not already stalking him. Not one of the horned cats, surely; they were apparently freed to roam the grounds at night. Something worse, then. Something more dangerous.

Or nothing. If there was an animal in the room, it was a silent one indeed. Even a serpent would have hissed by now, surely.

Silk got to his feet as quietly as he could and inched along the wall, his right hand grasping his hatchet, the fingers of his left groping what might have been splintered paneling.

A corner, as empty as the whole room seemed to be. He took a step, then another. If there were pictures, or even furniture, he had thus far failed to encounter them.

Another step; pull up the right foot to the left now. Pausing to listen, he could detect only his own whistling breath and the faint tinklings of the distant orchestra.

His mouth felt dry, and his knees seemed ready to give way beneath him; twice he was forced to halt, bracing his trembling hands against the wall. He reminded himself that he was actually in Blood's villa, and that it had not been as difficult as he had feared. The task to follow would be much harder: he would have to locate Blood without being discovered himself, and speak with him for some time in a place where they could talk without interruption. Only now was he willing to admit that it might prove impossible.

A second corner.

This vertical molding was surely the frame of a door; the pale rectangle of the window he had opened was on the opposite side of the room. His hand sought and found the latch. He pushed it down; it moved freely, with a slight rattle; but the door would not open.

"Have you been bad?"

He jerked the hatchet up, about to strike with deadly force at whatever might come from the darkness—about to kill, he told himself a moment later, some innocent sleeper whose bedchamber he had entered by force.

"Have you?" The question had a spectral quality; he could not have said whether it proceeded from a point within arm's reach or wafted through the open casement.

"Yes." To his own ears, the lone syllable sounded high and frightened, almost tremulous. He forced himself to pause and clear his throat. "I've been bad many times, I'm afraid. I regret them all."

"You're a boy. I can tell."

Silk nodded solemnly. "I used to be a boy, not so long ago. No doubt Maytera R—No doubt some of my friends would tell you that I'm a boy still in many respects, and they may well be right."

His eyes were adjusting to the darker darkness of the room, so that the skylight that played across the roof of the conservatory and the grounds in the distance, mottled though it was by the diffused shadows of broken clouds, made them appear almost sunlit. The light spilling through the open window showed clearly now the precise rectangle of flooring on which he had knelt, and dimly the empty, unclean room to either side. Yet he could not locate the speaker.

"Are you going to hurt me with that?"

It was a young woman's voice, almost beyond question. Again Silk wondered whether she was actually present. "No," he said, as firmly as he could. He lowered the hatchet. "I will do you no violence, I swear." Blood dealt in women, so Auk had said; now Silk felt that he had a clearer idea of what such dealings might entail. "Are you being kept here against your will?"

"I go whenever I want. I travel. Usually I'm not here at all."

"I see," Silk said, though he did not, in either sense. He pushed down the latchbar again; it moved as readily as it had before, and the door remained as stubborn.

"I go very far, sometimes. I fly out the window, and no one sees me."

Silk nodded again. "I don't see you now."

"I know."

"Sometimes you must go out through this door, though. Don't you?"

"No."

Her flat negative bore in its train the illusion that she was standing beside him, her lips almost brushing his ear. He groped for her, but his hand found only empty air. "Where are you now? You can see me, you say. I'd like to see you."

"I'll have to get back in."

"Get back in through the window?"

There was no reply. He crossed the room to the window and looked out, leaning on the sill; there was no one on the roof of the conservatory, no one but the talus in sight on the grounds beyond. His rope and limb lay where he had left them. Devils (according to legends no one at the schola had really credited) could pass unseen, for devils were spirits of the lower air, presumably personifications of destructive winds. "Where are you now?" he asked again. "Please come out. I'd like to see you."

Nothing. Thelxiepeia provided the best protection from devils, according to the Writings, but this was Phaea's day, not hers. Silk petitioned Phaea, Thelxiepeia, and for good measure Scylla, in quick succession before saying, "I take it you don't want to talk to me, but I need to talk to you. I need your help, whoever you are."

In Blood's ballroom, the orchestra had struck up "Brave Guards of the Third Brigade." Silk had the feeling that no one was dancing, that few if any of Blood's guests were even listening. Outside, the talus waited at the gate, its steel arms unnaturally lengthened, both its hands upon the ring.

Turning his back on the window, Silk scanned the room. A shapeless mass in a corner (one that he had not traversed when he had felt his way along the walls to the door) might conceivably have been a huddled woman. With no very great confidence he said, "I see you."

"To fourteen more my sword I pledged," sang the violins with desperate gaiety. Beardless lieutenants in brilliant green dress uniforms, twirling smiling beauties with plumes in their hair—but they were not there, Silk felt certain, no more than the mysterious young woman whom he himself was trying to address was here.

He crossed to the dark shape in the corner and nudged it with the toe of his shoe, then crouched, put aside his hatchet, and explored it with both hands—a ragged blanket and a thin, foul-smelling mattress. Picking up his hatchet again, he rose and faced the empty room. "I'd like to see you," he repeated. "But if you won't let me—if you won't even talk to me any more—I'm going to leave." As soon as he had spoken, he reflected that he had probably told her precisely what she wanted to hear.

He stepped to the window. "If you require my help, you

must say so now." He waited, silently reciting a formula of blessing, then traced the sign of addition in the darkness before him. "Good-bye, then."

Before he could turn to go, she rose before him like smoke, naked and thinner than the most miserable beggar. Although she was a head shorter, he would have backed away from her if he could; his right heel thumped the wall below the window.

"Here I am. Can you see me now?" In the dim skylight from the window her starved and bloodless face seemed almost a skull. "My name's Mucor."

Silk nodded and swallowed, half afraid to give his own, not liking to lie. "Mine's Silk." Whether he succeeded or was apprehended, Blood would learn his identity. "Patera Silk. I'm an augur, you see." He might die, perhaps; but if he did his identity would no longer matter.

"Do you really have to talk with me, Silk? That's what you said."

He nodded. "I need to ask you how to open that door. It doesn't seem to be locked, but it won't open."

When she did not reply, he added. "I have to get into the house. Into the rest of it, I mean."

"What's an augur? I thought you were a boy."

"One who attempts to learn the will of the gods through sacrifice, in order that he may—"

"I know! With the knife and the black robe. Lots of blood. Should I come with you, Silk? I can send forth my spirit. I'll fly beside you, wherever you go."

"Call me Patera, please. That's the proper way. You can send forth your body, too, Mucor, if you want."

"I'm saving myself for the man I'll marry." It was said with perfect (too perfect) seriousness.

"That's certainly the correct attitude, Mucor. But all I meant was that you don't have to stay here if you don't wish to. You could climb out of this window very easily and wait

out there on the roof. When I've finished my business with
Blood, we could both leave this villa, and I could take you
to someone in the city who would feed you properly and—
and take care of you."

The skull grinned at him. "They'd find out that my window opens, Silk. I wouldn't be able to send my spirit any
more."

"You wouldn't be here. You'd be in some safe place in
the city. There you could send out your spirit whenever you
wanted, and a physician—"

"Not if my window was locked again. When my window
is locked, I can't do it, Silk. They think it's locked now." She
giggled, a high, mirthless tittering that stroked Silk's spine
like an icy finger.

"I see," he said. "I was about to say that someone in the
city might even be able to make you well. You may not care
about that, but I do. Will you at least let me out of your
room? Open your door for me?"

"Not from this side. I can't."

He sighed. "I didn't really think you could. I don't suppose you know where Blood sleeps?"

"On the other side. Of the house."

"In the other wing?"

"His room used to be right under mine, but he didn't
like hearing me. Sometimes I was bad. The north addition.
This one's the south addition."

"Thank you," Silk stroked his cheek. "That's certainly
worth knowing. He'll have a big room on the ground floor,
I suppose."

"He's my father."

"Blood is?" Silk caught himself on the point of saying
that she did not resemble him. "Well, well. That may be
worth knowing, too. I don't plan to hurt him, Mucor,
though I rather regret that now. He has a very nice daugh-

ter; he should come and see her more often, I think. I'll mention it forcefully, if I get to talk with him."

Silk turned to leave, then glanced back at her. "You really don't have to stay here, Mucor."

"I know. I don't."

"You don't want to come with me when I leave? Or leave now yourself?"

"Not the way you mean, walking like you do."

"Then there's nothing I can do for you except give you my blessing, which I've done already. You're one of Molpe's children, I think. May she care for you and favor you, this night and every night."

"Thank you, Silk." It was the tone of the little girl she had once been. Five years ago, perhaps, he decided; or perhaps three, or less than three. He swung his right leg over the windowsill.

"Watch out for my lynxes."

Silk berated himself for not having questioned her more. "What are those?"

"My children. Do you want to see one?"

"Yes," he said. "Yes, I do, if you want to show him to me."

"Watch."

Mucor was looking out the window, and Silk followed her gaze. For half a minute he waited beside her, listening to the faint sounds of the night; Blood's orchestra seemed to have fallen silent. Ghost-like, a floater glided beneath the arch, its blowers scarcely audible; the talus let down the gate smoothly behind it, and even the distant rattle of the chain reached them.

A section of abatjour pivoted upward, and a horned head with topaz eyes emerged from beneath it, followed by a big, soft-looking paw.

Mucor said, "That's Lion. He's my oldest son. Isn't he handsome?"

Silk managed to smile. "Yes, he certainly is. But I didn't know you meant the horned cats."

"Those are their ears. But they jump through windows, and they have long teeth and claws that can hurt worse than a bull's horns."

"I imagine so." Silk made himself relax. "Lynxes? Is that what you call them? I've never heard of the name, and I'm supposed to know something about animals."

The lynx emerged from the abatjour and trotted over to stand beneath the window, looking up at them quizzically. If he had bent, Silk could have touched its great, bearded head; he took a step backward instead. "Don't let him come up here, please."

"You said you wanted to see them, Silk."

"This is close enough."

As if it had understood, the lynx wheeled. A single bound carried it to the top of the battlement surrounding the conservatory roof, from which it dived as though into a pool.

"Isn't he pretty?"

Silk nodded reluctantly. "I found him terrifying, but you're right. I've never seen a lovelier animal, though all Sabered Sphigx's cats are beautiful. She must be very proud of him."

"So am I. I told him not to hurt you." Mucor squatted on her heels, folding like a carpenter's rule.

"By standing beside me and talking to me, you mean." Gratefully, Silk seated himself on the windowsill. "I've known dogs that intelligent. But a—lynx? Is that the singular? It's an odd word."

"It means they hunt in the daytime," Mucor explained. "They would, too, if my father'd let them. Their eyes are sharper than almost any other animal's. But their ears are good, too. And they can see in the dark, just like regular cats."

Silk shuddered.

"My father traded for them, When he got them they were just little chips of ice inside a big box that was little on the inside. The chips are just like little seeds. Do you know about that, Silk?"

"I've heard of it," he said. For an instant he thought that he felt the hot yellow gaze of the lynx behind him; he looked quickly, but the roof was bare. "It's supposed to be against the law, though I don't think that's very strictly enforced. One could be placed inside a female animal of the correct sort, a large cat I'd imagine, in this case—"

"He put them inside a girl." Mucor's eerie titter came again. "It was me."

"In you!"

"He didn't know what they were." Mucor's teeth flashed in the darkness. "But I did, a long while before they were born. Then Musk told me their name and gave me a book. He likes birds, but I like them and they like me."

"Then come with me," Silk said, "and the lynxes won't hurt either of us."

The skull nodded, still grinning. "I'll fly beside you, Silk. Can you bribe the talus?"

"I don't think so."

"It takes a lot of money."

There was a soft scraping from the back of the room, followed by a muffled thump. Before the door swung open, Silk realized that what he had heard was a bar being lifted from it and laid aside. Nearly falling, he slid over the sill, and crouched as Mucor's window shut silently above his head.

For as long as it took him to run mentally through the formal praises of Sphigx, whose day was about to dawn (or so at least he felt), he waited, listening. No sound of voices reached him from the room above, though once he heard what might have been a blow. When he stood at last and peeped cautiously through the glass, he could see no one.

The panes that Lion had raised with his head yielded easily to Silk's fingers; as they rose, a moist and fragrant exhalation from the conservatory below invaded the dry heat of the rooftop. He reflected that it would be simple now—much easier than he had thought—to enter the conservatory from above, and the trees there had clearly supported Lion's considerable weight without damage.

Silk's fingertips described slow circles on his cheek as he considered it. The difficulty was that Blood slept in the other wing, if Mucor was to be believed. Entering here, he would have to traverse the length of the villa from south to north, finding his way though unfamiliar rooms. There would be bright lights and the armored guards he had seen in Auk's glass and on the highriders, Blood's staff and Blood's guests.

Regretfully Silk let down the movable section of the abatjour, retrieved his horsehair rope, and untied the rough limb that had served him so well. The merlons crowning the roof of the south annex would not have cutting edges, and a noose would make no dangerous noise. Three throws missed before the fourth snared a merlon. He tugged experimentally at the rope; the merlon seemed as solid as a post; drying his hands on his robe, he started up.

He had reached the roof of the wing and was removing his noose from the merlon when Mucor's spectral voice spoke, seemingly in his ear. There were words he could not quite hear, then, ". . . birds. Watch out for the whiteheaded one."

"Mucor?"

There was no reply. Silk looked over the battlement just in time to see the window close.

Although it was twenty times larger, this roof had no abatjour, and was in fact no more than a broad and extremely long expanse of slightly sloping tar. Beyond the parapet at its northern end, the lofty stone chimneys of the original structure stood like so many pallid sentries in the glimmering skylight. Silk had enjoyed several lively conversations with chimney sweeps since arriving at the manteion on Sun Street, and had learned (with many other things) that the chimneys of great houses were frequently wide enough to admit the sweep employed to clean and repair them, and that some had interior steps for his use.

Walking softly and keeping near the center so that he could not be seen from the ground, Silk walked the length of the roof. When he was near enough to look down on it, he saw that the more steeply pitched roof of the original structure was tiled rather than tarred. Its tall chimneys were clearly visible now; there were five, of which four appeared to be identical. The fifth, however—the chimney farthest but one from him—boasted a chimney pot twice the height of the rest, a tall and somewhat shapeless pot with a pale finial. For a moment, Silk wondered uneasily whether it could be the "white-headed one" Mucor had warned him against, and resolved to examine it only if he could not gain entry to any of the others.

Then another, more significant, detail caught his eye. The corner of some low projection, dark and distinct, could be seen beyond the third chimney, its angular outline in sharp contrast to the rounded contours of the tiles, and its top a cubit or so higher than theirs. He moved a few steps to his left to see it better.

It was, beyond question, a trapdoor; and Silk murmured a prayer of thanks to whatever god had arranged a generation ago that it should be included in the plan of the roof for his use.

Looping his rope around a merlon, he scrambled easily down onto the tiles and pulled the rope down after him. The Outsider had indeed warned him to expect no help; yet some other god was certainly siding with him. For a moment Silk speculated happily on which it might be. Scylla, perhaps, who would not wish her city to lose a manteion. Or grim and gluttonous Phaea, the ruler of the day. Or Molpe, since— No, Tartaros, of course. Tartaros was the patron of thieves of every kind, and he had prayed fervently to Tartaros (as he now remembered) while still outside Blood's wall. Moreover, black was Tartaros's color; all augurs and sibyls wore it in order that they might, figuratively if not literally, steal unobserved among the gods to overhear their deliberations. Not only was he himself clothed entirely in black, but the tarred roofs he had just left behind had been black as well.

"Terrible Tartaros, be thanked and praised most highly by me forever. Now let it be unlocked, Tartaros! But locked or not, the black lamb I pledged shall be yours." Recalling the tavern in which he had met Auk, he added in a final burst of extravagance, "And a black cock, too."

And yet, he told himself, it was only logical that the trapdoor should be precisely where it was. Tiles must break at times—must be broken fairly frequently by the violent hailstorms that had ushered in every winter for the past few years; and each such broken tile would have to be replaced. A trapdoor giving access to the roof from the attic of the villa would be much more convenient (as well as much safer) than a seventy-cubit ladder. A ladder of that size would very likely require a whole crew of workmen just to get it into place.

He tried to hurry across the intervening tiles to the trapdoor, but their glazed, convex, and unstable surfaces hindered him, quite literally at every stride. Twice tiles cracked beneath his impatient feet; and when he had nearly reached the trapdoor, he slipped unexpectedly and fell, and saved himself from rolling down the roof only by clutching at the rough masonry of the third chimney.

It was reassuring to note that this roof, like those of the

wings and the conservatory, was walled with ornamental battlements. He would have had a bad time of it if it had not been for the chimney; he was glad he had escaped it. He would have been shaken and bruised, and he might well have made enough noise to attract the attention of someone inside the villa. But at the end of that ignominious fall he would not have dropped from the edge of the roof to his death. Those blessed battlements (which had been of so much help to him ever since he had dashed from the wall across the grounds) were, now that he came to think of it, one of the recognized symbols in art of Sphigx, the lion-goddess of war; and *Lion* had been the name of Mucor's horned cat—of the animal she called her lynx, which had not harmed him. Taking all that into account, who could deny that Fierce Sphigx favored him also?

Silk caught his breath, made sure of his footing, and let go of the chimney. Here, not a hand's breadth from the toe of his right shoe, was the thing that he had slipped on—this blotch on the earthen-red surface of the roof. He stooped and picked it up.

It was a scrap of raw skin, an irregular patch about as large as a handkerchief from the pelt of some animal, still covered with coarse hair on one side and slimy with rotting flesh and rancid fat on the other, reeking with decay. He flung it aside with a snort of disgust.

The trapdoor lifted easily; below it was a steep and tightly spiraled iron stair. A more conventional stairway, clearly leading to the upper floor of the original villa, began a few steps from the bottom of the iron one. Briefly he paused, looking down at it, to savor his triumph.

He had been carrying his horsehair rope in an untidy coil, and had dropped it when he slipped. He retrieved it and wound it around his waist beneath his robe, as he had when he had set out from the manteion that evening. It was always possible, he reminded himself, that he would need it again. Yet he felt as he had during his last year at the schola, when he had realized that final year would actually be easier than the one before it—that his instructors no more wished him to fail after he had studied so long than he himself did, and that he would not be permitted to fail unless he curtailed his efforts to an almost criminal degree. The whole villa lay open before him, and he knew, roughly if not precisely, where Blood's bedchamber was located. In order to succeed, he had only to find it and conceal himself there before Blood retired. Then, he told himself with a pleasant sensation of virtue, he would employ reason, if reason would serve; if it would not . . .

It would not, and the fault would be Blood's, not his. Those who opposed the will of a god, even a minor god like the Outsider, were bound to suffer.

Silk was pushing the long handle of his hatchet through the rope around his waist when he heard a soft thump behind him. Dropping the trapdoor, he whirled. Leaping so that it appeared taller than many men, a huge bird flapped misshapen wings, shrieked like a dozen devils, and struck at his eyes with its hooked bill.

Instinctively, he threw himself backward onto the top of the trapdoor and kicked. His left foot caught the white-headed bird full in the body without slowing its attack in the least. Vast wings thundering, it lunged after him as he rolled away.

By some prodigy of good luck he caught it by its downy neck; but the carpels of its wings were as hard as any man's knuckles, and were driven by muscles more powerful than the strongest's. They battered him mercilessly as both tumbled.

The edge of the crenel between two merlons was like a wedge driven into his back. Still struggling to keep the bird's cruel, hooked beak from his face and eyes, he jerked the hatchet free; a carpal struck his forearm like a hammer, and the hatchet fell to the stone pavement of the terrace below.

The white-headed one's other carpal struck his temple, and the illusory nature of the world of the senses was made manifest: it narrowed to a miniature, artificially bright, which Silk endeavored to push away until it winked out.

Chapter 6

NEW WEAPONS

A whole whorl swam beneath Silk's flying, beclouded eyes—highland and tableland, jungle and dry scrub, savannah and pampa. The plaything of a hundred idle winds, buffeted yet at peace, he sailed over them all, dizzy with his own height and speed, his shoulder nudged by storm cloud, the solitary Flier three score leagues below him a darting dragonfly with wings of lace.

A black dragonfly that vanished into blacker cloud, into distant voices and the odor of carrion . . .

Silk choked on his own spew and spat; terror rose from the wheeling scene to foot him like a falcon, its icy talons in his vitals. He had blinked, and in that single blink the whorl had rolled over like a wind-tumbled basket or a wave-tossed barrel. The drifting skylands were *up* and the uneven, unyielding surface on which he lay, *down.* His head throbbed and spun, and an arm and both legs burned.

He sat up.

His mouth was wet with slime, his black robe discolored and stinking. He wiped them clumsily with numbed hands, then wiped his hand on his robe and spat again. The gray stone of the battlement had been crowding his left shoulder. The bird he had fought, the "white-headed one" of Mucor's warning, was nowhere to be seen.

Or perhaps, he thought, he had only dreamed of a terrible bird. He stood, staggered, and fell to his knees.

His eyes closed of themselves. He had dreamed it all, his tortured mind writhing among nightmares—the horrible bird, the horned beasts with their incandescent stares, the miserable mad girl, his dark rope reaching blindly again and again for new heights, the silent forest, the burly burglar with his hired donkeys, and the dead man sprawled beneath the swinging, hanging lamp. But he was awake now, awake at last, and the night was spent—awake and kneeling beside his own bed in the manse on Sun Street. It was shadeup and today was Sphigxday; already he should be chanting Stabbing Sphigx's morning prayer.

"O divine lady of the swords, of the gathering armies, of the swords . . ."

He fell forward, retching, his hands on the still-warm, rounded tiles.

The second time he was wiser, not attempting to stand until he was confident that he could do so without falling. Before he gained his feet, while he lay trembling beside the battlement, dawn faded and winked out. It was night again, Phaesday night once more—an endless night that had not yet ended and might never end. Rain, he thought, might wash him clean and clear his head, and so he prayed for rain, mostly to Phaea and Pas, but to Scylla as well, remembering all the while how many men (men better than himself) were imploring the gods as he did, and for better reasons: how long had they been praying, offering such small sacrifices as they could, washing Great Pas's images in orchards of dying trees and in fields of stunted corn?

It did not rain, or even thunder.

Excited voices drifted to him from somewhere far away; he caught the name Hierax repeated over and over. Someone or something had died.

"Hierax," Feather had replied at the palaestra a week or

two before, fumbling after some fact associated with the familiar name of the God of Death. "Hierax is right in the middle."

"In the middle of Pas and Echidna's sons, Feather? Or of all their children?"

"Of their whole family, Patera. There's only the two boys in it." Feather, also, was one of a pair of brothers. "Hierax and Tartaros."

Feather had waited fearfully for correction, but he, Patera Silk, had smiled and nodded.

"Tartaros is the oldest and Hierax is the youngest,"

Feather had continued, encouraged.

Maytera's cubit stick tapped her lectern. "The older, Feather. And the younger. You said yourself that there were only two."

"Hierax . . ." said someone far below the other side of the battlement.

Silk stood up. He head still throbbed, and his legs were stiff; but he did not feel as though he were about to gag again. The chimneys (they all looked the same now) and the beckoning trapdoor seemed an impossible distance away. Still reeling and dizzy, he embraced a merlon with both arms and peered over the battlement. As if it belonged to someone else, he noted that his right forearm was oozing blood onto the gray stones.

Forty cubits and more below, three men and two women were standing in a rough circle on the terrace, all of them looking down at something. For a slow half minute at least, Silk could not be certain what it was. A third woman pushed one of the others aside, then turned away as if in disgust. There was more talk until one of the armored guards arrived with a lamp.

The bird, Mucor's white-headed one, lay dead upon the flagstones, appearing smaller than Silk could have imagined, its unequal wings half spread, its long white neck bent back at an unnatural angle. He had killed it. Or rather, it had killed itself.

One of the men around the dead bird glanced upward, saw Silk watching him, pointed, and shouted something Silk could not understand. Rather too late (or so he feared), he waved as though he were a member of the household and retreated up the steep slope of the roof.

The trapdoor opened upon the dim and lofty attic he had glimpsed earlier, a cobwebbed cavern more than half filled with musty furniture and splintering crates. Feeble lights kindled at the muted clank of his foot upon the first iron step; he had hardly descended to the second when one winked out. It was a promising place in which to conceal himself, but it would no doubt be the first to be searched should the man on the terrace raise the alarm. Silk had rejected it by the time he reached the bottom of the spiraling steps, and with a pang of regret hurried straight to the wider wooden stair and ran down them to the upper floor of the original villa.

Here a narrow, tapestry-covered door opened onto a wide and luxuriously furnished corridor not far from a balustraded staircase up which cultured voices floated. A fat, formally dressed man sat in an elaborate red velvet and gilt armchair a few steps from the top of the staircase. His arms rested on a rosewood table, and his head upon his folded arms; he snored softly as Silk passed, jerked to wakefulness, stared uncomprehendingly at Silk's black robe, and lowered his head to his arms again.

The stair was thickly carpeted, its steps broad, and its slant gentle. It terminated in a palatial reception hall, in which five men dressed much like the sleeper stood deep in conversation. Several were holding tumblers, and none seemed alarmed. Some distance beyond them, the reception hall ended with wide double doors—doors that stood open at present, so that the soft autumn night itself appeared as a species of skylit hanging in Blood's hall. Beyond any question, Silk decided, those doors represented the principal entrance to the villa; the portico he had studied from the wall would be on the other side; and indeed when he had surveyed the scene below him for a moment—not leaning across the balustrade as he had so unwisely leaned across the battlement to stare down at the flaccid form of the white-headed one, but from the opposite side of the corridor, with his back against the nude, half again life-sized statue of some minor goddess—he could just make out the ghostly outlines of the pillars.

Unbidden, the manteion's familiar, fire-crowned altar rose before him as he stared at the open doors: the altar, the manse, the palaestra, and the shady arbor where he had sometimes chatted too long with Maytera Marble. Suppose that he were to walk down this staircase quite normally? Stroll through that hall, nodding and smiling to anyone who glanced toward him. Would any of them stop him, or call for guards? It seemed unlikely.

His own hot blood trickling down his right arm wet his fingers and dripped onto Blood's costly carpet. Shaking his head, Silk strode swiftly past the stair and seated himself in the matching red armchair on the other side. As long as his arm bled, he could be tracked by his blood: down the spiral stair from the roof, down the attic stair, and along this corridor.

Parting his robe, he started a tear above the hem of his tunic with his teeth and ripped away a strip.

Could not the blood trail be turned to his advantage? Silk rose and walked rapidly along the corridor, flexing his wrist and clenching his right hand to increase the bleeding, and entered the south wing by a short flight of steps; there he halted for a moment to wind the strip about his wound and knot it with his teeth just as Gib, the big man in the Cock, had. When he had satisfied himself that it would remain in place, he retraced his steps, passing the chair in which he had sat, the stairhead, the sleeper, and the narrow tapestry-covered door leading to the attic. Here, beyond paired icons of the minor deities Ganymedia and Catamitus, wide and widely spaced doors alternated with elaborately framed mirrors and amphorae overfilled with hothouse roses.

As Silk approached the entrance to the north wing, an officer in the uniform of the Guard emerged from an archway at the end of the corridor. The door nearest Silk stood half open; he stepped inside and shut it softly behind him.

He found himself facing a windowless pentagonal drawing room furnished in magnificent chryselephantine. For a moment he waited with his back to the corridor door, listening as he had listened so often that night. When he heard nothing, he crossed the thick carpet and opened one of the drawing room's ivory-encrusted doors.

This was a boudoir, larger and even more oddly shaped. There were wardrobes, two chairs, a rather tawdry shrine of Kypris whose smoldering thurible filled the room with the sweetness of frankincense, and a white dressing table before a glass whose pearlescent glow appeared to intensify as he entered. When he shut the door behind him, a swirl of colors danced across the glass. He fell to his knees.

"Sir?"

Looking up, Silk saw that the glass held only the gray face of a monitor. He traced the sign of addition. "Wasn't there a god? I saw . . ."

"I am no god, sir, merely the monitor of this terminal. What may I do to serve you, sir? Would you care to critique your digitally enhanced image?"

Disconcerted, Silk stood. "No. I—No, thank you." He struggled to recall how Auk had addressed the monitor in his glass. "I'd like to speak to a friend, if it isn't too much trouble, my son." That had not been it, surely.

The floating face appeared to nod. "The friend's name, please? I will attempt it."

"Auk."

"And this Auk lives where?"

"In the Orilla. Do you know where that is?"

"Indeed I do, sir. However, there are . . . fifty-four Auks resident there. Can you supply the street?"

"No, I'm afraid I have no idea." Suddenly weary, Silk drew out the dressing table's somewhat soiled little stool and sat down. "I'm sorry to have put you to so much trouble. But if you're—"

"There is an Auk in the Orilla with whom my master has spoken several times," the monitor interrupted. "No doubt he is the Auk you want. I will attempt to locate him for you."

"No," Silk said. "This Auk lives in what used to be a shop. So it must be on a shopping street, I suppose, with a lot of other stores and so on. Or at least on a street that used to have them." Remembering it, he recalled the thunder of the cartwheels. "A street paved with cobblestones. Does that help?"

"Yes. That is the Auk with whom my master speaks, sir. Let us see whether he is at home."

The monitor's face faded, replaced by Auk's disordered bed and jar of slops. Soon the image swelled and distorted, becoming oddly rounded. Silk saw the heavy wooden chair from which he had shriven Auk and beside which he had knelt when Auk shrived him. He found it heartening, somehow, to know that the chair was still there.

"I fear that Auk is unavailable, sir. May I leave a message with my similitude?"

"I—yes." Silk stroked his cheek. "Ask him, please, to tell Auk that I appreciate his help very, very much, and that if nothing happens to me it will be my great pleasure to tell Maytera Mint how kind he was. Tell him, too, that he's specified only one meritorious act thus far, while the penance he laid upon me called for two or three—for two at least. Ask him to let me know what the others should be." Too late, it occurred to Silk that Auk had asked that his name not be mentioned to the handsome boy who had spoken though Blood's glass. "Now then, my son. You referred to your master. Who is that?"

"Blood, sir. Your host."

"I see. Am I, by any chance, in Blood's private quarters now?"

"No, sir. These are my mistress's chambers."

"Will you tell Blood about the message I left for—for that man who lives in the Orilla?"

The monitor nodded gravely. "Certainly, sir, if he inquires."

"I see." A sickening sense of failure decended upon Silk. "Then please tell Auk, also, where I was when I tried to speak to him, and warn him to be careful."

"I shall, sir. Will that be all?"

Silk's head was in his hands. "Yes. And thank you. No." He straightened up. "I need a place to hide, a good place, and weapons."

"If I may say so, sir," remarked the monitor, "you require a proper dressing more than either. With respect, sir, you are dripping on our carpet."

Lifting his right arm, Silk saw that it was true; blood had already soaked through the strip of black cloth he had torn from his tunic a few minutes earlier. Crimson rivulets trickled toward his elbow.

"You will observe, sir, that this room has two doors, in addition to that through which you entered. The one to your left opens upon the balneum. My mistress's medicinal supplies are there, I believe. As to—"

Silk had risen so rapidly that he had knocked over the

stool. Darting through the left-hand door, he heard nothing more.

The balneum was larger than he had anticipated, with a jade tub more than big enough for the naked goddess at the head of the staircase and a separate water closet. A sizable cabinet held a startling array of apothecary bottles, an olla of violet salve that Silk recognized as a popular aseptic, a roll of gauze, and gauze pads of various sizes. A small pair of scissors cut away the blood-soaked strip; he smeared the ragged wound that the white-headed one's beak had left in his forearm with the violet salve, and at the second try managed to bandage it effectively. As he ruefully took stock of his ruined tunic, he discovered that the bird's talons had raked his chest and abdomen. It was almost a relief to wash and salve the long, bloody scratches, on which he could employ both his hands.

Yellowish encrustations were forming on his robe where he had wiped away his spew. He took it off and washed it as thoroughly as he could in the lavabo, wrung it out, smoothed it as well as he could, pressed it between two dry towels, and put it back on. Inspecting his appearance in a mirror, he decided that he might well pass a casual examination in a dim light.

Returning to the boudoir, he strewed what he took to be face powder over the clotted blood on the carpet.

The monitor watched him, unperturbed. "That is most interesting, sir."

"Thank you." Silk shut the powder box and returned it to the dressing table.

"Does the powder possess cleansing properties? I was unaware of it."

Silk shook his head. "Not that I know of. I'm only masking these, so visitors won't be unsettled."

"Very shrewd, sir."

Silk shrugged. "If I could think of something better, I'd

do it. When I came in, you said that you weren't a god. I knew you weren't. We had a glass in the—in a palaestra I attended."

"Would you like to speak to someone there, sir?"

"Not now. But I was privileged to use that glass once, and it struck me then—I suppose it struck all of us, and I remember some of us talking about it one evening—that the glass looked a great deal like a Sacred Window. Except for its size, of course; all Sacred Windows are eight cubits by eight. Are you familiar with them?"

"No, sir."

Silk righted the stool and sat down. "There's another difference, too. Sacred Windows don't have monitors."

"That is unfortunate, sir."

"Indeed." Silk stroked his cheek with two fingers. "I should tell you, then, that the immortal gods appear at times in the Sacred Windows."

"Ah!"

"Yes, my son. I've never seen one, and most people—those who aren't augurs or sibyls, particularly—can't see the gods at all. Although they frequently hear the voice of the god, they see only a swirl of color."

The monitor's face flushed brick red. "Like this, sir?"

"No. Not at all like that. I was going to say that as I understand it, those people who can see the gods first see the swirling colors as well. When the theophany begins, the colors are seen. Then the god appears. And then the colors reappear briefly as the god vanishes. All this was set down in circumstantial detail by the Devoted Caddis, nearly two centuries ago. In the course of a long life, he'd witnessed the theophanies of Echidna, Tartaros, and Scylla, and finally that of Pas. He called the colors he'd seen the Holy Hues."

"Fascinating, sir. I fear, however, that it has little to do with me. May I show you what it is I do, sir? What I do most frequently, I should say. Observe."

The monitor's floating face vanished, replaced by the image of a remarkably handsome man in black. Although the tunic of the man in the glass was torn and white gauze showed beneath it, Silk did not recognize this man as himself until he moved and saw the image move with him.

"Is that . . . ?" He leaned closer. "No. But . . ."

"Thank you, sir," his image said, and bowed. "Only a first attempt, although I think it a rather successful one. I shall do better next time."

"Take it away, please. I am already too much given to vanity, believe me."

"As you wish, sir," his image replied. "I intended no disrespect. I merely desired to demonstrate to you the way in which I most frequently serve my mistress. Would you care to see her in place of yourself? I can easily display an old likeness."

Silk shook his head. "An old unlikeness, you mean. Please return to your normal appearance."

"As you wish, sir." In the glass, Silk's face lost its blue eyes and brown cheeks, its neck and shoulders vanished, and its features became flatter and coarser.

"We were speaking of the gods. No doubt I told you a good deal that you already knew."

"No, sir. I know very little about gods, sir. I would advise you to consult an augur."

"Then let's talk about monitors, my son. You must know more than most about monitors. You're a monitor yourself."

"My task is my joy, sir."

"We're fortunate, then, both of us. When I was at—in the house of a certain man I know, a man who has a glass like this one, he clapped his hands to summon the monitor. Is that the usual method?"

"Clapping the hands or tapping on the glass, sir. All of us much prefer the former, if I may be excused for saying it."

"I see." Silk nodded to himself. "Aren't there any other methods?"

"We actually appear in response to any loud sound, sir, to determine whether there is something amiss. Should a fire be in progress, for example, I would notify my master or his steward, and warn his guests."

"And from time to time," Silk said, "you must look into this room although no one has called you, even when there has been no loud sound. Isn't that so?"

"No, sir."

"You don't simply look in to make certain everything's all right?"

"No, sir. My mistress would consider that an invasion of her privacy, I'm sure."

"When I entered this room," Silk continued, "I did not make any sound that could be called loud—or at least none that I'm aware of. Certainly I didn't clap my hands or tap on this glass; yet you appeared. There was a swirl of color, then your face appeared in the glass. Shortly afterward you told me you weren't a god."

"You closed the door, sir."

"Very gently," Silk said. "I didn't want to disturb your mistress.

"Most considerate, sir."

"Yet the sound of my shutting that door summoned you? I would think that in that case almost any sound would do, however slight."

"I really cannot say what summoned me, sir."

"That's a suggestive choice of words, my son."

"I concede that it may be, sir." The monitor's face appeared to nod. "Such being the case, perhaps I may proffer an additional suggestion? It is that you abandon this line of inquiry. It will not reward your persistence, sir. Prior to entering the balneum, you inquired about weapons, sir, and places of concealment. One of our wardrobes might do."

"Thank you." Silk looked into the nearest, but it was filled almost to bursting with coats and gowns.

"As to weapons, sir," the monitor continued, "you may discover a useful one in my lowest left drawer, beneath the stockings."

"More useful than this, I hope." Silk closed the wardrobe.

"I am very sorry, sir. There appear to have been many purchases of late of which I have not been apprised."

Silk hardly heard him—there were angry and excited voices in the corridor. He opened the door to the drawing room and listened until they faded away, his hand upon the glass latchbar of the boudoir door, acutely conscious of the thudding of his heart.

"Are you leaving, sir?"

"The left drawer, I think you said."

"Yes, sir. The lowest of the drawers to your left. I can guarantee nothing, however, sir. My mistress keeps a small needler there, or perhaps I should say she did so not long ago. It may, however . . ."

Silk had already jerked out the drawer. Groping under what seemed to be at least a hundred pairs of women's hose, his fingers discovered not one but two metal objects.

"My mistress is sometimes careless regarding the safety catch, sir. It may be well to exercise due caution until you have ascertained its condition."

"I don't even know what that is," Silk muttered as he gingerly extracted the first.

It was a needler so small that it lay easily in the palm of his hand, elaborately engraved and gold plated; the thumb-sized ivory grips were inlaid with golden hyacinths, and a minute heron scanned a golden pool for fish at the base of the rear sight. For a moment, Silk too knew peace, lost in the flawless craftsmanship that had been lavished upon every surface. No venerated object in his manteion was half so fine.

"Should that discharge, it could destroy my glass, sir."

Silk nodded absently. "I've seen needlers—I saw two tonight, in fact—that could eat this one."

"You have informed me that you are unfamiliar with the safety catch, sir. Upon either side of the needler you hold, you will observe a small movable convexity. Raised, it will prevent the needler from discharging."

"This," Silk said. Like the grips, each tiny boss was marked with a hyacinth, though these were so small that their minute, perfect florets were almost microscopic. He pushed one of the bosses down, and the other moved with it. "Will it fire now?"

"I believe so, sir. Please do not direct it toward my glass. Glasses are now irreplaceable, sir, the art of their manufacture having been left behind when—"

"I'm greatly tempted nevertheless."

"In the event of the destruction of this glass I should be unable to deliver your message to Auk, sir."

"In which case there'd be no need of it. This smooth bar inside the ring is the trigger, I suppose."

"I believe that is correct, sir."

Silk pointed the needler at the wardrobe and pressed the trigger. There was a sharp snap, like the cracking of a child's whip. "It doesn't seem to have done anything," he said.

"My mistress's wardrobe is not a living creature, sir."

"I never thought it was, my son." Silk bent to examine the wardrobe's door; a hole not much thicker than a hair had appeared in one of its polished panels. He opened the door again. Some, though not all, of the gowns in line with the hole showed ragged tears, as if they had been stabbed with a dull blade a little narrower than his index finger.

"I should use this on you, you know, my son," he told the monitor, "for Auk's sake. You're just a machine, like the scorer in our ball court."

"I am a machine, but not *just* a machine, sir."

Nodding mostly to himself, Silk pushed up the safety catch and dropped the little needler into his pocket.

The other object hidden under the stockings was shaped like the letter *T*. The stem was cylindrical and oddly rough, with a single, smooth protuberance below the crossbar; the crossbar itself seemed polished and slightly curved, and had upturned ends. The entire object felt unnaturally cold, as reptiles often do. Silk extracted it from the stockings with some difficulty and examined it curiously.

"Would it be convenient for me to withdraw, sir?" the monitor asked.

Silk shook his head. "What is this?"

"I don't know, sir."

He regarded the monitor narrowly. "Can you lie, under extreme provocation, my son? Tell an untruth? I know a chem quite well; and she can, or so she says."

"No, sir."

"Which leaves me not a whit the wiser." Silk seated himself on the stool again.

"I suppose not, sir."

"I think I know what this is, you see." Silk held the T-shaped object up for the monitor's inspection; it gleamed like polished silver. "I'd appreciate confirmation, and some instructions on how to operate it."

"I am afraid I cannot assist you, sir, although I would be glad to receive your own opinion."

"I think it's an azoth. I've never actually seen one, but we used to talk about them when I was a boy. One summer all of us made wooden swords, and sometimes we pretended they were azoths."

"Charming, sir."

"Not really," Silk muttered, scrutinizing the flashing gem in the pommel of the azoth. "We were as bloodthirsty as so many little tigers, and what's charming about that? But anyway, an azoth is supposed to be controlled by something called a demon. If you don't know about azoths, you don't know anything about that, I suppose."

"No, sir." The monitor's floating face swung from side to side, revealing that there was no head behind it. "If you wish to conceal yourself, sir, should you not do so at once? My master's steward and some of our guards are searching the suites on this floor."

"How do you know that?" Silk asked sharply.

"I have been observing them. I have glasses in some of the other suites, sir."

"They began at the north end of the corridor?"

"Yes, sir. Quite correct."

Silk rose. "Then I must hide in here well enough to escape them, and get into the north wing after they've left."

"You haven't examined the other wardrobe, sir."

"And I don't intend to. How many unsearched suites are there between us?"

"Three, sir."

"Then I've still got a little time." Silk studied the azoth. "When I made my sword, I left a nail sticking out, and bent it. That was my demon. When I twisted it toward me, the blade wasn't there any more. When I twisted it away from me, I had one."

"I doubt, sir—"

"Don't be too sure, my son. That may have been based on something supposedly true that I'd heard. Or I may have been imitating some other boy who'd gotten hold of a useful fact. I mean a fact that would be useful to me now."

The roughened stem of the *T* was the grip, obviously; and the crossbar was there to prevent the user's hand from contacting the blade. Silk tried to revolve the gem in the pommel, but its setting kept it securely in place.

The bent-nail demon of his toy sword had been one of those that had held the crosspiece; he felt certain of that. There was an unfacetted crimson gem (he vaguely remembered having heard a similar gem called a bloodstone) in the grip, just behind one of the smooth, tapering arms of the guard. It was too flat and much too highly polished to turn. He gripped the azoth as he had his wooden sword and pressed the crimson gem with his thumb.

Reality separated. Something else appeared between the halves, as a current divides a quiet pool. Plaster from the wall across the room fell smoking onto the carpet, revealing laths that themselves exploded in a shower of splinters with the next movement of his arm.

Involuntarily, he released the demon, and the azoth's blade vanished.

"Please be more careful with that, sir."

"I will." Silk pushed the azoth into the coiled rope about his waist.

"If it should be activated by chance, sir, the result might well be disastrous for you as well as others."

"You have to press the demon below the level of the grip, I think," Silk said. "It should be difficult for that to happen accidentally."

"I profoundly hope so, sir."

"You don't know where your mistress got such a weapon?"

"I did not even know she possessed it, sir."

"It must be worth as much as this whole villa. More, perhaps. I doubt that there are ten of them in the city." Silk turned toward the wardrobe and selected a blue winter gown of soft wool.

"They have left the suite they were searching earlier, sir. They are proceeding to the next."

"Thank you. Will you leave when I tell you to go?"

"Certainly, sir."

"I ought to destroy your glass." For a second, Silk stared at the monitor. "I'm tempted to do it. But if a god really visited it when I arrived . . ." He shrugged. "So I'm going to tell you to go instead, and cover your glass with a gown. Perhaps they won't notice it. Did they question the glasses in the other suites?"

"Yes, sir. Our steward summoned me to each glass. He is directing the searchers in person, sir."

"While you were here talking to me? I didn't know you could do that."

"I can, sir. One strives to best utilize lulls in the conversation, pauses, and the like. It is largely a matter of allocation, sir."

"But you didn't tell them where I was. You can't have. Why not?"

"He did not inquire, sir. As they entered each suite, he asked whether there was a stranger present."

"And you told them there wasn't?"

"No, sir. I was forced to explain that I could not be certain, since I am not perpetually present."

"Blood's steward—is that the young man called Musk?"

"Yes, sir. His instructions take precedence over all others, except my master's own."

"I see. Musk doesn't understand you much better than I do, apparently."

"Less well, perhaps, sir."

Silk nodded to himself. "I may remain in this suite after you've gone. On the other hand, I may leave, too, as soon as you're no longer here to watch what I'm doing. Do you understand what I've just told you?"

"Yes, sir," the monitor said. "Your future whereabouts will be problematical."

"Good. Now vanish at once. Go wherever it is that you go." Silk draped the glass, covering it completely in a way that he hoped would seem merely careless, and opened the door to his right.

For the space of a heartbeat, he thought the spacious, twilit bedchamber unoccupied; a faint moan from the enormous bed at its center revealed his mistake.

The woman in the bed writhed and keened aloud from the depths of her need. As he bent over her, something within him reached out to her; and though he had not touched her, he felt the thrill of touch. Her hair was as black as the night chough's wings, and as glossy. Her features, as well as he could judge in the uncertain glow, exquisite. She groaned softly, as though she knew he was looking down on her, and rolling her head upon her pillow, kissed it without waking.

Beyond the boudoir, the drawing room door opened.

He tore off his black robe and straw hat, ducked out of his torn tunic, kicked all three far under the big bed, and scrambled in, shoes and all. He was drawing up the gold-embroidered oversheet when he heard the door through which he had entered the boudoir open.

Someone said distinctly, "Nothing in here."

By then his thumb had found the safety catch. He sat up, leveling the needler, as the searchers entered.

"Stop!" he shouted, and fired. By the greatest good luck, the needle shattered a tall vase to the right of the door. The report brought the bedchamber's lights to their brightest.

The first armored guard halted, his slug gun not quite pointing at Silk; and the black-haired woman sat up abruptly, her slightly tilted eyes wide.

Without looking at her, Silk grated, "Go back to sleep, Hyacinth. This doesn't concern you." Faintly perfumed, her breath caressed his bare shoulder, deliciously warm.

"Sorry, Commissioner," the guard began, uncertainly. "I mean Patera—"

Too late, Silk realized that he was still wearing the old, blue-trimmed calotte that had once been Patera Pike's. He snatched it off. "This is unforgivable. Unforgivable! I shall inform Blood. Get out!" His voice was far too high, and mounting toward hysteria; surely the guard must sense how frightened he was. In desperation, he brandished the tiny needler.

"We didn't know—" The guard lowered his slug gun and took a step backward, bumping into the delicate-looking Musk, who had stepped through the boudoir behind him. "We thought everybody had— Well, just about everybody's already gone."

Silk cut him off. "Out! You've never seen me."

It had been (as he decided as soon as he had said it) the worst thing he could possibly have said, since Musk had certainly seen him only a few hours earlier. For an instant he felt certain that Musk would pounce upon it.

Musk did not. Silencing the sputtering guard with a shove, Musk said, "The outside door should've been locked. Take your time." He turned on his heel, and the guard shut the boudoir door quietly behind them.

Trembling, Silk waited until he heard the corridor door close as well before he kicked away the luxurious coverings and got out of the bed. His mouth was parched, and his knees without strength.

"What about me?" the woman asked. As she spoke, she pushed aside the oversheet and the red silk sheet, revealing remarkably rounded breasts and a small waist.

Silk caught his breath and looked away. "All right, what about you? Do you want me to shoot you?"

She smiled and threw her arms wide. "If it's the only thing you can do, why, yes." When Silk did not reply, she added, "I'll keep my eyes open, if that's all right with you. I like to see it coming." The smile became a grin. "Make it fast, but make it last. And make it good."

Both had spoken softly, and the lights were no longer glaring; Silk kicked the bed to re-energize them. "You have been given a philtre of some sort, I think. You'll feel very differently in the morning." Pushing up the safety catch, he dropped her needler back into his pocket.

"I was *given* nothing." The woman in the bed licked her lips, watching for his reaction. "I took what you're calling a philtre before the first ones got here."

"Rust?" Silk was on his knees beside the bed, groping for the clothing he had kicked beneath it. Fear was draining from him, and he felt immensely grateful for it. Lion-hearted Sphigx still favored him—nothing could be more certain.

"No." She was scornful. "Rust doesn't do this. Don't you know anything? On rust I'd have itched to kill them all, and I might've done it, too. Beggar's root's what they call it, and it turns a terrible bore into a real pleasure."

"I see." Wincing, Silk pulled out his ruined tunic and his second-best robe.

"Want me to give you some? I've got a lot more, and it only takes a pinch." She swung amazingly long legs over the side of the bed. "It's a lot more expensive than rust, and a lot harder to find, but I'm in a generous mood. I usually am—you'll see." She favored Silk with a sidelong smile that made his heart leap.

He stood up and backed away.

"They call it beggar's root because it makes you beg. I'm begging now, just listen to me. Come on. You'll like it."

Silk shook his head.

"Come sit next to me." She patted the rumpled sheet.

"That's all I'm asking for—right now, anyway. You were here in bed with me a minute ago."

He tried to pull his tunic over his head and failed, discovering in the process that even the slightest movement of his right arm was painful.

"You're the one that they were looking for, aren't you? Aren't you glad that I didn't tell them anything? You really ought to be, Musk can be awfully mean. Don't you want me to help you with that?"

"Don't try." He retreated another step.

Sliding off the bed, she picked up his robe. She was completely naked; he closed his eyes and turned away.

She giggled, and he was suddenly reminded of Mucor, the mad girl. "You really are an augur. He called you Patera—I'd forgotten. Do you want your little hat back? I stuck it under my pillow."

The uses to which Patera Pike's calotte might be put if it remained with her flashed through Silk's mind. "Yes," he said. "Please, may I have it back?"

"Sure, I'll trade you."

He shook his head.

"Didn't you come here to see me? You don't act like it, but you knew my name."

"No. I came to find Blood."

"You won't like him, Patera." Hyacinth grinned again. "Even Musk doesn't like him, not really. Nobody does."

"He has my sympathy." Silk tried to raise the tunic again, and was deterred by a flash of pain. "I've come to show him how he can be better liked, and even loved."

"Well, Patera, I'm Hyacinth, just like you said. And I'm famous. Everybody likes me, except you."

"I do like you," Silk told her. "That is one of the reasons I won't do what you want. It's a rather minor one, actually, but a real reason nonetheless."

"You stole my azoth, though, didn't you, Patera? I can see the end of it poking out of that rope."

Silk nodded. "I intend to return it. But you're quite right, I took it without your permission, and that's theft. I'm sorry, but I felt I'd better have it. What I'm doing is extremely important." He paused and waited for remonstrances that did not come. "I'll see that it's returned to you, and your needler as well, if I get home safely."

"You were afraid of the guards, weren't you? There in my bed. You were afraid of that one with Musk. Afraid that he'd kill you."

"Yes," Silk admitted. "I was terrified, if you want the truth; and now I'm just as terrified of you, afraid that I'll give in to you, disgrace my calling, and lose the favor of the immortal gods."

She laughed.

"You're right." Silk tried to put on his tunic again, but his right forearm burned and throbbed. "I'm certainly not brave. But at least I'm brave enough to admit it."

"Wait just a minute," she said. "Wait right here. I'm going to get you something."

He glimpsed the balneum through the door she opened. As she closed it behind her, it occurred to him that Patera Pike's calotte was still in the bed, under her pillow; moved by that weak impulse which turns back travelers to retrieve trifles, he rescued it and put it on.

She emerged from the balneum, naked still, holding out a gold cup scarcely larger than a thimble, half filled with brick-colored powder. "Here, Patera. You put it into your lip."

"No. I realize that you mean well, but I'd rather be afraid."

She shrugged and pulled forward her own lower lip. For a moment it made her ugly, and Silk felt a surge of relief. After emptying the little cup into the hollow between lip and gum, she grinned at him. "This is the best money can buy, and it works fast. Sure you don't want some? I've got a lot."

"No," he repeated. "I should go. I should have gone before now, in fact."

"All right." She was looking at the gem in the hilt of the azoth again. "It's mine, you know. A very important man gave it to me. If you're going to steal it, I ought to at least get to help you. Are you sure you're a real augur?"

Silk sighed. "It seems that I may not be much longer. If you're serious about wanting to help me, Hyacinth, tell me where you think Blood is likely to be at this hour. Will he have retired for the night?"

She shook her head, her eyes flashing. "He's probably downstairs saying good-bye to the last of them. They've been coming all night, commissioners and commissioners' flunkies. Every once in a while he sends a really important one up here for me. I lost count, but there must have been six or seven of them."

"I know." Silk tried to push the hilt of the azoth more deeply into the coil of rope. "I've lain between your sheets."

"You think I ought to change them? I didn't think men cared."

Silk knelt to fish his broad-brimmed straw hat from beneath the bed. "I doubt that those men do."

"I can call a servant."

"They're busy looking for me, I imagine." Silk tossed the hat onto the bed and readied himself for one last try at his tunic.

"Not the maids." She took his tunic from him. "You know, your eyes want to look at me. You ought to let them do it."

"Hundreds of men must have told you how beautiful you are. Would you displease the gods to hear it once more? I wouldn't. I'm still young, and I hope to see a god before I die." He was tempted to add that he might well have missed one by a second or less when he entered her chambers, but he did not.

"You've never had a woman, have you?"

Silk shook his head, unwilling to speak.

"Well, let me help you get this on, anyway." She held his tunic as high as she could stretch while he worked both arms into the sleeves, then snatched her azoth from the rope coiled around his waist and sprang toward the bed.

He gaped at her, stunned. Her thumb was upon the demon, the blade slot pointed at his heart. Backing away, he raised both hands in the gesture of surrender.

She posed like a duelist. "They say the girls fight like troopers in Trivigaunte." She parried awkwardly twice, and skewered and slashed an imaginary opponent.

By that time he had recovered at least a fraction of his composure. "Aren't you going to call the guards?"

"Don't think so." She lunged and recovered. "Wouldn't I make a fine swordsman, Patera? Look at these legs."

"No, I don't think so."

She pouted "Why not?"

"Because one must study swordsmanship, and practice day after day. There is a great deal to learn, or so I've been told. To speak frankly, I'd back a shorter, less attractive woman against you, assuming that she was less attracted to admiration and those bottles in your balneum, too."

Hyacinth gave no sign of having heard. "If you really can't do what I want—if you won't, I mean—couldn't you use this azoth instead? And kiss me, and pretend? I'd show you where I want you to put the big jewel, and after a while you might change your mind."

"Isn't there an antidote?" To prevent her from seeing his expression, he crossed the room to the window and parted the drapes. There was no one around the dead bird on the terrace now. "You have all those herbs. Surely you must have the antidote, if there is one."

"I don't want the antidote, Patera. I want you." Her hand was on his shoulder; her lips brushed his ear. "And if you go out there like you're thinking, the cats'll tear you to pieces."

The blade of the azoth shot past his ear, fifty cubits down to the terrace to slice the dead bird in two and leave a long, smoking scar across the flagstones. Silk flinched from it. "For Pas's love be careful!"

Hyacinth whirled off like a dancer as she pressed the demon again. Shimmering through the bedchamber like summer heat, the azoth's illimited discontinuity hummed of death, parting the universe, slitting the drapes like a razor and dropping a long section slabbed from wall and window frame at Silk's feet.

"Now you have to," she told him, and came at him with a sweeping cut that scarred half the room. "Say you will, and I'll give it back."

As he dove through the window, the azoth's humming blade divided the stone sill behind him; but all the fear he ought to have felt was drowned in the knowledge that he was leaving her.

Had he struck the flagstones head first, he would have been spared a great deal of pain. As it was, he turned head over heels in midair. There was only a moment of darkness, like that a bruiser knows when he is knocked to his knees. For what might have been seconds or minutes, he lay near the divided body of the white-headed one, hearing her voice call to him from the window without comprehending anything it said.

When at last he tried to stand, he found that he could not. He had dragged himself to within ten paces of the wall, and shot two of the horned cats Mucor called lynxes, when a guard in silvered armor took the needler from his hand.

After what seemed a very long time, unarmored servants joined him; these carried torches with which they kept the snarling lynxes at bay. Supervised by a fussy little man with a pointed, iron-gray beard, they rolled Silk onto a blanket and carried him back to the villa.

Chapter 7

THE BARGAIN

"It isn't much," the fussy little man said, "but it's mine for as long as he lets me have it."

"It" was a moderately large and very cluttered room in the north wing of Blood's villa, and the fussy little man was rummaging in a drawer as he spoke. He snapped a flask under the barrel of a clumsy-looking gun, pushed its muzzle through one of the rents in Silk's tunic, and fired.

Silk felt a sharp pain, as though he had been stung by a bee.

"This stuff kills a lot of people," the fussy little man informed him, "so that's to see if you're one of them. If you don't die in a minute or two, I'll give you some more. Having any trouble breathing?"

Clenching his teeth against the pain in his ankle, Silk drew a deep breath and shook his head.

"Good. Actually, that was a minimal dose. It won't kill you even if you're sensitive to it, but it'll take care of those deep scratches and make you sick enough to tell me I mustn't give you any more." The fussy little man bent to stare into Silk's eyes. "Take another deep breath and let it out."

Silk did so. "What's your name, Doctor?"

"We don't use them much here. You're fine. Hold out that arm."

Silk raised it, and the bee stung again.

"Stops pain and fights infection." The fussy little man squatted, pushed up Silk's trousers leg, and put the muzzle of his odd-looking gun against Silk's calf.

"It didn't operate that time," Silk told him.

"Yes, it did. You didn't feel it, that's all. Now we can take that shoe off."

"My own name is Patera Silk."

The fussy little man glanced up at him. "Doctor Crane, Silk. Have a good laugh. You're really an augur? Musk said you were."

Silk nodded.

"And you jumped out of that second-floor window? Don't do that again." Doctor Crane untied the laces and removed the shoe. "My mother hoped I'd be tall, you see. She was tall herself, and she liked tall men. My father was short."

Silk said, "I understand."

"I doubt it." Doctor Crane bent over Silk's foot, his pinkish scalp visible through his gray hair. "I'm going to cut away this stocking. If I pull it off, it might do more damage." He produced shiny scissors exactly like those Silk had found in Hyacinth's balneum. "She's dead now, and so's he, so I guess it doesn't matter." The ruined stocking fell away. "Want to see what he looked like?"

The absence of pain was intoxicating; Silk felt giddy with happiness. "I'd love to." He managed to add, "If you care to show me."

"I can't help it. You're seeing him now, since I look exactly like him. It's our genes, not our names, that make us whatever we are."

"It's the will of the gods." Silk's eyes told him that the little physician was probing his swollen right ankle with his fingers, but he could feel nothing. "Your mother was tall;

and if you were tall as well, you would say that it was because she had been."

"I'm not hurting you?"

Silk shook his head. "I don't resemble my own mother in the least; she was small and dark. I have no idea what my father looked like, but I know that I am the man that a certain god wished me to be before I was born."

"She's dead?"

Silk nodded. "She left us for Mainframe a month before I was designated."

"You've got blue eyes. You're only the second—no, the third person I've ever seen with them. It's a shame you don't know who your father was. I'd like to have a look at him. See if you can stand up."

Silk could and did.

"Fine. Let me take your arm. I want you up there on that table. It's a nice clean break, or anyway that's what it looks like, and I'm going to pin it and put a cast on it."

They were not planning to kill him. Silk savored the thought. They were not planning to kill him, and so there might still be a chance to save the manteion.

Blood was slightly drunk. Silk envied him that almost as much as his possession of the manteion. As though Blood had read his thoughts, he said, "Hasn't anybody brought you anything, Patera? Musk, get somebody to bring him a drink."

The handsome young man nodded and slipped out of the room, at which Silk felt somewhat better.

"We've got other stuff, Patera. I don't suppose you use them?"

Silk said, "Your physician's already given me a drug to ease the pain. I doubt that it would be wise to mix it with something else." He was very conscious of that pain, which was returning; but he had no intention of letting Blood see that.

"Right you are." Blood leaned forward in his big red leather chair, and for a moment Silk thought that he might actually fall out of it. "The light touch with everything—that's my motto. Always has been. Even with that enlightenment of yours, a light touch's best."

Silk shook his head. "In spite of what has happened to me, I cannot agree."

"What's this!" Grinning broadly, Blood pretended to be outraged. "Did enlightenment tell you to come out here and break into my house? No, no, Patera. Don't try to tell me that. That was greed, the same as you'd slang me for. Your tin sibyl told you I'd bought your place—which I have, and everything completely legal—so you figured I'd have things worth taking. Don't tell me. I'm an old hand myself."

"I came here to steal our manteion back from you," Silk said. "That's worth taking, certainly. You took it legally, and I intended to take it from you, if I could, in any way I could."

Blood spat, looked around for his drink, and finding the tumbler empty dropped it on the carpet. "What did you think you could do, nick the shaggy deed out of my papers? It wouldn't mean a shaggy thing. Musk's the buyer of record, and all he'd have to do is pay a couple of cards for a new copy."

"I was going to make you sign it over to me," Silk told him. "I intended to hide in your bedroom until you came, and threaten to kill you unless you did exactly as I ordered."

The door opened. Musk entered, followed by a liveried footman with a tray. The footman set the tray on an inlaid table at Silk's elbow. "Will that be all, sir?"

Silk took the squat, water-white drink from the tray and sipped. "Yes, thank you. Thank you very much, Musk."

The servant departed; Musk smiled bitterly.

"This's getting interesting." Blood leaned forward, his wide, red face redder than ever. "Would you really have killed me, Patera?"

Silk, who would not have, felt certain he would not be believed. "I hoped that it wouldn't be necessary."

"I see. I see. And it never crossed your mind that I'd yell for some friends in the City Guard the minute you left? That I wouldn't even have had to use my own people on you, because the Guard would do their work instead?" Blood laughed, and Musk concealed his smile behind his hand.

Silk sipped again, wondering briefly whether the drink was drugged. If they wanted to drug him, he reflected, they would have no need of subterfuge. Whatever it was, the drink was very strong, certainly. Drugged or undrugged, it might dull the pain in his ankle. He ventured a cautious swallow. He had drunk brandy already tonight, the brandy Gib had given him; it seemed a very long time ago. Surely Blood would make no charge for this drink, whatever else he might do. (Not once in a month did Silk drink anything stronger than water.)

"Well, didn't you?" Blood snorted in disgust. "You know, I've got a few people working for me that don't think any better than you do, Patera."

Silk returned his drink to the tray. "I was going to make you sign a confession. It was the only thing I could think of, so it was what I planned."

"Me? Confess to what?"

"It didn't matter." Fatigue had enfolded Silk like a cloak. He had never known that a chair could be as comfortable as this one, a chair in which he could sleep for days. "A conspiracy to overthrow the Ayuntamiento, perhaps.

Something like that." Recalling certain classroom embarrassments, he forced himself to breathe deeply so that he would not yawn; the faint throbbing in his foot seemed very far away, driven beyond the fringes of the most remote Vironese lands by the kindly sorcery of the squat tumbler. "I would have given it to one of my—to another augur, one I know well. I was going to seal it, and make him promise to deliver it to the Juzgado if anything happened to me. Something like that."

"Not too bad." Blood took Hyacinth's little needler from his waistband, thumbed off its safety catch, and aimed it carefully at Silk's chest.

Musk frowned and touched Blood's arm.

Blood chuckled. "Oh, don't worry. I only wanted to see how he'd behave in my place. It doesn't seem to bother him much." The needler's tiny, malevolent eye twitched to the right and spat, and the squat tumbler exploded, showering Silk with shards and pungent liquor.

He brushed himself with his fingers. "What would you like me to sign over to you? I'll be happy to oblige. Give me the paper."

"I don't know." Blood dropped Hyacinth's gold-plated needler on the stand that had held his drink. "What have you got, Patera?"

"Two drawers of clothing and three books. No, two; I sold my personal copy of the Writings. My beads—I've got those here, and I'll give them to you now if you like. My old pen case, but it's still in my robe up in that woman's room. You could have somebody bring it, and I'll confess to climbing onto your roof and entering your house without your permission, and give you the pen case, too."

Blood shook his head. "I don't need your confession, Patera. I have you.."

"As you like." Silk visualized his bedroom, over the kitchen in the manse. "Pas's gammadion. That's steel, of course, but the chain's silver and should be worth something. I also have an old portable shrine that belonged to Patera Pike. I've set it up on my dresser, so I suppose you could say it's mine now. There's a rather attractive triptych, a small polychrome lamp, an offertory cloth, and so on, with a teak case to carry them in. Do you want that? I had hoped—foolishly no doubt—to pass it on to my successor."

Blood waved the triptych aside. "How'd you get through the gate?"

"I didn't. I cut a limb in the forest and tied it to this rope." Silk pointed to his waist. "I threw the limb over the spikes on your wall and climbed the rope."

"We'll have to do something about that." Blood glanced significantly at Musk. "You say you were up on the roof, so it was you that killed Hierax."

Silk sat up straight, feeling as if he had been wakened from sleep. "You gave him the name of the god?"

"Musk did. Why not?"

Musk said softly, "He was a griffon vulture, a mountain bird. Beautiful. I thought I might be able to teach him to kill for himself."

"But it was no go," Blood continued. "Musk got angry with him and was going to knife him. Musk has the mews out back."

Silk nodded politely. Patera Pike had once remarked to him that you could never tell from a man's appearance what might give him pleasure; studying Musk, Silk decided that he had never accorded Patera Pike's sagacity as much respect as it had deserved.

"So I said that if he didn't want him, he could give him to me," Blood continued, "and I put him up there on the roof for a pet."

"I see." Silk paused. "You clipped his wings."

"I had one of Musk's helpers do it," Blood explained, "so he wouldn't fly off. He wouldn't hunt anyhow."

Silk nodded, mostly to himself. "But he attacked me, I suppose because I picked up that scrap of hide. We were next to the battlement, and in the excitement of the moment he—I will not call him Hierax, Hierax is a sacred name—forgot that he could no longer fly."

Blood reached for the needler. "You're saying I killed him. That's a shaggy lie! You did it."

Silk nodded. "He died by misadventure while fighting with me; but you may say that I killed him if you like. I was certainly trying to."

"And you stole this needler from Hyacinth before she drove you through the window with her azoth—must be about a thirty-cubit drop. Why didn't you shoot her?"

"Would you have," Silk inquired, "if you had been in my place?"

Blood chuckled. "And fed her to Musk's birds."

"What I have done to you already is surely much worse than anything that Hyacinth did to me; I say nothing of what I intended to do to you. Are you going to shoot me?" If he lunged, Silk decided, he might be able to wrestle the little needler from Blood in spite of his injured leg; and with the muzzle to Blood's head, he might be able to force them to let him go. He readied himself, calculating the distance as he edged forward in his chair.

"I might. I might at that, Patera." Blood toyed with the needler, palming it, flipping it over, and weighing it in his hand; he seemed nearly sober now. "You understand—or I hope you do, anyway—that we haven't committed any kind of a crime, not a one of us. Not me, not Musk here, not any of my people."

Silk started to speak, then decided against it.

"You think you know about something? All right, I'll guess. Tell me if I'm wrong. You've been talking with Hy, and so you think she's a whore. One of our guests tonight gave her that azoth. Quite a little present, plenty good enough for a councillor. Maybe she bragged on some of her other presents, too. Have I hit the target?"

Silk nodded guardedly, his eyes on the needler. "She'd had several . . . Visitors."

Blood chuckled. "He's blushing, Musk. Take a look at him. Yes, Patera, I know. Only they didn't pay, and that's what matters to the law. They were my guests, and Hy's one of my houseguests. So if she wants to show somebody a good time, that's her business and mine, but none of yours. You came out here to get back your manteion, you tell me. Well, we didn't take it away from you." Blood emphasized his point with the needler, jabbing at Silk's face. "If we're going to talk about what's not legal, we've got to talk about what's legal, too. And legally you never did own it. It belonged to the Chapter, according to the deed I've got. Isn't that right?"

Silk nodded.

"And the city took it from the Chapter for taxes owed. Not from you, because you never had it. Back last week that was, I think. Everything was done properly, I'm sure. The Chapter was notified and so on. They didn't tell you?"

"No." Silk sighed, and forced himself to relax. "I knew that it might happen, and in fact I warned the Chapter about it. I was never informed that it had happened."

"Then they ought to tell you they're sorry, Patera, and I hope they will. But that's got nothing to do with Musk and me. Musk bought your manteion from the city, and there was nothing irregular about it. He was acting for me, with my money, but there's nothing illegal about that either, it's just a business matter between him and me. Thirteen thousand cards we paid, plus the fees. We didn't steal anything, did we? And we haven't hurt you—or anybody—have we?"

"It will hurt the entire quarter, several thousand poor families, if you close the manteion."

"They can go somewhere else if they want to, and that's

up to the Chapter anyhow, I'd say." Blood gestured toward the welts on Silk's chest with the needler. "You got hurt some, and nobody's arguing about that. But you got banged up fighting my pet bird and jumping out a window. Hy was just defending herself with that azoth, something she's got every right in the whorl to do. You aren't planning to peep about her, are you?"

"Peep?"

"Go crying to the froggies."

"I see. No, of course not."

"That's good. I'm happy to hear you being reasonable. Just look at it. You broke into my house hoping to take my property—it's Musk's, but you didn't know that. You've admitted that to Musk and me, and we're ready to swear to it in front of a judge if we have to."

Silk smiled; it seemed to him a very long time since he had last smiled. "You aren't really going to have me killed, are you, Blood? You're not willing to take the risk."

Blood's finger found the trigger of the needler. "Keep on talking like that and I might, Patera."

"I don't believe so. You'd have someone else do it, probably Musk. You're not even going to do that, however. You're trying to frighten me before you let me go."

Blood glanced at Musk, who nodded and circled behind Silk's chair. Silk felt the tips of Musk's fingers brush his ears.

"If you go on talking to me like you have been, Patera, you're going to get hurt. It won't leave any marks, but you won't like it at all. Musk has done it before. He's good at it."

"Not to an augur. Those who harm an augur in any way suffer the displeasure of all the gods."

The pain was as sudden as a blow, and so sharp it left Silk breathless, an explosion of agony; he felt as though his head had been crushed.

"There's places behind your ears," Blood explained. "Musk pushes them in with his knuckles."

Gasping for air, his hands to his mastoids, Silk could not even nod.

"We can do that again and again if we have to," Blood continued. "And if we finally give up and go to bed, we can start over in the morning."

A red mist had blotted out Silk's vision, but it was clearing. He managed, "You don't have to explain my situation to me."

"Maybe not. I'll do it whenever I want to, just the same. So to get on with this—you're right, we'd just as soon not kill you if we don't have to. There's three or four different reasons for that, all of them pretty good. You're an augur, to start with. If the gods ever paid any attention to Viron, they quit a long time ago. Myself, I don't think there was ever anything in it except a way for people like you to get everything they wanted without working. But the Chapter looks after you, and if it ever got out that we did for you—I mean just talk, because they'd never be able to prove anything—it would get people stirred up and be bad for business."

Silk said, "Then I would not have died for nothing," and felt Musk's fingers behind his ears again.

Blood shook his head, and the contingent agony halted, poised at the edge of possibility. "Then too, we just bought your place so that might make some people think of us. Did you tell anybody you were coming?"

Here it was. Silk was prepared to lie if he must, but preferred to dodge if he could. He said, "You mean one of our sibyls? No, nothing like that."

Blood nodded, and the danger was past. "It could get somebody's attention anyway, and I can't be sure who's seen you. Hy has, and talked with you and so on. Probably even knows your name."

Silk could not remember, but he said, "Yes, she does. Can't you trust her? She's your wife."

Musk tittered behind him. Blood roared, his free hand slapping his thigh.

Silk shrugged. "One of your servants referred to her as his mistress. He thought that I was one of your guests, of course."

Blood wiped his eyes. "I like her, Patera, and she's the best-looking whore in Viron, which makes her a valuable commodity. But as for that—" Blood waved the topic aside. "What I was going to say is I'd rather have you as a friend." Seeing Silk's expression, he laughed again.

Silk strove to sound casual. "My friendship's easily gained." This was the conversation he had imagined when he had spied on the villa from the top of the wall; frantically he searched for the smooth phrases he had rehearsed. "Return my manteion to the Chapter, and I'll bless you for the rest of my life." A drop of sweat trickled from his forehead into his eyes. Fearing that Musk might think he was reaching for a weapon if he got out his handkerchief, he wiped his face on his sleeve.

"That wouldn't be what I'd call easy for me, Patera. Thirteen thousand I've laid out for your place, and I'd never see a card of it again. But I've thought of a way we can be friends that will put money in my pocket, and I always like that. You're a common thief. You've admitted it. Well, so am I." Blood rose from his chair, stretched, and seemed to admire the rich furnishings of the room. "Why should we, two of a kind, circle around like a couple of tomcats, trying to knife each other?"

Musk stroked Silk's hair; it made him feel unclean, and he said, "Stop that!"

Musk did.

"You're a brave man, Patera, as well as a resourceful one." Blood strode across the room to study a gray and gold painting of Pas condemning the lost spirits, one head livid with rage while the other pronounced their doom. "If I had been sitting where you are, I wouldn't have tried that with Musk, but you tried it and got away with it. You're young, you're strong, and you've got a couple of advantages besides that the rest of us haven't. Nobody ever suspects an augur, and you've had a pretty fair education—a better education than mine, I don't deny that. Tell me now, as one thief to another, didn't you know down in the cracks of your guts that it was wrong to try to steal my property?"

"Yes, of course." Silk paused to gather his thoughts. "There are times, however, when one must choose among evils. You're a wealthy man; stripped of my manteion, you would be a wealthy man still. Without my manteion, hundreds of families in our quarter—people who are already very poor—would be a great deal poorer. I found that a compelling argument." He waited for the crushing pain of Musk's knuckles. When it did not come he added, "You suggested that we speak as one thief to another, and I assumed that you intended for us to speak freely. To speak frankly, I find it just as compelling now."

Blood turned to face him again. "Sure you do, Patera. I'm surprised you couldn't come up with just as good a reason for shooting Hy. These gods of yours did worse pretty often, didn't they?"

Silk nodded. "Worse superficially, yes. But the gods are our superiors and may act toward us as they see fit, just as you could clip your pet's wings without guilt. I am not Hyacinth's superior."

Blood chuckled. "You're the only man alive who doesn't think so, Patera. Well, I'll leave morality to you. That's your business after all. Business is mine, and what we have here is a very simple little business problem. I paid the city thirteen thousand for your manteion. What do you think it's really worth?"

Silk recalled the fresh young faces of the children in the palaestra, and the tired, happy smiles of their mothers; the sweet smoke of sacrifice rising from the altar through the god-gate in the roof. "In money? It is beyond price."

"Exactly." Blood glanced at the needler he still held and dropped it into the pocket of his embroidered trousers. "That's how you feel, and that's why you came out here, even though you must have known there was a good chance you'd get killed. You're not the first who's tried to break in here, by the way, but you're the first who got inside the house."

"That is some consolation."

"So I admire you, and I think we might be able to do a little business. On the open market, Patera, your place is worth exactly thirteen thousand cards, and not one miserable cardbit more or less. We know that, because it was on the market just a few days ago, and thirteen thousand's what it brought. So that's the businessman's price. You understand what I'm telling you?"

Silk nodded.

"I've got plans for it, sure. Profitable plans. But it's not the only possible site, so here's my proposition. You say it's priceless. That's a lot of money, priceless." Blood licked his lips, his eyes narrowed, their gaze fixed on Silk's face. "So as a man that takes a lily profit wherever he can find one but never gouges anybody, I say we split the difference. You pay me twice what I paid, and I'll sell it to you."

Silk started to speak, but Blood raised a hand. "Let's pin it down like a couple of dimber thieves ought to. I'll sell it to you for twenty-six thousand flat, and I'll pay all costs. No tricks, and no splitting up the property. You'll get everything that I got."

Silk's hopes, which had mounted higher with every word, collapsed. Did Blood really imagine that he was rich? There were laymen, he knew, who thought all augurs rich. He said, "I've told you what I have; altogether, it wouldn't bring two hundred cards. My mother's entire estate amounted to a great deal less than twenty-six thousand cards, and it went to the Chapter irrevocably when I took my vows."

Blood smiled. "I'm flash, Patera. Maybe you'd like another drink?"

Silk shook his head.

"Well, I would."

When Musk had gone, Blood resumed his seat. "I know you haven't got twenty-six thousand, or anything close to it. Not that I'm swallowing everything you told me, but if you had even a few thousand you wouldn't be there on Sun Street. Well, who says that just because you're poor you've got to stay poor? You wouldn't think so to look at me, but I was poor once myself."

"I believe you," Silk said.

Blood's smile vanished. "And you look down on me for it. Maybe that made it easier."

"No," Silk told him. "It made it a great deal harder. You never come to the sacrifices at our manteion—quite a few thieves do, actually—but I was setting out to rob one of our own, and in my heart of hearts I knew that and hated it."

Blood's chuckle promised neither humor nor friendship. "You did it just the same."

"As you've seen."

"I see more than you think, Patera. I see a lot more than you do. I see that you were willing to rob me, and that you nearly brought it off. A minute ago you told me how rich you think I am, so rich I wouldn't miss four old buildings on Sun Street. Do you think I'm the richest man in Viron?"

"No," Silk said.

"No what?"

Silk shrugged. "Even when we spoke in the street, I never supposed that you were the wealthiest man in the city, although I have no idea who the wealthiest might be. I only thought that you were wealthy, as you obviously are."

"Well, I'm not the richest," Blood declared, "and I'm not the crookedest either. There are richer men than I am, and crookeder men than I am, lots of them. And, Patera, most of them aren't anywhere near as close to the Ayuntamiento as I am. That's something to keep in mind, whether you think so or not."

Silk did not reply, or even indicate by any alteration of his expression that he had heard.

"So if you want your manteion back, why shouldn't you get it from them? The price is twenty-six thousand, like I told you. That's all it means to me, so they've got it just as much as I have, and they'll be easier, most of them. Are you listening to me, Patera?"

Reluctantly, Silk nodded.

Musk opened the door as he had before and preceded the footman into the room. This time there were two tumblers on the footman's tray.

Blood accepted one, and the footman bowed to Silk. "Patera Silk?"

Everyone in the household must know of his capture by now, Silk reflected; apparently everyone knew who he was as well. "Yes," he said; it would be pointless to deny it.

With something in his expression Silk could not fathom, the footman bowed deeply and held out his tray. "I took the liberty, Patera. Musk said I might. If you would accept it as a favor to me . . . ?"

Silk took the drink, smiled, and said, "Thank you, my son. That was extremely kind of you." For an instant the footman looked radiant.

"If you're grabbed," Blood continued when the footman had gone, "I don't know you. I've never laid eyes on you, and I'd never suggest anything like this to anybody. That's the way it's got to be."

"Of course. But now, tonight, you're suggesting that I steal enough money to buy my manteion from you. That I, an augur, enter these other men's houses to steal, as I entered yours."

Blood sipped his drink. "I'm saying that if you want your manteion back, I'll sell it to you, and that's all I'm saying. How you get the money is up to you. You think the city asked where I got the price?"

"It is a workable solution," Silk admitted, "and it's the only one that has been proposed so far."

Musk grinned at him.

"Your resident physician tells me that my right ankle is broken," Silk continued. "It will be quite some time, I'm afraid, before it heals."

Blood looked up from his drink. "I can't allow you a whole lot of time, Patera. A little time, enough for a few jobs. But that's all."

"I see." Silk stroked his cheek. "But you'll allow me some—you'll have to. During the time you *will* allow, what will become of my manteion?"

"It's my manteion, Patera. You run it just like you did before, how's that? Only you tell anybody that wants to know that I own the property. It's mine, and you tell them so."

"I could say you've paid our taxes," Silk suggested, "as you have. And that you're letting us continue to serve the gods as an act of piety." It was a lie he hoped might eventually become the truth.

"That's good. But anything you take in over expenses is mine, and anytime I want to see the books, you've got to bring them out here. Otherwise it's no deal. How much time do you want?"

Silk considered, uncertain that he could bring himself to conduct the robberies Blood was demanding. "A year," he ventured. A great deal could happen in a year.

"Very funny. I bet they roar when you've got a ram for Scylsday. Three weeks—oh, shag, make it a month. That's the top, though. Will your ankle be all right in a month?"

"I don't know." Silk tried to move his foot and found as he had before that the cast immobilized it. "I wouldn't think it very likely."

Blood snorted. "Musk, get Crane in here."

As the door closed behind Musk, Silk inquired, "Do you always have a physician on the premises?"

"I try to." Blood set aside his tumbler. "I had a man for a year who didn't work out, then a brain surgeon who only stayed a couple of months. After that I had to look around quite a while before I found Crane. He's been with me . . ." Blood paused, calculating, "pretty close to four years now. He looks after my people here, naturally, and goes into the city three times a week to see about the girls there. It's handier, and saves a little money."

Silk said, "I'm surprised that a skillful physician—"

"Would work for me, taking care of my whores?" Blood yawned. "Suppose you'd seen a doctor in the city for that ankle, Patera. Would you have paid him?"

"As soon as I could, yes."

"Which would have been never, most likely. Working for me, he gets a regular salary. He doesn't have to take charity cases, and sometimes the girls'll tip him if they're flush."

The fussy little man arrived a moment later, ushered in by Musk. Silk had seen a picture of a bird of the crane kind not long before, and though he could not recall where it had been, he remembered it now, and with it Crane's self-mockery. The diminutive doctor no more resembled the tall bird than he himself did the shimmering fabric from which his mother had taken his name.

Blood gestured toward Silk. "You fixed him up. How long before he's well?"

The little physician stroked his beard. "What do you

mean by well, sir? Well enough to walk without crutches?"

Blood considered. "Let's say well enough to run fast. How long for that?"

"It's difficult to say. It depends a good deal on his heredity—I doubt that he knows anything useful about that—and on his physical condition. He's young at least, so it could be worse." Doctor Crane turned to Silk. "Sit up straight for a moment, young man. I want to listen to you again, now that you've had a chance to calm down."

He lifted Silk's torn tunic, put his ear against Silk's chest, and thumped his back. With the third thump, Silk felt something hard and cold slide into his waistband beneath the horsehair rope.

"Should've brought my instruments. Cough, please."

Already frantic with curiosity, Silk coughed and was rewarded with another thump.

"Good. Again, please, and deeper this time. Make it go deep."

Silk coughed as deeply as he could.

"Excellent." Doctor Crane straightened up, letting Silk's tunic fall back into place. "Truly excellent. You're a fine specimen, young man, a credit to Viron." The timbre of his voice altered almost imperceptibly. "Somebody up there likes you." He pointed jocularly toward the elaborately figured ceiling, where a painted Molpe vied with Phaea at bagatelle. "Some infatuated goddess, I should imagine."

Silk leaned back in his chair, although the hard object behind his spine made actual comfort impossible. "If that means I get less time from your employer, I would hardly call it evidence of favor, my son."

Doctor Crane smiled. "In that case, perhaps not."

"How long?" Blood banged his tumbler down on the stand beside his chair. "How long before it's as good as it was before he broke it?"

"Five to seven weeks, I'd say. He could run a little sooner

than that, with his ankle correctly taped. All this assumes proper rest and medical treatment in the interim—sonic stimulation of the broken bone and so forth."

Silk cleared his throat. "I cannot afford elaborate treatment, Doctor. All I'll be able to do is hobble about and pray that it heals."

"Well, you can't come here," Blood told him angrily. "Was that what you were hinting at?"

Doctor Crane began, "Possibly, sir, you might retain a specialist in the city—"

Blood sniffed. "We should've shot him and gotten it over with. By Phaea's sow, I wish the fall had killed him. No specialist. You'll see himself whenever you're in that part of the city. When is it? Sphigxday and Hieraxday?"

"That's right, and tomorrow's Sphigxday." Doctor Crane glanced toward an ornate clock on the opposite side of the room. "I should be in bed already."

"You'll see him then," Blood said. "Now get out of here."

Silk told Crane, "I sincerely regret the inconvenience, Doctor. If your employer will only give me a bit more time, it wouldn't be necessary."

At the door Crane turned and appeared, almost, to wink.

Blood said, "We'll compromise, Patera. Pay attention, because it's as far as I'm willing to go. Aren't you going to drink that?"

Feeling Musk's knuckles behind his ears, Silk took a dutiful sip.

"In a month—one month from today—you'll bring me a substantial sum. You hear that? I'll decide when I see it whether it's substantial enough. If it is, I'll apply it to the twenty-six thousand, and let you know how long you've got to come up with the rest. But if it isn't, you and that tin sibyl will have to clear out." Blood paused, his mouth ugly, swirling his drink in his hand. "Have you got anybody else living there? Maybe another augur?"

"There are two more sibyls," Silk told him. "Maytera Rose and Maytera Mint. You've met Maytera Marble, I believe. I am our only augur."

Blood grunted. "Your sibyls will want to come out here and lecture me. Tell them they won't get past the gate."

"I will."

"They're healthy? Crane could have a look at them when he comes to see you, if they need doctoring."

Silk warmed to the man. "That's exceedingly kind of you." There was always some good to be found in everyone, he reminded himself, the unnoted yet unfailing gift of ever-generous Pas. "Maytera Mint's quite well, as far as I know. Maytera Rose is as well as could be expected, and is largely prosthetic now in any case, I'm afraid."

"Digital arms and legs? That sort of thing?" Blood leaned forward, interested. "There aren't too many of those around any more."

"She got them some years ago; before I was born, really. There was some disease requiring amputations." It occurred to Silk that he should know more about Maytera Rose's history—about the histories of all three sibyls—than he did. "They were still easily found then, from what she says."

"How old is she?"

"I'm not sure." Silk berated himself mentally again; this was something he should know. "I suppose it's in our records. I could look it up for you, and I would be happy to do so."

"Just being polite," Blood told him. "She must be—oh, ninety, if she's got a lot of tin parts. How old would you say I am, Patera?"

"Older than you look, I suppose," Silk ventured. What guess would flatter Blood? It would not do to say something ridiculous. "Forty-five, possibly?"

"I'm forty-nine." Blood raised his tumbler in a mock toast. "Nearly fifty." Musk's fingers had twitched as Blood spoke, and Silk knew with an absolute certainty he could not have defended that Blood was lying: that he was at least five years older. "And not a part in my body that isn't my own, except for a couple teeth."

"You don't look it."

"Listen, Patera, I could tell you—" Blood waved the topic aside. "Never mind. It's late. How much did I say? In a month? Five thousand?"

"You said a substantial sum," Silk reminded him. "I was to bring you as much as I could acquire, and you would decide whether it was enough. Am I to bring it here?"

"That's right. Tell the eye at my gate who you are, and somebody will go out and get you. Musk, have a driver come around out front."

"For me?" Silk asked. "Thank you. I was afraid I'd have to walk—that is, I couldn't have walked, with my leg like this. I would have had to beg rides on farm carts, I'm afraid."

Blood grinned. "You're a thirteen thousand card profit to me, Patera. I've got to see you're taken care of. Listen now. You know how I said those sibyls of yours weren't to come out here and bother me? Well, that still goes, but tell that one—the old one, what's her name?"

"Maytera Rose," Silk supplied.

"Her. You tell Maytera Rose that if she's interested in getting another leg or something, and can raise the gelt, I might be able to help her out. Or if she's got something like that she'd like to sell, maybe to help you out. She won't get a better price anywhere."

"My thanks are becoming monotonous, I'm afraid," Silk said. "But I must thank you again, on Maytera's behalf and in my own."

"Forget it. There's getting to be quite a market for those

parts now, even the used ones, and I've got a man who knows how to recondition them."

Musk's sleek head appeared in the doorway. "Floater's ready."

Blood stood, swaying slightly. "Can you walk, Patera? No, naturally you can't, not good. Musk, fetch him one of my sticks, will you? Not one of the high-priced ones. Grab on, Patera."

Blood was offering his hand. Silk took it, finding it soft and surprisingly cold, and struggled to his feet, acutely conscious of the object Crane had put into his waistband and of the fact that he was accepting help from the man he had set out to rob. "Thank you yet again," he said, and clenched his teeth against a sharp flash of pain.

As his host, Blood would want to show him out; and if Blood were in back of him, Blood might well see the object under his tunic. Wishing mightily for the robe he had left behind in Hyacinth's bedchamber, half incapacitated by guilt and pain, Silk managed, "May I lean on your arm? I shouldn't have had so much to drink."

Side by side they staggered into the reception hall. Its wide double doors still let in the night; but it was a night (or so Silk fancied) soon to be gray with shadeup. A floater waited on the grassway, its canopy open, a liveried driver at its controls. The most eventful night of his life was nearly over.

Musk rattled the cast on Silk's ankle with a battered walking stick, smiled at his wince, and put the stick into his free hand. Silk discovered that he still detested Musk, though he had come, almost, to like Musk's master.

". . . floater'll take you back there, Patera," Blood was saying. "If you tell anyone about our little agreement, it's cancelled, and don't you forget it. A high stack next month, and I don't mean a few hundred."

The liveried driver had left the floater to help. In a

moment more, Silk was safely settled on the broad, cushioned seat behind the driver's, with Doctor Crane's chilly, angular mystery again gouging at his back. "Thank you," he repeated to Blood. "Thank you both." (He hoped that Blood would take his phrase to include Musk as well as Blood himself, though he actually intended Blood and the driver.) "I do appreciate it very much. You mentioned our agreement however. And—and I would be exceedingly grateful . . ." Tentatively, he put out his hand, palm up.

"What is it now, for Phaea's sake?"

"My needler, please. I hate to ask, after all you've done, but it's in your pocket. If you're not still afraid I might shoot you, may I have it back?"

Blood stared at him.

"You want me to bring you several thousand cards—I presume that's what you mean when you speak of a substantial sum. Several thousand cards, when I can scarcely walk. The least you can do is return my weapon, so that I've something to work with."

Blood giggled, coughed, then laughed loudly. Perhaps only because Silk heard it in the open air for the first time that night, Blood's laughter seemed to him almost the sound that sometimes rose, on quiet evenings, from the pits of the Alambrera. He was forced to remind himself again that this man, too, was loved by Pas.

"What a buck! He might do it, Musk. I really think he might do it." Blood fumbled Hyacinth's little needler out of his pocket and pushed its release; a score of silver needles leaped from its breach to shower like rain upon the closely cropped grass.

Musk leaned toward Blood, and Silk heard him whisper, "Lamp Street."

Blood's eyebrows shot up. "Excellent. You're right. You always are." He tossed the golden needler into Silk's lap. "Here you go, Patera. Use it in good health—yours, I mean. We're going to make a slight charge for it, though. Meet us about one o'clock at the yellow house on Lamp Street. Will you do that?"

"I must, I suppose," Silk said. "Yes, of course, if you wish me to."

"It's called Orchid's." Blood leaned over the door of the floater. "And it's across from the pastry cook's. You know exorcism? Know how it's done?"

Silk ventured a guarded nod.

"Good. Bring whatever you'll need. There've been, ah, problems there all summer. An enlightened augur may be just what we need. We'll see you there tomorrow."

"Good-bye," Silk said.

The canopy slid soundlessly out of the floater's sides as Blood and Musk backed away. When it latched, there was a muffled roar from the engine.

It felt, Silk thought, as if they were indeed floating; as if a flood had rushed invisibly to lift them and bear them off along the greenway, as if they were always about to spin away in the current, although they never actually spun.

Trees and hedges and brilliant flower beds reeled past. Here came Blood's magnificent fountain, with Soaking Scylla reveling among the crystal jets; at once it was gone and the main gate before them, the gate rising as the long, shining arms of the talus shrank. A dip and a wiggle and the floater was through, blown down the highway like a sere leaf, sailing through an eerie nightscape turned to liquid, leaving behind it a proud plume of swirling, yellow-gray dust.

The skylands still shone overhead, cut in two by the black bow of the shade. Far above even the skylands, hidden but present nonetheless, shone the myriad pinpricks of fire the Outsider had revealed; they, too, held lands unknowable in some incomprehensible fashion. Silk found himself more conscious of them now than he had been since that lifetime outside time in the ball court—colored spheres of flame, infinitely far.

The ball was still in his pocket, the only ball they had. He must remember not to leave it here in Blood's floater, or the boys would have no ball tomorrow. No, not tomorrow; tomorrow was Sphigxday. No palaestra. The day to prepare for the big sacrifice on Scylsday, if there was anything to sacrifice.

He slapped his pockets until he found Blood's two cards in the one that held the ball. He took them out to look at, then replaced them. They had been below the ball when he had been searched, and the ball had saved them. For what?

Hyacinth's needler had fallen to the floater's carpeted floor. He retrieved it and put it into his pocket with the cards, then sat squeezing the ball between his fingers. It was said to strengthen the hands. Minute lights he could not see burned on, burning beyond the skylands, burning beneath his feet, unwinking and remote, illuminating something bigger than the whorl.

Doctor Crane's mystery gouged his back. He leaned forward. "What time is it, driver?"

"Quarter past three, Patera."

He had done what the Outsider had wanted. Or at least he had tried—perhaps he had failed. As though a hand had drawn aside a veil, he realized that his manteion would live for another month now—a month at least, because anything might happen in a month. Was it possible that he had in fact accomplished what the Outsider had desired? His mind filled with a rollicking joy.

The floater leaned to the left as it rounded a bend in the road. Here were farms and fields and houses, all liquid, all swirling past as they breasted the phantom current. A hill rose in a great, brown-green wave, already breaking into a skylit froth of fence rails and fruit trees. The floater plunged down the other side and shot across a ford.

* * *

Musk adjusted the shutter of his dark lantern until the eight-sided spot of light remaining was smaller than its wick and oddly misshapen. His key turned softly in the well-oiled padlock; the door opened with a nearly inaudible creak.

The tiercel nearest the door stirred upon its perch, turning its hooded head to look at the intruder it could not see. On the farther side of a partition of cotton netting, the merlin that had been Musk's first hawk, unhooded, blinked and roused. There was a tinkle of tiny bells—gold bells that Blood had given Musk to mark some now-forgotten occasion three years ago. Beyond the merlin, the gray-blue peregrine might have been a painted carving.

The end of the mews was walled off with netting. The big bird sat its roweled perch there, immobile as the falcon, still immature but showing in every line a stength that made the falcon seem a toy.

Musk untied the netting and stepped in. He could not have said how he knew that the big bird was awake, and yet he did. Softly he said, "Ha, hawk."

The big bird lifted its hooded head, its grotesque crown of scarlet plumes swaying with the motion.

"Ha, hawk," Must repeated as he stroked it with a turkey feather.

Chapter 8

THE BOARDER ON
THE LARDER

As they sped across a field of stubble the driver inquired, "Ever ridden in one of these before, Patera?"

Drowsily, Silk shook his head before he realized that the driver could not see him. He yawned and attempted to stretch, brought up sharply by pain from his right arm and the gouged flesh of his chest and belly. "No, never. But I rode in a boat once. Out on the lake, you know, fishing all day with a friend and his father. This reminds me of that. This machine of yours is about as wide as the boat was, and only a little bit shorter."

"I like it better—boats rock too much for me. Where are we going, Patera?"

"You mean . . .?" The road (or perhaps another road) had appeared again. Seeming to gather its strength like a horse, the floater soared over the wall of dry-laid stones that had barred them from it.

"Where should I drop you? Musk said to take you back to the city."

Silk edged forward on the seat, knowing himself stupid with fatigue and struggling against it. "They didn't tell you?"

"No, Patera."

Where was it he wanted to go? He recalled his mother's house, and the wide, deep windows of his bedroom, with borage growing just beyond the sills. "At my manteion, please. On Sun Street. Do you know where it is?"

"I know where Sun Street is, Patera. I'll find it."

Here was a cartload of firewood bound for the market. The floater dipped and swerved, and it was behind them. The man on the cart would be first at the market, Silk thought; but what was the point of being first at the market with a load of firewood? Surely there would be wood there already, wood that had not sold the day before. Perhaps the man on the cart wanted to do a little buying of his own when he had disposed of his cargo.

"Going to be another hot one, Patera."

That was it, of course. The man on the cart—Silk turned to look back at him, but he was gone already; there was only a boy leading a mule, a laden mule and a small boy whom he had never noticed at all. The man on the cart had wanted to avoid the heat. He would sell what he had brought and sit drinking till twilight in the Cock or someplace like it. In the coolest tavern he could find, no doubt, and spend most of the money his wood had brought him, sleep on the seat of his cart as it made its slow way home. What if he, Silk, slept now on this capacious seat, which was so tantalizingly soft? Would not the driver, would not this old half-magical floater take him where he wanted to go in any event? Would the driver rob him while he slept, find Blood's two cards, Hyacinth's golden needler, and the thing that he still did not dare to look at, the thing—he felt he had guessed its identity while he still sat in that jewel box of a room to one side of Blood's reception hall. Would he not be robbed? Had the man upstairs, the man asleep in the chair near the stair ever gotten home, and had he gotten home safely? Many men must have slept in this floater, men who had drunk too heavily.

Silk felt that he himself had drunk too heavily; he had sipped from both drinks.

Blood was certainly a thief; he had admitted as much himself. But would Blood employ a driver who would rob his guests? It seemed unlikely. He, Silk, could sleep here—sleep now in safety, if he wished. But he was very hungry.

"All right," he said.

"Patera?"

"Go to Sun Street. I'll direct you from there. I know the way."

The driver glanced over his shoulder, a burly young man whose beard was beginning to show. "Where it crosses Trade. Will that be all right, Patera?"

"Yes." Silk felt his own chin, rough as the driver's looked. "Fine." He settled back in the soft seat, almost oblivious of the object beneath his tunic but determined not to sleep until he had washed, eaten, and wrung any advantage that might be gained from his present position. The driver had not been told he was Blood's prisoner; that was clear from everything he said, and it presented an opportunity that might not come again.

But in point of fact he was a prisoner no longer. He had been freed, though no fuss had been made about it, when Blood and Musk had taken him to this floater. Now, whether he liked it or not, he was a sort of factor of Blood's—an agent through whom Blood would obtain money. Silk weighed the term in his mind and decided it was the correct one. He had given himself wholly to the gods, with a holy oath; now his allegiance was inescapably divided, whether he liked it or not. He would give the twenty-six thousand cards he got (if indeed he got them) not to the gods but to Blood, though he would be acting in the gods' behalf. Certainly he would be Blood's factor in the eyes of the Chapter and the whorl, should either the Chapter or the whorl learn of whatever he would do.

Blood had made him his factor, creating this situation for his own profit. (Thoughtfully, Silk stroked his cheek, feeling the roughness of his newly grown beard again.) For Blood's own personal profit, as was only to be expected; but their relationship bound them both, like all relationships. He was Blood's factor whether he liked it or not, but also Blood's factor whether Blood liked it or not. He had made good use of the relationship already when he had demanded the return of Hyacinth's needler. Indeed, Blood had acknowledged it still earlier when he had told Doctor Crane to look in at the manteion.

Further use might be made of it as well.

A factor, but not a trusted factor to be sure; Blood might conceivably plan to kill him once he had turned over the entire twenty-six thousand, if he could find no further use for him; thus it would be wise to employ this temporary relationship to gain some sort of hold on Blood before it was ended. That was something more to keep in mind.

And the driver, who no doubt knew so many things that might be of value, did not know that.

"Driver," Silk called, "are you familiar with a certain house on Lamp Street? It's yellow, I believe, and there's a pastry cook's across the street."

"Sure am, Patera."

"Could we go past it, please? I don't think it will be very much out of our way."

The floater slowed for a trader with a string of pack mules. "I can't wait, Patera, if you're going to be inside very long."

"I'm not even going to get out," Silk assured him. "I merely wish to see it."

Still watching the broadening road, the driver nodded his satisfaction. "Then I'll be happy to oblige you, Patera. No trouble."

The countryside seemed to flow past. No wonder, Silk

thought, that the rich rode in floaters when distances were too great for their litters. Why, on donkeys this had taken hours!

"Have a good time, Patera? You stayed awfully late."

"No," Silk said, then reconsidered. "In a way I did, I suppose. It was certainly very different from everything I'm accustomed to."

The driver chuckled politely.

"I did have a good time, in a sense," Silk decided. "I enjoyed certain parts of my visit enormously, and I ought to be honest enough to admit it."

The driver nodded again. "Only not everything. Yeah, I know just what you mean."

"My view is colored, no doubt, by the fact that I fell and injured my ankle. It was really quite painful, and it's still something of a discomfort. A Doctor Crane very kindly set the bone for me and applied this cast, free of charge. I imagine you must know him. Your master told me that Doctor Crane has been with him for the past four years."

"Do I! The old pill-pounder and me have floated over a whorl of ground together. Don't make much sense sometimes, but he'll talk you deaf if you don't watch out, and ask more questions than the hoppies."

Silk nodded, conscious again of the object Crane had slipped into his waistband. "I found him friendly."

"I bet you did. You didn't ride out with me, did you, Patera?"

Blood had several floaters, obviously, just as he had implied. Silk said, "No, not with you. I came with another man, but he left before I did."

"I didn't think so. See, I tell them about Doc Crane on the way out. Sometimes they get worried about the girls and boys. Know what I mean, Patera?"

"I think so."

"So I tell them forget it. We got a doctor right there to

check everybody over, and if they got some kind of little problem of their own . . . I'm talking about the older bucks, Patera, you know? Why, maybe he could help them out. It's good for Doc, because sometimes they give him something. And it's good for me, too. I've had quite a few of them thank me for telling them, after the party."

"I fear I have nothing to give you, my son," Silk said stiffly. It was perfectly true, he assured himself; the two cards in his pocket were already spent, or as good as spent. They would buy a fine victim for Scylsday, less than two days off.

"That's all right, Patera. I didn't figure you did. It's a gift to the Chapter. That's how I look at it."

"I can give you my blessing, however, when we separate. And I will."

"That's all right, Patera," the driver said. "I'm not much for sacrifice and all that."

"All the more reason you may require it, my son," Silk told him, and could not keep from smiling at the sepulchral tones of his own voice. It was a good thing the driver could not see him! With Blood's villa far behind them, the burglar was fading and the augur returning; he had sounded exactly like Patera Pike.

Which was he, really? He pushed aside the thought.

"Now this here, this feels just like a boat, and no mistake. Don't it, Patera?"

Their floater was rolling like a barrel as it dodged pedestrians and rattling, mule-drawn wagons. The road had become a street in which narrow houses vied for space.

Silk found it necessary to grasp the leather-covered bar on the back of the driver's seat, a contrivance he had previously assumed was intended only to facilitate boarding and departure. "How high will these go?" he asked. "I've always wondered."

"Four cubits empty, Patera. Or that's what this one'll do,

anyhow. That's how you test them—run them up as high as they'll go and measure. The higher she floats, the better shape everything's in."

Silk nodded to himself. "You couldn't go over one of these wagons, then, instead of around it?"

"No, Patera. We got to have ground underneath to push against, see? And we'd be getting too far away from it. You remember that wall we cleared when I took the shortcut?"

"Certainly." Silk tightened his grip on the bar. "It must have been three cubits at least."

"Not quite, Patera. It's a little lower than that at the place where I went over. But what I was going to say was we couldn't have done it if we'd been full of passengers like we were coming out. We'd have had to stay on the road then."

"I understand. Or at any rate, I think I do."

"But look up ahead, Patera." The floater slowed. "See him lying in the road?"

Silk sat up straight to peer over the driver's liveried shoulder. "I do now. By Phaea's fair face, I hope he's not dead."

"Drunk more likely. Watch now, and we'll float right across him. You won't even feel him, Patera. Not no more than he'll feel you."

Silk clenched his teeth, but as promised felt nothing. When the prostrate man was behind them, he said, "I've seen floaters go over childen like that. Children playing in the street. Once a child was hit in the forehead by the cowling, right in front of our palaestra."

"I'd never do that, Patera," the driver assured Silk virtuously. "A child might hold up his arm and get it in the blowers."

Silk hardly heard him. He attempted to stand, bumped his head painfully against the floater's transparent canopy, and compromised on a crouch. "Wait! Not so fast, please.

Do you see that man with the two donkeys? Stop for a moment and let me out. I want a word with him."

"I'll just put down the canopy, Patera. That'll be a little safer."

Auk glanced sourly at the floater when it settled onto the roadway beside him. His eyes widened when he saw Silk.

"May every god bless you tonight," Silk began. "I want to remind you of what you promised in the tavern."

Auk opened his mouth to speak, but thought better of it.

"You gave me your word that you'd come to manteion next Scylsday, remember? I want to make certain you'll keep that promise, not only for your sake but for mine. I must talk to you again."

"Yeah. Sure." Auk nodded. "Maybe tomorrow if I'm not too busy. Scylsday for sure. Did you . . .?"

"It went precisely as you had predicted," Silk told him. "However, our manteion's safe for the time being, I believe. Good night, and Phaea bless you. Knock at the manse if you don't find me in the manteion."

Auk said something more; but the driver had overheard Silk's farewell, and the transparent dome of the canopy had risen between them; it latched, and Auk's voice was drowned by the roar of the blowers.

"You better watch your step, talking to characters like that, Patera," the driver remarked with a shake of his head. "That sword's just for show, and there's a needler underneath that dirty tunic. Want to bet?"

"You would win such a bet, I'm certain," Silk admitted, "but no needler can turn a good man to evil. Not even devils can do that."

"That why you want to see Orchid's place, Patera? I kind of wondered."

"I'm afraid I don't understand you." Crane's mystery had just given Silk a particularly painful job. He wiggled it into a new position as he spoke. Deciding that it would be harmless to reveal plans Blood knew of already, he added, "I'm to meet your master there tomorrow afternoon, and I want to be certain I go to the correct house. That's the yellow house, isn't it? Orchid's? I believe he mentioned a woman named Orchid."

"That's right, Patera. She owns it. Only he owns it, really, or maybe he owns her. You know what I mean?"

"I think so. Yes, of course." Silk recalled that it was Musk, not Blood, whose name appeared on the deed to his manteion. "Possibly Blood holds a mortgage upon this house, which is in arrears." Clearly Blood would have to protect his interest in some fashion against the death of the owner of record.

"I guess so, Patera. Anyhow, you talked about devils, so I thought maybe that was it."

The hair at the back of Silk's neck prickled. It was ridiculous (as if I were a dog, he said to himself later) but there it was; he tried to smooth it with one hand. "It might be useful if you would tell me whatever you know about this business, my son—useful to your master, as well as to me." How sternly his instructors at the schola had enjoined him, and all the acolytes, never to laugh when someone mentioned ghosts (he had anticipated the usual wide-eyed accounts of phantom footsteps and shrouded figures after Blood's mention of exorcism) or devils. Perhaps it was only because he was so very tired, but he discovered that there was not the least danger of his laughing now.

"I never seen anything myself," the driver admitted. "I hardly ever been inside. You hear this and that. Know what I mean, Patera?"

"Of course."

"Things get messed up. Like, a girl will go to get her best dress, only the sleeves are torn off and it's all ripped down the front. Sometimes people just, like, go crazy. You know? Then it goes away."

"Intermittent possession," Silk said.

"I guess so, Patera. Anyhow, you'll get to see it in a minute. We're almost there."

"Fine. Thank you, my son." Silk studied the back of the driver's head. Since the driver thought he had been a guest at Blood's, it would probably do no harm if he saw the object Crane had conveyed to him; but there was a chance, if only a slight one, that someone would question the driver when he returned to Blood's villa. Satisfied that he was too busy working the floater through the thickening stream of men and wagons to glance behind him, Silk took it out.

As he had suspected, it was an azoth. He whistled on a small footlight he had noticed earlier, holding the azoth low enough to keep the driver from seeing it, should he look over his shoulder.

The demon was an unfacetted red gem, so it was probably safe to assume it was the azoth he had taken from Hyacinth's drawer and she had snatched out of the coiled rope around his waist. It occurred to Silk as he examined the azoth that its demon should have been a blue gem, a hyacinth. Clearly the azoth had not been embellished in a style intended to flatter Hyacinth, as the needler in his pocket had been. It was even possible that it was not actually hers.

Rocking almost imperceptibly, the floater slowed, then settled onto the roadway. "Here's Orchid's place, Patera."

"On the right there? Thank you, my son." Silk slid the azoth into the top of the stocking on his good foot and pulled his trousers leg down over it; it was a considerable relief to be able to lean back comfortably.

"Quite a place, they tell me, Patera. Like I said, I've only been inside a couple times."

Silk murmured, "I very much appreciate your going out of your way for me."

Orchid's house seemed typical of the older, larger city

houses, a hulking cube of shiprock with a painted façade, its canary arches and fluted pillars the phantasmagoria of some dead artist's brush. There would be a courtyard, very likely with a dry fishpond at its center, ringed by shady galleries.

"It's only one story in back, Patera. You can get in that way, too, off of Music Street. That might be closer for you."

"No," Silk said absently. It would not do to arrive at the rear entrance like a tradesman.

He was studying the house and the street, visualizing them as they would appear by day. That shop with the white shutters would be the pastry cook's, presumably. In an hour or two there would be chairs and tables for customers who wished to consume their purchases on the spot, the mingled smells of maté and strong coffee, and cakes and muffins in the windows. A shutter swung back as Silk watched.

"In there," the driver jerked his thumb at the yellow house, "they'll be getting set to turn in now. They'll sleep till noon, most likely." He stretched, yawning. "So will I, if I can."

Silk nodded weary agreement. "What is it they do in there?"

"At Orchid's?" The driver turned to look back at him. "Everybody knows about Orchid's, Patera."

"I don't, my son. That was why I asked."

"It's a—you know, Patera. There's thirty girls, I guess, or about that. They put on shows, you know, and like that, and they have a lot of parties. Have them for other people, I mean. The people pay them to do it."

Silk sighed. "I suppose it's a pleasant life."

"It could be worse, Patera. Only—"

Someone screamed inside the yellow house. The scream was followed at once by the crash of breaking glass.

The engine sprang to life, shaking the whole floater as a

dog shakes a rat. Before Silk could protest, the floater shot into the air and sped up Lamp Street, scattering men and women on foot and grazing a donkey cart with a clang so loud that Silk thought for a moment it had been wrecked.

"Wait!" he called.

The floater turned almost upon its side as they rounded a corner, losing so much height that its cowling plowed the dust.

"That might be a—whatever the trouble is." Silk was holding on desperately with both hands, pain and the damage the white-headed one had done to his arm forgotten. "Go back and let me out."

Wagons blocked the street. The floater slowed, then forced its way between the wall of a tailor shop and a pair of plunging horses.

"Patera, they can take care of it. It's happened there before, like I told you."

Silk began, "I'm supposed—"

The driver cut him off. "You got a real bad leg and a bad arm. Besides, what if somebody saw you going in there—a place like that—at night? Tomorrow afternoon will be bad enough."

Silk released the leather-covered bar. "Did you really float away so quickly out concern for my reputation? I find that difficult to believe."

"I'm not going to go back there, Patera," the driver said stubbornly, "and I don't think you could walk back if you tried. Which way from here? To get to your manteion, I mean." The floater slowed, hovered.

This was Sun Street; it could not have been half an hour since they had floated past the talus and out Blood's gate. Silk tried to fix the Guard post and soiled statue of Councillor Tarsier in his memory. "Left," he said absently. And then, "I should have Horn—he's quite artistic—and some of the older students paint the front of our manteion. No, the palaestra first, then the manteion."

"What's that, Patera?"

"I'm afraid I was talking to myself, my son." They had almost certainly been painted originally; it might even be possible to find a record of the original designs among the clutter of papers in the attic of the manse. If money could be found for paint and brushes as well—

"Is it far, Patera?"

"Another six blocks perhaps."

He would be getting out in a moment. When he had left Blood's reception hall, he had imagined that the night was already gray with the coming of shadeup. Imagination was no longer required; the night was virtually over, and he had not been to bed. He would be getting out of the floater soon—perhaps he should have napped upon this soft seat after all, when he had the opportunity. Perhaps there was time for two or three hours sleep in the manse, though no more than two or three hours.

A man hauling bricks in a handcart shouted something at them and fell to his knees, but whatever he had shouted could not be heard. It reminded Silk that he had promised to bless the driver when they parted. Should he leave this walking stick in the floater? It was Blood's stick, after all. Blood had intended for him to keep it, but did he want to keep anything that belonged to Blood? Yes, the manteion, but only because the manteion was really his, not Blood's, no matter what the law, or even the Chapter, might say. Patera Pike had owned the manteion, morally at least, and Patera Pike had left him in charge of it, had made him responsible for it until he, too, died.

The floater was slowing again as the driver studied the buildings they passed.

Silk decided that he would keep the manteion and the stick, too—at least until he got the manteion back. "Up there, driver, with the shingled roof. See it?" He gripped the stick and made sure its tip would not slide on the floor of the floater; it was almost time to go.

The floater hovered, "Here, Patera?"

"No. One, two, three doors farther."

"Are you the augur everybody's talking about, Patera? The one that got enlightened? That's what somebody told me back at the estate."

Silk nodded. "I suppose so, unless there were two of us."

"You're going to bring back the caldé—that's what they say. I didn't want to ask you about it, you know? I hoped it would sort of come up by itself. Are you?"

"Am I going to restore the caldé? Is that what you're asking? No, that wasn't in my instructions at all."

"Instructions from a god." The floater settled to the roadway and its canopy parted and slid into its sides.

Silk struggled to his feet. "Yes."

The driver got out, to open the door for him. "I never thought there were any gods, Patera. Not really."

"They believe in you, however." Aided by the driver, Silk stepped painfully onto the first worn shiprock step in front of the street entrance to the manteion. He was home. "You believe in devils, it seems, but you do not believe in the immortal gods. That's very foolish, my son. Indeed, it is the height of folly."

Suddenly the driver was on his knees. Leaning on his stick, Silk pronounced the shortest blessing in common use and traced the sign of addition over the driver's head.

The driver rose. "I could help you, Patera. You've got a—a house or something here, don't you? I could give you a hand that far."

"I'll be all right," Silk told him. "You had better go back and get to bed."

Courteously, the driver waited for Silk to leave before restarting his blowers. Silk found that his injured leg was stiff as he limped to the narrow garden gate and let himself in, locking the gate behind him. By the time he reached the arbor, he was wondering whether it had not been foolish to refuse the driver's offer of help. He wanted very badly to rest, to rest for only a minute or so, on one of the cozy benches beneath the vines, where he had sat almost every day to talk with Maytera Marble.

Hunger urged him forward; food and sleep were so near. Blood, he thought, might have shown him better hospitality by giving him something to eat. A strong drink was not the best welcome to offer a man with an empty stomach.

His head pounded, and he told himself that a little food would make him feel better. Then he would go up to bed and sleep. Sleep until—why, until someone woke him. That was the truth: *until someone woke him.* There was no power but in truth.

The familiar, musty smell of the manse was like a kiss. He dropped into a chair, pulled the azoth from his stocking, and pressed it to his lips, then stared at it. He had seen it in her hand, and if the doctor was to be believed, it was her parting gift. How preposterous that he should have such a thing, so lovely, so precious, and so lethal! So charged with the forgotten knowledge of the earlier world. It would have to be hidden, and hidden well, before he slept; he was by no means sure that he could climb the steep and crooked stair to the upper floor, less sure that he could descend it again to prepare food without falling, but utterly certain that he would not be able to sleep at all unless the azoth was at hand—unless he could assure himself, whenever he was assailed by doubts, that it had not been stolen.

With a grunt and a muttered prayer to Sphigx (it was certainly Sphigxday by now, Silk had decided, and Sphigx was the goddess of courage in the face of pain in any event), he made his way slowly up the stair, got the rusty and utterly barren cash box that was supposed to secure the manteion's surplus funds from beneath his bed, locked the azoth in it, and returned the key to its hiding place under the water jug on his nightstand.

Descending proved rather easier than he had expected. By putting most of his weight on the stick and the railing, and advancing his sound foot one step at a time, he was able to progress quite well with a minimum of pain.

Giddy with success he went into the kitchen, leaned the stick in a corner, and after a brief labor at the pump washed his hands. Shadeup was peeping in through every window, and although he always rose early it was an earlier and thus a fresher morning than he had seen in some time. He really was not, he discovered with delight, so very tired after all, or so very sleepy.

After a second session with the pump, he splashed water over his face and hair and felt better still. He was tired, yes; and he was ravenously hungry. Still, he could face this new day. It might even be a mistake to go to bed after he had eaten.

His green tomatoes waited on the windowsill, but surely there had been four? Perplexed, he searched his memory.

There were only three there now. Might someone have entered the garden, intent upon the theft of a single unripe tomato? Maytera Marble cooked for the sibyls. Briefly Silk visualized her bent above a smoking pan, stirring his tomato into a fine hash of bacon and onions. His mouth watered, but nothing could possibly be less like Maytera Marble than any such borrowing.

Wincing with every step and amused by his own grimaces, he limped to the window and looked more closely. The remains of the fourth tomato were there, a dozen seeds and flecks of skin. Furthermore, a hole had been eaten— bored, almost—in the third.

Rats, of course, although this did not really look like the work of a rat. He pared away the damaged portion, sliced the remainder and the remaining pair, then belatedly realized that cooking would require a fire in the stove.

The ashes of the last were lifeless gray dust without a single gleam, as it seemed to Silk they always were. Others spoke of starting a new fire from the embers of the previous one; his own fires never seemed to leave those rumored, long-lived embers. He laid a few scraps of hoarded wastepaper on top of the cold ashes and added kindling from the box beside the stove. Showers of white-hot sparks from the igniter soon produced a fine blaze.

As he started out to the woodpile, he sensed a furtive movement, stopped, and turned as quickly as he could manage to look behind him. Something black had moved swiftly and furtively at the top of the larder. Too vividly he recalled the white-headed one, perched at the top of a chimney; but it was only a rat. There had been rats in the manse ever since he had come here from the schola, and no doubt since Patera Pike had left the schola.

The crackling tinder would not wait, rats or no rats. Silk chose a few likely-looking splits, carried them (once nearly falling) inside, and positioned them carefully. No doubt the rat was gone by now, but he fetched Blood's stick from its place in the corner anyway, pausing by the Silver Street window to study the indistinct, battered head at the end of the sharply angled handle. It seemed to be a dog's, or perhaps . . .

He rotated the stick, holding it higher to catch the grayish daylight.

Or perhaps, just possibly, a lioness's. After a brief uncertainty, he decided to consider it the head of a lioness; lionesses symbolized Sphigx, this was her day, and the idea pleased him.

Lions were big cats, and big cats were needed for rats, vermin too large and strong themselves for cats of ordinary size to deal with. Without real hope of success, he rattled the stick along the top of the larder. There was a flutter, and a sound he did not at once identify as a squawk. Another rattle, and a single black feather floated down.

It occured to Silk then that a rat might have carried the dead bird there to eat. Possibly there was a rat hole in the wainscotting up there, but the bird had been too large to be dragged through it.

He paused, listening. The sound he had heard had not been made by a rat, surely. After a moment he looked in the waste bin; the bird was no longer there.

If his ankle had been well, he would have climbed up on the stool; as things (and he himself) stood, that was out of the question. "Are you up there, bird?" he called. "Answer me!"

There was no reply. Blindly, he rattled Blood's stick across the top of the high larder again; and this time there was a quite unmistakable squawk. "Get down here," Silk said firmly.

The bird's hoarse voice replied, "No, no!"

"I thought you were dead."

Silence from the top of the larder.

"You stole my tomato, didn't you? And now you think I'll hurt you for that. I won't, I promise. I forgive you the theft." Silk tried to remember what night choughs were supposed to eat in the wild. Seeds? No, the bird had left the seeds. Carrion, no doubt.

"Cut me," the bird suggested throatily.

"Sacrifice you? I won't, I swear. The Writings warned me the sacrifice would be ineffectual, and I shouldn't have tried one after that. I've been punished very severely by one of your kind for it, believe me. I'm not such a fool as to try the same sacrifice again."

Silk waited motionless, listening. After a second or two, he felt certain that he could hear the bird's stealthy movements above the crack of whips and rumble of cartwheels that drifted through the window from Silver Street.

"Come down," he repeated.

The bird did not answer, and Silk turned away. The fire in the stove was burning well now, yellow flame leaping from the cook hole. He rescued his frying pan from the sink, wiped it out, poured the remaining oil into it—shaking the last lingering drop from the neck of the cruet—and put the pan on the stove.

His tomatoes would be greasy if he put them into the oil while it was still cold, unpleasantly flavored if he let the oil get too hot. Leaning Blood's stick against the door of the larder, he gathered up the stiff green slices, limped over to the stove with them, and distributed them with care over the surface of the pan, rewarded by a cloud of hissing, fragrant steam.

There was a soft cluck from the top of the larder.

"I can kill you whenever I want, just by banging around up there with my stick," Silk told the bird. "Show yourself, or I'll do it."

For a moment a long crimson bill and one bright black eye were visible at the top of the larder. "Me," the night chough said succinctly, and vanished at once.

"Good." The garden window was open already; Silk drew the heavy bolt of the Silver Street window and opened it as well. "It's shadeup now, and it will be much brighter soon. Your kind prefers the dark, I believe. You'd better leave at once."

"No fly."

"Yes, fly. I won't try to hurt you. You're free to go."

Silk watched for a moment, then decided that the bird was probably hoping that he would lay aside Blood's stick. He tossed it into a corner, got out a fork, and began turning the tomato slices; they sputtered and smoked, and he added a pinch of salt.

There was a knock at the garden door. Hurriedly, he snatched the pan from the fire. "Half a minute." Someone was dying, surely, and before death came desired to receive the Pardon of Pas.

The door opened before he could hobble over to it, and Maytera Rose looked in. "You're up very early, Patera. Is anything wrong?" Her gaze darted about the kitchen, her eyes not quite tracking. One was pupilless, and as far as Silk knew, blind; the other a prosthetic creation of crystal and fire.

"Good morning Maytera." Awkwardly, the fork and the smoking pan remained in Silk's hands; there was no place to put them down. "I suffered a little mishap last night, I'm afraid. I fell. It's still somewhat painful, and I haven't been able to sleep." He congratulated himself—it was all perfectly true.

"So you're making breakfast already. We haven't eaten yet, over in the cenoby." Maytera Rose sniffed hungrily, a dry, mechanical inhalation. "Marble's still fooling around in the kitchen. The littlest thing takes that girl forever."

"I'm quite certain Maytera Marble does the best she can," Silk said stiffly.

Maytera Rose ignored it. "If you want to give me that, I'll take it over to her. She can see to it for you till you come back."

"I'm sure that's not necessary." Sensing that he must eat his tomatoes now if he was to eat them at all, Silk cut the thinnest slice in two with his fork. "Must I leave this instant, Maytera? I can hardly walk."

"Her name's Teasel, and she's one of Marble's bunch." Maytera Rose sniffed again. "That's what her father says. I don't know her."

Silk (who did) froze, the half slice of tomato halfway to his mouth. "Teasel?"

"Her father came pounding on the door before we got

up. The mother's sitting with her, he said. He knocked over here first, but you didn't answer."

"You should have come at once, Maytera."

"What would have been the use when he couldn't wake you up? I waited till I could see you were out of bed." Maytera Rose's good eye was upon the half slice. She licked her lips and wiped her mouth on her sleeve. "Know where she lives?"

Silk nodded miserably, and then with a sudden surge of wholly deplorable greed thrust the hot half slice into his mouth, chewed, and swallowed. He had never tasted anything quite so good. "It's not far. I suppose I can walk it if I must."

"I could send Marble after Patera Pard when she's done cooking. She could show him where to go."

Silk shook his head.

"You're going to go after all, are you?" A moment too late, Maytera Rose added, "Patera."

Silk nodded.

"Want me to take those?"

"No, thank you," Silk said, miserably aware that he was being selfish. "I'll have to get on a robe, a collar and so forth. You'd better get back to the cenoby, Maytera, before you miss breakfast." He scooped up one of the smaller slices with his fork.

"What happened to your tunic?"

"And a clean tunic. Thank you. You're right, Maytera. You're quite right." Silk closed the door, virtually in her face, shot the bolt, and popped the whole sizzling slice into his mouth. Maytera Rose would never forgive him for what he had just done, but he had previously done at least a hundred other things for which Maytera Rose would never forgive him either. The stain of evil might soil his spirit throughout all eternity, for which he was deeply and sincerely sorry; but as a practical matter it would make little difference.

He swallowed a good deal of the slice and chewed the rest energetically.

"Witch," croaked a muffled voice.

"Go," Silk mumbled. He swallowed again. "Fly home to the mountains. You're free."

He turned the rest of the slices, cooked them half a minute more, and ate them quickly (relishing their somewhat oily flavor almost as much as he had hoped), scraped the mold from the remaining bread and fried the bread in the leftover liquid, and ate that as he once more climbed the stair to his bedroom.

Behind and below him, the bird called, "Good-bye!" And then, "Bye! Bye!" from the top of the larder.

Chapter 9

OREB AND OTHERS

Teasel lay upon her back, with her mouth open and her eyes closed. Her black hair, spread over the pillow, accentuated the pallor of her face. Bent above her as he prayed, Silk was acutely conscious of the bones underlying her face, of her protruding cheekbones, her eye sockets, and her high and oddly square frontal. Despite the mounting heat of the day, her mother had covered her to the chin with a thick red wool blanket that glowed like a stove in the sunbright room; her forehead was beaded with sweat, and it was only that sweat, which soon reappeared each time her mother sponged it away, that convinced him that Teasel was still alive.

When he had swung his beads and chanted the last of the prescribed prayers, her mother said, "I heard her cry out, Patera, as if she'd pricked her finger. It was the middle of the night, so I thought she was having a nightmare. I got out of bed and went in to see about her. The other children were all asleep, and she was still sleeping, too. I shook her shoulder, and she woke up a little bit and said she was thirsty. I ought to've told her to go get a drink herself."

Silk said, "No."

"Only I didn't, Patera. I went to the crock and got a cup of water, and she drank it and closed her eyes." After a moment Teasel's mother added, "The doctor won't come. Marten tried to get him."

Silk nodded. "I'll do what I can."

"If you'd talk to him again, Patera . . ."

"He wouldn't let me in last time, but I'll try."

Teasel's mother sighed as she looked at her daughter. "There was blood on her pillow, Patera. Not much. I didn't see it till shadeup. I thought it might have come out of her ear, but it didn't. She felt so cold."

Teasel's eyes opened, surprising them both. Weakly, she said, "The terrible old man."

Her mother leaned forward. "What's that?"

"Thirsty."

"Get her more water," Silk said, and Teasel's mother bustled out. "The old man hurt you?"

"Wings." Teasel's eyes rolled toward the window before closing.

They were four flights up, as Silk, who had climbed all four despite his painful right ankle, was very much aware. He rose, hobbled to the window, and looked out. There was a dirty little courtyard far below, a garret floor above them. The tapering walls were of unadorned, yellowish, sunbaked brick.

Legend had it that it was unlucky to converse with devils; Silk asked, "Did he speak to you, Teasel? Or you to him?"

She did not reply.

Her mother returned with the water. Silk helped her to raise Teasel to a half-sitting position; he had expected some difficulty in getting her to drink, but she drank thirstily, draining the clay cup as soon as it was put to her lips.

"Bring her more," he said, and as soon as Teasel's mother had gone, he rolled the unresisting girl onto her side.

When Teasel had drunk again, her mother asked, "Was it a devil, Patera?"

Silk settled himself once more on the stool she had provided for him. "I think so." He shook his head. "We have too much real disease already. It seems terrible . . ." He left the thought incomplete.

"What can we do?"

"Nurse her and feed her. See she gets as much water as she'll drink. She's lost blood, I believe." Silk took the voided cross from the chain around his neck and fingered its sharp steel edges. "Patera Pike told me about this sort of devil. That was—" Silk shut his eyes, reckoning. "About a month before he died. I didn't believe him, but I listened anyway, out of politeness. I'm glad, now, that I did."

Teasel's mother nodded eagerly. "Did he tell you how to drive it away?"

"It's away now," Silk told her absently. "The problem is to prevent it from returning. I can do what Patera Pike did. I don't know how he learned it, or whether it had any real efficacy; but he said that the child wasn't troubled a second time."

Assisted by Blood's stick, Silk limped to the window, seated himself on the sill, and leaned out, holding the side of the weathered old window frame with his free hand. The window was small, and he found he could reach the crumbling bricks above it easily. With the pointed corner of the one of the four gammadions that made up the cross, he scratched the sign of addition on the bricks.

"I'll hold you, Patera."

Teasel's father was gripping his legs above the knees. Silk said, "Thank you." He scratched Patera Pike's name to the left of the tilted X. Patera Pike had signed his work; so he had said.

"I brought the cart for you, Patera. I told my jefe about you, and he said it would be all right."

After a moment's indecision, Silk added his own name on the other side of the X. "Thank you again." He ducked back into the room. "I want you both to pray to Phaea. Healing is hers, and it would appear that whatever happened to your daughter happened at the end of her day."

Teasel's parents nodded together.

"Also to Sphigx, because today's hers, and to Surging Scylla, not only because our city is hers, but because your daughter called for water. Lastly, I want you to pray with great devotion to the Outsider."

Teasel's mother asked, "Why, Patera?"

"Because I told you to," Silk replied testily. "I don't suppose you'll know any of the prescribed prayers to him, and there really aren't that many anyway. But make up your own. They'll be acceptable to him as long as they're sincere."

As he descended the stairs to the street, one steep and painful step at a time, Mucor spoke behind him. "That was interesting. What are you going to do next?"

He turned as quickly as he could. As if in a dream, he glimpsed the mad girl's death's-head grin, and eyes that had never belonged to Teasel's stooped, hard-handed father. She vanished as he looked, and the man who had been following him down the stairs shook himself.

"Are you well, Marten?" Silk asked.

"I went all queer there, Patera. Don't know what come over me."

Silk nodded, traced the sign of addition, and murmured a blessing.

"I'm good enough now, or think I am. Worryin' too much about Sel, maybe. Rabbit shit on my grave."

In the past, Silk had carried a basin of water up the stairs to his bedroom and washed himself in decent privacy; that was out of the question now. After closing and locking both, he covered the Silver Street window with the dishrag and a dish towel, and the garden window (which looked toward the cenoby) with a heavy gray blanket he had stored on the highest shelf of the sellaria closet against the return of winter.

Retreating to the darkest corner of the kitchen, almost to the stair, he removed all his clothing and gave himself the cold bath he had been longing for, lathering his whole body from the crown of his head to the top of his cast, then sponging the suds away with clean, cool water fresh from the well.

Dripping and somewhat refreshed, yet so fatigued that he seriously considered stretching himself on the kitchen floor, he examined his discarded clothing. The trousers, he decided, were still salvageable: with a bit of mending, they might be worn again, as he had worn them before, while he patched the manteion's roof or performed similar chores. He emptied their pockets, dropping his prayer beads, Blood's two cards, and the rest on the scarred old kitchen table. The tunic was ruined, but would supply useful rags after a good laundering; he tossed it into the wash basket on top of his trousers and undershorts, dried those parts of himself that had not been dried already by the baking heat of the kitchen with a clean dish towel, and made his way up to bed. If it had not been for the pain in his ankle, he would have been half asleep before he passed the bedroom door.

His donkey was lost in the yellow house. Shards of the tumbler Blood broke with Hyacinth's golden needler cracked under the donkey's hooves, and a horned owl as big as a Flier circled overhead awaiting the moment to pounce. Seeing the double punctures the owl had left half concealed in the hair at the back of Teasel's neck, he shuddered.

The donkey fastened its teeth in his ankle like a dog. Though he flailed at it with Sphigx's walking stick, it would not let go.

Mother was riding Auk's big gray donkey sidesaddle—he saw her across the skylit rooftops, but he could not cry out. When he reached the place, her old wooden bust of the caldé lay among the fallen leaves; he picked it up, and it became the ball. He thrust it into his pocket and woke.

His bedroom was hot and filled with sunlight, his naked body drenched with sweat. Sitting up, he drank deeply from the tepid water jug. The rusty cash-box key was still in its place and was of great importance. As he lay down again, he remembered that it was Hyacinth whom he had locked away.

A black-clad imp with a blood-red sword stood upon his chest to study him, its head cocked to one side. He stirred and it fled, fluttering like a little flag.

Hard dry rain blew through the window and rolled across the floor, bringing with it neither wind nor respite from the heat. Silk groaned and buried his perspiring face in the pillow.

It was Maytera Marble who woke him at last, calling his name through the open window. His mind still sluggish with sleep, he tried to guess how long he had slept, concluding only that it had not been long enough.

He staggered to his feet. The busy little clock beside his triptych declared that it was after eleven, nearly noon. He struggled to recall the positions of its hands when he had permitted himself to fall into bed. Eight, or after eight, or possibly eight-thirty. Teasel, poor little Teasel, had been bitten by an owl—or by a devil. A devil with wings, if it had come in through her window, and thus a devil twice impossible. Silk blinked and yawned and rubbed his eyes.

"Patera? Are you up there?"

She might see him if he went near the window. Fumbling in a drawer for clean underclothes, he called, "What is it, Maytera?"

"*A doctor! He says he's come to treat you! Are you hurt, Patera?*"

"Wait a moment." Silk pulled on his best trousers, the only pair that remained, and crossed the room to the window, twice stepping painfully on pebbles.

Maytera Marble waited in the little path, her upturned face flashing in the hot sunshine. Doctor Crane stood beside her, a shabby brown medical bag in one hand.

"May every god favor you both this morning," Silk called down politely.

Crane waved his free hand in response. "Sphigxday and Hieraxday, remember? That's when I'm in this part of town! Today's Sphigxday. Let me in!"

"As soon as I get dressed," Silk promised.

With the help of Blood's lioness-headed walking stick, he hobbled downstairs. His arm and ankle seemed more painful than ever; he told himself firmly that it was only because the palliating effects of the drug Crane had given him the night before—and of the potent drinks he had imprudently sampled—had worn off.

Limping and wincing, he hurried into the kitchen. The heterogeneous collection of items he had left on the table there was rapidly transferred to his clean trousers, with only momentary hesitation over Hyacinth's gleaming needler.

"*Patera?*"

His blanket still covered the garden window; resisting the temptation to pull it down, he lurched painfully into the sellaria, flung open the door, and began introductions. "Maytera, this is Doctor Crane—"

Maytera Marble nodded demurely, and the physician said, "We've already met. I was tossing gravel through your window—I was pretty sure it was yours, since I could hear you snoring up there—when Marble discovered me and introduced herself."

Maytera Marble asked, "Did you send for him, Patera? He must be new to our quarter."

"I don't live here," Crane explained. "I only make a few calls here, two days a week. My other patients are all late sleepers," he winked at Silk, "but I hoped that Silk would be up."

Silk looked rueful. "I was a late sleeper myself, I'm afraid, today at least."

"Sorry I had to wake you, but I thought I might give you a ride when we're through—it's not good for you to walk too much on that ankle." By a gesture Crane indicated the sellaria. "I'd like to have you sitting down. Can we go inside?"

Maytera Marble ventured, "If I might watch you, Patera? Through the doorway . . . ?"

"Yes," Silk said. There should be ample opportunity to speak with Crane in private on the way to the yellow house. "Certainly, Maytera, if you wish."

"I hadn't known. Maytera Rose told Maytera Mint and me at breakfast, though she didn't seem to know a lot about it. You—you were testy with her, I think."

"Yes, very much so." Silk nodded sadly as he retreated into the sellaria, guilt overlaying the pain from his ankle. Maytera Rose had been hungry, beyond question, and he had turned her away. She had been inquisitive too, of course; but she could not help that. No doubt her intentions had been good—or at least no doubt she had told herself they were, and had believed it. How selflessly she had served the manteion for sixty years! Yet only this morning he had refused her.

He dropped into the nearest of the stiff old chairs, then stood again and shifted it two cubits so that Maytera Marble could watch from the doorway.

"All right if I put my bag on this little table here?" Crane stepped to his left, away from the doorway. There was no table there, but he opened his bag, held up a shapeless dark bundle so that Silk could see it (though Maytera Marble could not), dropped it on the floor, and set his bag beside it. "Now then, Silk. The arm first, I think."

Silk pushed up his sleeve and held out his injured arm.

Bright scissors Silk recalled from the previous night snipped away the bandages. "You probably think your ankle's worse, and in a way it is. But there's an excellent chance of blood-poisoning here, and that's no joke. Your ankle's not going to kill you—not unless we're playing in the worst sort of luck, anyway." Crane scrutinized the wounds under a tiny, brilliant light, muttered to himself, and bent to sniff them. "All right so far, but I'm going to give you a booster."

To keep his mind from the ampule, Silk said, "I'm very sorry I missed our prayers this morning. What time is it, Maytera?"

"Nearly noon. Maytera Rose said you had to—is that a bird, Patera?"

Crane snapped, "Don't jerk like that!"

"I was thinking of—of the bird that did this," Silk finished weakly.

"You could have broken off the needle. How'd you like me fishing around in your arm for that?"

"It *is* a bird!" Maytera Marble pointed. "It hopped back that way. Into your kitchen, I suppose, Patera."

"That's the stairwell, actually," Silk told her. "I'm surprised it's still here."

"It was a big black bird, and I think one of its wings must be broken. It wasn't exactly dragging it but it wasn't holding it right either, if you know what I mean. Is that the bird—? The one that—?"

"Just sit quietly," Crane said. He was putting a fresh bandage on Silk's arm.

Silk said, "No wonder it didn't fly," and Maytera Marble looked at him inquiringly.

"It's the one that I'd intended to sacrifice, Maytera. It had only fainted or something—had a fit, or whatever birds do. I opened the kitchen window for it this morning so it could fly away, but I suppose I must have broken its wing when I was poking around on top of the larder with my walking stick."

He held it up to show her. It reminded him of Blood, and Blood reminded him that he was going to have to explain to Maytera Marble—and if he was not extremely lucky, to Maytera Rose and Maytera Mint as well—exactly how he had received his injuries.

"On top of the larder, Patera?"

"Yes. The bird was up there then." Still thinking of the explanation the sibyls would expect, he added, "It had flown up there, I suppose."

Crane pulled a footstool into place and sat on it. "Up with your tunic now. Good. Shove your waistband down just a bit."

Maytera Marble turned her head delicately away.

Silk asked, "If I'm able to catch that bird, will you set its wing for me?"

"I don't know much horse-physic, but I can try. I've seen to Musk's hawks once or twice."

Silk cleared his throat, resolved to deceive Maytera Marble as little as possible without revealing the nature of his visit to the villa. "You see, Maytera, after I saw—saw Maytera Mint's friend, you know who I mean, I thought it might be wise to call on Blood. Do you remember Blood? You showed him around yesterday afternoon."

Maytera Marble nodded. "Of course, Patera. How could I forget?"

"And you had spoken afterward, when we talked under the arbor, about our buildings being torn down—or perhaps not torn down, but our having to leave. So I thought it might be wise for me to have a heart-to-heart talk with the new owner. He lives in the country, so it took me a good deal longer than I had anticipated, I'm afraid."

Crane said, "Lean back a little more." He was swabbing Silk's chest and abdomen with a blue solution.

Maytera Marble nodded dubiously. "That was very good of you, Patera. Wonderful, really, though I didn't get the impression that he—"

Silk leaned back as much as he could, pushing his hips forward. "But he did, Maytera. He's going to give me—to give us, I ought to say—another month here at least. And it's possible that we may never have to go."

"Oh, Patera!" Maytera Marble forgot herself so far as to look at him.

Silk hurried on. "But what I wanted to explain is that a man who works for Blood keeps several large birds as pets. I suppose there are several, at least, from the way that he and Blood talked about them."

Crane nodded absently.

"And he'd given this one to Blood," Silk continued. "It was dark, of course, and I'm afraid I got too close. Blood very graciously suggested that Doctor Crane come by today to see to my injuries."

"Why, Patera, how wonderful of him!" Maytera Marble's eyes positively shone with admiration for Silk's diplomatic skills, and he felt himself blush.

"All part of my job," Crane said modestly, replacing the stopper in the blue bottle.

Silk swallowed and took a deep breath, hoping that this was the proper moment. "Before we leave, Doctor, there's something I must bring up. A moment ago you said you would treat that injured bird if I was able to catch it. You were gracious about it, in fact."

Crane nodded warily as he rose. "Excuse me. Have to get my cutter."

"This morning," Silk continued, "I was called to bring the forgiveness of the gods to a little girl named Teasel."

Maytera Marble stiffened.

"She's close to death, but I believe—I dare to hope that she may recover, provided she receives the most basic medical attention. Her parents are poor and have many other children."

"Hold your leg out." Crane sat down on the footstool again and took Silk's foot in his lap. The cutter buzzed.

"They can't possibly pay you," Silk continued doggedly. "Neither can I, except with prayers. But without your help, Teasel may die. Her parents actually expect her to die— otherwise her father wouldn't have come here before shadeup looking for me. There are only two doctors in this quarter, and neither will treat anyone unless he's paid in advance. I promised Teasel's mother I'd do what I could to get her a doctor, and you're the only real hope I have."

Crane looked up. There was something in his eyes, a gleam of calculation and distant speculation, that Silk did not understand. "You were there this morning?"

Silk nodded. "That was why I got to bed so late. Her father had come to the cenoby before I returned from my talk with Blood, and when Maytera Rose saw that I had come home, she came and told me. I went at once." The memory of green tomatoes stung like a hornet. "Or almost at once," he added weakly.

Maytera Marble said, "You must see her, Doctor. Really you *must.*"

Crane ignored her, fingering his beard. "And you told them you'd try to get a doctor for whatshername?"

Hope blossomed in Silk. "Yes, I did. I'd be in your debt till Pas ends the whorl, and I'd be delighted to show you where she lives. We could stop there on the way."

Maytera Marble gasped. "Patera! All those steps!"

Crane bent over the cast again; his cutter whined and half of it fell away. "You're not going to climb a lot of stairs if I have anything to say about it. Not with this ankle. Marble here can show me—"

"Oh, yes!" Maytera Marble was dancing with impatience. "I've got to see her. She's one of mine."

"Or you can just give me the address," Crane finished. "My bearers will know where it is. I'll see to her and come back here for you." He removed the rest of the cast. "This hurt you much?"

"Not nearly as much as worrying about Teasel did," Silk told him. "But you've taken care of that, or at least taken care of the worst aspect of it. I'll never be able to thank you enough."

"I don't want your thanks," Crane said. He rose again, dusting particles of the cast from his trousers legs. "What I want is for you to follow my instructions. I'm going to give you a remedial wrapping. It's valuable and reusable, so I want it back when your ankle's healed. And I want you to use it exactly as I tell you."

Silk nodded. "I will, I promise."

"As for you, Marble," Crane turned to look at her, "you might as well ride along with me. It'll save you the walk. I want you to tell this girl's parents that I'm not doing this out of the goodness of my heart, because I don't want to be pestered night and day by beggars. It's a favor to Silk—Patera Silk, is that what you call him? And it's a one-time thing."

Maytera Marble nodded humbly.

The little physician went to his bag again and produced what looked like a wide strip of thin yellow chamois. "Ever see one of these?"

Silk shook his head.

"You kick them." Crane punted the wrapping, which

flew against the wall on the other side of the room. "Or you can just throw it a couple of times, or beat something smooth, like that footstool." He retrieved the wrapping, juggling it. "When you do, they get hot. You woke it up by banging it around. You follow me? Here, feel."

Silk did. The wrapping was almost too hot to touch, and seemed to tingle.

"The heat'll make your ankle feel better, and the sonic— you can't hear it, but it's there—will get the healing process going. What's more, it'll sense the break in your medial malleolus and tighten itself enough to keep it from shifting." Crane hesitated. "You can't get them any more, but I've got this one. Usually I don't tell people about it."

"I'll take good care of it," Silk promised, "and return it whenever you ask."

Maytera Marble ventured, "Shouldn't we be going?"

"In a minute. Wrap it around your ankle Patera. Get it fairly tight. You don't have to tie it or anything—it'll hold on as long as it senses the broken bone."

The wrapping seemed almost to coil itself about Silk's leg, its heat intense but pleasant. The pain in his ankle faded.

"You'll know when it's stopped working. As soon as it does, I want you to take it off and throw it against the wall like I showed you, or beat a carpet with it." The physician tugged at his beard. "Let's see. Today's Sphigxday. I'll come back on Hieraxday, and we'll see. Regardless, you ought to be walking almost normally a week from now. If I don't take it Hieraxday, I'll pick it up then. But until I do, I want you to stay off that ankle as much as you can. Get a crutch if you need one. And absolutely no running and no jumping. You hear me?"

Silk nodded. "Yes, of course. But you told Blood it would be five—"

"It's not as bad as I figured, that's all. A simple misdiagnosis. Your head augur . . . What do they call him, the Prolocutor? Haven't you noticed that when he gets sick I'm not the one he sends for? Well, that's why. Now and then I make a mistake. The sort of doctors he has in never do. Just ask them."

Maytera Marble inquired, "How does it feel, Patera?"

"Marvelous! I'm tempted to say as though my ankle had never been injured, but it's actually better than that. As if I'd been given a new ankle, a lot better than the one I broke."

"I could give you dozens of things that would make you *feel* better," Crane told him, "starting with a shot of pure and a sniff of rust. This will really make you better, and that's a lot harder. Now, what about this bird of yours? If I'm going to have to doctor it, I'd like to do it before we go. What kind of bird is it?"

"A night chough," Silk told him.

"Can it talk?"

Silk nodded.

"Then maybe I can catch it myself. Maytera, would you tell my bearers to come around to Sun Street? They're on Silver. Tell them you'll be coming with me, and we'll leave in a minute or two."

Maytera Marble trotted away.

The physician shook his finger at Silk. "You sit easy, young man. I'll find him."

He vanished into the stairwell. Soon, Silk heard his voice from the kitchen, though he could not make out what was being said. Silk called, "You told Blood that it would take so long to heal so that I'd get more time, didn't you? Thank you, Doctor."

There was no response. The wrapping was still hot, and oddly comforting. Under his breath Silk began the afternoon prayer to Sphigx the Brave. A fat, blue-backed fly sizzled through the open doorway, looked around for food, and bumped the glass of the nearer Sun Street window.

Crane called from the kitchen, "You want to come here a minute, Silk?"

"All right." Silk stood and walked almost normally to the kitchen door, his right foot bare and the wrapping heavy about his ankle.

"He's hiding up there." Crane pointed to the top of the larder. "I got him to talk a little, but he won't come down and let me see his wing unless you promise he won't be hurt again."

"Really?" Silk asked.

The night chough croaked from the top of the larder, and Crane nodded and winked.

"Then I promise. May Great Pas judge me if I harm him or permit others to do so."

"No cut?" croaked the bird. "No stick?"

"Correct," Silk declared. "I will not sacrifice you, or hurt you in any other fashion whatsoever."

"Pet bird?"

"Until your wing is well enough for you to fly. Then you may go free."

"No cage?"

Crane nudged Silk's arm to get his attention, and shook his head.

"Correct. No cage." Silk took the cage from the table and raised it over his head, high enough for the bird to see it. "Now watch this." With both hands, he dashed it to the floor, and slender twigs snapped like squibs. He stepped on it with his good foot, then picked up the ruined remnant and tossed it into the kindling box.

Crane shook his head. "You're going to regret that, I imagine. It's bound to be inconvenient at times."

With its sound wing flapping furiously, the black bird fluttered from the top of the larder to the table.

"Good bird!" Crane told it. He sat down on the kitchen stool. "I'm going to pick you up, and I want you to hold still for a minute. I'm not going to hurt you any more than I have to."

"I was a prisoner myself for a while last night," Silk remarked, more than half to himself. "Even though there was no actual cage, I didn't like it."

Crane caught the unresisting bird expertly, his hands gentle yet firm. "Get my bag for me, will you?"

Silk nodded and returned to the sellaria. He closed the garden door, then picked up the dark bundle that Crane had displayed to him. As he had guessed, it was his second-best robe, with his old pen case still in its pocket; it had been wrapped around his missing shoe. Although he had no stocking for his right foot, he put on both, shut the brown medical bag, and carried it into the kitchen.

The bird squawked and fluttered as Crane stretched out its injured wing. "Dislocated," he said. "Exactly like a dislocated elbow on you. I've pushed it back into place, but I want to splint it so he won't pop it out again before it heals. Meanwhile he'd better stay inside, or a cat will get him."

"Then he must stay in on his own," Silk said.

"Stay in," the bird repeated.

"Your cage is broken," Silk continued severely, "and I certainly don't intend to bake in here with all the windows shut, merely to keep you from getting out."

"No out," the bird assured him. Crane was rummaging in his bag.

"I hope not." Silk pulled the blanket from the garden window, threw it open, and refolded the blanket.

"What time are you supposed to meet Blood at the yellow house?"

"One o'clock, sharp." Silk carried the blanket into the sellaria; when he returned, he added, "I'm going to be late,

I imagine; I doubt that he'll do anything worse than complain about it."

"That's the spirit. He'll be late himself, if I know him. He likes to have everybody on hand when he shows up. I doubt if that'll be before two."

Stepping across to the Silver Street window, Silk took down the dishrag and the dish towel and opened it as well. It was barred against thieves, and it occurred to him that he was caged in literal fact, here in this old, four-room manse he had taught himself to call home. He pushed away the thought. If Crane's litter had been on Silver Street, it was gone now; no doubt Maytera Marble had performed her errand and it was waiting on Sun Street.

"This should do it." Crane was fiddling with a small slip of some stiff blue synthetic. "You'll be ready to go when I get back?"

Silk nodded, then felt his jaw. "I'll have to shave. I'll be ready then."

"Good. I'll be running late, and the girls get cranky if they can't go out and shop." Crane applied a final strip of almost invisible tape to keep the little splint in place. "This will fall right off after a few days. When it does, let him fly if he wants to. If he's like the hawks, you'll find that he's a pretty good judge of what he can and can't do."

"No fly," the bird announced.

"Not now, that's for sure. If I were you, I wouldn't even move that wing any more today."

Silk's mind was elsewhere. "It's diabolic possession, isn't it? At the yellow house?"

Crane turned to face him. "I don't know. Whatever it is, I hope you have better luck with it than I've had."

"What's been happening there? My driver and I heard a scream last night, but we didn't go inside."

The little physician laid a finger to his nose. "There are a thousand reasons why a girl might scream, especially one of those girls. Might have been a stain on her favorite gown, a bad dream, or a spider."

A tiny needle of pain penetrated the protection of the wrapping; Silk opened the cabinet that closed the kitchen's pointed north corner and got out the stool Patera Pike had used at meals. "I doubt that Blood wants me to exorcise his women's dreams."

Crane snapped his medical bag shut. "No one except the woman herself is really occupying the consciousness of what people like you choose to call a 'possessed' woman, Silk. Consciousness itself is a mere abstraction—a convenient fiction, actually. When I say that a man's unconscious, I mean no more than that certain mental processes have been suspended. When I say that he's regained consciousness, I mean that they've resumed. You can't occupy an abstraction as if it were a conquered city."

"A moment ago you said the woman herself occupied it," Silk pointed out.

With a last look at the injured bird, Crane rose. "So they really do teach you people something besides all that garbage."

Silk nodded. "It's called logic."

"So it is." Crane smiled, and Silk discovered to his own surprise that he liked him. "Well, if I'm going to look in on this sick girl of yours, I'd better scoot. What's the matter with her? Fever?"

"Her skin felt cold to me, but you're a better judge of diseases than I."

"I should hope so." Crane picked up his bag. "Let's see—through the front room there for Sun Street, isn't it? Maybe we can talk a little more on our way to Orchid's place."

"Look at the back of her neck," Silk said.

Crane paused in the doorway, shot him a questioning glance, then hurried out.

Murmuring a prayer for Teasel under his breath, Silk went into the sellaria and shut and bolted the Sun Street door, which Crane had left standing open. As he passed a window, he caught sight of Crane's litter. Maytera Marble reclined beside the bearded physician, her intent metal face straining ahead as though she alone were urging the litter forward by sheer force of thought. While Silk watched, its bearers broke into a trot and it vanished behind the window frame.

He tried to recall whether there was a rule prohibiting a sibyl from riding in a man's litter; it seemed likely that there was, but he could not bring a particular stricture to mind; as a practical matter, he could see little reason to object as long as the curtains were up.

The lioness-headed walking stick lay beside the chair in which he had sat for Crane's examination. Absently, he picked it up and flourished it. For as long as the wrapping functioned he would not need it, or at least would need it very little. He decided that he would keep it near at hand anyway; it might be useful, particularly when the wrapping required restoration. He leaned it against the Sun Street door, so that he could not forget it when he and Crane left for the yellow house.

A few experimental steps demonstrated once again that with Crane's wrapping in place he could walk almost as well as ever. There seemed to be no good reason for him not to carry a basin of warm water upstairs and shave as he usually did. He re-entered the kitchen.

Still on the table, the night chough cocked its head at him inquiringly. "Pet hungry," it said.

"So am I," he told it. "But I won't eat again until after midday."

"Noon now."

"I suppose it is." Silk lifted a stove lid and peered into the firebox; for once a few embers still glowed there. He breathed upon them gently and added a handful of broken twigs from the ruined cage, reflecting that the night chough was clearly more intelligent than he had imagined.

"Bird hungry."

Flames were flickering above the twigs. He debated the need for real firewood and decided against it. "Do you like cheese?"

"Like cheese."

Silk found his washbasin and put it under the nozzle of the pump. "It's hard, I warn you. If you're expecting nice, soft cheese, you're going to be disappointed."

"Like cheese!"

"All right, you can have it." A great many vigorous strokes of the pump handle were required before the first trickle of water appeared; but Silk half filled his basin and set it on the stove, and as an afterthought replenished the night chough's cup.

"Cheese now?" the night chough inquired. "Fish heads?"

"No fish heads—I haven't got any." He got out the cheese, which was mostly rind, and set it next to the cup. "You'd better watch out for rats while I'm away. They like cheese too."

"Like rats." The night chough clacked its crimson beak and pecked experimentally at the cheese.

"Then you won't be lonely." The water on the stove was scarcely warm, the twigs beneath it nearly out. Silk picked up the basin and started for the stair.

"Where rats?"

He paused and turned to look back at the night chough. "Do you mean you like them to eat?"

"Yes, yes!"

"I see. I suppose you might kill a rat at that, if it wasn't too big. What's your name?"

"No name." The night chough returned its attention to the cheese.

"That was supposed to be my lunch, you know. Now I'll have to find lunch somewhere or go hungry."

"You Silk?"

"Yes, that's my name. You heard Doctor Crane use it, I suppose. But we need a name for you." He considered the matter. "I believe I'll call you Oreb—that's a raven in the Writings, and you seem to be some sort of raven. How do you like that name?"

"Oreb."

"That's right. Musk named his bird after a god, which was very wrong of him, but I don't believe that there could be any objection to a name from the Writings if it weren't a divine name, particularly when it's a bird's name there. So Oreb it is."

At his washstand upstairs, he stropped the big, bone-handled razor that had waited in his mother's bureau until he was old enough to shave, lathered his face, and scraped away his reddish-blond beard. As he wiped the blade clean, it occurred to him, as it did at least once a week, that the razor had almost certainly been his father's. As he had so many times before, he carried it to the window to look for some trace of ownership. There was no owner's name and no monogram, not even a maker's mark.

As often in this weather, Maytera Rose and Maytera Mint were enjoying their lunch at a table carried from the cenoby and set in the shade of the fig tree. When he had dried his face, Silk carried the basin back to the kitchen, poured out his shaving water, and joined the two sibyls in the garden.

By a gesture, Maytera Rose offered him the chair that would normally have been Maytera Marble's. "Won't you join us, Patera? We've more than enough here for three."

It stung, as she had no doubt intended. Silk said, "No, but I ought to speak with you for a moment."

"And I with you, Patera. I with you." Maytera Rose began elaborate preparations for rising.

He sat down hurriedly. "What is it, Maytera?"

"I had hoped to tell you about it last night, Patera, but you were gone."

A napkin-draped basket at Silk's elbow exuded the very perfume of Mainframe. Maytera Marble had clearly baked that morning, leaving the fruit of her labor in the cenoby's oven for Maytera Mint to remove after she herself had left with Crane. Silk swallowed his saliva, muttered, "Yes," and left it at that.

"And this morning it had quite escaped my mind. All that I could think of was that awful man, the little girl's father. I will be sending Horn to you this afternoon for correction, Patera. I have punished him already, you may be sure. Now he must acknowledge his fault to you—that is the final penalty of his punishment." Maytera Rose paused to render her closing words more effective, her head cocked like the night chough's as she fixed Silk with her good eye. "And if you should decide to punish him further, I will not object. That might have a salutary effect."

"What did he do?"

The synthetic part of Maytera Rose's mouth bent sharply downward in disgust; as he had on several similar occasions, Silk wondered whether the aged, disease-ridden woman who had once been Maytera Rose was still conscious. "He made fun of you, Patera, imitating your voice and gestures, and talking foolishness."

"Is that all?"

Maytera Rose sniffed as she extracted a fresh roll from the basket. "I would say it was more than enough."

Maytera Mint began, "If Patera himself—"

"Before Patera was born, I endeavored to inculcate a

decent respect for the holy calling of augur, a calling—like that of we sibyls—established by Our Sacred Scylla herself. I continue that effort to this day. I try, as I have always tried, to teach every student entrusted to my care to respect the cloth, regardless of the man or woman who wears it."

"A lesson to us all." Silk sighed. "Very well, I'll talk to him when I can. But I'm leaving in a few minutes, and I may not be back until late. That was what I wanted to tell you—to tell Maytera Mint particularly."

She look up, a question in her melting brown eyes.

"I'll be engaged, and I can't say how long it may take. You remember Auk, Maytera. You must. You taught him, and you told Maytera Marble about him yesterday, I know."

"Oh, Patera, I do indeed." Maytera Mint's small, not uncomely face glowed.

Maytera Rose sniffed, and Maytera Mint dropped her eyes again.

"I spoke to him last night, Maytera, very late."

"You did, Patera?"

Silk nodded. "But I'm forgetting something I should tell you. I'd seen him earlier that evening, and shriven him. He's trying, quite sincerely I believe, to amend his life."

Maytera Mint looked up again, her glance bright with praise. "That's truly wonderful, Patera!"

"It is indeed; and it's far more your doing, and Patera Pike's, than it is mine. What I wanted to say, Maytera, is that when I last spoke with him, he indicated that he might come here today. If he does, I'm sure he'll want to pay his respects to you."

He waited for her to confirm it. She did not, sitting with folded hands and downcast eyes.

"Please tell him that I'm anxious to see him. Ask him to wait, if he can. I doubt that he'll come before supper. If I haven't returned, tell him that I'll be back as soon as possible."

Spreading rich yellow butter on another golden roll, Maytera Rose said, "Last night you had gone already by the time Horn had finished working for his father. I'll tell him that he'll have to wait, too."

"I'm certain you will, Maytera. Thank you both." Silk stood up, wincing when he put too much weight on his injured ankle. For a formal exorcism he would need the Chrasmologic Writings from the manteion, and images of the gods—of Pas and Scylla particularly. And of Sphigx the patroness of the day. The thought reminded him that he had never completed her prayers; hardly the way to gain favor.

He would take the triptych his mother had given him; her prayers might follow it. As he tramped upstairs again, more conscious of his ankle than he had been since before Crane's visit, he reflected that he had been trained only in dealing with devils who did not exist. He recalled how startled he had been when he had realized that Patera Pike credited them, and even spoke with gruff pride of personal efforts to frustrate them.

Before he reached the top of the stair, he regretted leaving Blood's walking stick in the sellaria. Sitting on his bed, he unwound the wrapping; it was distinctly cool to the touch. He dashed it against the wall as violently as he could and replaced it, then removed his shoe and put on a clean stocking.

Blood would meet him at the yellow house on Lamp Street. Musk, or someone as bad as Musk, might come with Blood. Silk folded up the triptych, laid it in its baize-lined teak case, buckled the straps, and pulled out its folding handle. This and the Writings, which he would have to get before he left; Pas's gammadion was about his neck already, his beads in his pocket. It might be prudent to take a holy lamp, oil, and other things as well. After considering and rejecting half a dozen possibilities, he got the key from beneath his water jug.

With the young eagle on his gauntleted left arm, Musk stood on the spattered white pavement by Scylla's fountain and looked about him, his head as proudly poised, and his back as straight, as any Guardsman's. They were watching from the deep shade of the portico: Blood, Councillor Lemur and his cousin Councillor Loris, Commissioner Simuliid, and half a dozen others. Mentally, Musk shook the dice cup.

The eagle had been trained to wrist and to the lure. It knew his voice and had learned to associate it with food. When he removed its hood, it would see the fountain, flowing water in a countryside in which water of any kind was now a rarity. The time had come for it to learn to fly—and he could not teach it that. It would return for the lure and the hackboard. Or it would not. Time to throw the dice.

Blood's voice came to him faintly through the plashing of the fountain. "Don't rush him."

Someone had asked what he was waiting for. He sighed, knowing he could not delay much longer. To hold on to this moment, in which the bird that he might never see again was still his.

The sky was empty or seemed so, the skylands invisible behind the endless, straight glare of the sun. Fliers, if there were any, were invisible too. Above the tops of the trees on the other side of the wall, distant fields curved upward, vanishing in a blue haze as they mounted the air. Lake Limna seemed a fragment of mirror set into the whorl, like a gaud into a cheap picture frame.

Time to throw.

As though it knew what was about to happen, the young

eagle stirred. Musk nodded to himself. "Come back to me," he whispered. "Come back to me."

And then, as if somebody else (an interfering god or Blood's mad daughter) controlled it, his right arm went up. Self-willed, his hand grasped the scarlet-plumed hood and snatched it away.

The young eagle lifted its wings as though to fly, then folded them again. He should have worn a mask, perhaps. If the eagle struck at his face now, he would be scarred for life if he was not killed; but his pride had not permitted it.

"Away, Hawk!" He lifted his arm, tilting it to tip the bird into the air. For a split second he thought it was not going to fly at all.

The great wings seemed to blow him back. Slowly and clumsily it flew, its wingtips actually brushing the lush grass at every downstroke—out to the wall and left, past the gate and left again up the grassway. For a moment he thought it was returning to him.

Into the portico, scattering the watchers there like quail. If it turned right at the end of the wing, mistook the cat pen for the mews—

Higher now, as high as the top of the wall, and left again. Left until it passed overhead, its wings a distant thunder. Higher now, and higher still, still circling and climbing, riding the updraft from the baking lawn and the scorching roofs. Higher the young eagle rose and higher, black against the glare, until it, like the fields, was lost in the vastness of the sky.

When the rest had gone Musk remained, shading his eyes against the pitiless sun. After a long while, Hare brought him binoculars. He used them but saw nothing.

Chapter 10

THE CAT WITH THE
RED-HOT TAIL

Lamp Street was familiar and safe once more, stripped of the mystery of night. Silk, who had walked it often, found that he recognized several shops, and even the broad and freshly varnished door of the yellow house.

The corpulent woman who opened it in response to Crane's knock seemed surprised by his presence. "It's awfully early, Patera. Just got up myself." She yawned as if to prove it, only tardily concealing her mouth. Her pink peignoir gaped in sympathy, its vibrant heat leaving the bulging flesh between its parted lips a deathly white.

The air of the place poured past her, hot and freighted with a hundred stale perfumes and the vinegar reek of wasted wine. "I was to meet Blood here at one o'clock," Silk told her. "What time is it?"

Crane slipped past them into the reception room beyond.

The woman ignored him. "Blood's always late," she said vaguely. She led Silk through a low archway curtained with clattering wooden beads and into a small office. A door and a window opened onto the courtyard he had imagined the night before, and both stood open; despite them, the office seemed hotter even than the street outside.

"We've had exorcists before." The corpulent woman took the only comfortable-looking chair, leaving Silk an armless one of varnished wood. He accepted it gratefully, dropping his bag to the floor, laying the cased triptych across his thighs, and holding Blood's lioness-headed stick between his knees.

"I'll have somebody fetch you a pillow, Patera. This is where I talk to my girls, and a hard chair's better. It keeps them awake, and the narrow seat makes them think that they're getting fat, which is generally the case."

The memory of his fried tomatoes brought Silk a fresh pang of guilt, well salted with hunger. Could it be that some god spoke through this blowsy woman? "Leave it as it is," he told her. "I, too, need to learn to love my belly less, and my bed."

"You want to talk to all the girls together? One of the others did. Or I can just tell you."

Silk waved the question aside. "What these particular devils may have done here is no concern of mine, and paying attention to their malicious tricks would risk encouraging them. They are devils, and unwelcome in this house; that is all I know, and if you and—and everyone else living here are willing to cooperate with me, it is all I need to know."

"All right." The corpulent woman adjusted her own chair's ample cushions and leaned back. "You believe in them, huh?"

Here it was. "Yes," Silk told her firmly.

"One of the others didn't. He said lots of prayers and had the parade and all the rest of it anyway, but he thought we were crazy. He was about your age."

"Doctor Crane thinks the same," Silk told her, "and his beard is gray. He doesn't phrase it quite as rudely as that, but that's what he thinks. He thinks that I'm crazy too, of course."

The corpulent woman smiled bitterly. "Uh-huh, I can guess. I'm Orchid, by the way." She offered her hand as though she expected him to kiss it.

He clasped it. "Patera Silk, from the manteion on Sun Street."

"That old place? Is it still open?"

"Yes, very much so." The question reminded Silk that it soon might not be, although it was better not to mention that.

"We're not now," Orchid told him. "Not until nine, so you've got plenty of time. But tonight's our biggest night, usually, so I'd appreciate it if you were finished by then." At last noticing his averted eyes, she tugged ineffectually at the edges of the pink peignoir.

"It should take me no more than two hours to perform the initial rites and the ceremony proper, provided I have everyone's cooperation. But it may be best to wait until Blood arrives. He told me last night that he would meet me here, and I feel sure that he will wish to take part."

Orchid was eyeing him narrowly. "He's paying you?"

"No. I'm performing this exorcism as a favor to him—I owe him much more, really. Did he pay the other exorcists you spoke of?"

"He did or I did, depending."

Silk relaxed a little. "In that case, it's not to be wondered at that their exorcisms were ineffectual. Exorcism is a sacred ceremony, and no such ceremony can be bought or sold." Seeing that she did not understand, he added. "They cannot be sold—my statement is true in the most literal sense of its words—because once sold the ceremony loses all its sacred character. What is sold is then no more than a profane mummery. That is not what we will carry out here today."

"But Blood could give you something, couldn't he?"

"Yes, if he wished. No gift affects the nature of the

ceremony. A gift is given freely—if one is given at all. The point upon which the efficacy of the ceremony turns is that there must be no bargain between us; and there is none. I would have no right to complaint if a promised gift were not forthcoming. Am I making this clear?"

Orchid nodded reluctantly.

"In point of fact, I expect no gift at all from Blood. I owe him several favors, as I said. When he asked me to do this, I was—as I remain—eager to oblige."

Orchid leaned toward him, the peignoir yawning worse than ever. "Suppose this time it works, Patera. I could give you something, couldn't I?"

"Of course, if you choose. However, you will owe me nothing."

"All right." She hesitated, considering. "Sphigxday's our big night, like I said—that's why Blood comes around, usually, today. To check up on us before we open up. We're closed Hieraxday, so not then either. But come in any other day and I'll give you a pass. How's that?"

Silk was stunned.

"You know what I mean, right, Patera? Not me. I mean with any of the girls, whoever you want. If you'd like to give her a little something for herself, that's all right. But you don't have to, and there won't be anything to the house." Orchid considered again. "Well, a card in a cart, huh? All right, that's a lay a month for a year." Seeing his expression she added, "Or I can get you a boy if you'd rather have that, but let me know in advance."

Silk shook his head.

"Because if you do, you don't get to see the gods? Isn't that what they say?"

"Yes." Silk nodded. "Echidna forbids it. One may see the gods when they appear in our Sacred Windows. Or one may be blessed by children of the body. But not both."

"Nobody's talking about sprats, Patera."

"I know what we're talking about."

"The gods don't come any more anyhow. Not to Viron, so why not? That last time was when I was—wasn't even born yet."

Silk nodded. "Nor I."

"Then what do you care? You're never going to see one anyway."

Silk smiled ruefully. "We're getting very far from the subject, aren't we?"

"I don't know." Orchid scratched her head and examined her nails. "Maybe. Or maybe not. Did you know that this place used to be a manteion?"

Stunned again, Silk shook his head.

"It did. Or anyhow, some of it did, the back part on Music Street. Only the gods didn't come around very much any more, even if they still did it once in a while back then. So they closed it down, and the ones that owned this house then bought it and tore down the back wall and joined the two together. Maybe that's why, huh? I'll get Orpine to show you around. Some of the old stuff's still back there, and you can have it if there's anything you want."

"That's very kind of you," Silk said.

"I'm a nice person. Ask anybody." Orchid whistled shrilly. "Orpine'll be along in a minute. Anything you want to know, just ask her."

"Thank you, I will. May I leave my sacra here until I require them?" The prospect of separation from his triptych made Silk uneasy. "Will they be safe?"

"Your sack? Better than the fisc. You could leave that box thing, too. Only I've been wondering, you know about the old manteion in back. We call it the playhouse. Could that be why it's happening?"

"I don't know."

"I asked one of the others and he said not. But I kind of

wonder. Maybe the gods don't like some of the stuff we do here."

"They do not," Silk told her.

"You haven't even seen anything, Patera. We're not as bad as you think."

Silk shook his head. "I don't think you bad at all, Orchid, and neither do the gods. If they thought you bad, nothing that you could do would dismay them. They detest all the evil that you do—and all that I do—because they see in us the potential to do good."

"Well, I've been thinking maybe they sent this devil to get even with us." Orchid whistled again. "What's keeping that girl!"

"The gods do not send us devils," Silk told her, "and indeed, they destroy them wherever they meet them, deleting them from Mainframe. That, at least, is the legend. It's in the Writings, and I have them here in my bag. Would you like me to read the passage?" He reached for his glasses.

"No. Just tell me so I can understand it."

"All right." Silk squared his shoulders. "Pas made the whorl, as you know. When it was complete, he invited his queen, their five daughters and their two sons, and a few friends to share it with him. However—"

From the other side of the sun-bright doorway, someone screamed in terror.

Orchid lunged out of her chair with praiseworthy speed. Limping a little and repeating to himself Crane's injunction against running, Silk trailed after her, walking as quickly as he could.

The courtyard was lined with doorways on both floors. As he searched for the source of the disturbance, it seemed to him that whole companies of young women in every possible stage of undress were popping in and out of them, though he paid them little attention.

The dead woman lay halfway up a flight of rickety steps thrown down like a ladder by the sagging gallery above; she was naked, and the fingers of her left hand curled about the hilt of a dagger jutting from her ribs below her left breast. Her head was angled so sharply in Silk's direction that it almost appeared that her neck was broken. He found her oddly contorted face at once horrible and familiar.

Against all his training, he covered that face with his handkerchief before beginning to swing his beads.

It quieted the women somewhat, although the dagger, the wound it had made, and the blood that had so briefly spurted from that wound were still visible.

Orchid shouted, "Who did this? Who stabbed her?" and a puffy-eyed brunette, nearly as naked as the woman sprawled on the steps, drawled, "She did, Orchid—she killed herself. Use your head. Or if you won't, use your eyes."

Kneeling on a blood-spattered step just below the dead woman's head, Silk swung his beads, first forward-and-back, then side-to-side, thus describing the sign of addition. "I convey to you, my daughter, the forgiveness of all the gods. Recall now the words of Pas, who said, 'Do my will, live in peace, multiply, and do not disturb my seal. Thus you shall escape my wrath. Go willingly, and any wrong that you have ever done shall be forgiven.' O my daughter, know that this Pas and all the lesser gods have empowered me to forgive you in their names. And I do forgive you, remitting every crime and wrong. They are expunged." With his beads, Silk traced the sign of subtraction. "You are blessed." Bobbing his head nine times, as the ritual demanded, he traced the sign of addition.

A female voice breathed curses somewhere to his right, blasphemy following obscenity. "Hornbuss Pas shag you Pas whoremaster Pas hornswallow 'Chidna sick-licker Pas . . ." It sounded to Silk as though the speaker did not know what she was saying, and might well be unaware that she was speaking at all.

"I pray you to forgive us, the living," he continued, and once again formed the sign of addition with his beads above the dead woman's handkerchief-shrouded head. "I and many another have wronged you often, my daughter, committing terrible crimes and numerous offences against you. Do not hold them in your heart, but begin the life that follows life in innocence, all these wrongs forgiven." He made the sign of subtraction again.

A statuesque girl spat; her tightly curled hair was the color of ripe raspberries. "What are you doing that for? Can't you see she's stiff? She's dead, and she can't hear a shaggy word you're saying." At the final phrase her voice cracked, and Silk realized that it was she whom he had heard swearing.

He gripped his beads more tightly and bent lower as he reached the effectual point in the liturgy of pardon. The sun beating down upon his neck might have been the burning iron hand of Twice-Headed Pas himself, crushing him to earth while ceaselessly demanding that he perfectly enunciate each hallowed word and execute every sacred rubric faultlessly. "In the name of all the gods, you are forgiven forever, my daughter. I speak here for Great Pas, for Divine Echidna, for Scalding Scylla . . ." Here it was allowable to halt and take a fresh breath, and Silk did so. "For Marvelous Molpe, for Tenebrous Tartaros, for Highest Hierax, for Thoughtful Thelxiepeia, for Fierce Phaea, and for Strong Sphigx. Also for all lesser gods."

Briefly and inexplicably, the glaring sun might almost have been the swinging, smoking lampion in the Cock. Silk whispered, "The Outsider likewise forgives you, my daughter, for I speak here for him, too."

After tracing one final sign of addition, he stood and turned toward the statuesque young woman with the raspberry hair; to his considerable relief, she was clothed. "Bring me something to cover her with, please. Her time in this place is over."

Orchid was questioning the puffy-eyed brunette. "Is this her knife?"

"You ought to know." Fearlessly, the brunette reached beneath the railing to pull the long dagger from the wound. "I don't think so. She'd have showed it to me, most likely, and I've never seen it before."

Crane came down the steps, stooped over the dead woman, and pressed his fingers to her wrist. After a second or two, he squatted and laid an ausculator to her side.

(We acknowledge this state we call death with so much reluctance, Silk thought, not for the first time. Surely it can't be natural to us.)

Withdrawing the dagger had increased the seepage from the wound; under all the shrill hubbub, Silk could hear the dead woman's blood dripping from the steps to the crumbling brick pavement of the courtyard, like the unsteady ticking of a broken clock.

Orchid was peering nearsightedly at the dagger. "It's a man's. A man called Cat." Turning to face the courtyard, she shouted, "Shut up, all of you! Listen to me! Do any of you know a cull named Cat?"

A small, dark girl in a torn chemise edged closer. "I do. He comes here sometimes."

"Was he here last night? How long since you've seen him?"

The girl shook her head. "I'm not sure, Orchid. A month, maybe."

The corpulent woman waddled toward her, holding out the dagger, the younger women parting before her like so many ducklings before a duck. "You know where he lives? Who's he get, usually?"

"No. Me. Orpine sometimes, if I'm busy."

Crane stood up, glanced at Silk and shook his head, and put away his ausculator.

Blood's bellow surprised them all. "What's going on here?" Thick-bodied and a full head taller than most of the women, he strode into the courtyard with something of the air of a general coming onto a battlefield.

When Orchid did not answer, the raspberry-haired girl said wearily, "Orpine's dead. She just killed herself." She had a clean sheet under her arm, neatly folded.

"What for?" Blood demanded.

No one replied. The raspberry-haired girl shook out her sheet and passed a corner up to Crane. Together, they spread the sheet over the dead woman.

Silk put away his beads and went down the steps to the courtyard. Half to himself he muttered, "She didn't—not forever. Not even as long as I."

Orchid turned to look at him. "No, she didn't. Now shut up."

Musk had taken the dagger from her. After scrutinizing it himself, he held it out for Blood's inspection. Orchid explained, "A cully they call Cat comes here sometimes. He must've given it to her, or left it behind in her room."

Blood sneered. "Or she stole it from him."

"My girls don't steal!" As a tower long subverted by a hidden spring collapses, Orchid burst into tears; there was something terrible, Silk felt, in seeing that fat, indurated face contorted like a heartsick child's. Blood slapped her twice, forehand and backhand, without effect, though both blows echoed from the walls of the courtyard.

"Don't do that again," Silk told him. "It won't help her, and it may harm you."

Ignoring him, Blood pointed to the still form beneath the sheet. "Somebody get that out of sight. You there. Chenille. You're plenty big enough. Pick her up and carry her to her room."

The raspberry-haired woman backed away, trembling, the roughed spots on each high cheekbone glaring and unreal.

"May I see that, please?" Deftly, Silk took the dagger from Musk. Its hilt was bleached bone; burned into the bone with a needle and hand-dyed, a scarlet cat strutted with a tiny black mouse in its jaws. The cat's fiery tail circled the hilt. Following the puffy-eyed brunette's example, Silk reached under the railing and retrieved his handkerchief from beneath the sheet. The slender, tapering blade was highly polished, but not engraved. "Nearly new," he muttered. "Not terribly expensive, but not cheap either."

Musk said, "Any fool can see that," and took back the dagger.

"Patera." Blood cleared his throat. "You were here. Probably you saw her do it."

Silk's mind was still on the dagger. "Do what?" he asked.

"Kill herself. Let's get out of this sun." With a hand on Silk's elbow, Blood guided him into the spotted shade of the gallery, displacing a chattering circle of nearly naked women.

"No, I didn't see it," Silk said slowly. "I was inside, talking to Orchid."

"That's too bad. Maybe you want to think about it a little more. Maybe you saw it after all, through a window or something."

Silk shook his head.

"You agree that this was a suicide, though, don't you, Patera? Even if you didn't see it yourself?" Blood's tone made his threat obvious.

Silk leaned back against the spalled shiprock, sparing his broken ankle. "Her hand was still on the knife when I first saw her body."

Blood smiled. "I like that. In that case, Patera, you agree that there's no reason to report this."

"I certainly wouldn't want to if I were in your place." To himself, Silk reluctantly admitted that he felt sure the dead woman had been no suicide, that the law required that her death by violence be reported to the authorities (though he had no illusions about the effort they would expend upon the death of such a woman), and that if he were somehow to find himself in Blood's place he would leave it as rapidly as possible—though neither honor nor morality required him to say any of these things, since saying them would be futile and would unquestionably endanger the manteion. It was all perfectly reasonable and nicely reasoned; but as he surveyed it, he felt a surge of self-contempt.

"I think we understand each other, Patera. There are three or four witnesses I could produce if I needed them—people who saw her do it. But you know how that is."

Silk forced himself to nod his agreement; he had never realized that even passive assent to crime required so much resolution. "I believe so. Three or four of these unhappy young women, you mean. Their testimony would not carry much weight, however; and they would be apt to presume upon your obligation afterward."

Under Musk's direction, a burly man with less hair even than Blood had picked up the dead woman's body, wrapping it in the sheet. Silk saw him carry it to the door beyond the entrance to Orchid's office, which Musk opened for him.

"That's right. I couldn't have put it better myself." Blood lowered his voice. "We've been having way too much trouble here as it is. The Guards have been in here three times in the past month, and they're starting to talk about closing us down. Tonight I'll have to come up with some way to get rid of it."

"To dispose of that poor woman's body, you mean. You know, I've been terribly slow about this, I suppose because these aren't the sort of people I'm accustomed to. She was

Orpine, wasn't she? One of these women mentioned it. She must have had the room next to Orchid's office. Musk and another man have taken her body there, at any rate."

"Yeah, that was Orpine. She used to help out Orchid now and then, running the place." Blood turned away.

Silk watched him stride across the courtyard. Blood had called himself a thief the night before; it struck Silk now that he had been wrong—had been lying, in fact, in order to romanticize what he really did, though he would steal, no doubt, if given an opportunity to do so without risk; he was the sort of person who would consider theft clever, and would be inclined to boast of it.

But the fact was that Blood was simply a tradesman—a tradesman whose trades happened to be forbidden by law, and were inescapably colored by that. That he himself, Patera Silk, did not like such men probably meant only that he did not understand them as well as his own vocation required.

He strove to reorder his thoughts, shifting Blood (and himself as well) out of the criminal category. Blood was a tradesman, or a merchant of sorts; and one of his employees had been killed, almost certainly not by him or even under his direction. Silk recalled the pictured cat on the dagger; it reminded him of the engraving on the little needler, and he took it out to re-examine. There were golden hyacinths on each ivory grip because it had been made for a woman called Hyacinth.

He dropped it back into his pocket.

Blood's name . . . If the dagger had been made for him, the picture on its hilt would have shown blood, presumably: a bloody dagger of the same design, perhaps, or something of that sort. The cat had held a mouse in its jaws, and mice thus caught by cats bled, of course; but he could recall no blood in the picture, and the captive mouse had been quite small. He was no artist, but after putting himself in the place of the one who had drawn and tinted that picture, he decided that the mouse had been included mostly to indicate that the cat was in fact a cat, and not some other cat-like animal, a panther for example. The mouse had been a kind of badge, in other words.

The cat itself had been scarlet, but hardly with blood; even a large mouse would not have bled as much as that, and the cat had presumably been tinted to indicate that it was somehow burning. Its upright tail had actually been tipped with fire.

He took a step away from the wall and was punished by a flash of pain. On one knee, he pulled down his stocking and unwound Crane's wrapping, then flogged the guiltless wall he had just deserted.

When the wrapping was back in place, he went into the room next to Orchid's cramped office. It was larger than he had expected, and its furnishings were by no means devoid of taste. After glancing at a shattered hand mirror and a blue dressing gown he picked up from the floor, he uncovered the dead woman's face.

He found Blood in a private supper room with Musk and the burly man who had carried Orpine's body, discussing the advisability of keeping the yellow house closed that night.

Uninvited, Silk pulled up a chair and sat down. "May I interrupt? I have a question and a suggestion. Neither one should take long."

Musk gave him an icy stare.

Blood said, "They'd better not."

"The question first. What's become of Doctor Crane? He was out there with us a moment ago, but when I looked for him after you left I couldn't find him."

When Blood did not answer, the burly man said, "He's

checking out the girls so they don't give anybody anything he hasn't got already. You know what I mean, Patera?"

Silk nodded. "I do indeed. But where does he do it? Is there some sort of infirmary—"

"He goes to their rooms. They got to undress and wait in their rooms until he gets there. When he's through with them, they can go out if they want to."

"I see." Silk stroked his cheek, his eyes thoughtful.

"If you're looking for him, he's probably upstairs. He always does the upstairs first."

"Fine," Blood said impatiently. "Crane's gone back to work. Why shouldn't he? You'd better do the same, Patera. I still want this place exorcised, and in fact it needs it now more than ever. Get busy."

"I am about my work," Silk told him. "This is it, you see, or at least it's a part of it, and I believe that I can help you. You spoke of disposing of that poor girl's—of Orpine's—body. I suggest that we bury it."

Blood shrugged. "I'll see about doing something—she won't be found, and she won't be missed. Don't worry about it."

"I mean that we should inter it as other women's bodies are interred," Silk explained patiently. "There must be a memorial sacrifice for her at my manteion first, of course. Tomorrow's Scylsday, and I can combine the memorial service with our weekly Scylsday sacrifice. We've a man in the neighborhood who has a decent wagon. We've used him before. If none of these women are willing to wash and dress their friend's body, I can provide one who will take care of that as well."

Grinning, Blood thumped Silk on the arm. "And if some shaggy hoppy sticks his nose in, why we didn't do anything irregular. We had an augur and a funeral, and buried the poor girl in respectable fashion—he's intruding on our grief. You're a real help, Patera. When can you get your man here?"

"As soon as I return to my manteion, I suppose, which will be as soon as I've exorcised this house."

Blood shook his head. "I want to get her out of here. What about that sibyl I talked to yesterday? Couldn't she get him?"

Silk nodded.

"Good." Blood turned to the handsome young man beside him. "Musk, go down to the manteion on Sun Street and ask for Maytera Marble—"

Silk interrupted. "She'll probably be in the cenoby. The front door's on Silver Street, or you could go through the garden and knock at the back."

"And tell her there's going to be a funeral tomorrow. Have her get this man with the wagon for you. What's his name, Patera?"

"Loach."

"Get Loach and his wagon, or if he's not available, get somebody else. You don't know what happened to Orpine. A doctor's looked at her, and she's dead, and Patera here is going to take care of the funeral for us, and that's all you know. Get the woman, too. I don't think any of these sluts could face up to it."

"Moorgrass," Silk put in.

"Get her. You and the woman ride in the wagon so you can show this cully Loach where it is. If the woman has to have anything to work with, see that she brings it with her. Now get going."

Musk nodded and hurried away.

"Meantime you can get back to your exorcism, Patera. Have you started yet?"

"No. I'd hardly arrived when this happened, and I want to find out a great deal more about the manifestations they have experienced here." Silk paused, stroking his cheek. "I said that I'd just arrived, and that is true; but I've had time enough to make one mistake already. I told Orchid that I didn't care what the devils—or perhaps I should say *the devil*, because she spoke as though there were only one— had been up to. I said it because it was what they taught us to say in the schola, but I believe it may be an error in this case. I should speak with Orchid again."

The burly man grunted. "I can tell you. Mostly it's breakin' mirrors."

"Really?" Silk leaned forward. "I would never have guessed it. What else?"

"Rippin' up the girls' clothes."

The burly man looked toward Blood, who said, "Sometimes they're not as friendly as we'd like them to be to the bucks. The girls aren't, I mean. A couple times one's talked crazy, and naturally the buck didn't like it. Maybe it was just nerves, but the girls got hurt."

"And we don't like that," the burly man said. "I got both those culls pretty good, but it's bad for business."

"You have no idea what may be doing this?"

"Devils. That's what everybody says." The burly man looked toward Blood again. "Jefe?"

"Ask Orchid," Blood told Silk. "She'll know. I only know what she tells me, and if an exorcism makes everybody feel better . . ." He shrugged.

Silk rose. "I'll speak to Orchid if I can. I realize she's upset, but I may be able to console her. That, too, is a part of my work. Eventually, I'd like a talk with Chenille as well. That's the tall woman with the fiery hair, isn't it? Chenille?"

Blood nodded. "She's probably gone by now, but she'll be back around dinner. Orchid's got a walk-up upstairs over the big room out front."

Chenille opened the door to Orchid's rooms and showed Silk in. Still wearing the pink peignoir, Orchid was sitting on a wide green-velvet couch in the big sellaria, her hard, heavy face as composed as it had been when they had talked in the cramped office downstairs.

Chenille waved toward a chair. "Have a seat, Patera." She herself sat down next to Orchid and put her arm around her shoulders. "He says Blood sent him up to talk to us. I said all right, but he'll probably come back later if you'd rather."

"I'm fine," Orchid told her.

Looking at her, Silk could believe it; Chenille herself seemed more in need of solace.

"What do you want, Patera?" Orchid's voice was harsher than he remembered. "If you're here to tell me how she's gone to Mainframe and all that, save it till later. If you still want somebody to show you around my place, Chenille can do it."

There was a glass on the wall to the left of the couch. Silk was watching it nervously, but no floating face had yet appeared. "I'd like to speak with you in private for a few minutes, that's all."

To Chenille he added, "I was going to say that it would give you a chance to get dressed—so many of you here are not—but I see that you're dressed already."

"Go out," Orchid said. And then, "It was nice of you to worry about me, Chenille. I won't forget this."

The tall girl rose, smoothing her skirt. "I was going to look for a new gown, before this happened."

"I have to speak to you, too," Silk told her, "and this should only take a few minutes. You can wait for me, if you prefer. Otherwise, I would appreciate it very much if you came to my manteion this evening."

"I'll be in my room."

Silk nodded. "That will be better. Please pardon me for not rising; I injured my ankle last night." He watched

Chenille as she went out, waiting until she had closed the door behind her.

"Nice-looking, isn't she?" Orchid said. "Only she'd bring in more if she wasn't so tall. Maybe you like them that way. Or is it the hips?"

"What I like hardly matters."

"Good hips, nice waist for a girl as big as she is, and the biggest boobs in the place. Sure you won't change your mind?"

Silk shook his head. "I'm surprised you didn't mention her kind disposition. There must be a great deal of good in her, or she wouldn't have come here to comfort you."

Orchid stood up. "You want a drink, Patera? I've got wine and whatnot in the cabinet here."

"No, thank you."

"I do." Orchid opened the cabinet and filled a small goblet with straw-colored brandy.

"She seemed quite depressed," Silk ventured. "She must have been a close friend of Orpine's."

"Chenille's a real rust bucket, to hand you the lily, Patera, and they're always pretty far down anytime they're straight."

Silk snapped his fingers. "I knew I'd heard that name before."

Orchid resumed her seat, swirled her brandy, inhaled its aroma, and balanced the goblet precariously on the arm of the couch. "Somebody told you about her, huh?"

"A man I know happened to mention her, that's all. It doesn't matter." He waved the question away. "Aren't you going to drink that?" After he had spoken, he realized that Blood had asked the same question of him the previous night.

Orchid shook her head. "I don't drink until the last buck's gone. That's my rule, and I'm going to stick to it, even today. I just want to know it's there. Did you come here to talk about Chen, Patera?"

"No. Can we be overheard here? I ask for your sake, Orchid, not for my own."

She shook her head again.

"I've heard that houses like this often have listening devices."

"Not this one. And if it did, I wouldn't have any in here."

Silk indicated the glass. "The monitor doesn't have to appear to overhear what is said in a room, or so one's given me to understand. Does the monitor of that glass report to you alone?"

Orchid had the brandy goblet again, swirling the straw-colored fluid until it climbed the goblet to the rim. "That glass has never worked for as long as I've owned this house, Patera. I wish it did."

"I see." Silk limped across the room to the glass and clapped his hands loudly. The room's lights brightened, but no monitor answered his summons. "We have a glass like this in Patera Pike's bedroom—I mean in the room that he once occupied. I should try to sell it. I would think that even an inoperable glass must be worth something."

"What is it you want with me, Patera?"

Silk returned to his chair. "What I really want is to find some more tactful way of saying this. I haven't found it. Orpine was your daughter, wasn't she?"

Orchid shook her head.

"Are you going to deny her even in death?"

He had not known what to expect: tears, or hysteria, or nothing—and had felt himself ready for them all. But now Orchid's face appeared to be coming apart, to be losing all cohesion, as if her mouth and her bruised and swollen cheeks and her hard hazel eyes no longer obeyed a common will. He wanted her to hide that terrible face in her hands; she did not, and he turned his own away.

There was a window on the other side of the couch. He went to it, parted its heavy drapes, and threw it open. It overlooked Lamp Street, and though he would have called the day hot, the breeze that entered Orchid's sellaria seemed cool and fresh.

"How did you know?" Orchid asked.

He limped back to his chair. "That's what's wrong with this place, not enough open windows. Or one thing, anyhow." Wanting to blow his nose, he took out his handkerchief, saw Orpine's blood on it just in time, and put it away hastily.

"How did you know, Patera?"

"Don't any of the others know? Or at least guess?"

Orchid's face was still out of control, afflicted with odd, almost spastic twitchings. "Some of them have probably thought about it. I don't think she ever told anybody, and I didn't treat her any better than the rest." Orchid gulped air. "Worse, whenever there was any difference. I made her help me, and I was always yelling at her."

"I'm not going to ask you how this happened; it's none of my affair."

"Thanks, Patera." Orchid sounded as though she meant it. "Her father took her. I couldn't have, not then. But he said—he said—"

"You don't have to tell me," Silk repeated.

She had not heard. "Then I found her on the street, you know? She was thirteen, only she said fifteen and I believed her. I didn't know it was her." Orchid laughed, and her laughter was worse than tears.

"There's really no need for you to torment yourself like this."

"I'm not. I've been wanting to tell somebody about it ever since Sphigx was a cub. You already know, so it can't do any harm. Besides, she's—she's—"

"Gone," Silk supplied.

Orchid shook her head. "Dead. The only one alive, and I'll never have any more now. You know how places like this work, Patera?"

"No, and I suppose I should."

"It's pretty much like a boarding house. Some places, the girls are pretty much like in the Alambrera. They don't hardly ever let them out, and they take all their money. I was in a place like that once for almost two years."

"I'm glad that you escaped."

Orchid shook her head again. "I didn't. I got sick and they kicked me out—it was the best thing that ever happened to me. What I wanted to say, Patera, is I'm not like that here. My girls rent their rooms, and they can go anytime. About the only thing they can't do is bring in a buck without his paying. Are you with me?"

"I'm not sure I am," Silk admitted.

"Like if they meet him outside. If they bring him back here, he has to pay the house. So do those that come here looking. Tonight, we'll have maybe fifty or a hundred come. They pay the house, and then we show them all the girls that aren't busy, downstairs in the big room."

"Suppose that I were to come," Silk said slowly. "Not dressed as I am now, but in ordinary clothes. And I wanted a particular woman."

"Chenille."

Silk shook his head. "Another one."

"How about Poppy? Little girl, pretty dark."

"All right," Silk said. "Suppose I wanted Poppy, but she didn't want to take me to her room?"

"Then she wouldn't have to," Orchid said virtuously, "and you'd have to pick somebody else. Only if she did that very often, I'd kick her out."

"I see."

"Only she wouldn't, Patera. Not to you. She'd jump at you. Any of these girls would."

Orchid smiled, and Silk, confronted by the effect of her bruises, wanted to strike Blood. Hyacinth's azoth was under his tunic—he thrust the thought away.

Orchid had seen and misinterpreted his expression; her smile vanished. "I didn't get to finish telling you about Orpine, Patera. All right if I go on about her?"

Silk said, "Certainly, if you wish."

"I found her on the street, like I told you. That's something I do sometimes, go around looking for somebody if I've got an empty room. She said her name was Pine—you don't hardly ever get a straight name out of them—and she was fifteen, and it never hit me. It just didn't."

"I understand," Silk said.

"Somebody dusted her dial, you know what I mean? So I said, listen, lots of girls live with me, and nobody lays a finger on them. You come along, and we'll give you a good hot meal, free, and you'll see. So she said she didn't have the rent money, like they always do, and I said I'd trust her for the first month. That's what I always say.

"After she'd been here nearly a year, she ducked out of the big room. I said what's wrong, and she said her father had come in and he'd made her do certain things for him when she was little, and that was why she'd run out on him. You know what I mean, Patera?"

Silk nodded, his fists clenched.

"She told me his name, and I went out and looked at him again, and it was him. So then I knew who she was, and by and by I told her all about it." Orchid smiled; it seemed strange to Silk that the identical word should indicate her earlier expression as well.

"I'm glad I did it now. Real glad. I told her not to expect any favors, and I didn't give her any. Or at least, not very often. What I did, though—what I did—"

Silk waited patiently, his eyes averted.

"What I did was start having cake on the birthdays, so we

could have it on hers. And I called her Orpine instead of Pine, and pretty soon everybody did." Orchid daubed at her eyes with the hem of the pink peignoir. "All right, that's it. Who told you?"

"Your faces, to begin with."

Orchid nodded. "She was beautiful. Everybody said so."

"Not when I saw her, because there was something in her face that didn't belong there. Still it struck me that her face was a younger version of your own, although that could have been coincidence or my imagination. A moment later I heard her name—Orpine. It sounds a great deal like yours, and it seemed to me that it was such a name as a woman named Orchid might choose, especially if she had lost an earlier daughter. Did you? You don't have to tell me about it."

Orchid nodded.

"Because orpines, which only sound like orchids, have another name. Country people call them live-forevers; and when I thought of that other name, I said, more or less to myself, that she had not; and you agreed. Then when Blood suggested that she might have stolen the dagger that killed her, you burst into tears and I knew. But to tell you the truth, I was already nearly certain."

Orchid nodded slowly. "Thanks, Patera. Is that all? I'd like to be alone for a little while."

Silk rose. "I understand. I wouldn't have disturbed you if I hadn't wanted to let you know that Blood's agreed that your daughter should be buried with the rites of the Chapter. Her body will be washed and dressed—laid out, as the people who do it say—and carried to my manteion, on Sun Street. We'll hold her service in the morning."

Orchid stared at him incredulously. "Blood's paying for this?"

"No." Silk actually had not considered the matter of expenses, though he knew only too well that some of those connected with the final offices of the dead could not be avoided. His mind whirled before he recalled Blood's two cards, which he had set aside for the Scylsday sacrifice in any event. "Or rather, yes. Blood gave me—gave my mante-ion, I should say, a generous gift earlier. We'll use that."

"No, not Blood." Orchid rose heavily. *"I'll* pay it, Patera. How much?"

Silk compelled himself to be scrupulously honest. "I should tell you that we often bury the poor, and sometimes they have no money at all. The generous gods have always seen to it—"

"I'm not poor!" Orchid flushed an angry red. "I been pretty flat sometimes, sure. Hasn't everybody? But I'm not flat now, and this's my sprat. The other girl, I had to—Oh, shag you, you shaggy butcher! How much for a good one?"

Here was opportunity. Not merely to save the manteion the cost of Orpine's burial, but to pay for earlier graves bought but never paid for; Silk jettisoned his scruples to seize the moment. "If it's really not inconvenient, twenty cards?"

"Let's go into the bedroom, Patera. That's where the book is. Come on."

She had opened the door and vanished into the next room before he could protest. Through the doorway he could see a rumpled bed, a cluttered vanity table, and a chaise longue half buried in gowns.

"Come on in." Orchid laughed, and this time there was real merriment in the sound. "I bet you've never been in a woman's bedroom before, have you?"

"Once or twice." Hesitantly, Silk stepped through the doorway, looking twice at the bed to assure himself that no one lay dying there. Presumably Orchid thought of it as a place for rest and lust, and possibly even for love. Silk could only too easily imagine his next visit, in ten years or twenty. All beds became deathbeds at last.

"Your mama's. You've gone into your mama's bedroom, I bet." Orchid plumped herself down before the vanity table, swept a dozen colored bottles and jars aside, and elevated an ormolu inkstand to the place of honor before her.

"Oh, yes. Many times."

"And looked through her things when she was out of the house. I know how you young bucks do." There were twenty bedraggled peacock quills at least wilting in the rings of the ormolu inkstand. Orchid selected one, then wrinkled her nose at it.

"I can sharpen that for you, if you like." Silk got out his pen case.

"Would you? Thanks." Revolving on the vanity stool, she handed the peacock quill to him. "Did you ever try on her underwear?"

Silk looked up from the quill, surprised. "No, I never even thought of it. I did open a drawer once and peep into it, though. I felt so bad about it that I told her the next day. Do you have something to catch the shavings?"

"Don't worry about them. You had a nice mama, huh? Is she still alive?"

Silk shook his head. "Would you prefer a broad nib?" Orchid did not reply, and he, contemplating the splayed and frowzy one before him, decided to give her one anyway. A broad nib used more ink, but she would not mind that; and broad nibs lasted longer.

"Mine died when I was little. I guess she was nice, but I really don't remember her very well. When somebody's dead, Patera, can they come back and see people they care about, if they want to?"

"It depends on what is meant by *see.*" With the slender blade of the long-handled penknife, Silk sliced yet another whitish sliver from the nib. He was accustomed to goose and crow quills; this was larger than either.

"Talk to them. Visit with them a while, or just let them see you."

"No," Silk said.

"Just no? Why not?"

"Hierax forbids it." He returned the quill to her and snapped his pen case shut. "If he did not, the living would live at the direction of the dead, repeating their mistakes again and again."

"I used to wonder why she never came to see me," Orchid said. "You know, I haven't thought about that in years, and now I'll think about Orpine, hoping that Hierax will let her out once or twice so I can see her again. Have a seat there on the bed, Patera. You're making me jittery."

Reluctantly, Silk smoothed the canary-colored sheet and sat down.

"A minute ago, you said twenty cards. That's about as cheap as they come, I bet."

"It would be modest," Silk admitted, "but certainly not contemptible."

"All right, what about fifty? What would she get for that much?"

"Gods!" He considered. "I can't be absolutely sure. A better sacrifice and a much better casket. Flowers. A formal bier with draperies. Perhaps a—"

"I'll make it a hundred," Orchid announced. "It will make me feel better. A hundred cards, and everything the best." Orchid plunged her quill into the inkwell.

Silk opened his mouth, closed it again, and put his pen case away.

"And you can say that I was her mother. I want you to say it. What do you call that thing where they stand up and talk in the manteion?"

"The ambion," Silk said.

"Right. I never told them here, because I knew—we both knew—what sort of things the other girls would say about her, and me too, behind our backs. You tell them tomorrow. From the ambion. And put it on her stone."

Silk nodded. "I will."

With florid sweeps of her quill, Orchid was writing the draft. "Tomorrow, right? When'll it be?"

"I had thought at eleven."

"I'll be there, Patera." Orchid's face hardened. "We all will."

Silk was still shaking his head as he closed Orchid's door behind him. Chenille was waiting in the hall outside; he wondered whether she had been eavesdropping, and if so how much she had heard.

She said, "You wanted to talk to me?"

"Not here."

"I waited in my room. You never came, so I came over here to see what was up."

"Of course." Orchid's draft for a hundred cards was still in his hand; he folded it once and thrust it into the the pocket of his robe. "I told you I'd be there in a few minutes, didn't I? We were a great deal longer than that, I'm afraid. I can only apologize."

"You still want to talk in my room?"

Silk hesitated, then nodded. "We must speak privately, and I'd like to see where it is."

Chapter 11

SUMMONED

"What Orchid's got used to be for the owner and his wife," Chenille explained. "Then their sprats had rooms close to theirs, then upper servants, then maids, I guess. I'm about halfway on the inside. That's not so bad."

Turning left, Silk followed her down the musty hallway.

"Half look out on the court like mine does. That's not as good as it sounds, because they have big parties in there sometimes and it gets pretty noisy unless you stay till the end, and usually I don't. You take those drunks up to your room and they get sick—then you never get the smell out. Maybe you think it's gone, but wait for a rainy night."

They turned the corner.

"Sometimes they chase the girls along the gangways and make lots of noise. But the outside rooms on this side have windows on the alley. There's not much light, and it smells bad."

"I see," Silk said.

"So that's not so good either, and they have to have bars on their windows. I'd rather hang on to what I've got." Chenille halted, pulled a key on a string from between ample breasts, and opened a door.

"Are the rooms beyond yours vacant?"

"Huh-uh. I don't think there's an empty room in the

place. She's been turning them away for the last month or so. I've got a girlfriend that would like to move in, and I've got to tell her as soon as somebody goes."

"Perhaps she might occupy Orpine's room." Chenille's was less than half the size of Orchid's bedroom, with most of its floorspace taken up by an oversized bed. There were chests along the wall, and an old wardrobe to which a hasp and padlock had been added.

"Yeah. Maybe. I'll tell her. You want me to leave the door open?"

"I doubt that it would be wise."

"All right." She closed it. "I won't lock us in. I don't lock when there's a man in here, it's not a good idea. You want to sit on the bed with me?"

Silk shook his head.

"Suit yourself." She sat down, and he lowered himself gratefully onto one of the chests, the lioness-headed stick clamped between his knees.

"All right, what is it?"

Silk glanced toward the open window. "I should imagine it would be easy for someone to stand there on the gallery, just out of sight. It would be prudent for you to make sure no one is."

"Look here." She aimed a finger at him. "I don't owe you one single thing, and you're not paying me, not even a couple bits. Orpine was kind of a friend of mine, we didn't fight much, anyhow, and I thought it was nice, what you did for her, so when you said you wanted to talk to me, I said fine. But I've got things to do, and I'll have to come back here tonight and sweat it like a sow. So talk, and I better like what you're going to say."

"What would you do if you didn't, Chenille?" Silk asked mildly. "Stab me? I don't think so; you've no dagger now."

Her brightly painted mouth fell open then clamped shut again.

Silk leaned back against the wall. "It wasn't terribly obscure. If the Civil Guard had been notified, as I suppose it should have been, I'm certain they would have understood what happened at once. It took me a minute or two, but then I know very little about such things."

Her eyes blazed. "She did it herself! You saw it. She stabbed herself." Chenille gestured toward her own waist.

"I saw her hand on the hilt of your dagger, certainly. Did you put it there? Or was it only that she was trying to pull it out when she died?"

"You can't prove anything!"

Silk sighed. "Please don't be foolish. How old are you? Honestly now."

"What does that have to do with anything?"

"Nothing, I suppose. It's only that you make me feel very old and wise, just as the children at our palaestra do. You're not much older than some of them, I believe."

For several seconds Chenille gnawed her lip. At last she said, "Nineteen. That's the lily word, too, or anyhow I think it is. As well as I can figure, I'm about nineteen. I'm older than a lot of the girls here."

"I'm twenty-three," Silk told her. "By the way, may I ask you to call me Patera? It will help me to remember who I am. What I am, if you prefer."

Chenille shook her head. "You think I'm some cank chit you can get to suck any pap you want to, don't you? Well, listen, I know a lot you never even dream about. I didn't stick Orpine. By Sphigx, I didn't! And you can't prove I did, either. What're you after, anyhow?"

"Fundamentally I'm after you. I want to help you, if I can. All the gods—the Outsider knows that someone should have, long ago."

"Some help!"

Silk raised his shoulders and let them drop. "Little help

so far, indeed; but we've hardly begun. You say that you know much more than I. Can you read?"

Chenille shook her head, her lips tight.

"You see, although you know a great deal that I do not—I'm not denying that at all—what it comes down to is that we know different things. You are wise enough to swear falsely by Sphigx, for example; you know that nothing will happen to you if you do that, and I'm beginning to feel it's something I should learn, too. Yesterday morning I wouldn't have dared to do it. Indeed, I would hardly dare now."

"I wasn't lying!"

"Of course you were." Silk laid Blood's stick across his knees and studied the lioness's head for a moment. "You said that I couldn't prove what I say. In one sense, you're quite correct. I couldn't prove my accusation in a court of law, assuming that you were a woman of wealth and position. You're not, but then I have no intention of making my case in any such court. I could convict you to Orchid or Blood easily, however. I'd add that you've admitted your guilt to me, as in fact you have now. Orchid would have the bald man who seems to live here beat you, I suppose, and force you to leave. I won't try to guess what Blood might do. Nothing, perhaps."

The raspberry-haired girl, still seated on the bed, would not meet his eyes.

"I could convince the Civil Guard, also, if I had to. It would be easy, Chenille, because no one cares about you. Very likely no one ever has, and that's why you're here now, living as you do in this house."

"I'm here because the money's good," she said.

"It wouldn't be. Not any longer. The big, bald man—I never learned his name—would knock out a tooth or two, I imagine. What Musk might do if Blood allowed him a free hand I prefer not to speculate on. I don't like him, and it may be that I'm prejudiced. You know him much better, I'm sure."

The girl on the bed made a slight, almost inaudible sound.

"You don't cry easily, do you?"

She shook her head.

"I do." Silk smiled and shrugged again. "Another of my all too numerous faults. I've been close to tears since I first set foot in this place, and the pain in my ankle is no help, I'm afraid. Will you excuse me?"

He pushed down his black stocking and took off Crane's wrapping. It was warm still to his touch, but he lashed the floor with it and replaced it. "Shall I explain to you what happened, or would you prefer to tell me?"

"I'm not going to tell you anything."

"I hope to change your mind about that. It's necessary that you tell me a great deal, eventually." Silk paused to collect his thoughts. "Very well, then. This unhappy house has been plagued by a certain devil. We'll call her that for the present at least, though I believe that I could name her. As I understand it, several people have been possessed at one time or another. Did they all live here, by the way? Or were patrons involved as well? Nobody's talked about that, if some were."

"Only girls."

"I see. What about Orchid? Has she been possessed? She didn't mention it."

Chenille shook her head again.

"Orpine? Was she one of them?"

There was no reply. Silk asked again, with slightly more emphasis, *"Orpine?"*

The door opened, and Crane looked in. "There you are! They said you were still around somewhere. How's your ankle?"

"Quite painful," Silk told him. "The wrapping you lent me helped a great deal at first, but—"

Crane had crouched to touch it. "Good and hot. You're walking too much. Didn't I tell you to stay off your feet?"

"I have," Silk said stiffly, "insofar as possible."

"Well, try harder. As the pain gets worse you will anyhow. How's the exorcism coming?"

"I haven't begun. I'm going to shrive Chenille, and that's far more important."

Looking at Crane, Chenille shook her head.

"She doesn't know it yet, but I am," Silk declared.

"I see. Well, I'd better leave you alone and let you do it." The little physician left, closing the door behind him.

"You were asking about Orpine," Chenille said. "No, she was never possessed that I know of."

"Let's not change the subject so quickly," Silk said. "Will you tell me why that doctor takes such an interest in you?"

"He doesn't."

Silk made a derisive noise. "Come now. He obviously does. Do you think I believe he came here to inquire about my leg? He came here looking for you. No one but Orchid could have told him I was here, and I left her only a few moments ago; almost the last thing she said to me was that she wanted to be alone. I just hope that Crane's interest is a friendly one. You need friends."

"He's my doctor, that's all."

"No," Silk said. "He is indeed your doctor, but that's not all. When Orchid and I heard someone scream and went out into the courtyard, you were fully dressed. It was very noticeable, because you were the only woman present who was."

"I was going out!"

"Yes, precisely. You were going out, and thus dressed, which I found a great relief—sneer if you like. I didn't begin, of course, by asking myself why you were dressed, but why the others weren't; and the answers were harmless and straightforward enough. They'd been up late the previous night. Furthermore, they expected to be examined by Crane, who would make them disrobe in any event, so there was no reason for them to dress until he'd left.

"Crane and I had arrived together just a few minutes earlier, yet you were fully dressed, which was why I noticed you and asked you to bring something to cover poor Orpine's body. The obvious inference is that you had been examined already; and if so, you must certainly have been first. It seemed possible that Crane had begun at the far end of the corridor, but he didn't—this room is only halfway to the old manteion at the back of the house. Why did he take you first?"

"I don't know," Chenille said. "I didn't even know I was. I was waiting for him, and he came in. If nothing's wrong, it only takes a second or two."

"He sells you rust, doesn't he?"

Surprised, Chenille laughed.

"I see I'm wrong—so much for logic. But Crane has rust; he mentioned it to me this morning as something that he could have given me to make me feel better. Orchid and a friend who knows you have both told me you use it, and neither has reason to lie. Furthermore, your behavior when you encountered Orpine confirms it."

Chenille appeared about to speak, and Silk waited for her to do so while silence collected in the stuffy room. At last she said, "I'll level with you, Patera. If I give you the lily word, will you believe me?"

"If you tell me the truth? Yes, certainly."

"All right. Crane doesn't sell me, or anybody, rust. Blood would have his tripes if he did. If you want it, you're supposed to buy it from Orchid. But some girls buy it outside sometimes. I do myself, once in a while. Don't tell them."

"I won't," Silk assured her.

"Only you're dead right, Crane's got it, and sometimes he gives me some, like today. We're friends, you know what I mean? I've done him a few favors and I don't charge him. So he looks at me first, and sometimes he gives me a little present."

"Thank you," Silk said. "And thank you for calling me Patera. I noticed and appreciated that, believe me. Do you want to tell me about Orpine now?"

Chenille shook her head stubbornly.

"Very well, then. You said that Orpine had never been possessed, but that was mendacious —she was possessed at the time of her death, in fact." The moment had come, Silk felt, to stretch the truth in a good cause. "Did you really think that I, an anointed augur, could view her body and not realize that? When Crane had gone you took some of the rust he'd given you, dressed, and left your room by that other door, stepping out onto the gallery, which you call the gangway." Silk paused, inviting contradiction.

"I don't know where you had your dagger, but last year we found that one of the girls at our school had a dagger strapped to her thigh. At any rate, while you were coming down those wooden steps, you came face-to-face with Orpine, possessed. If you hadn't taken the rust Crane gave you, you would probably have screamed and fled; but rust makes people bold and violent. That was how I hurt my ankle last night, as it happens; I encountered a woman who used rust.

"In spite of the rust, Orpine's appearance must have horrified you; you realized you were confronting the devil all of you have come to fear, and your only thought was to kill her. You drew your dagger and stabbed her once, just below the ribs with the blade angled up."

"She said I was beautiful," Chenille whispered. "She tried to touch me, to stroke my face. It wasn't Orpine— I might have knifed Orpine, but not for that. I backed away.

She kept coming, and I knifed her. I knifed the devil, and then it was Orpine lying there dead."

Silk nodded. "I understand."

"You figured out my dagger, didn't you? I didn't think of it until it was too late."

"The picture representing your name, you mean. Yes, I did. I had been thinking about Orpine's name ever since I'd heard it. There's no point in going into that here, but I had. Crane gave you the dagger, isn't that right? You said a moment ago that he occasionally makes you a present. Your dagger must have been one of them."

"You think he gave it to me to get me into trouble," Chenille said. "It wasn't like that at all."

"What was it like?"

"One of the other girls had one. She has, most of us have—do you really care about all this?"

"Yes," Silk told her. "I do."

"So she went out that night. She was going to meet him someplace to eat, I guess, only a couple of culls jumped her and tried to pull her down. She plucked, and cut them both. That's what she says. Then she beat the hoof, only she'd got blood on her.

"So I wanted to get one for when I go out, but I don't know much about them, so I asked Crane where I could get a good one, where they wouldn't cheat me. He said he didn't know either, but he'd find out from Musk, because Musk knows all about knives and the rest of it, so next time he brought me that one. He'd got it specially made for me, or anyhow the picture put on."

"I see."

"Do you know, Patera, I'd never even seen chenille, not to know it was my flower anyway, till he brought me a bouquet for my room last spring? And I love it—that's when I did my hair this color. He said sometimes they call it burning cattail. We laugh about it, so when I asked he gave me the dagger. Bucks buy dells things like that pretty often, to show they trust her not to do anything."

"Is Doctor Crane the friend you mentioned?"

"No. That's somebody younger. Don't make me tell you who, unless you want to get me hurt." Chenille fell silent, tight-lipped. "That's abram. This's going to hurt me a lot more, isn't it? But if I don't tell, he might help me if he can."

"Then I won't ask you again," Silk said. "And I'm not going to tell Orchid or Blood, unless I must to save someone else. If the Guard were investigating, I suppose I'd have to tell the officer in charge, but I believe it might be a far worse injustice to turn you over to Blood than to permit you to go unpunished. Since that's the case, I'll let you go unpunished, or almost unpunished, if you'll do as I ask. Orpine's service will take place at eleven tomorrow, at my manteion on Sun Street. Orchid's going to demand that all of you to attend it, and doubtless many of you will. I want you to be among those who do."

Chenille nodded. "Yeah. Sure, Patera."

"And while the service is in progress, I want you to pray for Orpine and Orchid, as well as for yourself. Will you do that as well?"

"To Hierax? All right, Patera, if you'll tell me what to say."

Silk gripped Blood's walking stick, flexing it absently between his hands. "Hierax is indeed the god of death and the caldé of the dead, and as such is the most appropriate object of worship at any such service. It will be Scylsday, however, and thus our sacrifice cannot be his alone."

"Uh-huh. That's about the only prayer I know—what they call her short litany. Will that be all right?"

Silk laid aside the stick and leaned toward Chenille, his decision made. "There is one more god to whom I wish you to pray—a very powerful one who may be able to help you,

as well as Orchid and poor Orpine. He is called the Outsider. Do you know anything about him?"

She shook her head. "Except for Pas and Echidna, and
the days and months, I don't even know their names."

"Then you must open your heart to him tomorrow," Silk
told her, "praying as you've never prayed before. Praise
him for his kindness toward me, and tell him how badly
you—how badly all of us in this quarter need his help. If
you do that, and your prayers are heartfelt and truthful, it
won't matter what you say."

"The Outsider. All right."

"Now I'm going to shrive you, removing your guilt in the
matter of Orpine's death and any other wrongs that you
have done. Kneel here. You don't have to look at me."

Half the abandoned manteion had been converted into a
small theater. "The old Window's still back there," Chenille explained, pointing. "It's the back of the stage, sort
of, only we always keep a drop in front of it. There's four
or five drops, I think. Anyhow, we go in back of the Window
to towel off and powder, and there's a lot of hoses on the
floor and hanging down back there."

Silk was momentarily puzzled until he realized that the
"hoses" were in actuality sacred cables. "I understand," he
said, "but what you describe could be dangerous. Has anyone been hurt?"

"A dell fell off the stage and broke her arm once, but she
was pretty full."

"The powers of Pas must indeed have departed from this
place. And no wonder. Very well." He put his bag and the
triptych on seats. "Thank you, Chenille. You may go out
now if you wish, although I would prefer that you remain
to take part in the exorcism."

"If you want me I'll stay, Patera. All right if I grab something to eat?"

"Certainly."

He watched her go, then shut the door to the courtyard behind her. Her mention of food had reminded him not only that he had given the cheese he had intended for his lunch to the bird, but of his fried tomatoes. No doubt Chenille would go to the pastry shop across the street. He shrugged and opened his bag, resolved to divert his mind from food.

There seemed to be a kitchen in the house, however; if Blood had not yet eaten, it was quite possible that he would invite him to lunch when the exorcism had been concluded. How long had it been since he had sat beneath the fig tree, watching Maytera Rose consume fresh rolls? Several hours, surely, but he had failed to share his breakfast with her; he was justly punished.

"I will not eat," he muttered to himself as he unpacked the glass lamps and the little flask of oil, "until someone invites me to a meal; then and only then shall I be free of this vow. Strong Sphigx, hardship is yours! Hear me now."

Perhaps Orchid would wish to speak to him again about the arrangements for tomorrow; judging from her appearance (and thus, as he reminded himself, very possibly unfairly) Orchid ate often and well. She might easily fancy a bowl of grapes or a platter of peach fritters . . .

Largely to take his mind off food, he called, "Are you here, Mucor? Can you hear me?"

There was no reply.

"I know it was you, you see. You've been following me, as you said you would last night. I recognized your face in Teasel's father's face this morning. Was it you that drank her blood? This afternoon I saw your face again, in poor Orpine's."

He waited but there was no whisper at his ear, no voice except his own echoing from the bare shiprock walls.

"Say something!"

A gravid silence filled the deserted manteion.

"That woman screaming in this house last night while I was outside in the floater—it was too apposite for mere chance. The devil was there because I was, and you're that devil, Mucor. I don't understand how you do the things you do, but I know it's you that do them."

He had packed the glass lamps in rags. As he unwrapped one, he caught sight of what might almost have been Mucor's death's-head grin. Carrying a lamp in each hand, he limped to the stage to look more closely at the painted canvas—it was presumably what Chenille had called a drop—behind it.

The scene was a crude mockery of Campion's celebrated painting of Pas enthroned. As depicted here, Pas had two erections as well as two heads; he nursed one in each hand. Before him, worshipful humanity engaged in every perversion that Silk had ever heard of, and several that were entirely new to him. In the original painting, two of Pas's taluses, mighty machines of a peculiarly lovely butter yellow, were still at work upon the whorl, planting a sacred goldenshower in back of Pas's throne. Here the taluses were furnished with obscene war rams, while Pas's blossom-freighted holy tree had been replaced by a gigantic phallus. Overhead the vast, dim faces of the spiritual Pas leered and slavered.

After carefully setting the blue lamps on the edge of the stage, Silk extracted Hyacinth's azoth from beneath his tunic. He wanted to slash the hateful thing before him to ribbons, but to do so would certainly destroy whatever might remain of the Window behind it. He pressed the demon, and with one surgical stroke slit the top of the painted canvas from side to side. The detestable painting vanished with a thump, in a cloud of dust.

Blood came in while he was setting up his triptych in front of the blank, dark face of the Window. Votive lamps burned again before that abandoned Window now, their bright flames stabbing upward from the blue glass as straight as swords; thuribles lifted slender pale columns of sweet smoke from the four corners of the stage.

"What did you do that for?" Blood demanded.

Silk glanced up. "Do what?"

"Destroy the scenery." Blood mounted the three steps at one side of the stage. "Don't you know what that stuff costs?"

"No," Silk told him. "And I don't care. You're going to make a profit of thirteen thousand cards on my manteion. You can use a fraction of it to replace what I've destroyed, if you choose. I don't advise it."

Blood kicked the pile of canvas. "None of the others did anything like this."

"Nor were their exorcisms effective. Mine will be—or so I have reason to believe." With the triptych centered between the lamps to his satisfaction, Silk turned to face Blood. "You are afflicted by devils, or one devil at least. I won't bother to explain just who that devil is now, but do you know how a place or a person—any person—falls into the power of devils?"

"Pah! I don't believe in them, Patera. No more than I do in your gods."

"Are you serious?" Silk bent to retrieve the walking stick Blood had given him. "You said something of the sort yesterday morning, but you have a fine effigy of Scylla in front of your villa. I saw it."

"It was there when I acquired the property. But if it hadn't been, I might have put up something like that anyway, I admit. I'm a loyal son of Viron, Patera, and I like to show it." Blood stooped to examine the triptych. "Where's Pas?"

Silk pointed.

"That whirlwind? I thought he was an old man with two heads."

"Any representation of a god is ultimately a lie," Silk explained. "It may be a convenient lie, and it may even be a reverent one; but it's ultimately false. Great Pas might choose to appear as your old man, or as the spiraling storm which is his eldest representation. Neither image would be more nearly true than the other, or more true than any other—merely more appropriate."

Blood straightened up. "You were going to tell me about devils."

"But I won't, not at present at least. It would take some time, and you wouldn't believe me in any case. You've saved me a decidedly unwelcome walk, however. I want you to assemble every living person in this house in this theater. Yourself, Musk if he's come back, Crane, Orchid, Chenille, the bald man, all the young women, and anyone else who may be present. By the time you get them in here, I will have completed my preparations."

Blood mopped his sweating face with a handkerchief. "I don't take orders from you, Patera."

"Then I will tell you this much about devils." Silk freed his imagination and felt it soar. "They are here, and one person has died already. Once they have tasted blood, they grow fond of it. I might add that it is by no means unusual to find them acting upon merely verbal resemblances, notions that you or I might consider only puns. It's apt to occur to them that if ordinary blood is good, the blood of Blood should be much better. You'd be wise to keep that in mind."

The women arrived by twos and threes, curious and more or less willingly driven by Musk and the muscular bald man, whose name seemed to be Bass; soon they were joined by Loach and Moorgrass from Silk's own manteion, both frightened and very glad to see him. Eventually Crane and a dry-eyed, grim Orchid took seats in the last row. Silk waited for Blood, Bass, and Musk to join them before he began.

"Let me describe—"

His words were drowned by the chattering of the women.

"Quiet!" Orchid had risen. "Shut up, you sluts!"

"Let me describe," Silk began again, "what has happened here and what we will be trying to accomplish. The entire whorl was originally under the protection of Great Pas, the Father of the Gods. Otherwise it could never have existed."

He paused, studying the faces of the twenty-odd young women before him intently, and feeling rather as if he were addressing Maytera Mint's class in the palaestra. "Great Pas planned every part of it, and it was constructed by his slaves under his direction. In that way were the courses of all our rivers charted, and Lake Limna itself dug deep. In that way were the oldest trees planted, and the manteions through which we are to know him built. You are sitting, of course, in one such manteion. When the whorl was complete, Pas blessed it."

Silk paused again, counting silently to three, as he so often had at the ambion, while he searched the faces of his audience for one that had come to resemble the mad girl's, however subtly. "Even if you're inclined to dispute what I've said, I require that you accept it for the present, for the sake of this exorcism. Is there anyone here who *cannot* accept it? If so, please stand." He stared hard at Blood, but Blood did not rise.

"Very well," Silk continued. "Please understand that it was not merely the whorl as a whole that received Pas's blessing and with it his protection. Each individual part received it as well, and most have it still.

"At times, however, and for good reasons, Pas withdraws

his protection from certain parts of this whorl he created. It may be a tree, a field, an animal, a person, or even an entire city. In this instance, it is surely a building—the one we are in now, the one that has since become a part of this house, so that Pas's protection has departed from the entire house."

He let that sink in while his eyes roved from face to face. All of Orchid's women were relatively young, and one or two were strikingly beautiful; many if not most were more than ordinarily good-looking. None resembled Mucor in the least.

"What, you may ask, does that mean? Does it mean that the tree dies or the city burns? No, it does not. Suppose that one of you owned a cat, one that bit and scratched you until at last, in disgust, you thrust your cat out into the street and shut your door. That cat, which once was yours, would not die—or at least, it would not die immediately. But when dogs attacked it, there would be no one to defend it, and any passerby who wished to stone it or lay claim to it could do so with impunity.

"So it is with those of us from whom Pas's blessing has been taken. Some of you, I know, have suffered possession here, and in a few moments I am going to ask one of you who has been possessed to describe it."

A small dark woman at one end of the first row grinned, and though little in her face had changed, it seemed to Silk that he could see the skull that underlay it. He relaxed, and realized that his palms were running with sweat, that the carved handle of Blood's walking stick was slippery with it, his forehead beaded with perspiration that threatened to run into his eyes. He wiped it away with the sleeve of his robe.

"This object behind me was once a Sacred Window—I doubt that there is anyone present who is so ignorant that she does not know that. Through the Window that this once was, Lord Pas spoke to mankind. So it is with the gods, as every one of you must know—they speak to us by means of the Windows that Great Pas built for them and us. They have other ways as well, of course, of which augury is but one. That doesn't alter the fact that the Windows are the primary means. Is it any wonder, then, that when we permitted this one to fall into disrepair, Pas withdrew his blessing? I say we, because I include myself; we, every man and every woman in Viron, let this devilish thing happen.

"In preparation for this exorcism, I did everything that I could to repair your Window. I cleaned and tightened its connections, spliced and reconnected its broken cables, and attempted certain other more difficult repairs. As you see, I failed. Your Window remains lightless and lifeless. It remains closed to Pas, and we can only hope that he will take the will for the deed and restore his blessing to this house, as we pray."

Several of the young women traced the sign of addition in the air.

Silk nodded approvingly, then looked straight at the dark woman. "Now I am going to speak directly to the devil who has come among us, for I know that it is here, and that it hears me.

"That very great god the Outsider has placed you in my power. You, also, have a window, as we both know. I can close it, and lock it against you, if I choose. Depart from this house forever, or I will so choose." Silk struck the stage with Blood's stick. *"Be gone!"*

The young women started and gasped, and the dark one's grin faded. It was (Silk told himself) as though she'd had a fever; the fever was draining away as he watched, and her delirium with it.

"Now I have spoken enough for the present. Orchid, I asked Chenille a while ago whether you'd been possessed, and she said you hadn't. Is that correct?"

Orchid nodded.

"Stand up, please, and speak loudly enough for all of us to hear you."

Orchid rose and cleared her throat. "No, Patera. It's never happened to me. And I don't want it to."

Several of the young women tittered.

"It will never happen to any of you again. I believe that I can promise you that, and I do. Orchid, you know to whom it has already happened. Who are they?"

"Violet and Crassula."

Silk gestured with the walking stick. "Will they stand up, please?"

Reluctantly, they did so, Violet taller than most, with sleek black hair and flashing eyes; Crassula thin and almost plain.

Silk said, "This isn't all. I know that there's one more at least. If you've been possessed, please stand up, even if Orchid did not name you."

Blood was smiling in the back row; he nudged Musk, who smiled in return as he cleaned his nails with a long-bladed knife. The women stared at one another; a few whispered. Slowly, the small, dark woman rose.

"Thank you, my daughter," Silk said. "Yes, you're the one. Has the devil gone now?"

"I think so."

"So do I. What's your name, my daughter?"

"Poppy, Patera. Only I still don't feel quite like I did before."

"I see. You know, Poppy, Orchid mentioned you to me when we were talking earlier, I suppose—" He was on the point of saying that it had probably been because she was Chenille's opposite physically; at the last possible moment he substituted, "because you're very attractive. That may have had something to do with your possession, although I can't be certain. When were you possessed, Poppy?"

"Just now."

"Speak louder, please. I don't believe everyone can hear you."

Poppy raised her voice. "Just now, until you said be gone, Patera."

"And how did it feel, Poppy?"

The small, dark girl began to tremble.

"If it frightens you too much, you don't have to tell us. Would you rather sit back down?"

"I felt like I was dead. I didn't care any more about anything, and I was right here but far away. I was seeing all the same things, but they meant different things, and I can't explain. People were hollow, like clothes nobody was wearing, all of them except you."

Violet said, "I had my best pins in my hair, and I laid one on the washstand. I didn't want to, but I did, and the drain sort of reached up and ate it, a real good pin with a turquoise head, and I thought it was funny."

Silk nodded. "And for you, Crassula?"

"I wanted to fly, and I did. I stood up in the bed and jumped off and sort of flew around the room. He hit me, but I didn't care."

"Was this last night? One of you was possessed last night. Was it you, Crassula?"

The thin woman nodded wordlessly.

"Was it you who screamed last night? I was here then— outside the house, on Lamp Street, and I heard someone scream."

"That was Orpine. It had come back and I was throwing things. The flying was the first time, last month."

Silk nodded, looking thoughtful. "Thank you, Crassula. I should also thank Poppy and Violet, and I do. I've never had the opportunity to speak with anyone who's been possessed before now, and what you've told me may be helpful to me."

Mucor was gone, or at least he could no longer see her in any of the faces before him. When they had met in Sun Street, Blood had told him that there were human beings who could possess others; he wondered whether Blood did not at least suspect that the devil who had troubled this house was his daughter. Silk decided that it might be best not to give him more time in which to think of it.

"Now we're going to sing the song that we will sing in the course of the ceremony. Stand up, all of you, and join hands. Blood, you and Musk and the rest must sing with us. Come to the front and join hands."

Most of them did not know the *Hymn to Every God*, but Silk taught them the chorus and the first three verses, and eventually achieved a creditable performance, to which Musk, who so seldom spoke, supplied a more than adequate tenor.

"Good! That was our rehearsal, and in a moment we'll begin the ceremony. We'll start outside. This little jar of paint and this brush—" Silk displayed them, "have been blessed and consecrated already. Five of you, chosen from among those who live in this house, will participate in the restoration of the voided cross over the Music Street door, while the rest of us sing. It would be best if the three who have been possessed were among that five. After that, we'll circle the house three times in procession, and then assemble in here once more for the final casting out."

Outside, while surprised urchins stared and pointed at the women, many of whom were still only half dressed, Silk chose the additional representatives, selecting two who were slight of build from among those who seemed to be taking the proceedings most seriously. The *Hymn to Every God* sounded faint and thin in the open air of Music Street, but a score of watching loungers removed their hats as Blood and Bass gravely lifted each of the five in turn on their shoulders. Gammadion by gammadion the nearly effaced voided cross was restored to prominence. When the base line had been added beneath it, Silk burned the brush and the remainder of the paint in the largest thurible.

"Aren't you going to sacrifice?" Orchid asked. "The others did."

"I've just done so," Silk told her. "A sacrifice need not be of a living beast, and you've just witnessed one that wasn't. Should a second exorcism be required, we will offer a beast, and retrace the sacred design in its blood. Do you understand the sacrifice, and why we're doing all this? I'm assuming that the evil being entered your house through this Music Street door, since it is the only outside entrance to the profaned manteion."

Orchid nodded hesitantly.

"Good." Silk smiled. "As the second part proper of this exorcism, we will march in solemn procession, making a threefold circuit of the entire structure, while I read from the Chrasmologic Writings. It might be best if you were to walk behind me, and for the four men to take positions from which they can maintain order."

He raised his voice for the benefit of the listening women. "It will not be necessary for you to keep in step like troopers. It *will* be necessary that you remain in a single file and pay attention to what I read."

He got out his glasses, wiped them on his sleeve, and put them on. One of the young women tittered nervously.

Would Hyacinth laugh so, if she were to see him with these small and always somewhat smeared lenses before his eyes? Surely she would—she had laughed at less ridiculous things when they had been together. For the first time it struck him that she might have laughed as she had because she had been happy. He himself had been happy then, though for no good reason.

As he cleared his throat, he sought to recollect those emotions. No, not happy—joyful.

Joyous. Silk endeavored to imagine his mother offering Hyacinth the pale, greenish limeade that they had drunk each year during the hottest weather, and failed utterly.

" 'A devil does violence to itself, first of all, when it becomes an abscess and, as it were, a cancer in the whorl, as far as it can; for to be enraged at anything in the whorl is to separate oneself from that whorl, and its ultimately semi-divine nature, in some part of which the various natures of all other things whatsoever are contained. Secondly, a devil does violence to itself when it turns away from any good man, and moves against him with the intention of doing harm.' "

Silk risked a glance behind him. Orchid's hands were clasped in prayer, and the younger women were following in decent order, though a few seemed to be straining to hear. He elevated his voice.

" 'Thirdly, a devil does violence to itself whenever it succumbs to the pleasure of pain. Fourthly, when it plays a part, whether acting or speaking insincerely or untruthfully. Fifthly, when it acts or moves, always aimlessly . . .' "

They had completed half of the third and final circuit when a window shattered above their heads, subjecting Crane, near the end of their straggling line, to a shower of glass. "Just the devil departing," he assured the women around him. "Don't start yelling."

Orchid had stopped to stare up at the broken window. "That's one of my rooms!"

A feminine voice from the window, vibrant and firm, spoke like thunder. "Send up your augur to me!"

Chapter 12

DINNER ON AUK

Hers was the most beautiful face that Silk had ever seen. It hovered behind the glass in Orchid's sellaria, above a suggestion of neck and shoulders; and its smile was at once innocent, inviting, and sensual, the three intermingling to form a new quality, unknown and unknowable, desirable and terrifying.

"I've been watching you . . . Watching for you. Silk? Silk. What a lovely name! I've always, always loved silk, Silk. Come to me and sit down. You're limping, I've seen you. Draw up a chair to the glass. You mended our broken Window, mended it a little bit, anyway, and that's part of this house now, you said, Silk."

He had knelt, head bowed.

"Sit down, please. I want to see your face. Aren't you paying me honor? You should do what I ask."

"Yes, O Great Goddess," he said, and rose. This wasn't Echidna, surely; this goddess was too beautiful, and seemed almost too kind. Scylla had eight, or ten, or twelve arms; but he could not see her arms. Sphigx—it was Sphigxday—

"Sit down. There's a little chair behind you, Silk. I can see it. It was very nice of you to mend our terminal."

Her eyes were of a color he had never seen before, a blue so deep that it was almost black, without being truly black or even dark, their lids so heavy that she seemed blind.

"I would have revealed myself to you then, if I could. I could see and hear you, but not that. There's no power for the beam, I think. It still won't light. So disappointing. Perhaps you can do something more?"

He nodded, speechless.

"Thank you. I know you'll try. In mending that, you mended this, I think. It's dusty." She laughed, and her laughter was the chiming of bells far away, bells cast of a metal more precious than any gold. "Isn't it funny? I could break that window. By making the right sound. And holding it until the glass broke. Because I could hear you outside reading something. You didn't stop the first time I called. I suppose you didn't hear me?"

He wanted to run but shook his head instead. "No, Great Goddess. I'm terribly sorry."

"But I can't wipe the glass. Wipe this glass for me, Silk. And I'll forgive you."

"If you'll— My handkerchief has blood on it, Great Goddess. Perhaps in there—"

"I won't mind. Unless it's still wet. Do as I asked. Won't you, please?"

Silk got out his handkerchief, stained with Orpine's blood. At each step he took toward the glass, he felt that he was about to burst into flames or dissolve into the air like smoke.

"I watched him kill a thousand once. Men, mostly. It was in the square. I watched from my balcony. They made them kneel facing him, and some still knelt when they were dead."

It seemed the depth of blasphemy to whisk his ragged, bloodstained handkerchief up and down those lovely features, which when the dust was gone seemed more real than he. Not Molpe; Molpe's hair fell across her face. Not—

"I wanted to faint. But he was watching me from his

balcony. Much higher up, with a flag over the thing there. The little wall. I was staying at his friend's house then. I saw so much then. It doesn't bother me any more. Have you sacrificed to me today? Or yesterday? Some of those big white bunnies, or a white bird?"

The victims identified her. "No, Kypris," Silk said. "The fault is mine; and I will, as soon as I can."

She laughed again, more thrilling than before. "Don't bother. Or let those women do it. I want other services from you. You're lame. Won't you sit down now? For me? There's a chair behind you."

Silk nodded and gulped, finding it very difficult to think of words in the presence of a goddess, harder still when his eyes strayed to her face. He struggled to recall her attributes. "I hurt my ankle, O Great Goddess Kypris. Last night."

"Bouncing out of Hyacinth's window." Her smile grew minutely wider. "You looked like a big black rabbit. You really shouldn't have. You know, Silk? Hy wouldn't have hurt you. Not with that big sword or any other way. She liked you, Silk. I was in her, so I know."

He took a deep breath. "I had to, Gentle Kypris, in order to preserve the anipotence by which I behold you."

"Because Echidna lets you see us in our Sacred Windows, then. Like a child."

"Yes, Gentle Kypris; by her very great kindness to us, she does."

"And am I the first, Silk? Have you never seen a god before?"

"No, Gentle Kypris. Not like this. I had hoped to, perhaps when I was old, like Patera Pike. Then yesterday in the ball court— And last night. I went into that woman's dressing room without knocking and saw colors in the glass there, colors that looked like the Holy Hues. I've still never seen them, but they told us—we had to memorize the descriptions, actually, and recite them." Silk paused for breath. "And it seemed to me—it has always seemed to me, ever since I used the glass at the schola, that a god might use a glass. May I tell them about this at the schola?"

Kypris was silent for a moment, her face pensive. "I don't think . . . No. No, Silk. Don't tell anybody."

He made a seated bow.

"I was there last night. Yes. But not for you. Only because I play with Hy sometimes. Now she reminds me of the way I used to be, but all that will be over soon. She's twenty-three. And you, Silk? How old are you?"

"Twenty-three, Gentle Kypris."

"There. You see. I prompted you. I know I did." She shook her head almost imperceptibly. "All that abstinence! And now you've seen a goddess. Me. Was it worth it?"

"Yes, Loving Kypris."

She laughed again, delighted. "Why?"

The question hung in the silence of the baking sellaria while Silk tried to kick his intellect awake. At length he said haltingly, "We are so much like beasts, Kypris. We eat and we breed; then we spawn and die. The most humble share in a higher existence is worth any sacrifice."

He waited for her to speak, but she did not.

"What Echidna asks isn't actually much of a sacrifice, even for men. I've always thought of it as a token, a small sacrifice to show her—to show all of you—that we are serious. We're spared a thousand quarrels and humiliations, and because we have no children of our own, all children are ours."

The smile faded from her lovely face, and the sorrow that displaced it made his heart sink. "I won't talk to you again, Silk. Or at least not very soon. No, soon. I am hunted . . ." Her perfect features faded to dancing colors.

He rose and found that he was cold in his sweat-soaked tunic and robe, despite the heat of the room. Vacantly, he stared at the shattered window; it was the one he had opened when he had spoken with Orchid. The gods—Kypris herself—had prompted him to throw it open, perhaps; but Orchid had closed it again as soon as he left, as he should have known she would.

He trembled, and felt that he was waking from a dream. An awful silence seemed to fill the empty house, and he remembered vaguely that it was said that haunted houses were the quietest of all, until the ghost walked. Everyone was outside, of course, waiting on Lamp Street where he had left them, and he would be able to tell them nothing.

He visualized them standing in their silent, straggling line and looking at one another, or at no one. How much had they overheard through the window? Quite possibly they had heard nothing.

He wanted to jump and shout, to throw Orchid's untasted goblet of brandy out the window or at the empty glass. He knelt instead, traced the sign of addition, and rose with the help of Blood's stick.

Outside, Blood demanded to know who had summoned him. Silk shook his head.

"You won't tell me?"

"You don't believe in the gods, or in devils, either. Why should I tell you something at which you would only scoff?"

A woman whose hair had been bleached until it was as yellow as Silk's own, exclaimed, "That was no devil!"

"You must keep silent about anything you heard," Silk told her. "You should have heard nothing."

Blood said, "Musk and Bass were supposed to have found every woman in the place and made them come to this ceremony of yours. If they missed any of them, I want to know about it." He turned to Orchid. "You know your girls. Are they all here?"

She nodded, her face set. "All but Orpine."

Musk was staring at Silk as though he wanted to murder him; Silk met his eyes, then turned away. Speaking loudly to the group at large, he said, "We've never completed our third circuit. It is necessary that we do so. Return to your places, please." He tapped Blood's shoulder. "Go back to your place in the procession."

Orchid had kept the Writings for him, her finger at the point at which he had stopped reading. He opened the heavy volume there and began to pace and read again, a step for each word, as the ritual prescribed: "Man, himself, creates the conditions necessary for advance by struggling with and yielding to his animal desires; yet nature, the experiences of the spirit, and materiality need never be. His torment depends upon himself, yet the effects of that torment are always sufficient. You must consider this."

The words signified nothing; the preternaturally lovely face of Kypris interposed itself. She had seemed completely different from the Outsider, and yet he felt that they were one, that the Outsider, who had spoken in so many voices, had now spoken in another. The Outsider had cautioned him to expect no help, Silk reminded himself as he had so many times since that infinite instant in the ball court; he felt that he had received it nevertheless, and was about to receive more. His hands shook, and his voice broke like a boy's.

". . . has of all merely whorlly intellectual ambition and aspiration."

Here was the door of the derelict manteion, with Pas's voided cross fresh and bright above it in black paint that had not yet dried. He closed the Writings with a bang and opened the door, led the way in and limped up the steps to the stage that had once been a sanctuary.

"Sit down, please. It doesn't matter whom you sit with, because we won't be long. We're almost finished."

Leaning on Blood's walking stick, he waited for them to get settled.

"I am about to order the devil forth. I see that the last person in our procession—Bass, I suppose—shut the door behind him. For this part of the ceremony it should be open." Providentially, he remembered the thin woman's name. "Crassula, you're sitting closest. Will you open it for us, please?

"Thank you. Since you were one of the possessed, it might be well to begin this final act of exorcism with you. Do you have a good memory?"

Crassula shook her head emphatically.

"All right. Who does?"

Chenille stood up. "I do, Patera. Pretty good, and I haven't had a drop since last night."

Silk hesitated.

"Please?"

Slowly, Silk nodded. This was to be a meritorious act, of course; he could only hope that she was capable. "Here's the formula all of us will use: *'Go, in the names of these gods, never to return.'* Perhaps you'd better repeat it."

"Go, in the names of these gods, never to return."

"Very good. I hope that everyone heard you. When I've finished, I'll point to you. Pronounce your own name loudly, then recite the formula—'Go in the names of these gods, never to return.' Then I'll point out the next person, the woman beside you, and she is to say her own name and repeat the formula she'll have just heard you use. Is there anyone who doesn't understand?"

He scanned their faces as he had earlier, but found no trace of Mucor. "Very well."

Silk forced himself to stand very straight. "If there is anything in this house that does not come in the name of the gods, may it be gone. I speak here for Great Pas, for Strong Sphigx, for Scalding Scylla . . ." The sounding

names seemed mere words, empty and futile as the sighings
of the hot wind that had blown intermittently since spring;
and he had not been able to make himself pronounce that
of Echidna. "For the Outsider, and for Gentle Kypris. I,
Silk, say it! *Go, in the names of these gods, never to return.*"

He pointed toward the woman with the raspberry-col-
ored hair, and she said loudly, "Chenille! Go, in the names
of these gods, never to return!"

"Mezereon. Go, in the names of these gods, never to
return."

Orchid spoke after the younger women, in a firm, clear
voice. After her, Blood positively thundered—there was,
Silk decided, a broad streak of actor in the man. Musk was
inaudible; Silk could not help but feel that he was calling
to devils, rather than casting them out.

Silk waited on the uppermost of the three steps as he
pointed to Bass, who stammered as he pronounced his own
name and rumbled out the formula.

Silk started down the steps, hurrying despite his pain.

Doctor Crane, the final speaker, said, "Crane. Go, in the
names of these gods, never to return. And now—"

Silk slammed shut the door to Music Street and shot the
bolt.

"—I've got to go myself. I'm late already. Stay off that
ankle!"

"Good-bye," Silk told him, "and thank you for the ride
and your treatment." He raised his voice. "All of you may
leave. The exorcism is complete."

Suddenly very weary, he sat down on the second step and
unwound the wrapping. All the young women had begun
to talk at once. He flailed the dull red tiles of the floor with
the wrapping, and then, recalling Crane, flung it as hard as
he could against the nearest wall.

A hush fell as the chattering women streamed out into
the courtyard; by the time he had replaced the wrapping,

he thought himself alone; he looked up, and Musk stood before him, as silent as ever, his hands at his sides.

"Yes, my son. What is it?"

"You ever see how a hawk kills a rabbit?"

"No. I spent all but one year of my boyhood here in the city, I'm afraid. Did you wish to speak to me?"

Musk shook his head. "I wanted to show you how a hawk kills a rabbit."

"Very well," Silk said. "I'm watching."

Musk did not respond; after half a minute or more Silk rose, gripping Blood's stick. The long-bladed knife seemed to come from nowhere—to appear in Musk's hand as though called forth by a nod from Pas. Musk thrust, and Silk felt an explosion of pain in his chest. He staggered and dropped the walking stick; one heel struck the step behind him, and he fell.

By the time that he was able to pull himself up, Musk was gone. Hyacinth's azoth was in Silk's hand, though he could not recall drawing it. He stared at it, dropped it clattering to the floor, clutched his chest, then opened his robe.

His tunic showed no tear, no blood. He pulled it up and touched the spot gingerly; it was inflamed and very painful. A single drop of darkly crimson blood appeared on the surface and trickled away.

He let his tunic fall again, and picked up the azoth to examine its pommel, running his fingers across the faceted gem there. That was it, and there had been no miracle. Musk had reversed his knife with a motion too swift to be seen as he had thrust, striking hard with its pommel, which must itself be in some fashion pointed or sharply angled.

And he himself, Patera Silk, the Outsider's servant, had been ready to kill Musk, believing that Musk had killed him. He had not known that he could come so easily to murder. He would have to watch his temper, around Musk particularly.

The gem, which he had supposed colorless, caught a ray of sunlight from the god-gate in the roof and flashed a watery green. For some reason, it reminded him of her eyes. He put it to his lips, his thoughts full of things that could never be.

To spare his broken ankle, he had waited until Moorgrass had finished washing and dressing the body, so that he might ride back to the manteion in Loach's wagon.

They would need a coffin, and ice. Ice was very costly, but having accepted a hundred cards from Orchid, he could not refuse her daughter ice. Mutes could be engaged easily and cheaply. On the other hand—

Loach's wagon lurched to a stop, and Silk looked up in surprise at the weather-stained façade of his own manteion. Loach inquired, "Lay her on the altar for now, Patera?"

He nodded; it was what they always did.

"Let me help you down, Patera. About my pay—"

The fisc was closed, of course, and would not open at all on Scylsday. "See me after sacrifice tomorrow," Silk said. "No, on Molpsday. Not before then." The icemongers might cash Orchid's draft for him if he bought enough ice, but there was no point in relying on that.

Auk came out of the mantion, waved, and wedged the door open; the sight of him snapped Silk out of his calculations. "I'm sorry I'm late," he called. "There was a death."

Auk's heavy, brutal face took on what seemed intended as an expression of concern. "Friend of yours, Patera?"

"No," Silk said. "I didn't know her."

Auk smiled. He helped Loach carry Orpine's shrouded body inside, where a new coffin, plain but sturdy-looking, waited on a catafalque.

Maytera Marble rose from the shadows, the silver gleam of her face almost ghostly. "I arranged for these, Patera.

The man you sent said that we'd require them. They can be returned, if they're not suitable."

"We'll need a better casket tomorrow." Silk fumbled in his pockets, and at length produced Orchid's draft. "Take this, please. It's payable to bearer. Get ice, half a load of ice, and see if they'll cash it for you. Flowers, too. Arrange for a grave, if it's not too late."

A tiny, but abrupt and uncoordinated, movement of her head as she glanced at the draft betrayed Maytera Marble's surprise.

"You're right." Silk nodded as she looked up at him. "It's a great deal. I'll get the victims in the morning, a white heifer if I can find one, and a rabbit for Kypris—several, I ought to say. And a black lamb and a black cock for Tartaros; I pledged those last night. But we must have the ice tonight, and if you could take care of it, Maytera, I would be exceedingly grateful."

"For Kypris the—? All right, Patera. I'll try." She hurried away, the rapid taps of her footfalls like the soft rattle of a snare drum. Silk shook his head and looked about for Loach, but Loach had already left, unobserved.

Auk said, "If there's ice left in Viron, she'll find it. She teach you, Patera?"

"No. I wish now that she had—she and Maytera Mint. But I should have asked her to arrange for mutes. Well, it can be taken care of tomorrow. Can we talk here, Auk, or would you prefer to go to the manse?"

"Have you eaten yet, Patera? I was hoping you'd have a bite of supper with me while you told me what happened last night."

"I couldn't pay my share, I'm afraid."

"I asked you, Patera. I wouldn't let you pay if you wanted to. But you listen here." Auk's voice dropped to a whisper. "I'm in this as much as you are. It was me that helped you. I got a right to know."

"Of course. Of course." Silk sank wearily into a seat near the catafalque. "Sit down, please. It hurts my ankle to stand. I'll tell you whatever you want to know. To tell the truth, I need to tell someone—to talk all of it over, and other things, too. Everything that happened today. And I'd like very much to go to dinner with you. I'm beginning to like you, and I'm terribly hungry; but I can't walk far. Much as I appreciate your generosity, perhaps we should dine together some other night."

"We don't have to leg it over to the Orilla. There's a nice place right down the street. They got the tenderest, juiciest roasts you ever cut on the side of your flipper." Auk grinned, showing square, yellow teeth that looked fully capable of severing a human hand at the wrist. "Suppose I was to buy an augur—one that really needed it—a dimber uphill dinner. Whatever he wanted. That'd be a meritorious act, wouldn't it?"

"I suppose so. Nevertheless, you must consider that he may not deserve one."

"I'll keep it in mind." Auk strolled to the coffin and pulled down the shroud. "Who is she?"

"Orchid's daughter Orpine. That was nicely done, but you knew her, I'm sure."

"Her *daughter?*" Leaving Orpine's body, Auk took Silk's arm. "Come on, Patera. If we don't get over there, we'll have to eat in the public room."

Musk had caught sight of his eagle before he stepped out of the floater. She was at the top of a blasted pine, silhouetted against the brightening skylands.

She was looking at the hackboard, Musk knew. She could see the hackboard more clearly from half a league away than he had ever seen the palms of his own hands. She would be ravenous by now; like a falcon (as Musk reminded himself) an eagle would have to learn to fly before it could learn to hunt. Apparently, she had not yet gone after lambs, though she might tomorrow—it was his greatest fear.

He circled the villa. The meat bound to the hackboard had been there all day; it was nearly dry now, and blanketed with flies. He kicked the board to dislodge them before he brought out the lure and a bag of cracked maize.

The lure whistled as he spun it on its five-cubit line.

"Ho, hawk! Ho, hawk!"

Once he imagined that he heard the faint jingle of her bells, though he knew it was impossible. He scattered maize nearly to the wall, then returned to the hackboard and swung the lure again while he waited. It was late— perhaps too late. It would be dark very soon, and when it was she would not fly.

"Ho! Ho, hawk!"

As well as Musk could judge, the eagle on the remote snag had not stirred so much as a feather; but a plump brown wood weaver was settling on the cropped grass near the wall to peck at the maize.

He dropped the lure and crouched, his needler gripped with both hands and his left elbow braced on his left knee. It would be a long shot, in poor light.

The wood weaver fell, fluttered up, cannoned into the wall, and fell again. Before it could fly a second time, he had it. Back at the hackboard, he loosened the nose in the lure line and let the red-and-white lure fall to the ground. With the noose tight about the wood weaver's right leg, he twirled it, producing a fine and almost invisible shower of blood.

"Ha, hawk!"

The wide wings spread. For a moment Musk, watching the eagle, still twirling the dying wood weaver in its ten-cubit circle, felt that he more than possessed it.

Felt that he himself was the great bird, and was happy.

*   *   *

"You seen what they wrote on that wall, Patera." Auk sat down, having chosen a chair from which he could watch the door. "Some sprat from the palaestra, like you say. But I'd talk to them about it, if I was you. Could be trouble."

"I'm not responsible for every boy who finds a piece of chalk." This eating house had seemed remote indeed to Silk, though it was almost in sight of his manteion. He lowered himself into the capacious armchair the host was holding for him and looked around him at the white-washed shiprock walls. Their private dining room was smaller even than his bedroom in the manse, still crowded after a waiter had removed two superfluous chairs.

"All of them good and thick," Auk said, answering the question Silk had not asked, "and so's the door. This was the Alambrera back in the old days. What do you like?"

Silk scanned the neatly lettered slate. "I'll have the chops, I think." At eighteen cardbits, the chops were the least expensive meal; and even if there were in fact only a single chop, this dinner would be his most bountiful meal of the week.

"How'd you get over the wall?" Auk asked when the host had gone. "Have any trouble?"

And so Silk told the whole story, from the cutting of his horsehair rope by a spike to his ride back to the city in Blood's floater. Auk was roaring with laughter when the waiter brought their dinners, but he had grown very serious by the time Silk reached his interview with Blood.

"You didn't happen to mention me any time while you were talking to him?"

Silk swallowed a luscious mouthful of chop. "No. But I very foolishly tried to speak with you through the glass in Hyacinth's boudoir, as I told you."

"He may not find out about that." Auk scratched his chin thoughtfully. "The monitors lose track after a while."

"But he may," Silk said. "You'll have to be on guard."

"Not as much as you will, Patera. He'll want to know what you wanted to talk to me about, and since you didn't, he can't get it from me. What are you going to tell him?"

"If I tell him anything at all, I'll tell him the truth."

Auk laid down his fork. "That I helped you?"

"That I knew you were concerned about my safety. That you had warned me about going out so late at night, and that I wanted to let you know I had not come to harm."

Auk considered the matter while Silk ate. "It might go, Patera, if he thinks you're crazy enough."

"If he thinks I'm honest enough, you mean. The best way to be thought honest is to be honest—or at any rate that's the best that I've ever found. I try to be."

"But you're going to try to steal twenty-six thousand for him, too."

"If that's what I must do to save our manteion, and I can get it in no other way, yes. I'll be forced to choose between evils, exactly as I was last night. I'll try to see that no one is hurt, of course, and to take the money only from those who can well afford to lose it."

"Blood will take your money, Patera. And have a good laugh over it."

"I won't let him take it until he furnishes safeguards. But there's something else I ought to tell you about. Did I mention that Blood wanted me to exorcise the yellow house?"

"Orchid's place? Sure. That's where that girl Orpine lived, only I never knew she was Orchid's daughter."

"She was." There was butter and soft, fresh bread in the middle of the table; Silk took a slice and buttered it, wishing that he might take the whole loaf home to the manse. "I'm going to tell you about that, too. And about Orpine, who died possessed."

Auk grunted. "That's your lay, Patera, not mine."

"Possession? It's really no one's now. Perhaps there was a time when most augurs believed in devils, as Patera Pike certainly did. But I may be the only augur alive who believes in them now, and even now I'm not certain that I believe in them in the same sense he did—as spirits who crept into the whorl without Pas's permission and seek to destroy it."

"What about Orpine? Was she really Orchid's daughter?"

"Yes," Silk said. "I spoke to Orchid about her and she admitted it. Practically boasted of it, in fact. What was Orpine like?"

"Good-looking." Auk hesitated. "I don't feel right talking about this stuff to you, Patera. She could be a lot of fun, because she didn't care what she did or what anybody thought about it. You know what I mean? She would've made more money if she'd been better at making people think she liked them."

Silk chewed and swallowed. "I understand. I wanted to know because I've been wondering about personalities, and so on—whether there's a particular type of person who's more prone to be possessed than another—and I never saw Orpine alive. I had been talking to her mother; we heard a scream and hurried outside, and found her lying there on the stair. She had been stabbed. Someone suggested that she might have stabbed herself. Her face— Have you ever seen a possessed person?"

Auk shook his head.

"Neither had I until this morning, shortly before I saw Orpine's body." Silk patted his lips with his napkin. "At any rate, she was dead; but even in death it seemed that her face was not quite her own. I remember thinking that there was something horrible about it, and a good deal that was familiar, as well. At first, the familiar part seemed quite easy. After I'd thought about it for a moment—the eyes and the shape of her nose and lips and so on—I realized that she looked rather like Orchid, the woman I'd just been speaking to. I asked her about it afterward, and she told me that Orpine had been her daughter, as I said."

"Maybe I should've known, too," Auk said, "but I never guessed. Orpine was a lot younger."

Silk shrugged. "You know a great deal more about women than I do, I'm sure. Perhaps I saw as much as I did mostly because I know so little about them. When one knows little about a subject, what one sees are apt to be the most basic things, if one sees anything at all. What I wanted to say, however, was that even the horrible element in her face was familiar."

"Go on." Auk refilled his wineglass. "Let's hear it."

"I'm hesitating because I'm fairly certain you won't believe me. Orpine reminded me of someone else I had been talking with not long before—of Mucor, the mad girl in Blood's villa."

Auk laid aside his fork, the steaming beef on its tines still untasted. "You mean the same devil had taken 'em both over, Patera?"

Silk shook his head. "I don't know, but I felt that I ought to tell you. I believe that Mucor has been following me in spirit. And I am coming to believe that she can, in some fashion, possess others, just as devils—and the gods, for that matter—are said to do at times. This morning I felt sure that I had glimpsed her in the face of an honest working man; and I think that she was possessing Orpine when Orpine died. Later I recognized her in another woman.

"If I'm correct, if she can really do such things and if she has been following me, you're running a substantial risk just by sitting with me at this table. I'm very grateful for this truly remarkable dinner, and even more grateful for your help last night. Furthermore, I'm hoping to ask you a few questions before we separate; and all of that puts me heavily in debt to you. I was too tired—and too hungry, I suppose—to consider the danger to which I was subjecting you when we spoke in the manteion. Now that I have, I feel obliged to warn you that you too may suffer possession if you remain in my company."

Auk grinned. "You're an augur, Patera. If she was to grab hold of me while we're sitting here, couldn't you make her beat the hoof?"

"I could try; but I have only one threat to use against her, and I've used it. You're not leaving?"

"Not me. I think I'll have another dumpling instead, maybe with a little of this gravy on it."

"Thank you. I hope you won't regret it. You haven't yet commented on my somewhat uneven performance last night. If you're afraid I might be insulted, I assure you that you could not be more severe with me than I've already been with myself."

"All right, I'll comment." Auk sipped his wine. "In the first place, I think if you can raise even a thousand, you'd better make sure Blood signs the manteion over to you before you cough up your goldboys. You were going on about safeguards a minute ago. I don't think you ought to trust in any safeguards except the deed, signed and witnessed by a couple dimber bucks who got nothing to do with Blood."

"You're right, I'm sure. I've been thinking much the same thing."

"You better. Don't trust him, even if something that he does makes you think you can."

"I'll be very careful." Silk's chops were bathed in a piquant, almost black sauce he found unspeakably delicious; he wiped some from his plate with another slice of bread.

"And I think you've probably found your true calling." Auk grinned. "I don't think I could've done much better, and I might not've done as good. This was your first time, too. By number ten I'll be begging to come along, just to watch you work."

Silk sighed. "I hope there won't be a tenth, for both our sakes."

"Sure there will. You're a real son of Tartaros. You just don't know it yet. Third or fourth, or whatever it is, I want to see what it is a dimber bucko like you needs a hand from me on. You want to go back to Blood's tonight and get your hatchet?"

Silk shook his head ruefully. "I won't be able to work on the roof until my ankle's healed, and it's more than half finished anyway. Do you recall what I said about Hyacinth's needler?"

"Sure. And the azoth. A nice azoth ought to bring a couple thousand cards, Patera. Maybe more. If you want to sell it, I can steer you to somebody who'll give you a lily price."

"I can't, because it isn't mine. Hyacinth intended to lend it to me, I'm sure. As I told you, I had told her that I was borrowing those weapons, and I promised that I would return them when I no longer required them. I feel certain she would not have sent the azoth to me by Doctor Crane if I had not said that earlier."

When Auk did not reply, Silk continued miserably, "Two thousand cards, if I actually received that much, would be an appreciable fraction of the twenty-six thousand that we require. More than five percent, in fact. You'll laugh at me—"

"I ain't laughing, Patera."

"You should. A thief who can't bring himself to steal! But Hyacinth trusted me. I cannot believe that the—that any god would wish me to betray a friendless woman's trust."

"If she lent it to you, I wouldn't sell it either," Auk told him. "Just to start out, she's there in Blood's house, and if you've got yourself a friend on the inside, that's not anything you want to fight clear of. You got any notion why this doctor would take on something as risky as that for her?"

"Perhaps he's in love with her."

"Uh-huh. It could be, but I'll bet he's got some kind of lock. It'd be worth your while to find out what it is, and I'd like to hear about it when you do. I'd like to see this azoth you got from her, too. Suppose I come around tomorrow night. Would you let me see it?"

"You may look at it now, if you like." Silk pulled the azoth from beneath his tunic and passed it across the table to Auk. "I brought it to Orchid's today because I feared I might require some sort of weapon."

Auk whistled softly, then held the azoth up, admiring the play of light along its gleaming grip. "Twenty-eight hundred easy. Might bring three thousand. Whoever gave it to her probably paid five or six for it."

Silk nodded. "I believe I may have some idea who that was, although I don't know where he could have gotten that much money." Auk regarded him quizzically, but Silk shook his head. "I'll tell you later, if it appears that I may be correct."

He held out his hand for the azoth, which Auk returned with a final grunt of admiration.

"I want to ask you about Hyacinth's needler. Blood took out the needles before he gave it back to me. Can you tell me where I might buy more without a brevet?"

"Sure, Patera. No problem at all. Have you got that with you, too?"

Silk took Hyacinth's engraved needler from his pocket and passed it to Auk.

"The smallest they make. I know 'em." He returned the

needler and rose. "Listen, can you get by without me for a minute? I got to—you know."

"Of course." Silk directed his attention to his chops; there had been three, and hungry though he was, he had thus far eaten only the first. He attacked the second without neglecting the tender dumplings, buttered squash with basil, and shallots in oil and vinegar that the eating house had provided (apparently at no additional charge) to accompany them.

Mere worry, mere concern, would not save the manteion. It would be necessary to devise a plan, and that plan need not necessarily involve stealing twenty-six thousand cards. Enlisting the sympathy of some magnate might do as well, for example, or . . .

Silk was discovering that he had devoured his third and final chop without realizing he had finished the second when Auk returned.

Chapter 13

SILK FOR CALDÉ

Doctor Crane shut and bolted the door of his infirmary. It had been a hard day; he was glad to be back again, very glad that Blood (who had put in a grueling day as well) would not entertain tonight. With luck, Crane thought, he might get a good night's sleep, an uninterrupted night's sleep, a night in which the cats clawed no one, Musk's hawks refrained from footing Musk and his helper—most of all, a night in which none of the fools that Viron called women decided that some previously unnoticed mole was in fact the first symptom of a fatal disease.

Shuffling into his bedroom, which had no door to the hall, he closed the door to the infirmary and bolted it as well. Let them call him through the glass, if they wanted him. He removed his shoes and flung his stockings onto the pile of soiled clothing in a corner, reminding himself again that he must take those clothes to the laundry in the other wing.

Had he put the black stocking he'd cut off that fellow Silk in there? No, he'd thrown it away.

In bare feet, he padded to the window and stood staring out through the grille at the shadowy grounds. The weather had been fine all summer, glowing with the hot, dry heat of home; but it would be autumn soon. The sun would dim, and the winds bring chill, drenching rains. The calendar called it autumn already. He hated rain and cold, snow, and coughs and runny noses. For a month or more, the thermometer would fluctuate between ten and ten below, as if chained to the freezing point. Human beings were never intended for such a climate.

When he had pulled down the shade, he glanced at the calendar, his eyes following his thought. Tomorrow would be Scylsday; the market would be closed, officially at least, and nearly empty. That was the best time for turning in a report, and the trader would be leaving on Hieraxday. There were still five of the little carved Sphigxes left.

He squared his shoulders, reminding himself that he too was a trooper of a sort, brought out his pen case, the black ink, and several sheets of very thin paper. As always, it would be necessary to write in a way that would not reveal his identity, should his report be intercepted.

And to report sufficient progress to prevent his being withdrawn. Tonight that would not be difficult.

Not that he would not like to go home, he told himself, and particularly to go home before the rains arrived, though they said that home had once been as wet as this place. Or rather, as wet as this place normally was.

He chose a crow quill and meticulously touched up its point. "There is a movement to restore the Charter. It is centered upon one Silk, a young augur of no family. He is said to have been the object of miracles, attributed to Pas or Scylla. Thus far it seems confined to the lower orders. The watchword 'Silk for caldé' is written on walls, although not" (it was a guess, but Crane felt confident of his ground) "on the Palatine. I am in contact with him and am gaining his trust. I have seen to it that he has an azoth. This can be reported if it proves necessary to destroy him."

Crane grinned to himself; that had been pure luck, but it would open their eyes.

"The Civil Guard is being expanded again. All units are at or over full strength. There is talk of forming a reserve brigade, officered by veterans."

For nearly half a minute, he sat staring at what he had written; better to say too little than too much. He dipped the crow quill for the twentieth time. "The bird has been freed. Its trainer says this is necessary. He will try to lure it back within the next few days. Lemur and Loris are reported to have observed its release."

And to have emerged from the subcellar, as upon several previous occasions, Crane reminded himself. Unquestionably the Ayuntamiento was making extensive use of the half-flooded construction tunnels, though its headquarters was not there.

Or could not be located if it was, although so many had perished there searching for it. Besides Viron's dormant army, there were Vironese soldiers in those tunnels, as well as several taluses.

Crane shook his head, then smiled at the thought of the Rani's reward. Turning to his glass, he clapped his hands. "Monitor!"

The floating face appeared.

"Code. Snakeroot. What have you got for me?"

Blood's fleshy features filled the glass. "Councillor Lemur ought to hear this."

Blood's face was replaced by the deceptively cheerful-looking visage of Potto. "You can give me the message."

"I'd rather—"

Crane smiled at Blood's reluctance.

"That doesn't matter. What is it?"

Crane edged nearer the glass.

When Blood had faded and the monitor reappeared to tell him there were no further exchanges of interest, Crane dipped his quill again. "Later. The bird has come back of its own volition. It is said to be in good condition."

He wiped the quill carefully and returned it to his pen case, blew on the paper, and folded and refolded it until it was scarcely larger than his thumbnail. When he pressed it into Sphigx's swordless left hand, the hand closed upon it.

Crane smiled, put away his pen case and the remaining paper, and considered the advisability of a long soak in the tub before bed. There was a good light in the bathroom— he had installed it himself—and if he read for an hour, the tightly folded sheet would have taken on the brown hue of the elaborately carved wood before he retired. He always liked seeing that, enjoyed making sure. He was, as he had to be, a very careful man.

"Thanks," Auk said as he resumed his seat. "I feel better now. Listen, Patera, do you know how to use that thing?"

"The needler?" Silk shrugged. "I fired it, as I told you. Not other than that."

Auk refilled his goblet. "I meant the azoth. No, naturally you don't, but I'll tell you about the needler anyhow."

He drew his own needler, twice the size of the engraved and gold-plated weapon in Silk's pocket. "Notice I got the safety on? There's a lever like this on both sides."

"Yes," Silk said. "So it won't shoot. I know about that."

"Fine." Auk pointed with his table knife. "This pin here, sticking out? You call this the status pin. If it's pushed out like that, you've got needles left."

Silk took Hyacinth's needler from his pocket again. "You're right, it's flush with the side."

"Now watch. I can empty mine by pulling this loading knob back."

A silver fountain of needles sprang from the breach of Auk's needler and scattered over the table. Silk picked one up.

"There's not much to see," Auk said. "Just little rods of

solid alloy—some kind of stuff that a lodestone pulls a lot better than steel."

Silk tested the tip with his finger. "I thought they'd be sharper."

"Huh-uh. They wouldn't work as good. If a thing as little as that went straight through somebody, it probably wouldn't do much damage. You want it to slew around so it cuts sidewise. The point's rounded just a shade to make it feed into the barrel, but not much."

Silk put down the needle. "What makes the noise?"

"The air." Auk smiled at Silk's surprise. "When you were a sprat, didn't some other sprat ever sling a rock at you and almost hit you? So you heard the rock go past your ear?"

Silk nodded.

"All right, there wasn't a bang like with a slug gun, was there? It was just a rock, and the other sprat threw it with his sling. What you heard was the rock going through the air, just like you might hear the wind in the chimney. The bigger the rock was, and the faster it was going, the more noise it would make."

"I see," Silk murmured, and with the words the entire scene returned, glowing with the vivid colors and hot shame of youth: the whizzing stones, his futile defense and final flight, the blood that had streamed from his face down his best white tunic to dye its embroidered flowers.

"All right, a needle's just a tiny little thing, but when it's shot out it goes so fast that the rock might just as well be traveling backwards. So it makes that noise you heard. If it had got slewed around before it hit that jug you shot, it would have screeched like a tomcat." Auk swept his needles into a pile with his hands. "They drop down inside the handle. See? All right. Right under my finger is a little washer with a hole in the middle and a lot of sparks in it."

Silk raised his eyebrows, more than ready to grasp at any distraction. "Sparks?"

"Just like you see if you pet a cat in the dark. They got put into the washer when this needler was made, and they chase each other around and around the hole in that washer till you need them. When I close the breech, that'll stick the first needle into the barrel, see?" Auk flicked on the safety. "If I'd have pulled the trigger, that would tap off some sparks for the coil. And as long as it's got sparks, that coil works like a big lodestone. It's up front here looped around the barrel, and it sucks the needle to it real fast. You'd think it would stay right there after it gets there, wouldn't you?"

Silk nodded again. "Or be drawn back to the coil, if it overshot."

"Right. Only it don't happen, because the last spark is through the coil before the needle ever gets there. Are you finished, Patera? I've told you just about everything I know."

"Yes, and the entire meal was delightful. Superb, in fact. I'm extremely grateful to you, Auk. However, I do have one more question before we go, though no doubt it will seem a very silly one to you. Why is your needler so much bigger than this one? What advantages are secured by the increase in size?"

Auk weighed his weapon in his hand before thrusting it away. "Well, Patera, for one thing mine holds a lot more needles. Full up, there's a hundred and twenty-five. I'd say your little one there most likely only holds fifty or sixty. Mine are longer, too, which is why I can't give you some of mine to use in yours. Longer needles mean a wider cut when they slew around, and a wider cut takes your cull out of the fight quicker. My barrel's longer, too, and the needles are a hair thicker. All that gives 'em half a dog's cheek more speed, so they'll go in deeper."

"I understand." Silk had drawn back the loading knob of

Hyacinth's needler and was peering at the rather simple-looking mechanism revealed by the open breech.

"A needler like yours is all right inside a house or a place like this, but outside you'd better be up close before you pull the trigger. If you're not, your needle's going to start slewing around in the air before it ever gets to your cull, and once it starts doing that, don't even Pas's sprats—your pardon, Patera—know where it's going to end up."

Looking thoughtful, Silk got out one of Blood's cards. "If you would allow me, Auk. I'm heavily indebted to you."

"I already paid, Patera." Auk rose, pushing back his chair until it thumped the wall. "Some other time, maybe." He grinned. "Now then. You remember I said don't even the gods know where your needles are going?"

"Of course." Silk rose as well, finding his ankle less painful than he had anticipated.

"Well, maybe they don't. But I do, and I'll tell you soon as we get outside. I know where you and me are going to go, too."

"I should return to my manteion." By an effort of will, Silk was able to walk almost normally.

"This won't take more than a couple hours, and I got two or three surprises I want to show you."

The first was a litter for one, with a pair of bearers. Silk climbed into it with some trepidation, wondering whether there would be any such conveyance to carry him to the manse when the business of the evening was done. The shade had risen until no sliver of gold remained, and a dulcet breeze whispered soothingly that the dust and heat of vanquished day had been but empty lies. It fanned Silk's flushed cheeks, and the sensual pleasure it gave him told him he had drunk one goblet of wine too many. Sadly, he resolved to watch himself more strictly in the future.

Auk strode along beside the litter, his grin flashing in the semidarkness. Silk felt something small, squarish, and heavy thrust into his hand.

"What we was talking about, Patera. Put 'em in your pocket."

By that time, Silk's fingers had told him that it was a paper-wrapped packet, tightly tied with string. "How . . . ?"

"The waiter. I had a word with him when I stepped out, see? They ought to fit, but don't try them here."

Silk dropped the packet of needles into the pocket of his robe. "I— Thank you again, Auk. I don't know what to say."

"I had him whistle out this trot-about for you, and he sent a pot boy off after those. If they don't fit, tell me tomorrow. Only I think they will."

The litter halted much sooner than Silk had expected, before a tall house whose lower and third stories were dark, though the windows between them blazed with light. When Auk knocked, the door was opened by a lean old man with a small, untidy beard and white hair more disordered even than Silk's own.

"Aha! Good! Good!" The old man exclaimed. "Inside! Inside! Just shut the door. Shut the door, and follow me." He went up the stair two steps at a time, with a speed that Silk would have found astonishing in someone half his age.

"His name's Xiphias," Auk told him when he had finished paying the bearers. "He's going to be your teacher."

"Teacher of what?"

"Hacking. Thirty years ago, he was best. The best in Viron, anyhow." Turning, Auk led Silk inside and closed the door. "He says he's better now, but the younger men won't accept his challenges. They say they don't want to show him up, but I don't know." Auk chuckled. "Think how they'd feel if the old goat beat them."

Nodding and content to wonder for a few minutes longer what "hacking" might be, Silk seated himself on the second step and removed Crane's wrapping; it was cold, and though he could not be certain in the dimness of the hallway, he thought that he could feel actual ice crystals in the nap of its cloth covering. He struck the floor with it. "Do you know about these?"

Auk stooped to look more closely. "I don't know. What you got?"

"A truly wonderful bandage for my ankle." Silk lashed the floor again. "It winds itself around the broken bone almost like a serpent. Doctor Crane lent it to me. You're supposed to kick it or something until it gets hot."

"Can I see it for a minute? I can do that better, standing up."

Silk handed him the wrapping.

"I heard of them, and I saw one once, only I didn't get to touch it. Thirty cards they wanted for it." Auk slapped the wall with the wrapping; when he squatted to help Silk replace it, it felt hot enough to smoke.

The stair was as steep and narrow as the house itself, covered with torn carpeting so threadbare as to be actually slick in spots; but helped manfully by Auk and urged forward by curiosity, jaw set and putting as much weight as possible on Blood's lioness-headed stick, Silk climbed it almost as quickly as he might have with two sound legs.

The door at the top opened upon a single bare room that occupied the entire second story; its floor was covered with worn sailcloth mats, its walls decorated with swords, many of them of shapes that Silk had never seen or never noticed, and long cane foils with basketwork hilts.

"You're lame!" Xiphias called. "Limping!" He danced toward them, thrusting and parrying.

"I injured my ankle," Silk told him. "It should be better in a few weeks."

Xiphias pushed his foil into Silk's hands. "But you must start now! Begin your lessons this very evening! Do you know how to hold that? You're left-handed? Good! Very good! I'll teach you the right, too, eventually. Keep your stick in your right, eh? You may parry, but not thrust or cut with it. Is that understood? May I have a stick too? You agree that's fair? No objection? Where—Over there!" An astonishing bound carried him to the nearest wall, from which he snatched two more foils and a yellow walking stick so slender that it was scarcely more than a wand; like the foils it was of varnished bamboo.

Silk told him, "I can't engage you with this bad ankle, sir, and the Chapter frowns upon all such activities—not that I'd be an even match or anything like a match for you. Besides, I have no funds to pay for a lesson."

"Aha! Auk's your friend? Your word on his score, Auk? It's not just to get him killed, is it?"

Auk shook his head.

"He's my friend, and I'm his." As soon as Silk spoke, he realized that it was no more than the truth. He added, "Because I am, I won't let him pay."

Xiphias's voice dropped to a whisper. "You won't fight, you say, with your cloth and gimp leg. But what if you were attacked? You'd have to. Have to . . . And since Auk's your friend, he'd fight too, wouldn't he? Fight for you? You say you don't want him to pay. Don't you think he feels the same way?"

He tossed Auk a foil. "Not made of money are you, Auk? A good thief but a poor man, isn't that what they say about you? Wouldn't you—wouldn't you both like to save Auk all that money? Yes! Oh, yes! I know you would."

Auk unbuckled his hanger and laid it against the wall. "If we beat him, he won't charge me."

"That's right!" Xiphias sprang away. "Will you excuse me, Patera, while I remove my trousers?"

They fell as he spoke; one spindle-thin leg was black synthetic and gleaming steel. At the touch of the old man's fingers, it too fell away, leaving him swaying on a single, natural, knotted, blue-veined leg. "What do you think of my secret? Five it took!" He hopped toward them, balancing himself precariously with his foil and the yellow walking stick. "Five I found!"

Almost too late, Silk blocked a wide, whistling cut at his head.

"Too many parts? Scarcely enough!" Another swinging slash. "Don't cringe!"

Auk lunged at the old man. His parry was too swift for the eye to follow; the crack of his foil against Auk's skull sounded louder than Auk's shot in the Cock. Auk sprawled on the sailcloth mat.

"Now, Patera! Guard yourself!"

For the space of a brief prayer that seemed half the night, that was all Silk did, frantically fending off cut after cut, forehand, backhand, to the head, to the neck, to the arms, the shoulders, the waist. There was no time to think, no time to do anything but react. Almost in spite of himself, he began to sense a certain pattern, a rhythm that governed the old man's slashing attack. Despite his ankle, he could move faster, turn faster, than the old man on his one leg.

"Good! Good! After me! Good!"

Xiphias was on the defensive now, parrying the murderous cuts Silk launched at his head and shoulders.

"Use the point! Watch this!" The old man lunged, his slender stick the leg he lacked, the end of his foil between Silk's legs, then under his left arm. Silk himself thrust desperately. Xiphias's parry sent his point awry. Silk cut at his head and lunged when he backed away.

"Where'd you study, lad?"

Auk was on his feet once more, grinning and rubbing his head. Feeling that he had been betrayed, Silk thrust and parried, cut, and parried the old man's cuts. There was no time to speak, no time to think, no time to do anything but fight. He had dropped the lioness-headed stick, but it did not matter—the pain in his ankle was remote, the pain of somebody else far off, of some body that he hardly knew.

"Good! Oh, very nice!"

The *clack, clack, clack* of the foils was the beating of the Sphigxdrum that called men to war, the rattle of crotala that led the dance, a dance in which every movement had to be as quick as possible.

"I'll take him, Auk! I'll teach him! He's mine!"

Hopping and half falling, propped by his slender stick, the old man met each attack with careless ease, his mad eyes burning with joy.

Maddened too, Silk thrust at them. His bamboo blade flew wide, and the slender walking stick struck a single, paralyzing blow to his wrist. His foil dropped to the mat, and Xiphias's point thumped his breastbone. "You're dead, Patera!"

Silk stared at him, rubbed his wrist, and at last spat at the old man's feet. "You cheated. You said I couldn't hit with my stick, but you hit me with yours."

"I did! Oh, yes!" The old man flung it into the air and parried it as it fell. "But aren't I sorry? Isn't my heart torn? Overflowing with remorse? Oh, it is, it is! I weep! Where would you like to be buried?"

Auk said quietly, "There ain't any rules, Patera, not when we fight. Somebody lives, somebody dies. That's all there is."

Silk started to speak, thought better of it, swallowed, and said, "I understand. If I'd considered something that happened this afternoon more seriously—as I should have before now—I would have understood sooner. You're right, of course, sir. You're both right."

"Where did you study?" Xiphias asked. "Who's your old master?"

"No one," Silk told him truthfully. "We used to fence with laths when I was a boy, sometimes; but I'd never held a real foil before."

Xiphias cocked a bushy eyebrow at him. "Like that, eh? Or perhaps you're still angry because I tricked you?" He hopped over to Blood's fallen walking stick, snatched it up (practically falling himself) and tossed it to Silk. "Want to hit me back? Punish me for trying to save you? Do your worst!"

"Of course not. I'd rather thank you, Xiphias, and I do." Silk rubbed the crusted bruise Musk had left on his ribs. "It was a lesson I needed. When may I come for my next?"

While the old man was considering, Auk said, "He'll be a good contact for you, Patera. He's a master-of-arms, not just of the sword. He was the one that sold the boy your needles, see?"

"Mornings, afternoons, or evenings?" Xiphias inquired. "Would evenings be all right? Good! Can we say Hieraxday, then?"

Silk nodded again. "Hieraxday after shadelow, Master Xiphias."

Auk brought the old man his prosthetic leg and helped him keep his balance while he closed its socket about his stump.

"You see," Xiphias asked, tapping it with his foil, "that I've earned the right to do what I did? That I was cheated once myself? That I paid the price when I was as young and strong as you are today?"

Outside, in the hot, silent street, Auk said, "We'll find you a litter before long, Patera. I'll pay 'em, but then I'll have to get going."

Silk smiled. "If I can fight with that marvelous old madman on this ankle, I can certainly walk home on it. You may leave me now, Auk, and Pas's peace go with you. I won't try to thank you for everything you've done for me tonight. I couldn't, even if I talked until morning. But I'll repay you whenever I get the chance."

Auk grinned and clapped him on the back. "No hurry, Patera."

"Down this little street—it's String Street, I know it—and I'll be on Sun Street. A few steps east, and I'll be at the manteion. You have business of your own to attend to, I'm certain. And so good night."

He took care to stride along normally until Auk was out of sight, then permitted himself to limp, leaning on Blood's stick. His bout with Master Xiphias had left him drenched with sweat; fortunately the night wind had no edge to it.

Autumn was nearly over. Was it only yesterday that it had rained? Silk assured himself that it was. Winter was almost upon them, though there was only that shower to prove it. The crops were in—meager crops, most peasants said, hardly worth the work of harvest; the parched dead of summer seemed to last longer each year, and this year the heat had been terrible. As it still was, for that matter.

Here was Sun Street; wide though it was, he had almost missed the turning. The funeral tomorrow—Orpine's final rites, and very likely her first as well. He recalled what Auk had said about her and wished that he had known her, as perhaps Hyacinth had. Had Maytera been able to cash Orchid's draft? He would have to find out—perhaps she had left him a note. He wouldn't have to tell her to sweep the manteion. Could rue still be had cheaply in the market? No, could rue be had at any price? Almost certainly, yes. And . . .

And there was the manse, with the manteion beyond it; but he had barred the Sun Street door.

He hobbled diagonally across Sun Street to the garden gate, unlocked and opened it, and locked it again carefully behind him. As he went along the narrow path to the manse, where no one slept or ate or lived except himself, voices floated into the garden through the open window. One was harsh, rising almost to a shout, then sinking to a mutter. The other, speaking of Pas and Echidna, of Hierax and Molpe and all the gods, was in some odd fashion familiar.

He paused for a moment to listen, then sat down on the old worn step. It was—surely it was—his own.

". . . who makes the crops to shoot forth from dirt," said this second voice. "You sprats have all seen it, and you'd think it wonderfully wonderful if you hadn't."

It was his talk at manteion from Molpsday, or rather a parody of it. But perhaps he had really sounded like that, had sounded that foolish. No doubt he sounded that foolish still.

"Thus when we see the trees dancing in the breeze we are to think of her, but not only of her, of her mother, too, for we would not have her without her mother, or the trees, or even the dance."

He had said that, surely. Those had been his precise words—that babble. The Outsider had not only spoken to him, but had somehow split him in two: the Patera Silk who lived here and was speaking now in the musty sellaria, and he himself, Silk the failed thief—Silk the foe and tool of Blood, Silk who was Auk's friend, who had in his waistband an azoth lent him by a whore and her trumpery needler in his pocket.

Silk who longed to see her again.

The harsh voice: "Silk good!"

Perhaps. But was it that Silk or this one, himself? Was it this one, with Hyacinth's azoth in its hand, drawn unconsciously? This Silk who feared and hated Musk, and ached to kill him?

Of whom was he afraid? That other Silk would not have

harmed a mouse, had postponed getting the ratsnake he needed again and again, visualizing the suffering of—rats. And yet it would be a fearful thing to meet that Silk whom he had been, and was a fearful thing to meet him now, in voice and memory. Had he truly become someone else?

He tore open the heavy, paper-wrapped packet Auk had put into his hand, dropping several needles. More filled the open breech of the needler like water; he released the loading knob and the breech closed. The needler would fire now if he needed it.

Or perhaps would not.

Patera Silk, and Silk nightside. He found that he, the latter, was contemptuous of the former, though envious, too.

His own voice echoed from the manse. "In the names of all the immortal gods, who give us all we have."

Strange gifts, at times. He had saved this manteion, or had at least postponed its destruction; now, hearing the voice of its augur, he knew that it had never really been worth saving—though he had been sent to save it. Grim-faced, he rose, thrust the azoth back into his waistband and dropped the needler into his pocket again with what remained of the packet of needles, and dusted the back of his robe.

Everything had changed because he himself was changed. How had it happened? When he climbed Blood's wall? When he had entered the manteion to get the hatchet? Long ago, when he had helped force the window, with the other boys? Or had Mucor laid some spell on him, there in her filthy, lightless room? Mucor was one who might lay spells, if any did; Mucor was a devil, in so far as devils were. Was it she who had drunk poor Teasel's blood?

"Mucor," Silk whispered. "Are you here? Are you still following me?" For a moment he seemed to hear an answering whisper, as the night wind stirred the dry leaves of the fig tree.

Gabbling now, his voice from the window: "Here hear what the Writings here have to Say-ilk. Here hear the high hopes of Horrible Hierax."

"Here axe," repeated the harsh voice, as though mocking his finding the hatchet, and Silk recognized it.

No, it had not been Mucor, or his deciding to take the hatchet or any such thing. All gods were good, but might not the unfathomable Outsider be good in a dark way? As Auk was, or as Auk might be? Suddenly Silk remembered the whorl outside the whorl, the Outsider's immeasurable whorl beneath his feet. So dark.

Yet lit by scattered motes.

With one hand on the needler in his pocket, he opened the door of the manse and stepped inside.

Coming soon from Tor Books . . .

LAKE OF THE LONG SUN

The Second Volume of
The Book of the Long Sun

by Gene Wolfe

Available in Hardcover, January '94.
ISBN 0-312-85494-3 $21.95

Enjoy the following preview!

Chapter 1

THEY HAD SCIENTISTS

Silence fell, abrupt as a shouted command, when Patera Silk opened the door of the old, three-sided manse at the slanted intersection where Sun Street met Silver. Horn, the tallest boy in the palaestra, was sitting bolt upright in the least comfortable chair in the musty little sellaria; Silk felt sure he had dropped into it hastily when he heard the rattle of the latch.

The night chough (Silk had stepped inside and shut the door behind him before he remembered that he had named the night chough Oreb) was perched on the high, tapestried back of the stiff "visitor's" chair.

" 'Lo, Silk," Oreb croaked. "Good Silk!"

"And good evening to you. A good evening to you both. Tartaros bless you."

Horn had risen as silk entered; Silk motioned for him to sit again. "I apologize. I'm terribly sorry, Horn. I truly am. Maytera Rose told me she meant to send you to talk to me this evening, but I forgot all about it. So much as been—O Sphigx! Stabbing Sphigx, have pity on me!"

This last had been in response to sudden, lancing pain in his ankle. As he limped to the room's sole comfortable chair, the one in which he sat to read, it occurred to him that its seat was probably still warm; he considered feeling the cushion to make sure, rejected the idea as embarrassing to Horn, then (propping himself with Blood's lioness-headed walking stick) laid his free hand on the seat anyway out of sheer curiosity. It was.

"I sat down there for a minute, Patera. I could see your bird better from there."

"Of course." Silk sat, lifting his injured ankle onto the hassock. "You've been here half the night, no doubt."

"Only a couple hours, Patera. I sweep out for my father while he empties the till and—and—locks the money up."

Silk nodded approvingly. "That's right. You shouldn't tell me where he keeps it." He paused, recalling that he had intended to steal this very manteion from Blood. "I wouldn't steal it, because I'd never steal anything from you or your family; but you never know who may be listening."

Horn grinned. "Your bird might tell, Patera. Sometimes they take shiny things, that's what I've heard. Maybe a ring or a spoon."

"No steal!" Oreb protested.

"I was thinking of a human eavesdropper, actually. I shrove an unhappy young woman today, and I believe there was someone listening outside her window the whole time. There was a gallery out there, and once I felt certain I heard the boards creak when he shifted his weight. I was tempted to get up and look, but crippled as I am at present, he would've been gone before I could have put my head out of the window—and back again, no doubt, the moment I sat down." Silk sighed. "Fortunately she kept her voice quite low."

"Isn't listening like that a major offense against the gods, Patera?"

"Yes. Not that he cares, I'm afraid. The worst part of the whole affair is that I know the man—or at least, I'm beginning to know him—and I've liked what I've seen of him. There's a great deal of good in him, I feel certain, though he tries so hard to conceal it."

Oreb fluttered his sound wing. "Good Crane!"

"I didn't mention his name," Silk told Horn, "nor did you hear any name."

"No, Patera. Half the time I can't make out what that bird's saying."

"Fine. Perhaps it would be even better if you had as much difficulty understanding me."

Horn colored. "I'm sorry, Patera. I didn't want to—It wasn't because—"

"I didn't mean that," Silk explained hastily. "Not at all. We haven't even begun to talk about that yet, though we will. We must. I merely meant that I shouldn't even have mentioned shriving that woman. I'm much too tired to keep a proper watch on my tongue. And now that Patera Pike has left us—well, I still have Maytera Marble to confide in. I'd go mad, I think, if it weren't for her."

He leaned forward in the soft old chair, struggling to concentrate his surging thoughts. "I was going to say that though he's a good man, or at least a man who might be good, he has no faith in the gods; yet I'm going to have to get him to admit he listened, so I can shrive him of the guilt. It's sure to be difficult, but I've been examining the matter from all sides, Horn, and I can see no way to evade my duty."

"Yes, Patera."

"I don't mean this evening. I've been entirely too busy this evening, and this afternoon, too. I saw—something I can't tell you about, unfortunately. But I've been thinking about this particular man and the problem he presents ever since I came in. Seeing that blue thing on the bird's wing reminded me."

"I was wondering what that was, Patera."

"A splint, I suppose you'd call it." Silk glanced at the clock. "Your mother and father will be frantic."

Horn shook his head. "The rest of the sprats'll tell them where I went, Patera. I told them before I left."

"By Sphigx, I hope so." Silk leaned forward and drew up his injured leg, pushed down his stocking, and unwound the chamois-like wrapping. "Have you seen one of these, Horn?"

"A strip of leather, Patera?"

"It's much more than that." Silk tossed it to him. "I want you to do something for me, if you will. Kick it hard, so that it flies against the wall."

Horn gawked.

"If you're afraid you'll break something, throw it down hard three or four times. Not here on the carpet, I think. Over there on the bare boards. Hard, mind."

Horn did as he was told, then returned the wrapping to Silk. "It's getting hot."

"Yes, I thought it would." Silk rewound it about his aching ankle and smiled with satisfaction as it tightened. "It isn't just a strip of leather, you see, although it may be that its exterior actually is leather. Inside there's a mechanism, something as thin as the gold labyrinth in a card. When that mechanism is agitated, it must take up energy. At rest, it excretes a part of it as heat. The remainder emerges as sound, or so I was told. It makes a noise we can't hear, I suppose because it's too soft or perhaps because it's pitched too high. Can you hear it now?''

Horn shook his head.

''Neither can I, yet I could hear sounds that Patera Pike could not—the squeaking of the hinges on the garden gate, for example, until I oiled them.''

Silk relaxed, soothed by the wrapping and the softness of his chair. ''These wonderful wrappings were made in the Short-Sun Whorl, I imagine, like glasses and Sacred Windows, and so many other things that we have but can't replace.''

''They had scientists there, Patera. That's what Maytera Rose says.''

Oreb croaked, ''Good Crane!''

Silk laughed. ''Did he teach you to say that while he was treating your wing, you silly bird? Very well, Doctor Crane's a scientist of sorts, I suppose; he knows medicine at least, which is more science than most of us know, and he let me borrow this, though I must return it in a few days.''

''A thing like that must be worth twenty or thirty cards, Patera.''

''More than that. Do you know Auk? A big man who comes to sacrifice on Scylsdays?''

''I think so, Patera.''

''Heavy jaw, wide shoulders, big ears. He wears a hanger and boots.''

''I don't know him to talk to, Patera, but I know who you mean.'' Horn paused, his handsome young face serious. ''He's trouble, that's what everybody says, the kind who knocks down people who get in his way. He did that to Teasel's father.''

Silk had taken out his beads; he drew them through his fingers absently as he spoke. ''I'm sorry to hear it. I'll try to speak to him about it.''

''You'd better keep away from him, Patera.''

Silk shook his head. ''I can't, Horn. Not if I'm to do my duty. In fact, Auk's precisely the sort of person I must get close to. I don't believe that even the Outsider— And it's too late for that in any case. I was going to tell you that I showed this wrapping to Auk, and he indicated that it was worth a great deal more.

That isn't important, however. Have you ever wondered why so much knowledge was left behind in the Short-Sun Whorl?''

"I guess the ones that knew about those things didn't come to our whorl, Patera.''

"Clearly they did not. Or if they did, they can't have settled here in Viron. Yet they knew many things that would be very valuable to us, and certainly they would have had to come if Pas had instructed them to.''

"The Fliers know how to fly, Patera, and we don't. We saw one yesterday, remember? Just after the ball game. He was pretty low. That's what I'd like to know. How to fly like they do, like a bird.''

"No fly!'' Oreb announced.

Silk studied the voided cross dangling from his beads for a moment, then let the beads fall into his lap. "This evening I was introduced to an elderly man who has a really extraordinary artificial leg, Horn. He had to buy up five broken or worn-out legs to build it, but it's an artificial leg such as the first settlers had—a leg that might have been brought from the Short-Sun Whorl. When he showed it to me, I thought how marvelous it would be if we could only make things like that now for Maytera Rose and Maytera Marble, and for all the beggars who are blind or crippled. It would be marvelous to fly, too, of course. I've always wanted to do it myself, and it may be that they are the same secret. If we could build wonderful legs like that for the people who need them, perhaps we could build wonderful wings as well for everyone who wanted to have them.''

"That would be great, Patera.''

"It may come to pass. It may yet come to pass, Horn. If people in the Short-Sun Whorl could teach themselves to do such things . . .'' Silk shook himself and yawned, then rose with the help of Blood's stick. "Well, thank you for coming by. It's been a pleasure, but I'd better go up to bed.''

"I was supposed—Maytera said—''

"That's right.'' Silk put away his beads. "I'm supposed to punish you. Or lecture you, or something. What was it you did that made Maytera Rose so angry?''

Horn swallowed. "I was just trying to talk like you do, Patera. Like in manteion. It wasn't even today, and I won't do it again.''

"Of course.'' Silk settled back into his chair. "But it *was* today, Horn. Or at least, today was one of several such days. I heard you before I opened the door. I sat down on the step for a minute to listen, in fact. You imitated me so well that for a while I actually thought that your voice was my own; it was like hearing myself. You're very good at it.''

"Good boy," Oreb croaked. "No hit."

"I won't," Silk told the bird, and it lurched through the air to his lap, then hopped from his lap to the arm of the chair, and from the arm to his shoulder.

"Maytera Rose hits us sometimes, Patera."

"Yes, I know. It's very courageous of her, but I'm not at all certain it's wise. Let's hear you again, Horn. Out on the step, I couldn't hear everything you said.''

Horn muttered, and Silk laughed. "I couldn't hear you that time, either. Surely I don't sound like that. When I'm at the ambion, I can hear my bray echo from the walls.''

"No, Patera."

"Then say it again, just as I would. I won't be angry, I promise you.''

"I was only . . . You know. Like the things you say."

"No talk?" Oreb inquired.

Silk ignored him. "Fine. Let me hear it. That's what you came to talk about, and I feel sure it will be a valuable corrective for me. I tend to get above myself, I'm afraid.''

Horn shook his head and stared at the carpet.

"Oh, come now! What sorts of things do I say?"

"To always live with the gods, and you do it any time you're happy with the life they've given you. Think about who's wise and act like he does.''

"That was well said, Horn; but you didn't sound in the least like me. It's my own voice I want to hear, just as I heard it on the step. Won't you do that?''

"I guess I've got to stand up, Patera."

"Then stand, by all means.''

"Don't look at me. All right?"

Silk shut his eyes.

For half a minute or more there was silence. Through his eyelids, Silk could detect the fading of the light (the best in the manse) behind his chair. He welcomed it. His right forearm, torn by the hooked beak of the white-headed one the night before, felt hot and swollen now; and he was so tired that his entire body ached.

"Live with the gods," his own voice directed, "and he does live with the gods who consistently shows them that his spirit is satisfied with what has been assigned to him, and that it obeys all that the gods will—the spirit that Pas has given every man as his guardian and guide, the best part of himself, his understanding and his reason. As you intend to live hereafter, it is in your power to live here. But if men do not permit you, . . ."

Silk stepped on something that slid beneath his foot, and fell with a start to the red clay tiles.

". . . think of wisdom only as great wisdom, the wisdom of a prolocutor or a councillor. That itself is unwise. If you could talk this very day with a councillor or His Cognizance, either would tell you that wisdom may be small, a thing quite suited to the smallest children here, as well as great. What is a wise child? It is a child who seeks out wise teachers, and hears them."

Silk opened his eyes. "What you said first was from the Writings, Horn. Did you know it?"

"No, Patera. It's just something I've heard you say."

"I was quoting. It's good that you've got that passage by heart, even if you learned it only to make fun of me. Sit down. You were talking about wisdom. Well, no doubt I must have spouted all that foolishness, but you deserve to learn better. Who are the wise, Horn? Have you really considered that question? If not, do so now. Who are they?"

"Well—You, Patera."

"NO!" Silk rose so abruptly that the bird squawked. He strode to the window and stood staring out through the bars at the ruts of Sun Street, black now under a flood of uncanny skylight. "No, I'm not wise, Horn. Or at least, I've been wise for a moment only—one moment out of my whole life."

He limped across the room to Horn's chair and crouched before it, one knee on the carpet. "Allow me to tell you how foolish I have been. Do you know what I believed when I was your age? That nothing but thought, nothing except wisdom, mattered. You're good at games, Horn. You can run and jump, and you can climb. So was I and so did I, but I had nothing but contempt for those abilities. Climbing was nothing to boast of, when I couldn't climb nearly as well as a monkey. But I could think better than a monkey—better than anyone else in my class, in fact." He smiled bitterly, shaking his head. "And that was how I thought! Pride in nonsense."

"Isn't thinking good, Patera?"

Silk stood. "Only when we think rightly. Action, you see, is the end that thought achieves. Action is its only purpose. What else is it good for? If we don't act, it's worthless. If we can't act, useless.''

He returned to his chair, but did not sit down. ''How many times have you heard me talk about enlightenment, Horn? Twenty or thirty times, surely, and you remember very well. Tell me what I said.''

Horn glanced miserably at Oreb as though for guidance, but the bird merely cocked his head and fidgeted on Silk's shoulder as if eager to hear what Horn had to say. At last he managed, ''It—it's wisdom a god sort of pours into you. That doesn't come from a book or anything. And—and—''

''Perhaps you'd do better if you employed my voice,'' Silk suggested. ''Stand up again and try it. I won't watch you if it makes you nervous.''

Horn rose, lifting his head, rolling his eyes toward the ceiling, and drawing down the corners of his mouth. ''Divine enlightenment means you know without thinking, and that isn't because thinking's bad but because enlightenment is better. Enlightenment is sharing in the thinking of the god.''

He added in his normal voice, ''That's as close as I can come, Patera, without more time to remember.''

''Your choice of words might be improved upon,'' Silk told him judiciously, ''but your intonation is excellent, and you have my speech mannerisms almost pat. What is of much, much more importance, nothing that you said was untrue. But who gets it, Horn? Who receives enlightenment?''

''People who've tried to live good lives for a long time. Sometimes they do.''

''Not always?''

''No, Patera. Not always.''

''Would you believe me, Horn—credit me fully without reservation—if I told you that I myself have received it? Yes or no.''

''Yes, Patera. If you say so.''

''That I received it only yesterday?''

Oreb whistled softly.

''Yes, Patera.''

Silk nodded, mostly to himself it seemed. ''I did, Horn, and not through any merit of mine. I was about to say that you were with me, but it wouldn't be true. Not really.''

''Was it before manteion, Patera? Yesterday you said you wanted to make a private sacrifice. Was it for that?''

''Yes. I've never made it, and perhaps I never will—''

"No cut!"

"If I do, it won't be you," Silk told Oreb. "Probably it won't be a live animal at all, although I'm going to have to sacrifice a lot of them tomorrow, and buy them as well."

"Pet bird?"

"Yes, indeed." Silk lifted Blood's lioness-headed stick to shoulder height; and Oreb hopped onto it, turning his head to watch Silk from each eye.

Horn said, "He wouldn't let me touch him, Patera."

"You had no reason to touch him, and he didn't know you. All animals hate the touch of a stranger. Have you ever kept a bird?"

"No, Patera. I had a dog, but she died."

"I was hoping to get some advice. I wouldn't want Oreb to die—although I'd imagine that night choughs are hardy creatures. Hold out your wrist."

Horn did, and Oreb hopped onto it. "Good boy!"

"I wouldn't try to hold him," Silk said. "Let him hold you. You can't have had many toys as a child, Horn."

"Not many. We were—" Suddenly, Horn smiled. "There was one. My grandfather made it, a wooden man with a blue coat. It had strings, and if you did them right, you could make him walk and bow."

"Yes!" Silk's eyes flashed, and the tip of the lioness-headed stick thumped the floor. "That's exactly the sort of toy I mean. May I tell you about one of mine? You may think I'm straying from the topic; but I won't be, I promise you."

"Sure, Patera. Go ahead."

"There were two dancers, a man and a woman, very neatly painted. They danced on a little stage, and when I wound it up, music played. And they danced, the little woman quite gracefully, and the little man somersaulting and spinning and cutting all sorts of capers. There were three tunes—you moved a lever to choose the one you wanted—and I used to play with it for hours, singing songs I'd made up for myself and imagining things for him to say to her, and for her to say to him. Silly things, most of them, I'm afraid."

"I understand, Patera."

"My mother died during my last year at the schola, Horn. Possibly I've already told you that. I'd been cramming for an examination, but the Prelate called me into his chambers again and told me that after her last sacrifice I would have to go home anu remove my personal belongings. Our house—her whole estate, but it was mostly the house—went to the Chapter, you understand. One signs an agreement before one enters the schola."

"Poor Silk!"

He smiled at the bird. "Perhaps, though I didn't think so at the time. I was miserable on account of my mother's death, but I don't believe that I ever felt sorry for myself. I had books to read, and friends, and enough to eat. But now I really am wandering from the subject.

"To hurry back to it, I found that toy in the back of my closet. I had been at the schola for six years, and I doubt that I'd so much as laid eyes on it for years before I left. Now here it was again! I wound it up, and the dancers danced once more, and the music played exactly as it had when I was a little boy. The tune was 'First Romance,' and I'll never forget that song now."

Horn coughed. "Nettle and me talk about that sometimes, Patera. You know, when we're older."

"Nettle and I," Silk corrected him absently. "That's good, Horn. It's very good, and you'll both be older much sooner than you imagine. I'll pray for you both.

"But I had intended to say that I cried then. I hadn't at her rites; I hadn't been able to, not even when her casket was put into the ground. But I did then, because it seemed to me that for the dancers no time at all had passed. That they couldn't know that the man who wound them now was the boy who had wound them the last time, or that the woman who had bought them on Clock Street was dead. Do you follow what I'm saying, Horn?"

"I think so, Patera."

"Enlightenment is like that for the whole whorl. Time has stopped for everyone else. For you, there is something outside it—a peri-time in which the god speaks to you. For me, that god was the Outsider. I don't think I've said much about him when I've talked to the palaestra, but I will be saying a great deal about him in the future. Maytera Mint said something to me this afternoon that has remained with me ever since. She said that he was unlike the other gods, who take council with one another in Mainframe; that no one save himself knew his mind. Maytera Mint has great humility, but she has wisdom, too. I must remember not to let the first blind me to the second."

"Good girl!"

"Yes, and great goodness, too. Humility and purity."

Horn said, "About enlightenment, Patera. Yours, I mean. Is that why somebody's writing things about you getting to be caldé?"

Silk snapped his fingers. "I'm glad you mentioned that—I had intended to ask you about it. I knew I'd forgotten something. Someone had chalked, 'Silk for caldé,' on a wall; I saw it on the way home. Did you do that?"

Horn shook his head.

"Or one of the other boys?"

"I don't think it was one of us sprats at all, Patera. It's on two places. There on the slop shop, and then over on Hat Street, on that building Gosseyplum lives in. I've looked at them both, and they're pretty high up. I could do it without standing on anything and I think maybe Locust could, but he says he didn't."

Silk nodded to himself. "Then I believe you're correct, Horn. It was because I've been enlightened. Or rather it's happened because I told someone about it, and was overheard. I've told several persons now, yourself included, and perhaps I shouldn't have."

"What was it like, Patera? Besides everything stopped, like you said?"

For several tickings of the clock on the mantel, Silk sat silent, contemplating for the hundredth time the experience he had by this time revolved in his mind so often that it was like a water-smoothed stone, polished and opaque. At last he said, "In that moment I understood all that I'll ever truly need to know. It's erroneous, really, for me to call it a moment, when it was actually outside time. But I, Horn," (he smiled) "I am inside time, just as you are. And I find that it takes time for me to comprehend everything that I was told in that moment that was not a moment. It takes time for me to assimilate it. Am I making myself clear?"

Poor Horn nodded hesitantly. "I think so, Patera."

"That may be good enough." Silk paused again, lost in thought. "One of the things I learned was that I'm to be a teacher. There's only one thing that the Outsider wishes me to do—I am to save our manteion. But it is as a teacher that he wishes me to do it.

"There are many callings, Horn, the highest being pure worship. That isn't mine; mine is to teach, and a teacher has to act as well as think. The old man I met this evening—the man with the wonderful leg—was a teacher, too; and yet he's all action, an activity, as old as he is, and one-legged, too. He teaches swordfighting. Why do you think he is as he is? All action?''

Horn's eyes shone. ''I don't know, Patera. Why?''

''Because a fight with swords—still more, with azoths—affords no time for reflection; thus to be all action is a part of what he has to teach. Listen carefully now. *He has thought about that.* Do you understand? Even though fighting with a sword must be all action, teaching others that kind of fighting requires thought. The old man had to think not only about what he was to teach, but about how he could best teach it.''

Horn nodded. ''I think I understand, Patera.''

''In the same way, Horn, you must think about imitating me. Not merely about how I can be imitated, but about what to imitate. And when to do it. Now go home.''

Oreb flapped his sound wing. ''Wise man!''

''Thank you. Go, Horn. If Oreb wishes to go with you, you may keep him.''

''Patera?''

Silk rose as Horn did. ''Yes. What is it?''

''Are you going to study swordfighting?''

For a moment Silk considered his reply. ''There are more important things to learn than swordfighting, Horn. Whom to fight, for example. One of them is to keep secrets. Someone who holds in confidence only those secrets he has been told not to reveal can never be trusted. Surely you understand that.''

''Yes, Patera.''

''And there is more to be learned from any good teacher than the subject taught. Tell your father and mother that I didn't keep you so late in order to punish you, but through carelessness, for which I apologize.''

''No go!'' Fluttering frenziedly, Oreb half flew and half fell from Horn's shoulder to the lofty back of the tapestried chair. ''Bird stay!''

Horn's hand was already on the latch. ''I'll tell them we were just talking, Patera. I'll say you were teaching me about the Outsider and a lot of other things. It'll be the truth.''

Oreb croaked, ''Good-bye! Bye, boy!''

''You foolish bird,'' Silk said as the door closed behind Horn, ''what have you learned from all this? A few new words, perhaps, which you will misapply.''

''Gods' ways!''

''Oh, yes. You're very wise now.'' Although it was still warm,

Silk unwound the wrapping. After beating the hassock with it, he wrapped it around his forearm over the bandage.

"Man god. My god."

"Shut up," his god told him wearily.

He had thrust his arm into the glass, where Kypris was kissing it. Her lips were as chill as death, but it was a death he welcomed at first. In time he grew frightened and struggled to withdraw it, but Kypris would not release it. When he shouted for Horn, no sound issued from his mouth. Orchid's sellaria was in the manse, which did not seem odd at all; a wild wind moaned in the chimney. He remembered that Auk had foretold such a wind, and tried to recall what Auk had said would happen when it blew.

Without relinquishing her grip on his arm, the goddess revolved, her own arms upraised; she wore a clinging gown of liquid spring. He was acutely conscious of the roundness of her thighs, the double globosity of her hips. As he stared, Blood's orchestra played "First Romance" and Kypris became Hyacinth (though Kypris still) and lovelier than ever. He kicked and tumbled, his feet above his head, but his hand clasped hers and would not be torn from it.

He woke gasping for breath. The lights had extinguished themselves. In the faint skylight from a curtained window, he saw Oreb hop out and flap away. Mucor stood beside his bed, naked in the darkness and skeletally thin; he blinked; she faded to mist and was gone.

He rubbed his eyes.

A warm wind moaned as it had in his dream, dancing with his ragged, pale curtains. The wrapping on his arm was pale too, white with frost that melted at a touch. He unwound it and whipped the damp sheet with it, then wound it about his newly painful ankle, telling himself that he should not have climbed the stairs without it. What would Doctor Crane say when he told him?

The whipping had evoked a spectral glow from the lights, enough for him to distinguish the hands of the busy little clock beside his triptych. It was after midnight.

Leaving his bed, he lowered the sash. Not until it was down did he realize that he could not have seen Oreb fly out—Oreb had a dislocated wing.

Downstairs, he found Oreb poking about the kitchen in search of something to eat. He put out the last slice of bread and refilled the bird's cup with clean water.

"Meat?" Oreb cocked his head and clacked his beak.

"You'll have to find some for yourself if you want it," Silk told him. "I haven't any." After a moment's thought—he added, "Perhaps I'll buy a little tomorrow, if Maytera cashed Orchid's draft, or I can myself. Or at least a fish—a live one I could keep in the washtub until whatever's left over from the sacrifices runs out, and then share with Maytera Rose. And Maytera Mint, of course. Wouldn't you like some nice, fresh fish, Oreb?"

"Like fish!"

"All right, I'll see what I can do. But you have to be forthcoming with me now. No fish if you're not. Were you in my bedroom?"

"No steal!"

"I didn't say that you stole," Silk explained patiently. "Were you there?"

"Where?"

"Up there." Silk pointed. "I know you were. I woke up and saw you."

"No, no!"

"Of course you were, Oreb. I saw you myself. I watched you fly out the window."

"No fly!"

"I'm not going to punish you. I simply want to know one thing. Listen carefully now. When you were upstairs, did you see a woman? Or a girl? A thin young woman, unclothed, in my bedroom?"

"No fly," the bird repeated stubbornly. "Wing hurt."

Silk ran his fingers through his strawstack hair. "All right, you can't fly. I concede that. Were you upstairs?"

"No steal." Oreb clacked his beak again.

"Nor did you steal. That is understood as well."

"Fish heads?"

Silk threw caution to the winds. "Yes, several. Big ones, I promise you."

Oreb hopped onto the window ledge. "No see."

"Look at me, please. Did you see her?"

"No see."

"You were frightened by something," Silk mused, "though it may have been my waking. Perhaps you were afraid that I'd punish you for looking around my bedroom. Was that it?"

"No, no!"

"This window is just below that one. I *thought* I saw you fly, but

I really saw you hop out the window and drop down into the black-berries. From there it would have been easy for you to get back here into the kitchen through the window. Isn't that what happened?''

"No hop!"

"I don't believe you, because—" Silk paused. Faintly, he had heard the creak of Patera Pike's bed; he felt a pang of guilt at having awakened the old man, who always labored so hard and slept so badly—although he had dreamed (only dreamed, he told himself firmly) that Pike was dead, as he had dreamed, also, that Hyacinth had kissed his arm, that he had talked to Kypris in an old yellow house on Lamp Street: to Lady Kypris, the Goddess of Love, the whores' goddess.

Shaken by doubt, he went back to the pump and worked its handle again until clear icy water gushed into the stoppered sink, splashed his sweating face again and again, and soaked and resoaked his un-tidy hair until he was actually shivering despite the heat of the night.

"Patera Pike is dead," he told Oreb, who cocked his head sympathetically.

Silk filled the kettle and set it on the stove, starting the fire with an extravagant expenditure of wastepaper; when flames licked the sides of the kettle, he seated himself in the unsteady wooden chair in which he sat to eat and pointed a finger at Oreb. "Patera Pike left us last spring; that's practically a year ago. I performed his rites myself, and even without a headstone, his grave cost more than we could scrape together. So what I heard was the wind or something of that sort. Rats, perhaps. Am I making myself clear?''

"Eat now?"

"No." Silk shook his head. "There's nothing left but a little maté and a very small lump of sugar. I plan to brew myself a cup of maté and drink it, and go back to bed. If you can sleep too, I advise it."

Overhead (above the sellaria, Silk felt quite certain) Patera Pike's old bed creaked again.

He rose. Hyacinth's engraved needler was still in his pocket, and before he had entered the manse that evening he had charged it with needles from the packet Auk had bought for him. He pulled back the loading knob to assure himself that there was a needle ready to fire, and pressed down the safety catch. Crossing the kitchen to the stair, he called, "Mucor? Is that you?''

There was no reply.

"If it is, cover yourself. I'm coming up to talk to you."

The first step brought a twinge of pain from his ankle. He wished for Blood's stick, but it was leaning against the head of his bed.

Another step, and the floor above creaked. He mounted three more steps, then stopped to listen. The night wind still sighed about the manse, moaning in the chimney as it had in his dream. It had been that wind, surely, that had made the old structure groan, that had caused him—fool that he was—to think that he had heard the old augur's bed creak, had heard it squeak and readjust its old sticks and straps as Patera rolled his old body, sitting up for a moment to pray or peer out through the empty, open windows before lying down again on his back, on his side.

A door shut softly upstairs.

It had been his own, surely—the door to his bedroom. He had paid it no attention when he had put on his trousers and hurried downstairs to look for Oreb. All the doors in the manse swung of their own accord unless they were kept latched, opening or shutting in walls that were no longer plumb, cracked old doors in warped frames that had perhaps never been quite right, and certainly were not square now.

His finger was closing on the trigger of the needler; recalling Auk's warning, he put his fingertip on the trigger guard. "Mucor? I don't want to hurt you. I just want to talk to you. Are you up there?"

No voice, no footfall, from the upper floor. He went up a few more steps. He had shown Auk the azoth, and that had been most imprudent; an azoth was worth thousands of cards. Auk broke into larger and better defended houses than this whenever he chose. Now Auk had come for the azoth or sent an accomplice, seen his opportunity when the kitchen lights kindled.

"Auk? It's me, Patera Silk."

There came no answering voice.

"I've got a needler, but I don't want to have to shoot. If you raise your hands and offer no resistance, I won't. I won't turn you over to the Guard, either."

His voice had energized the single dim light above the landing. Ten steps remained, and Silk climbed them slowly, his progress retarded by fear as much as pain, seeing first the black-clad legs in the doorway of his bedroom, then the hem of the black robe, and at last the aged augur's smiling face.

Patera Pike waved and melted into silver mist; his blue-trimmed black calotte dropping softly onto the uneven boards of the landing.